REQUIE

Requiem in Red
www.amazon.com/dp/1975608119

NORMA ROTH

The Fates stroked their weaving
"The clock ticks," said Lachesis, who sings of the things that were.
"Now," said Clotho, who sings of the things that are.
"Wait," said Atropos, who wept about the things that were to be
                                                                -Unknown

Chapter 1
June 1952

Myrna Schroeder wiped the sink one last time and glanced at the small round clock above it. A half hour to catch the bus. Her big, floppy purse and her lunch in a small brown paper sack were ready on the kitchen table. "Scarlett, are you dressed?" she called.

Her small daughter, curly red hair glowing in the late afternoon sun, stood in the doorway to the bedroom. Her white sleeveless blouse was buttoned askew over red shorts, and Myrna knelt to straighten it. "Mama. Do I have a daddy?"

Myrna had practiced how to answer that question almost all of Scarlett's five years, but it still took her breath. She rebuttoned the blouse and put her arm around her daughter. "Your daddy died in the war," she said, the lie sliding easily off her tongue.

"What's a war?"

Myrna took a deep breath. "A really bad man killed a lot of people and wanted to kill a lot more, so he had to be stopped. A whole lot of men, called an army, went to where he lived and fought with the bad man's army until they stopped trying to kill people. Good men were killed, too, and your daddy was one of them. He didn't even know you were going to be born, but he would have really loved you."

"What's his name?"

"Bob," Myrna replied, as she stood. "Now, let's go. The bus comes soon and I have to go to work and you have to go to Mrs. Neumann's."

"Can I tell Mrs. Neumann about my daddy?"

"Yes." Mrs. Neumann already knew Scarlett had no daddy. Everybody knew Scarlett had no daddy. Nobody knew that Scarlett existed because of a rape. Nobody knew the identity of Scarlett's "daddy," and Myrna made sure he didn't know. He didn't deserve any part of that precious life.

"I don't want to go to Mrs. Neumann's." Scarlett crossed her arms over her breast and planted her feet apart.

"Scarlett, I don't have time for this. I don't want to go to work, either, but if I don't we won't eat and we won't have any place to live. I don't think you'd like that."

Scarlett made a big sigh, and walked to the door. She walked down the long flight of outside steps ahead of Myrna. Mrs. Neumann stood beside the porch railing on the ground floor of the two-story house.

"Good afternoon, Myrna. Scarlett, would you like to go to the grocery store with me?" she said, in her heavy German accent.

"My daddy died in the war," Scarlett announced. "His name was Bob."

Mrs. Neumann raised her eyebrows and looked at Myrna, who nodded. "That is sad that he died," she said.

Myrna opened her purse and removed a worn black billfold, opened it and took out two bills. She handed them to Mrs. Neumann. "Twenty for rent and five for babysitting."

"Danke," said Mrs. Neumann, as she tucked the money into her apron pocket.

"Well, I'll see you tonight," Myrna said, then she bent and kissed Scarlett on the cheek. 'Love you, sweetie." She turned and walked down the sidewalk where she could see the blue and yellow city bus waddling up the street, a half-block away from the corner where she waited. It wheezed to a stop when it reached her and the door flapped open.

"Afternoon, Bill," she said to the driver as she dropped her dime into the coin box.

"Hi, Myrna. Ready for another night at Weston Switch?"

"Oh, yeah. Eight hours in that sweat box. Would you believe only three fans in the whole department? Let the big shots in their air conditioned offices come down and spend their work time in the same place we do. I bet we would have air conditioning in two days." The driver smiled, shifted gears and the bus moved into the traffic, while Myrna worked her way back to a seat.

Myrna slid into a seat beside a window, and sighed. Sweat crawled down her scalp in tiny rivers and beaded around her hairline, pooled under her arms in the sleeveless white blouse, and trickled between her breasts. After the long, cold winter and a brief pleasant spring, summer with all its fierce heat and smothering humidity, had arrived to spend a couple of months in northern Illinois.

The bus reeked of sour bodies, cigarette smoke, stale and fresh, and vehicle exhaust. Ahead was another night to sweat through, going deaf from the rattle of riveters and the thump-thump-thump of small punch presses. All for assembling the innards of automatic switches so she could feed Scarlett and herself and provide a roof over their heads.

The view through the bus window showed buildings of sagging wood, paintless gray with age, or worn brick, windows hidden under years of grime. The sidewalk was empty. Few people walked in this part of Newport City.

The bus thumped over the last of the four sets of railroad tracks seconds before a warning bell clanged and the crossing gates came down. A shudder went through Myrna when an air horn's wail crescendoed. Twin diesel locomotives, giant drive wheels a blur, their sharp edges like those that long ago decapitated her sixteen-year-old mother, blasted through the crossing. The long train of rocking, clacketing freight cars carried its freight a hundred miles east to Chicago.

On the other hand, she would give a lot to be on a train going anywhere but to the two-block-square, gray concrete building across the tracks on the right side of the street: Weston Automatic Switch Company. The bus rocked over a pothole, then wheezed to a stop half-way down the block at the entrance to Weston Switch. Myrna pried herself off the seat; she'd sweat so much her skirt stuck to it. She

3

shuffled down the aisle behind a woman who stank of sweat and unwashed hair. *Is that where I'll be in twenty years?*, she thought, as she stepped down to the sidewalk. The bus door flapped shut behind her, and the vehicle belched a cloud of exhaust and waddled down the street in its faded blue and yellow paint, tired and worn as its passengers.

A male voice behind Myrna said, "What's a good-lookin' broad like you doin' on nights?" He chuckled. "You oughta go for a transfer upstairs to a nice cushy job. I hear the big boss, Weston himself, has an eye for a good lookin' woman. He might even take you home in his fancy Rolls Royce. Course he'd probably stop off at a hotel somewhere for a little fun first. "

Myrna's face burned, but she ignored the voice and pulled open the heavy glass door to the plant. She'd heard it all before.

The company guard sat inside the door, his gut pressed against the edge of a card table. His name, "Harry," was embroidered in black above the gray shirt pocket, and "Marchand Security" was stamped on a black metal band above the black visor of his gray hat.

Myrna fished through her big floppy cloth purse for her badge. Her thumb found the open pin on it. "Ouch." She jerked her hand out and stuck her pricked thumb in her mouth until it stopped hurting. More carefully, she retrieved the badge, and flashed it at the guard. He barely glanced at it, and Myrna pushed open the door behind him to the concrete steps beyond it.

She trudged up the steps in grooves made by thousands of other workers over the eighty years of the building's life. It had been Weston Switch for the last fifteen. She pulled open the door at the second floor and coughed as the first whiff of the acrid machine oil caught in her throat. On her left, pea soup green machines sat idle behind a wire fence, like caged creatures from an alien planet.

On the industrial green wall to her right, a square gray time clock hung between two large racks filled with cards. Myrna pulled her card from the "OUT" slot, slipped it into the clock's slot, pulled it out after it was stamped and slid it into the "IN" slot. Two forty-eight. She was early. That was the good part. The bad part was that it meant she had to sit in the break room and listen to Betty Brown and her mouth ten minutes longer.

The break room, where the women of Department 21 waited for the shift to begin, was still twenty feet away, but Betty's deep voice and braying laugh echoed down the hall. "Eddie smacked me in the face once, and I smacked him right back, rocked him right on his heels. He never laid a hand on me again. That's what you oughta do to your old man, Edna," the voice said.

Myrna huffed. Edna Heflin was a mousy little woman with straight brown hair turning gray, who worked to support five kids and a good-for-nothing boozer of a husband. He couldn't hold a job and he beat her up when he was in a bad mood,

Myrna tried to slip in unnoticed, but she barely got through the door before Betty bawled, "Hey, Myrn. You're early. Bus too full for the driver to pull off and get a little nooky on the way down?" She roared with laughter. A smattering of titters responded.

Betty was a good five foot nine and weighed about two hundred pounds. She always wore slacks with a knife-edged crease and plaid shirts. Her dark brown hair was cut like a man's and she had a man's paunch. Only the slight bulge of her little breasts betrayed her sex. Not that she was a butch or anything. She and Eddie had been married for twenty years and had three grown sons.

Myrna ignored Betty's comment and walked to the rank of gray lockers set against the wall next to the bathroom. She worked the combination lock, opened the locker and put her purse and lunch sack inside. She was about to close the door when Betty shouted again.

"Hey, Myrn, I'm talkin' to you."

Myrna closed the locker door, twisted the padlock with deliberate care and walked slowly to an empty chair beside the door.

"Cat got yer tongue, Myrn?"

Some twenty-five women sat on an assortment of chairs, leftovers from offices and factory departments, set against three walls of the big, room with its pea green walls. Late afternoon sun forced its way through the years of grime on the ceiling-high, many-paned window behind Betty, silhouetting her against the hazy light. The room smelled of metal and machine oil, sweat and unwashed bodies.

"Did you mean me?" Myrna replied. "I don't answer to somebody else's name. My name is Myrn-*ah*. You know, like Myrn-*ah* Loy, my mama's favorite movie star, who she named me after."

Betty put on a nasty grin and looked at her friends. "Oh, now, it's a movie star. La-de-dah!" The grin morphed into a scowl. "Well, I like Myrn, and that's what I'll keep callin' you. No broad with a bastard kid's got any call to think she's better than anybody else. Sure as hell not a movie star. And from what I hear, you ain't much different from your slut mama."

Myrna clenched her jaw until she nearly broke her teeth. Lillie Schroeder's spectacular death under the wheels of a locomotive some twenty-five years ago was still cause for conversation among many of the 25,000 folks in Newport City, Illinois. Myrna said nothing. Betty was right, except that Myrna didn't think she was better than anybody else. Aunt Ada never stopped telling her what a no-good tramp she was, that her mother had been even worse, and since Scarlett was born the name-calling and ugly remarks got worse. A third generation of whores, Ada had screamed.

When Myrna didn't respond, Betty picked up a newspaper from a nearby card table that tilted on a half-folded leg. "Humph! Ain't this town and this state ever gonna be rid of the goddamn Holmans?"

Myrna sucked in a quick breath and held it.

"Who're the Holmans?" asked Martha Schwartz, a widow with two kids.

"Read the paper once in a while and you'd know what was going on," Betty snapped.
Martha's husband had been killed when he touched a hot wire on the job as an electric company lineman. Martha didn't pay much attention to anything but trying to survive.

"The Holmans have had their dirty fingers in politics in this town for nearly a hundred years," Betty went on. "The old man was Chief Justice of the Illinois Supreme Court, way back. The father is head of the state Senate, and now the playboy son is runnin' for the U-nited States House of Representatives."

"What's his name?" Sally Untermeyer asked.

"David. David Holman, the Third," Betty sneered. I ain't never seen him. He was too good to go to high school here. They shipped him out east to some high-falutin' boarding school where the old man and the grandfather and everybody before him went. I hear he's got the reddest hair in the state. It's the family trademark. All of 'em have red hair, but his is s'posed to be redder than all of 'em put together. See, here's his pitcher." She turned the paper so the front page faced the room, displaying a two-column black-and-white photograph of a good-looking young man with tightly curled hair.

Myrna wanted to scream. Why couldn't he stay out of her life? Not that he was in it, but now people would be talking about him all the time and asking her if she'd vote for him. Nobody knew he was Scarlett's father. Nobody. Definitely, not David Holman. A sudden thought made her blood run cold. Scarlett looked just like him. Now that he was in the papers, somebody might make the connection.

Betty's voice droned on, reading the article. "Holman, the—uh—sky-on—of Newport City's most prom-i-nent family, is married to the former Carol Rasmuss . . .."

Betty stopped, and everyone facing the door made a collective gasp and stared as if a Martian had appeared there. Myrna turned and stared, too, and for a moment forgot David Holman. Jack Sweeney, their boss, stood in the doorway, Beside him stood a young woman, tall and slim, dressed in black pants pressed to a crease that rivaled Betty's and a simple white cotton sleeveless shirt, perfect complement to skin the color of coffee with a dollop of cream.
"Ladies," Jack announced, "I'd like you to meet Lydia McIntire, who starts work in our department tonight." Lydia McIntire parted full lips in a tentative smile. "Since I can't invade this female bastion," he continued "I'll let Betty introduce Lydia to the rest of the girls." He turned and left.

7

Lydia McIntire, her head held high, stepped inside the room. Betty's grin squished her tiny eyes to slits. "Since when did Weston Switch start hirin' niggers? Or ain't you a nigger? McIntire. Maybe black Irish. Ha! Ha! What part of Ireland you come from?"

The new girl's hands fisted, but she grinned, a grin that was no smile. "My great-great grandmother's master came from Glasgow. That's in Scotland. He took a shine to the fourteen-year-old house nigger."

Except for clanks from machinery and distant male voices shouting and laughing, the room fell silent. Twenty-four pairs of eyes shifted away from the door. Betty cleared her throat. Lydia McIntire said nothing, holding Betty's gaze with her own, her full lips pressed thin. Betty broke the eye contact, sighed and pointed. "That there girl next to the door is Myrn-ah. The one next to the empty chair beside her is Sadie, and next to her is Liz, and . . ."

Myrna wanted to cheer. Not often did anyone get the best of Betty Brown.

When Betty finished the introductions, Lydia McIntire sat beside Myrna, in the only empty chair in the room. "You're Myrna?" she asked.

"Myrna Schroeder."

"Have you worked here long?"

"About two years. I was laid off last year for about six months and I've only been back since January."

"Is it a good place to work?"

Myrna shrugged. "It's a job."

Lydia McIntire chuckled. "I guess that's what they all boil down to. You have to earn money. Doesn't make much difference how."

"You're right."

The klaxon began to honk, startling Myrna as usual. Why did she always jump when that thing went off, especially since she heard it a half-dozen times every night?

"What's that?" Lydia asked.

"It's time to go to work. We line up out there by the double doors and Tim Forrester, the set-up man, reads us our machine assignments."

Myrna stood and got in the ragged line behind a half-dozen other women, Lydia McIntire right behind her. The line snaked through Department 43 with its milling machines that poured stinking machine oil over switch parts, as the women operators drilled holes in the parts.

"What do I do?" Lydia McIntire whispered in Myrna's ear.

"Just wait until Tim tells you. Clyde, the other set-up guy, will show you where to go and what to do," Myrna replied. She turned back toward Tim.

Tim Forrester stood beside the door, clipboard in hand, snapping out assignments. The line dwindled as the women disappeared one by one through the big door to the machines they'd been assigned. Now, only Belle Crosson stood between Myrna and Tim. He glanced at his clipboard and made a check mark. "It's screwdriver four tonight, Belle," he said.

Belle had worked in Department 43 for years, and the constant exposure to the machine oil had turned her face with its network of wrinkles into lightly tanned leather. When her hands cracked open from the oil, they'd transferred her to Department 21. Now, the wrinkles converged, making her face smaller and meaner. "Four?"

Myrna cringed. Screwdriver 1 belonged to Belle. Everybody knew that. There'd be hell to pay all night if she was taken off. Don't even think 'hell', Myrna told herself. You might accidentally say in it front of Scarlett.

"Can't help it," Tim said. "It's down. Been down since before noon, Jack says."
"

"That shit-ass Harriet. She never can run the damn thing right," Belle said.

"She runs a better rate than you do," Tim retorted.

"Yeah. She pushes it up so nobody else can make it, and then the machine breaks and I get stuck with four. Wouldn't put it past her to do it a' purpose," Belle growled.

"Cool it, Belle. Get in there." He looked at his clipboard again and Belle stalked toward the door, muttering.

"Won't she get fired for talking like that to the boss?" Lydia whispered.

"Tim's no boss, and she talks like that all the time. Nobody pays any attention to her," Myrna replied."

"Let's see. Myrna?" Tim grinned. "Hey, how about I take you home tonight. Them cabs is pretty crowded, and maybe we could take a little detour. I know a nice little country school house and I've got a blanket." Tim was married and the father of four children.

Myrna clenched her teeth, but said nothing. It didn't do any good, they'd just be after her all the more. Why did they always say dirty things to her? He never talked like that to Christine Hagerman. Although Christine could call herself "Mrs.," her husband had married her just because she was pregnant. He never even lived with her and divorced her as soon as the baby was born, but nobody made dirty remarks to Mrs. Perfect.

Tim checked the clipboard again. "Well, I guess I've got a kick press for you tonight, Myrna. Number five."

Kick press. The worst job in the place, the only machine that didn't run powered, and you could hurt your back if you kicked it wrong.

As she walked into Department 21, she heard Tim say, "Well, well. Look what we've got here. Lydia McIntire, ain't it? Jack told me about you. We'll start you on the bench, and see if you can figure out how to put the parts together." He turned so his head was inside the door.

"Hey, Clyde, got one for you to babysit."

Myrna went into the department. The room was sixty feet long by twenty wide, the walls covered with the ubiquitous green paint. Two rows of fluorescent tubes ran down the center of the ceiling, the length of the room. Three tall floor fans, scattered around the room, hummed in a futile attempt to cool the air. It smelled like metal and grease and leftover sweat.

The ten, woman-high, punch presses that lined the west wall wore the same pea green, but on them it was scratched and scuffed, and big spots of shiny bare metal showed through. The presses, with their angled oval covers, looked like so many tattered green soldiers at present arms. Only the boss's pets, like Christine Hagerman, ran the three automatic machines on the other side of the doors. She was supposed to be the best operator in the department.

The foreman's office, a box of plasterboard and wood with four large windows so he could see the whole department, was set in the middle of the room. It was just big enough for a desk, file cabinet, desk chair and a visitor's chair. In front of the boss's office sat the four screwdrivers that looked like a row of tall, skinny metal giraffes from some futuristic movie. Operators sat on high stools to run them. Next to them,

Myrna pulled out the green chair with its round wood seat at kick press 5, and sat down, shifting around on the hard seat as if comfort were possible. Belle sat beside her on a high stool at screwdriver 4, muttering to herself, her face set in a sour mask, her hands a blur as she fed parts into the die, tripped the pedal, and swept the finished part into the bin beside the machine.

Across the narrow space in the next row, Betty Brown and Sadie Mitchell powered up the riveters, and their machine gun rattle filled the room. The small power presses behind her began their floor-shaking "thunk-thunk-thunk." Across the room, behind the riveters, Myrna saw the new girl, Lydia, sitting at the assembly bench, her head tilted toward Clyde as he explained how to put the parts together. She had a smart look about her, like she knew what he would say before he said it. Then again, she was new. In six months, she'd probably

11

have that glazed-over look in her eyes and the stooped shoulders of everyone else.

Myrna looked down at the half-cylinder tray in front of her, filled with switch springs, each U-shaped piece of thin copper, about an inch long and a half-inch wide. One end was cut into two legs about three-quarters of an inch long. The solid end was bent at an angle with a hole in the center. A small box at her right held silver rivets that looked like short fat straight pins and glittered like expensive jewelry. She poured some into a tiny tray and with a touch of her forefinger slid one through an opening in the tray to the die seat. She fit the spring over it and stomped hard on the big iron pedal; the jolt ricocheted all the way up her legs through her backbone to her head. The hammer dropped with a clunk, flattened the rivet to the spring, and her forefinger flicked the part into the box behind the machine.

Seven hours, fifty-eight minutes and one thousand four hundred and ninety-nine kicks to go.

Chapter 2

Three floors above where Department 21's night shift was getting ready for supper break, Mark Weston pulled open the right-hand drawer on his massive glass-and-chrome desk and took out a decanter of Glen Livet. Fiery rays of late afternoon sun leaked through the blinds, turned the Glen Livet gold, and sent rainbow shards of light from the intricate design cut into the heavy glass. A matching tumbler sat on the desktop. A row of similar bottles and decanters graced the bar on the west wall, but this supply Mark kept close at hand. He poured the Scotch slowly into the glass, made a silent toast to the sun, brought the glass to his lips and swallowed it, neat. He poured another, leaned back in the black leather Eames chair and let this one take its time. The smooth liquor ironed out all the kinks and annoyances of the day.

The room was a twin of Department 21 in size, but polished oak hid the concrete floor that gleamed under the red and blue oriental rugs scattered over it. Behind the thin wood blinds and white silk draperies with dark red valances, four windows sparkled like the liquor decanters. Heavy oak paneling covered the concrete block walls. Opposite the windows, a pair of black leather sofas flanked a thick glass cocktail table that held business magazines placed in three neat stacks. The air was like a cool spring breeze.

An antique grandfather clock stood in the corner opposite the desk, a little out of place in a room filled with contemporary furniture. Mark smiled as he looked at it over his glass. How many hours had he spent as a little boy lying on his stomach on the soft red rug in front of the clock in its niche in Gramps' grand foyer? An ancestor had brought the clock from England right after the Revolution. It didn't fit Noreen's interior designer's plans for their home. Neither did the rug, so both were relegated to the office. That suited him just fine.

Now, he sat in his own throne room, king of an empire that had been born in his brain. The sound of his kingdom made a barely felt vibration through the soles of his custom-made loafers. The new automatic press on the ground level, the only place strong enough to support it, punched out fifty thousand springs an hour from long narrow strips of copper sheeting. It cost a hundred thousand dollars, but it needed only one operator per shift, replacing ten smaller machines and their operators and quadrupling their output.

Each stamp vibrated through the building like a machine gun firing hundred-pound iron balls into a padded wall. It was a good reminder of what the building was really about to everyone who worked in the sheltered executive office suite.

Mark replaced the cut-glass stopper and returned the decanter to its home, then went to the bar sink, washed the glass, returned and set it beside the bottle, closed the drawer, and pushed the button lock. Now, he could face his empress, Noreen.

"Joanne," he said into the intercom on his desk. "I'm leaving."

"Yes, Mr. Weston. Have a nice evening."

Mark got into the small elevator in the corner behind the desk, and let the heavy oak doors slide shut. He leaned against the paneled walls; gray carpet cradled his feet. What excuse could he manufacture to delay going home to Noreen? Noreen, who reminded him almost daily for the past fifteen years whose money, rather, whose father's money, made Weston Automatic Switch Company possible. And that father owned fifty-two per cent of the stock, and would until he died. And when the old man died, his only child would inherit that fifty-two per cent.

"Keep it in the family forever," Ed Best had said with a wink when the papers were signed. Mark wasn't considered part of the family. Ed had hopes of a grandson to carry on the business. His daughter did not share those hopes. Just the thought of pregnancy, childbirth and spending the rest of her life with the resulting product made her nauseous. It was the only thing she disagreed with her father about.

The elevator walls seemed to shrink around Mark when he remembered that signing, to squeeze him, making him momentarily immobile. The car eased to a stop and the door whispered open. The hot, heavy air hit him in the face like a wall. A man could suffocate in this heat. He stepped out and crossed the industrial green hallway in two strides. He shoved the heavy metal door open. It swung and bumped something.

"Oh!" The voice was high, and the cry was followed immediately by a sound of something scraping concrete.

Mark stepped out onto the stoop. "Omigod!" A woman sprawled on the asphalt parking lot beside the stoop, her blue skirt around her hips. That stoop was at least four feet high. She had to be hurt. Her left arm

14

was flung out above her head at a peculiar angle. A small brown paper bag lay just beyond her hand, and what looked like a sandwich was near it. An apple rolled toward Tom Anderson's car. She noticed Mark and brushed her skirt lower with her right arm, then struggled to sit up, her face twisting in pain as she tried to move her left arm.

"Wait. Let me help you," Mark called, and he ran down the steps, almost tripping over a big, fabric handbag on the bottom step. He knelt beside her. She struggled to sit up again, and her eyes, like dark sapphires, widened like a startled deer. "Don't move. It looks like you could have broken your arm. I'll get help."

"I'm all right. I don't need help." She set her jaw and tried to stand, bracing herself with her right arm. Her face twisted with pain.

The door was near the corner of the building where it met the drive into the parking lot, and Mark reached the drive in a few steps. At the street end of the drive, an eight-foot steel post held the hinge end of a steel mesh gate that stretched twelve feet across the drive to another post. A small square white building with a flat roof stood beside the gate opening.

"Guard," he shouted. He waited a moment, but there was no response, so he shouted again.

A gray hat with a black visor appeared in the open door and pointed across the gate past the front of the building. Mark's next shout was lost as a semi rumbled past in a cloud of choking black exhaust. The hat turned toward the street and the truck.

"Guard," Mark shouted again, taking a few steps toward the gate. The hat turned toward him. When he saw who was calling him, the guard wearing the hat stepped outside the shack and started down the drive.

"No," Mark called, waving him back. "Call the ambulance. There's been an accident."

The guard hesitated a moment, the hat bobbed affirmative, and disappeared into the shack.

Mark strode back to the girl, pulled off his jacket, folded it into a square and knelt beside her. "Help will be here soon." He raised her head and slipped the jacket under it.

"I don't need an ambulance. I have to get back to work."

"Not before you're checked out at the hospital."

Her eyes widened. "I can't go to the hospital."

"You can't NOT go to the hospital," he snapped. "I'm no doctor, but I think if your arm's broken it will have to be set and a cast put on it." He looked at the ground. "I'm sorry. I didn't mean to growl at you. Force of habit. And while I'm at it, I'm really sorry to have caused this. I had no idea anyone was outside that door. No one is ever on that landing."

"It's so hot and it was shady on the steps, and kind of quiet. It seemed like a better place to eat supper than in the cafeteria." she said.

"I see," he said. "By the way, I'm Mark Weston." Her eyes got the frightened deer look again.

"What's your name and where do you work?"

"Myrna Schroeder. I work in Department 21"

"The small press department, right?"

She nodded, and Mark suddenly saw someone other than a thin girl wearing a cheap blue skirt and white blouse, who smelled of sweat. She wasn't really young, not a kid, she was a woman, a beautiful woman when you got a good look at her. She was the image of Disney's Snow White, with her heart-shaped face and hair like heavy black satin. A small, straight nose and full red lips finished the Snow White look. Snow White had been Mark Weston's fantasy woman since he'd first seen the movie as a boy. Noreen spent thousands just trying to look that good. The old familiar twinge stirred in Mark's groin. He took a deep breath. "How long have you worked with us?"

"About two years."

"Does your husband work here, too?"

Her eyes widened. "I'm not married," she said.

A siren wailed, coming closer until it growled into silence at the gate. Mark got up and went to the drive. The guard was opening the gate and the long white vehicle operated by Eichberger's Funeral Home

16

rolled down the slight incline to where Mark stood. Once, the sick and injured of Newport City traveled to the hospital and/or the cemetery in the same black hearse. When doctors stopped making house calls and people got used to using Eichberger's for ambulance service, they bought the fancy white one with its oscillating red light and siren on the top.

"She's over there. She fell off that stoop and I think she broke her arm," Mark told the driver and the man who sat in the passenger seat.

Both men got out of the ambulance, and the passenger went to the back, opened the door and pulled out a rolling stretcher. The driver walked to where Myrna lay, and knelt beside her.

"Hello. I'm George Seitz. How are you feeling?"

"I'm fine, really. My arm hurts a little, but that's all. I can go back to work."

George Seitz ran his hand lightly down the injured arm and shook his head. "You won't be going back to work just yet. The bone in your lower arm feels like it isn't lined up right."

The other man laid the stretcher on the asphalt beside Myrna and looked at his partner. "Looks like we've got a broken arm here," George Seitz said, then turned back to Myrna. "We're going to lift you a little to get you on the stretcher. It might hurt, but we'll try to be real careful."

"But I can't go to the hospital," Myrna said, the frightened deer look on her face. "I can't miss work."

Mark stood at Myrna's right side, watching the men. What was the matter with the girl? She seemed to be panicked at the idea of missing work. He didn't think putting parts together on a punch press was such thrilling work that somebody would be afraid to miss a few days or a week.

Seitz looked up at Mark. "Lady, this guy's the big cheese here. He can fix it so you don't get laid off or lose your pay."

Mark's face burned. Of course, she was afraid of losing her job if she didn't go to work. Why didn't he know that? Maybe he'd better pay some attention to employee relations. "Don't even think about it, Miss

Schroeder. I'll talk to your foreman. It's Jack Sweeney, isn't it?" The girl nodded.

Seitz stood beside the door, clipboard in hand. "Miss., I need your name, age, address and telephone number?" Seitz continued. Myrna gave him the information. He wrote it on the clipboard, closed the door and turned toward the front.

The ambulance crew lifted Myrna carefully to the stretcher, and Mark followed them to the ambulance. "I'll talk to Jack, then I'll go to the hospital," he told Myrna.

Mark touched Seitz's arm, and said. "I'll pay for everything." Seitz nodded and got behind the wheel. Mark stepped back as Seitz maneuvered the long vehicle into a turn and drove up the inclined driveway. The siren whined to life and the red light flashed as it turned left into the street and sped toward the hospital.

Mark stared at the empty driveway in a mental fog. He felt like he'd just stepped off a cliff and was spinning in midair. All because of a little factory girl who looked like Snow White.

"You okay Mr. Weston?"

Mark started. The guard was looking at him strangely. "I'm fine. This all happened so fast."

"Stuff like that usually does," the guard replied. "Well, I'll get back to my post."

Mark nodded, then walked back to his coat on the ground, picked it up, brushed it and folded it over his arm. The brown paper bag still lay on the ground, the sandwich wrapped in waxed paper halfway out of it. The apple was nowhere in sight, probably under Anderson's car. He picked up the bag and sandwich and tossed them into a nearby trash container, then reached into his pocket and pulled out a small black instrument, pressed a button on it. The door to the wood frame one-car garage in the corner of the parking lot began to slide up. He owned the only automatic garage door opener in town.

Inside the garage, he unlocked the door to the Rolls Royce Silver Wraith, tossed his jacket and the girl's handbag into the back seat and slid behind the steering wheel. The car was warm, but the garage spared it from the suffocating heat. He pulled the door shut and wiped an imaginary speck of dust off the dash, turned the key in the ignition and touched the accelerator lightly with his foot. The Rolls Royce's engine woke quietly, purring like a tiger.

"Oh, shit. I forgot to tell her foreman," Mark said aloud, as he backed the Rolls out of the garage. He closed the garage door, turned the car and headed toward the gate. The guard was outside, ready to open the gate, and Mark stopped. "Can you hand me the phone?" The guard ran back into his shack and stretched the phone cord to Mark, who called Jack Sweeney, returned the phone and turned into the street toward the hospital.

Ten minutes later, Mark pulled into the emergency entrance to the hospital, found a parking place and angled the Rolls between two cars. Inside the waiting room, he strode to a corner desk. "A young woman named Myrna Schroeder was brought in by ambulance about twenty minutes ago," he said to the nurse behind the desk. "Can you tell me how she is?"

The woman flipped through file folders, frowned and picked up a phone. "This is Joyce in admitting. Do you have a patient named. . .?" She looked up at Mark. He repeated the name. "Myrna Schroeder," she said. "There's a man here asking about her." She looked up again. "Are you a relative?" Mark shook his head. "May I have your name and your connection with the patient?"

Mark sighed. "My name is Mark Weston. I was responsible for her injury."

The woman repeated the information into the phone, listened and then hung up. "She has a broken arm, but it's not serious. They're setting it now. Someone will be out to speak to you when they're finished. You can have a seat in the waiting room."

"Thank you," he replied, and crossed the room to a row of wooden folding chairs. He sat in one beside a table littered with magazines. Nobody else was in the room. He propped his right ankle on his left knee, brushed the cuff of his charcoal summer wool pants, pulled at a wrinkle in his black silk calf-high sock and rubbed at a slight scuff on the toe of his black loafer. He picked up a magazine at random, a *Life*, dated June 12, 1949. Good God! Three years old! He tossed it back on the table.

What the hell am I doing here? The assistant foreman, what was his name, Sweeney, could have brought her. A thought trickled out of a deep recess in his brain. Would I have done all this if she was forty, weighed two hundred pounds and had a face like a gargoyle? One corner of his mouth turned up in a half-smile. Hell, I'd give Sweeney a bonus to take care of it.

He finally became aware of the hospital smell: urine and feces washed over by strong antiseptic, and his stomach turned over. Disgusting. He stood and went to a window beside the double entry doors. Branches from a tree covered a third of the window, but beyond it he could see bright yellow lily-like flowers along the driveway and a hedge behind them. It was strange, way too quiet. He thought a hospital emergency room would be full of people and ambulances roaring up with sirens blaring. Of course, Eichberger's was the only ambulance in town.

As if on command, he heard a wail in the distance that came closer, then stopped. A moment later, the Eichberger ambulance appeared in the drive, turned and backed up to the open emergency room double doors. Seitz and his partner jumped out and ran to the rear, opened the door and pulled out a stretcher. A man wrapped in blankets with some kind of black rubber mask on his face lay on the stretcher. A nurse appeared at the patient's side and spoke to him. Seitz and the other man rolled the stretcher through the doors, the nurse still beside the patient, talking to him.

"Mark?" Mark turned to face Dr. Karl Steinhart, a sometime golfing partner, who wore a white shapeless gown and a cap that covered his hair. A surgical mask hung around his neck, and he held a clipboard. "What are you doing here? They said you asked about . . ." he consulted the clipboard, "Myrna Schroeder."

"Yes. How is she?"

"She's fine. Just a simple fracture of the ulna."

"What's that?"

"The in the forearm. We set it and put a cast on it. Your *friend* will be fine."

Mark caught the implication in the word and focused on Steinhart's eyes, an action that usually caused Harvard educated corporate vice presidents to break out in a sweat and stammer. Ten years of medical school and twenty of private practice immunized Dr. Steinhart against intimidation, but still he paused. "She's not my friend," Mark said. "She's my employee. I'm responsible for her accident."

"I see," the doctor replied. "She said she fell off a stoop at the plant. How did that happen?"

"She decided to eat her lunch at the top of the steps outside the door that leads to my elevator. The landing's about four feet off the ground. I opened the door, felt some resistance and pushed it harder. I heard her cry out. When I got outside, she was lying on the ground with her arm at a funny angle. I had the guard call the ambulance."

"Lucky she didn't hit her head."

"Yes," Mark replied absently. "What comes next?"

Steinhart listed things Myrna had to do.

"How long will she be off work?"

"I'd say at least a week. She can go back and do light work until the cast comes off in about six weeks."

"Send the bill to my office,'

"You want to cover this? Doesn't she have insurance?"

"She's covered by the company policy, but this was my fault. I'll cover all expenses."

"She said she doesn't have a family doctor. I gathered it's because she can't afford one. God, Mark, don't you pay your people enough that they can go to the doctor?"

Mark glared at Steinhart. "They get decent salaries and they have insurance. Will you take her as your patient?"

Steinhart shrugged, and grinned. "Sure. If you're paying I may be able to take that trip to California I've been thinking about."

Mark's tension disappeared. "Just don't jack up your fees too high— and thanks. Is she ready to go home now?"

Steinhart nodded. "She should have someone with her for a day or two. I'll tell her and call somebody to pick her up."

"I'll take her home."

Steinhart's right eyebrow arced toward the edge of his. "Some ambulance, a Silver Wraith Rolls Royce. Or is it the Mercedes today?

I'll go tell the nurse to bring her out. She may be a little wobbly." He turned and crossed the room and disappeared through the door.

Moments later, the padded double doors to the emergency room opened and Myrna, in a wheelchair, was rolled across the floor by a student nurse in a blue and white striped dress. Myrna's left arm was wrapped in a large white sling and Mark could see the end of a plaster cast. Her fair skin was translucent, and she acknowledged Mark with a wan smile.

Mark went to her. "How are you feeling?"

"A little woozy, but they said it would go away soon."

"I'll get the car and bring it to the door," he said, and turned to the nurse. "You can bring her outside when I drive up."

A blanket of heat and humidity struck him when he left the air-conditioned waiting room and he strode quickly to the Rolls, automatically inspecting it for scratches or dings. As soon as he closed the door, he turned on the air conditioning, cranking the window open to exhaust the hot air.

The nurse helped Myrna get into the car and closed the door. "Your purse is in the back seat," Mark said, as he pulled away from the curb. "Are you in pain?"

She shook her head. "Not right now. The doctor said the drugs would wear off later and it would probably hurt a lot then. He gave me a bottle of pain pills." She held up a bottle filled with small white pills.

"I can't tell you how sorry I am about this," he said. "You don't have to worry about expenses. I'll pay for it all. Dr. Steinhart said you don't have a family doctor, but he agreed to be your doctor. Okay?"

"I guess so."

He stopped for the stop sign at the end of the emergency drive. "By the way, where do you live?"

Myrna gave Mark her address and leaned back against the soft seat. The car seats were all gray and smelled like leather. They probably were leather, she thought. The dashboard was real wood, polished as shiny as Ada's dining room table. The car was cool, as if it was air conditioned. Imagine. An air conditioned car.

22

She sneaked a look at him as he drove. He was tall, probably at least six feet. When she had first seen him from where she lay on the parking lot, he looked like a giant. He was good looking for an older guy, with strong features, tanned from the sun. Finely shaped brows framed his eyes, which were as black as midnight, with crinkles around the outer edges. His nose had a little bump in the middle. Lines from both sides of his nose reached a mouth that probably frowned more easily than it smiled. He had a Pepsodent smile, his teeth were even except for one on the side that lapped over its neighbor a bit.

"How's the arm now?" he asked, turning toward her.

"It's all right," she said. "You turn left at the next corner."

Mark braked for a stop light, and while he waited, ran one hand through his hair, ruffling the neatly combed dark waves, shot through with silver, frosted around his ears and at his temples. He'd loosened his tie and unbuttoned the stiff, crisp collar of his white shirt. It may have been the tousled hair, the beautiful blue tie askew and a few dark hairs peeking out of the "V" of his shirt, but suddenly the mask came off. He wasn't the rich man who owned the town. He was just a hot, tired guy at the end of a working day.

"Whew! It's sure been a hot one today," he said.

"It's nice and cool in the car, though," Myrna said. "It feels real good."

"Air conditioning is a great invention," he said, steering the car through the intersection and into a left turn.

Chapter 3

Kids scattered from a baseball game in the middle of the street and gawked at the big car as it passed. Folks, mostly men, sat on their porch steps with an after-supper smoke or beer and stared at the car, wondering what a Rolls was doing in this neighborhood. Man, what was it like to be behind the wheel?

"It's the big house on the right, the one with the stairs on the outside," Myrna said. Mr. Weston nodded and steered toward the curb.

Although it was still daylight at eight o'clock, Myrna's kitchen light was on the side of the house away from the sun and was usually dark by this time. Now, a light shone through the window, and there weren't any in Mrs. Neumann's apartment downstairs. Scarlett must still be up. She hadn't even thought about that. She'd told Mr. Weston she wasn't married. How could she explain Scarlett? Could he fire her because she had an illegitimate child?

"Is that your apartment with the lights on?" Mr. Weston asked as he parked at the curb. She nodded. "Do you always leave your lights on when you go to work?"

"People will think I'm home and won't break in."

"Break in?" Newport City was a town where doors were never locked. "You mean thieves would come in while you're gone?"

"Sometimes." She realized the car had stopped and fumbled for the door latch.

Before she got the door open, Mr. Weston was around the car and opening the door for her. "Here. Give me your hand and just ease yourself across the seat." His hand was soft, not like the hard, working men's hands she knew. When she reached the edge of the seat, he stooped and put his arm around her, supporting the cast. "Okay. Now swing your legs around."

"I can get out by myself."

"Not with that awkward cast. The last thing you need is to fall down again."

When her feet touched the ground, her knees didn't want to hold her. His arm gripped her and he urged her to take a step. How could she have gotten this weak in the few minutes from the hospital?

"The shock is wearing off," he said, as if reading her mind. He slammed the car door and helped her to the steps.

"I'm stronger now," she said. "I can make it up the steps." She tried to pull away, but he tightened his hold.

"Like hell you can." He moved to her other side and supported the cast. "Now, you take the handrail and I'll hold you under the cast."

Myrna nodded, too tired to disagree. Even with Mr. Weston's help, each step seemed to be a mile high. The landing at the top looked like it was in the clouds. By the time they had reached half-way, Myrna was breathing hard. She'd never make it to the top. Then what would she do? She'd die before she let him carry her.

The door opened. "Who is there?" Mrs. Neumann called.

"It's me," Myrna replied, then to Mr. Weston. "You can go now. Mrs. Neumann can help me the rest of the way."

"You're really trying hard to get rid of me, aren't you?" Mr. Weston replied with a chuckle. "Well, I'm here until I get you inside and make sure you'll be taken care of." He called, "Mrs. Neumann. I'm Mark Weston and Myrna's been hurt. It's hard for her to get up the stairs so I'm helping her. Just hold the door open and we'll be there in a second."

Mrs. Neumann's silhouetted head peered over the railing. "Myrna? What happened?"

"I'll tell you about it when I get upstairs," Myrna said, gritting her teeth against the pain and the effort it took to get up the next step.

"Stupid old fool," Mr. Weston muttered in her ear.

"No, she's not. She's a nice lady and she helps me a lot. She's just nosey and she talks a lot."

They finally reached the landing, both puffing. Mr. Weston still held her as they paused to catch their breath.

"Mama. Mama. You're home already. Even before I went to bed." Scarlett stopped in the doorway and her smile turned to a puzzled frown. "What's that on your arm?"

"I'll tell you about it when I get inside," Myrna said, then to Mr. Weston, "I can manage now. Thank you for all your help."

"I told you I wasn't leaving until I was sure you were all right. Now, come on." He guided her through the door.

Mark was sweating. There must have been thirty steps and that cast made Myrna heavy. He helped her through the door, past the placid shape of Mrs. Neumann, into a tiny kitchen. Fastened to the wall on his left was an old-fashioned sink with a long drainboard. A small four-burner stove sat against the wall perpendicular to the sink, a white painted cabinet, like something he'd seen in an antique shop, stood against the wall opposite the sink, with a small refrigerator next to it. A white table, covered with a red checked cloth, and two chairs took up the middle of the room. The room smelled of bleach and looked clean enough to do surgery.

The little red-haired girl stood back, staring wide-eyed at Myrna and him, her right forefinger in her mouth. Mrs. Neumann suddenly pulled a chair away from the table, as if she'd just realized Myrna needed to sit down. He eased her into the chair and let go.

Myrna looked up at him with a wan smile. "I keep saying thank you, but I can't think of any other way to tell you how much I appreciate your help."

He grinned. "I haven't had the opportunity to be a knight in shining armor for a long time. I just wish you hadn't been hurt."

"Oh, where are my manners. Mrs. Neumann, this is Mr. Mark Weston."

The woman's eyes made saucers. "From da fac-to-ry?" she asked, in a heavy German accent he noticed for the first time.

"Yes," he replied, and turned to the child, who hung back. If Myrna was Snow White, this child was Orphan Annie, with her tumble of fire-red curls and strange lime green eyes, both of which looked oddly familiar. She'd called Myrna, "Mama", but Myrna had said she wasn't married. Maybe she was divorced. Some people, some lucky people, did get divorced. He knelt to the child's level. "Hi, I'm Mark. What's your name?"

The youngster looked at Myrna, who nodded, and then pulled the finger out of her mouth. "Scarlett."

"That's a pretty name, especially for a little girl with such red hair. Do you go to school?"

Scarlett shook her head.

"She'll be in kindergarten next fall," Myrna said.

Those strange green eyes locked onto Mark's, and with a solemn face, Scarlett said, "You're pretty."

Behind him, Mark heard Myrna gasp, "Scarlett."

Mark nearly lost his balance and grasped the edge of the table for support. He began to laugh until he almost overbalanced again, but one look at the small face sobered him.

"I'm sorry," he said. "I shouldn't have laughed. What you said was very nice and I really like it. Nobody in my whole, entire, long life ever told me I was pretty. Thank you. I laughed because I know a lot of people who would faint dead a way to hear somebody say that to me. Most people think I'm kind of scary. "

"Know something?" Scarlett shook her head. "You're pretty yourself. I am very pleased to meet you," he said and stood, painfully aware of creaking knees. He was getting too old to be helping damsels in distress, even if they did look like Snow White and Little Orphan Annie.

"You'll spoil her with that kind of talk," Myrna said.

"Nonsense. Pretty girls need to be told they are."

Scarlett had her finger back in her mouth and stared at him, solemn as a small judge, and then she wrapped a lopsided smile around the finger. She looked up at her mother. "Can I sit on your lap, Mama?"

Myrna reached out with her right arm. "Of course, baby." Scarlett wriggled onto her mother's lap, careful of the cast that rested on the table.

Mark turned to speak to Myrna but Mrs. Neumann had her mouth open, ready for the first question. Mark didn't give her the opportunity. "I accidentally opened a door into Myrna and pushed her off a rather high stoop, and she broke her arm. We've just come from the hospital. She'll be in that cast for several weeks and will need a lot of help. Right now, she's tired and needs some rest. Can you stay with her?"

"Of course. There is just me downstairs."

"And Scarlett, can you help take care of your Mama?"

Scarlett's eyes widened and she nodded, then turned to Myrna

"I'll set up the appointment with Karl Steinhart in the morning and call you. Mark said."

The women exchanged glances. "I don't have a telephone," Myrna said.

Mark covered his shock. If she didn't have a doctor, why would he assume she had a telephone?

"I have a telephone, Mr. Weston," said Mrs. Neumann.

Mark said, "May I call you in the morning then, Mrs. Neumann?"

"Ja. My number is Blue 555-6428."

Mark repeated it. "Thank you. Now, I'll leave you to get Myrna settled. She really needs some rest." He turned to Myrna. "I'll be by tomorrow to take you to the doctor."

"But I . . ."

Mark shook his head. "No 'buts.' I'll be here."

"I don't know what to say."

He smiled. "'Yes, Mark,' would be fine. It was nice meeting you, Mrs. Neumann. Scarlett, take good care of your Mama, and I'll see you tomorrow."

Mark ran down the stairs and across the narrow yard and got into the car. He sat there for a moment, recalling a heart-shaped face, a blue skirt showing a slim thigh. Nice piece of ass, he thought. A bit stiff, a bit cold, except the way she cuddled the little girl and defended the old woman. A hint of fire there. He chuckled. It might be fun to light the fire. He started the car, stepped on the clutch, pulled back the stick, fed the engine with a gentle touch of his foot on the accelerator and pulled away from the curb, smiling.

Then he remembered the little redhead with her finger in her mouth. Again, something stirred in his brain. The hair and those strange green eyes. Why were they familiar? Well, a child was a complication he didn't need. Why hadn't Myrna told him about the child? Something was fishy there. He'd have Joanne check her records tomorrow.

Chapter 4

Fifteen minutes later and a mile and a half across town, the Rolls Royce drove between the square stone pillars that flanked the driveway to Mark's home, and he sighed. Pull yourself together, old boy, and pretend it never happened. Her highness awaits, he thought. He slowed the Rolls into the driveway, around to the front door, and got out.

Noreen waited in the living room, standing beside the white marble fireplace like a movie star, wearing a floor-length ice blue satin gown that accentuated her height and her anorexic body, pale blonde hair coiffed to perfection, short and slightly bouffant, her long pink-tipped fingers around the stem of a half-full martini glass on the white marble mantel.

"Are we going somewhere?" Mark asked, as he turned to the bar.

"We were expected at Mother's twenty minutes ago. Don't tell me you forgot? It is Wednesday, after all."

Mark went to the sideboard and poured a finger of Scotch into his glass, replaced the smooth round stopper in the heavy crystal decanter, and sauntered to the opposite corner of the fireplace. "Guess I did. Strange, after spending every Wednesday night for the past fifteen years at your parents' table. I must be getting old."

Noreen's teeth gleamed between bright red lips. "You said it." She took a sip of her martini. "Enduring Mother's weekly dinners shouldn't be too much to show your gratitude for their generosity."

Mark swallowed his drink. It burned pleasantly. "Their generosity has been amply repaid. How much have they made above their investment in my idea?"

Noreen smiled. "Of course, but it would have been an idea never realized had they not been so generous. And—if you had never met me."

"Oh, I'd have met you, or somebody else with a rich and greedy father."

Noreen flinched as if he had struck her, tossed down the rest of her drink and placed the empty glass on the mantel. "Now that you have that out of your system, please go change. I'll call Mother and tell her we're on our way. By the way, why you are so late?"

Mark placed his glass on the large antique Chinese trunk that served as a coffee table. "An accident at the plant."

"That made you three hours late? What happened? I didn't hear about an explosion."

"I opened a door into a woman who was eating her lunch on the rear doorstep and knocked her onto the parking lot. She broke her arm. I took her to the hospital and then home."

Noreen laughed. "How gallant. She must have been attractive."

"It was the only decent thing to do, and I hope it headed off a lawsuit. Now, if you'll excuse me, my dear, I'll go make myself presentable for your parents."

"Just hurry. We're going to be almost an hour late, and you know how Mother hates having her schedule upset." Noreen's Radcliffe accent had overtones of a fishwife.

In his room, Mark grimaced into the mirror, fumbling with the black bow tie. After all these years, you'd think he'd learn how to tie the damn thing. He gave it a final twitch, shrugged into his white dinner jacket and ran down the wide curving staircase.

Noreen gave him a silent inspection. "You'll do." She swept across the room to the front door.

"I'll do," Mark mocked. "You sound like a female Professor 'enry 'iggins."

"Oh, don't be tiresome. You're not the only one who's read Bernard Shaw. Now, get the car."

The ornate iron gates of the Best estate were open and Mark turned into the drive. Beside him, Noreen smoothed her hair, then her dress, opened her satin bag and rummaged through it, coming out with a lipstick. She pulled down the sun visor and frowned into its mirror, touching the lipstick to her already perfectly made up lips. Mark stopped at the entry steps, and Noreen got out. "I'll wait here for you," she said.

"Why? I've been inside before. I know my way around."

"Mark!"

All right." He parked the car in the circular drive and joined Noreen. "You're as jumpy as a cat. What's going on?"

"Why wouldn't I be jumpy? Thanks to you, I'll be treated to a lengthy dissertation on what delay does to a perfectly prepared meal, and how could I be so inconsiderate, and couldn't I train you better?"

"Woof!" Mark replied softly. Noreen glared and lifted her skirt to go up the steps.

They reached the huge foyer, and Noreen rearranged her face into a charming smile. At the far end, Ed Best was showing his favorite sculpture, a copy of the Venus de Milo, to a man who could have been the butt of short man jokes. But nobody made jokes about Miles Endicott, president of American Electric, one of the five largest corporations in the world. What was he doing here? Mark wondered.

Ed wore his Congenial Host smile and swept his right arm toward Mark and Noreen. "Miles, my daughter, Noreen Best Weston, and her husband, Mark, the brain behind the Weston Automatic Switch."

The little man, barely five feet tall, wearing an impeccably tailored white silk dinner jacket, black trousers and black tie, bowed his head with its halo of white hair over Noreen's hand. "Charmed, my dear. You are the image of your lovely mother. Ed, my friend, you are truly blessed to have two such beautiful women in your life." The small hand then gripped Mark's with the precise amount of strength and steel gray eyes drilled into Mark's. "I know all about Mark Weston, Boy Wonder, who practically won the war in a little factory in the middle of nowhere."

He turned to the woman who had joined them. "Mark Weston, my wife, Delores." Delores Endicott was at least ten inches taller than her husband, and twenty years younger, every blonde hair in her shoulder length page boy on its best behavior. Cool sea blue eyes assessed him while the soft rose lips smiled a subtle invitation.

Seems like she thinks I'll do, Mark thought. He inclined his head and made polite noises, then turned to his mother-in-law, tall and silver gray from her hair down her long satin gown to the toes of shoes that peered politely from under the dress. "Good evening, Eleanor. You look lovely, as usual." Another twenty years, and Noreen would look just like her, even more of an icicle.

"I'm pleased you could finally find your way here," she replied as she held up her cheek for the ritual kiss.

Banal conversation over cocktails and dinner finally ended, and the three women went into the living room for coffee. Ed led the way to his den, a room designed to mimic a British men's club. He held the big black leather armchair for Miles Endicott, who ignored it and found another that fit him. Ed left Mark to fend for himself and enthroned himself behind the enormous mahogany desk. Andrew, the Best's general factotum, poured brandy, served them and left.

Ed cradled the brandy snifter in his palms, inhaled the aroma, smiled and swallowed, closing his eyes and exhaling a satisfied, "A-a-ah!" Mark and Miles Endicott followed, without the "A-a-ah!" When they finished the ritual, Ed leaned back in his outsized desk chair, which gave a genteel twang. "Well, Miles, I'll let you tell Mark here the good news."

Endicott smiled. "I won't beat around the bush, Mark. I've been watching Weston Automatic Switch for a long time, and I suggested to my board that the company might make a nice addition to our line. They agreed, and I've been talking with Ed for several months." Mark shot a look at Ed, catching the smug expression on his face, and felt his blood pressure surge. Endicott smiled, understanding. "Ed didn't want to bother you with it. He preferred to have it a done deal, or at least, most of the details worked out, before he said anything. Those details have been settled among all the lawyers, with approval of both boards. Everything's ready for your stamp of approval.

Mark clamped his fingers around the glass, then carefully set it on the table beside him, leaned toward Endicott and said softly: "Which boards approved what? I don't recall any offer from American Electric discussed at any board meeting I attended."

Ed harrumphed. "We had an emergency meeting the week you were in New York with the bankers."

"And you just didn't bother to tell the president of the company about it and the president of the company just happened not to get the minutes of this 'emergency meeting.' Isn't that a bit unusual?"

"I didn't want you distracted when you were working on that government contract. We had more than a quorum. And I am chairman of the board."

Mark leaned back and picked up his brandy snifter. "Well, whatever you decided, I disapprove, and I'll take you to court if necessary."

"Gentlemen, please," Endicott said, shooting a daggered look at Ed, then turned to Mark. "Mark, I deeply regret that you were not kept informed of these proceedings. Ed assured me you'd be pleased. If I'd been aware you wouldn't agree, things would have been done quite differently. Nevertheless, I am here because American Electric is prepared to offer twelve million dollars for Weston Automatic Switch Co., plus stock and a number of lesser, but generous, incentives. Ed drove a hard bargain, but he agrees that it is a good deal."

Mark stared into Endicott's cold gray gaze, at his wary expression. He turned to Ed, who still lounged back in his chair, playing with the brandy snifter, apparently relaxed. Mark knew better. He was tense as a coiled snake. "Is Noreen in on this? How much has she been involved?"

Ed stared into his brandy snifter. "We've discussed it. She is my heir, after all."

"You discussed it with my wife, and said nothing to me. You seem to have this all wrapped, tied and ready for delivery." He paused. "Does he know the part about the patent?"

Ed's chair made a loud twang as he sat up, breathing hard, his face red as a ripe boil, and set the brandy snifter on the desk very gently, pasting a smile on his face as he turned to Miles Endicott.

"The boy will have his jokes," he said and barked a laugh.

Endicott swirled his brandy in the glass. "Boys do joke. But I don't see any boys here. Would you explain yourself, Mark?"

"I thought you made a thorough investigation. Isn't that why you made your deal with Ed?" He turned to Ed. "You may have the board chairmanship locked up in perpetuity, but the patents for the Weston automatic switch are registered to me, and to me alone. So, go ahead and make all the deals you want, but not with the rights to the patents."

Ed pasted on a smile. "Please, Mark. We don't want to discuss family problems before our guest."

"Since your guest wants to buy the company, it's more than a family problem."

"Gentlemen." Endicott's voice was soft, controlled, like the buzz of a rattler. "Ed, my friend. Surely you didn't intend to mislead me. Anson said you told him the patent situation would all be taken care of, that you guaranteed that Mark would be happy to be associated with us." Ed opened his mouth, but shut it when Endicott raised a cautioning hand. "I'd like to hear Mark's version."

Mark smiled, and eased back in his chair. "As you undoubtedly know, Ed put up the seed money for the company in return for fifty-two per cent of the stock and keeping the board in the family with him as chairman in perpetuity. When he dies, the chairmanship goes to my wife." Mark picked up the brandy snifter, cuddled it in his hands, rocked it gently, and inhaled deeply, then put the glass to his lips and swallowed what remained. "But I invented the switch and made it what it is today, and I'll make it what it will be in the future. Or I'll trash it. It's mine. And I won't sell – to Ed, to Noreen, or to you." Mark stood. "I'm sorry you made the trip for nothing Mr. Endicott. It's been a pleasure to meet you. Good night."

He reached the study door in two steps, opened it, stepped into the central hall and closed it softly behind him, and grinned. For once, he had Ed Best by the balls and he would squeeze until the old bastard screamed.

He didn't remember Noreen until he saw the pillars flanking his driveway. No matter, she'd probably want to stay with Mother and Daddy tonight to discuss how they would pull this particular fat out of the fire. He showered, wrapped his robe around him, and settled into his club chair in the bedroom with the Wall Street Journal and a nightcap.

The phone rang, and he reached for it on the end table.

"Miles Endicott, here."

"Yes?"

"I want to see you in the morning, 9:30. I have to be in San Francisco by 5:00 their time. I'll meet you in the coffee shop of this fleabag called the Premium Inn. I assume you know where it is."

"Oh, now you want to talk to me."

"I wish I'd talked to you before this. I must be getting senile to let Ed Best con me like this," Endicott said.

Mark said nothing for a long moment. "What do you have in mind?"

"I'll tell you when I see you."

"Sorry it's so late. If I'd known you were coming, I'd have set you up at Pleasant Meadows, a place I have in the country. At any rate, I'd rather meet you there instead of the coffee shop where anyone in town can see and hear us." Mark gave him the directions to the farm.

"I'll see you there at 9:30 sharp." Before Mark could reply, there was a click in his ear.

Mark settled back in his chair, stretched his legs and tucked his chin onto his steepled fingers. What was the wily old fox up to? Mark smiled. Now, that sounded interesting.

He picked up the drink and swallowed, set the glass back on the table and unfolded the Journal to the article the phone call had interrupted.

Chapter 5

A big drum thundered. Myrna snuggled deeper into the covers, but the pounding wouldn't go away. She squeezed her eyes tight, but the noise went on. There was no escape. She opened her eyes just enough to see that the sun was shining, but squinted against the light. The noise continued. She made herself open her eyes again, this time all the way. There wasn't a place in her body that didn't hurt, but especially her left arm. She closed her eyes. Maybe if she could sleep a little longer the pain would go away. She tried to reach Scarlett, who always slept at her left side, but something got in the way. She wriggled around until she could reach Scarlett. The space was empty. Scarlett wasn't there.

Now, Myrna was wide-awake. Where was Scarlett? Was she kidnapped? Who took her? Why couldn't she wake up? She struggled to sit up, and when the cast on her left arm held her down, she remembered. Mrs. Neumann had put Scarlett to bed on the living room couch so Myrna wouldn't accidentally hit her with the cast in the night.

Myrna had sent Mrs. Neumann home. She'd fussed, but Myrna insisted. In truth, she didn't want her around with all her questions. That way, she was almost as bad as Ada.

Scarlett appeared in the bedroom doorway. "Mama, somebody's coming up the steps."

"Oh, baby. I woke up and you weren't in bed, and I got so scared. Come here and let me give you a big kiss."

Scarlett jumped onto the bed, sending a lance of pain through Myrna's body, but she ignored it and pulled Scarlett to her with her right arm and deposited a kiss on the chubby little cheek.

The noise had stopped. Whoever came up the stairs had reached the top.

"Be real quiet," Myrna said. "If they think nobody's home, they'll go away. Probably only a 'cyclopedia salesman."

There was a polite rap on the door. Myrna put her finger to her lips to hush Scarlett. Another rap, louder. Myrna held her breath.

"Myrna. Miss Schroeder. Are you all right?"

Myrna felt faint. Mr. Weston. What was he doing here?

Myrna put her finger to her lips again. "Don't say anything. Don't even move," she whispered.

"Miss Schroeder?" he shouted and pounded on the door. "Are you there?"

Oh, God! He'll think I'm out running around when I'm supposed to be home sick. He'll tell Jack and I'll get fired.

"Scarlett. I have to go to the door. It's my boss. You know. The man who brought me home last night. I'm going to close this door, and you stay right here."

Scarlett's curls bounced up and down. "I'll hide under the covers."

Myrna struggled out of bed. The cast seemed determined to keep her there. She worked her right arm into the sleeve of her thin cotton housecoat, pulled the other side over her arm and held it fast. Her hair was a mess, but she couldn't hold the housecoat shut and comb her hair at the same time. He'd just have to see her with messy hair.

"Thank God," Mr. Weston said as soon as she opened the door. "You had me frightened out of my wits. I was about to call the police to see whether you had taken a turn for the worse, or fallen and couldn't get up or something equally bad."

Myrna pulled the housecoat tighter. "I'm sorry. I was asleep. What time is it?"

"It's eight o'clock." He hit himself in the forehead. "I'm forty kinds of a fool. I just didn't think. You work nights, so you're used to sleeping late. I'm sorry I woke you. Go on back to bed. By the way, where's Mrs. Neumann? I thought she was going to stay."

"I sent her home after she got Scarlett settled. I just wanted to be by myself. She talks a lot."

He made a rueful grin. "I can understand that. Anyway, I worried about you all night. I called Karl Steinhart as soon as I dared this morning—and here I am." He looked at the gleaming black tips of his shoes for a second, like a little boy caught in mischief.

"What do you want?"

"I wanted to make sure you were all right and to tell you that I'd made an appointment with Karl for you. He said he had an opening at three this afternoon."

"At three," she said. "Where is his office?"

"I said . . ."

A car door slammed in front of the house, and a moment later, a second door closed. Myrna felt the blood drain from her face. The sounds were familiar; Ernie's old green Chevy. Myrna looked over Mr. Weston's shoulder. Sure enough, Ada was plowing across the grass toward the stairs and Ernie had stopped to check out Mr. Weston's car. She looked down and saw her bare feet sticking out from under the housecoat. "Oh, no," she said.

"What's wrong?"

"It's my aunt and uncle. Mrs. Neumann must have called them. They'll see you here and me in my housecoat with bare feet. How will I ever explain?"

"Explain what?" he asked. The words scarcely left his mouth when the landing shuddered, and he turned to see a large square-shaped woman grab the railing and plant one foot on the steps and begin to climb. She wore a shapeless dress with the color faded out of it and her iron gray hair was skewered into a bun at the nape of her neck. He couldn't see her eyes, but her mouth was set into a thin, straight line. A short, chunky man with a fringe of white hair, wearing baggy black pants and a blue work shirt, was bent over, peering into the Mercedes.

"What the hell?"

"Please. You'll have to go," Myrna said, her eyes wide with panic.

"I can't," he said, as the shaking increased with the woman's heavy, determined steps. "I'll have to wait until your aunt gets up here. What is your uncle doing at my car? I don't like people pawing over it."

Myrna bit her lips and half-turned into the house. "I have to go inside. I can't let her see me like this."

Mark frowned. What was going on? She'd been cool as a cucumber last night, but the sight of this old woman clumping up the stairs had her terrified.

The woman reached the step below the landing, and Mark stepped back to give her room. Her look, from tiny beige pig eyes, raked over his face before she turned to Myrna. "I thought you was hurt. Mrs. Neumann said you broke your arm. Don't look like you broke it so bad you couldn't get it on with this guy."

Mark resisted an impulse to shove her back down the stairs. "Now, wait a minute. What are you insinuating?"

She turned back to him; those little eyes squinted to slits. "You, get your hide out of here. You don't have to stand out here and advertise your business with Myrna."

Mark clenched his fists and set his mouth, an expression that made numerous underlings urgently want to be somewhere else. "I understand you're Miss Schroeder's aunt," he said in a quiet, measured tones.

"*Miss* Schroeder is the right of it," the woman said.

"I'm being respectful of Miss Schroeder," he replied. "I don't like the insinuation you just made about her and me."

The woman didn't flinch. She crossed her arms over her ample breasts, stuck out the top layer of her chins and said, "I ain't in-sin-u-atin' nothing. You sure know what this little slut has . . ."

"Ada, please," Myrna said barely above a whisper.

Ada jerked her head to face Myrna. "You shut up. This john in his fine clothes and fancy car don't need me to tell him what you are."

"Don't say another word," Mark said in a voice as quiet and deadly as a cobra. "If you do, I may not escort you down the stairs. I'll throw you off this porch, if I can pick you up. I haven't done any weight lifting lately." Ada opened her mouth, but closed it quickly when Mark continued. "Take a good look at your niece. She was severely injured last night. Does she usually wear a heavy cast on her left arm?"

Ada interrupted. "She's wearin' almost nothing'."

Mark ignored her. "She's so afraid of you she's shaking like a leaf. That isn't going to help her recover. Now, you take yourself back down these stairs and pry your husband away from my car and get out of here."

40

"Who do you think you are to order me away from my own kin?"

"My name's Mark Weston."

"He owns Weston Switch, Ada," Myrna said quietly. "He's my boss."

Ada's expression altered slightly, although it was hard for Mark to identify the change. Maybe her mouth relaxed a little. "I know who Mark Weston is. His name's all over town, just as much of a slut as you are, if men were sluts." She said. "Well, at least you can pay her good."

"You filthy-minded old bitch," Mark muttered. He turned to Myrna. "Go inside. I'll help your aunt and uncle to their car, and then I have to go to a meeting I can't get out of. I'll tell Mrs. Neumann to come up and stay with you and Scarlett and I'll be back at 2:30 to take you to the doctor. Okay?"

Myrna shook her head. "No. Please. I'd rather not have Mrs. Neumann come up."

"Are you sure you'll be all right?" Without waiting for an answer, he took her good arm and helped her inside.

Mark followed Myrna's aunt down the stairs, one step behind, to make sure she couldn't turn around, followed her to the car and opened the door. She glared at him as she turned and wedged herself into the seat. The car made a decided list to the right.

"You'll hear about this," she hissed. "I'll get me a lawyer and make it real nasty for you."

Mark ignored her and slammed the door.

"Hey, mister. Is this a real Mercedes Benz?" The little man ran an appreciative hand across the top of Mark's car.

"Yes, it is, and I don't like having people pawing over it. Get in your own car and take that wife of yours out of here."

"Aw! Never mind Ada. She's got a mouth on her, but she don't mean nothin'. What kinda job you got to have a car like this?"

"I told you, get your hands off my car and get out of here. And so you don't forget, my name's Mark *Weston*, and I own *Weston* Automatic Switch."

Ernie sidled away from the Mercedes to his Chevy and opened the door. "I didn't mean nothin'. I just like nice cars and I never seen a Mercedes up close before. Like I said about Ada, she's all bark."

"And I said get out of here, and if I hear about her or you bothering Miss Schroeder again, you will regret it."

"Okay. Okay." Ernie slid behind the wheel and slammed the door.

Mark stood on the grassy strip between the sidewalk and the street until the old green car pulled away from the curb and was out of sight. He got into the Mercedes and started the car, letting the deep purr of the German crafted engine work its magic on his temper. He let black beauty glide into the driving lane of the squalid little street lined with squalid little houses inhabited by squalid little people like the two who just left.

The girl wasn't squalid, though. She had more class than Noreen.

He eased on the brake pedal at a stop sign where kids wearing white belts stood on the corners with other kids lined up behind them. When the street was clear in both directions, the young guards dropped their arms and kids streamed across to the school nearby, just a block from a small park. Wonder what it would be like to have kids of your own, to send them off to school and be there when they came home? A boy to teach how to take a clock apart and put it back together, a girl to dress in pretty clothes, like Myrna's little girl, a redhead, a sweetheart.

The crossing cleared and the guards beckoned him on. No, Myrna Schroeder wasn't a piece of ass. Except for the incident with the old bitch, she was strong, but with a certain innocent vulnerability. Mark had never met a woman quite like her.

Chapter 6

A smile spread across Mark's face as he approached the sprawling Victorian era house a quarter-mile ahead of him, his "Halloween House." It was painted a cheerful cream, and the lacy edges of the pointed tower and numerous gables were trimmed in dark green. Mark still imagined it sitting alone on top of a hill silhouetted against a glowering sky in a horror movie. Noreen hated it and wouldn't come near. Occasionally, he rented it to visiting businessmen, such as Endicott, or to friends who wanted a place for a romantic assignation with someone other than their wives.

A cloud of greige dust had trailed the Mercedes since it turned off the highway onto the gravel road three miles back. It collapsed as Mark slowed to turn onto the paved driveway. The gate in the weathered rail fence was open and Mark followed the curved, paved drive into the garage in the barn. He got out of the car, ran up the steps and strode across the wide porch to the door. The screen door opened as he reached for the handle, and a tall blonde woman, who could have graced the cover of Vogue, held it open and smiled at him. "Good morning Mark."

The sun lit a scattering of silver threads in her wheat blonde hair, which was brushed straight back and braided into an elaborate figure eight at the nape of her neck, the only hint that she was not in her mid-twenties. Her perfect oval face was smooth and creamy with a hint of pink in the cheeks. Large ice blue eyes sparkled with wit and intelligence, and her full lips were parted in a wide, white smile.

"Lovely morning, Inge, and you look radiant as usual," he said as he stepped through the opening. "How's Christer?"

"Christer is fine. He's just this moment removing some croissants from the oven, for you and your guest."

Mark closed the screen behind him and entered the cool, dark foyer. A whiff of warm sugar came from the direction of the kitchen at his right.

"Mr. Endicott is waiting for you in the study," Inge added, and turned toward the kitchen. "I'll bring the coffee and croissants in a few moments."

"Christer's croissants and your excellent coffee. What more could a man ask?" Mark said, and strode into the sun-filled study with its rich fragrance of leather, books and lemon oil.

Miles Endicott sat in a Windsor chair, bent over a pile of papers spread on the low coffee table in front of him. The large bay window beside him framed a field of rich soil, black as coal, with small green shoots showing through at regular spaces, corn just beginning to poke through the ground. Mark wondered at Endicott's wool navy blazer with brass buttons on what promised to be a hot day, then remembered Endicott was on his way to San Francisco. His own memories of San Francisco in the summer made him shiver. Endicott's rimless glasses rested low on his nose.

"Morning, Miles," Mark said, said, pulling out a chair and sitting opposite the billionaire. "Have any trouble finding this place?"

Endicott looked up, startled, and removed the glasses. "Oh, Mark. I didn't hear you come in. No, your directions were excellent. The driver had no problem finding it." He glanced at his watch. "He'll be back in an hour."

"Those papers must really be interesting. Inge and I weren't exactly silent," said Mark.

"They are, my boy, they are, as you will soon find out."

Mark turned at a discreet rap on the doorframe, and Inge came in, following the sweet buttery fragrance of warm croissants. She carried a large silver tray that held a basket of Mark's favorite pastry, wrapped in a gleaming white napkin, a pair of thin china cups and saucers, dessert plates, a silver coffee server and matching creamer and sugar. She set the tray on the table, served the men and left.

"Nice place you have here." Endicott leaned back, his feet coming an inch off the floor. "Quiet, comfortable. Your housekeeper is a knockout. I didn't know household help came looking like movie stars. Mine sure don't."

Mark picked up his coffee cup and took a sip. "I doubt your wife would hire a top dollar Chicago call girl as a housekeeper."

Endicott's head snapped up, his gray eyes wide. "A call girl? You keep your own personal bimbo?"

44

"Inge is not my personal bimbo. She gave up the life and is very married to Christer, who was the head chef in the hotel where she worked. They wanted to make a new start away from the city, and I needed a housekeeper and a chef. It's worked out well."

"Humph," Endicott said, and thrust the papers at Mark, who had just placed a croissant on his plate. He dusted the powdered sugar from his fingers and took the papers. He picked up his coffee cup and slid back in the chair. "Look this over," he said, and swallowed a big gulp of the hot coffee without a change of expression. Mark was impressed. The coffee was hot enough to scald his esophagus.

Endicott set the coffee cup on the table. "I left Ed's place not long after you did last night. I was too angry to sit there and be sociable. I was up half the night planning how to make things right for you."

"Right for me? There's nothing wrong for me."

"I negotiated in good faith. Your father-in-law didn't. That means a whole different ball game. I'm sure we can work something out about the patent without him."

"Such as?" Mark shuffled the papers.

"Read those first. I think they'll explain."

The papers were neatly typed. "This looks like you had it ready when you came here," Mark said.

"My wife was once my secretary. She's an excellent typist, and I usually take a portable typewriter on business trips. Never know when I might need something typed."

Mark took a bite of croissant, washed it down with a sip of coffee and wiped the sugar from his finger on a napkin, then leaned back in his chair and scanned the first page. He was careful to keep his expression neutral, but as he read he felt his blood pressure rise. That pig thinks he can trick me into selling my patent with an offer like this? He has more hooks and loopholes there than in a Chinese puzzle.

When he finished, he put the papers on the table and folded his hands in his lap. "This is fascinating. First, you make an end run around me and deal exclusively with Ed, and now you're ready to scuttle Ed to deal with me."

"That's uncalled for," Endicott snapped.

Mark picked up the papers and shook them at Endicott. "This is what you came up with after staying up all night?" He slapped the papers down. "In exchange for a patent valued at more than your total net worth, you're going to give me the opportunity to operate one of your companies at a salary that's about half of what I take in now. That's real nice of you. Also, real smart. You have the original patent, and you have me under your thumb to create more ideas that you can patent in your name." He pushed the dishes aside, placed his elbows on the table so he faced Endicott on the same level, and folded his hands. "Whatever gave you the idea that I was that stupid? Because I let Ed Best pretend he controls my company?"

"You knew you could twist Ed around like a pretzel," Mark continued. "He's so greedy, he'd grab a bone from a dog's jaws if he thought he'd get a good price for it. You thought you'd get everything signed, sealed and delivered before the dumb son-in-law ever caught on."

Endicott's face turned the color of a ripe tomato.

"Why the hell are you so eager to buy my company? Nothing in your background has anything to do with automatic switches."

Endicott slid forward in his chair so his feet were firmly on the floor. "It's a good product and we need to diversify. I don't plan to make any changes. It's making money and that's all that matters."

"That's a good story. Tell me another. A man like you doesn't go around throwing money into projects without a plan."

Endicott touched his fingertips to his lips and sighed. "Everybody knows automation is the future. Your switch has a head start. I want to be ready."

"And you thought I was too stupid to know that and not have my own plans for the future of the switch?"

Endicott leaned toward Mark. "Enough of this bullshit. That offer gives you, alone, a cool million for the patent, over and above the three million for your share of the company."

"How are you going to explain that to Ed Best?"

"Ed controls the board. You control the patent. The company is worthless without the patent."

Mark leaned across the table. "That won't make Ed very happy. He might decide to sue."

"He could sue himself bankrupt and nothing would change."

Mark smiled. "I think I know why you're so anxious to get my company. I believe rumors, and I've heard a lot recently about some interesting things that are in the pipeline. You want to position yourself to grab the ball early on."

Endicott's face remained blank.

"You know, Miles, if you had come to me as the operating executive of this company and laid your plans on the table instead of trying an end run around me with Ed Best, we might have been able to do business. As it is, you could offer me the entire inventory in Fort Knox and I would still turn you down." Endicott looked toward the door, as if to escape. When his face had faded to red and his breathing had slowed, he pushed back the chair and stood. "Thank you for your hospitality," and stalked out of the room, Napoleon in civilian clothes.

Mark heard voices in the foyer and the screen door slammed. Moments later, a powerful motor purred to life and tires crunched on the gravel road. He picked up the croissant and took a bite. The rich, sweet flakes melted in his mouth, like the victory he'd just scored on Miles Endicott.

He wiped his mouth and hands on a napkin, stood, crossed the room to the desk and picked up the phone. He gave a number and waited through the rings. When in hell is this hick town ever going to get dial service? "Joanne," he said when his secretary answered. "I'd like you to call Alex McLaughlin in Seattle," and gave her a number. "Have him call me back as soon as possible at Pleasant Meadow. Thanks."

Five minutes later the phone rang, and he picked it up. "Hello, Alex. How are you? Thought I'd better give you a heads-up. Miles Endicott just left here. I think he's gotten wind of your project. He's trying to buy my company." Mark then explained what had happened. After McLaughlin replied, Mark said, "We need to meet. Denver's about half way. On Saturday? Good. At the Brown Hotel. I'll have Joanne get back to your girl with the details. Thanks. Good to talk to you. See you Saturday."

He cradled the phone, and stood, grinning. The blood sang through his veins. He felt like he could take on a pride of lions single-handed. Nothing like a good battle to rev up the juices. Almost as good as sex.

At the thought of sex, Mark's mind segued to an image of Myrna standing on the miniscule porch, her right hand clutching the thin pink robe pulled awkwardly over her cast, her neat, small bare toes peeping out, just right for nibbling.

After Mark closed the door, Myrna leaned against it and closed her eyes, feeling the vibrations from Ada's heavy tread as her aunt and Mr. Weston descended the stairs. Her legs seemed unwilling to hold her up, and the pain ratcheted up with every beat of her heart.

What's wrong with me? she thought. No matter what I do, it always turns out bad. Why didn't I go to the cafeteria like everybody else? It's air conditioned. Why did I decide to sit on that stoop? I saw the door. Why didn't I have enough sense to know that somebody might open it? I'm just plain stupid."

Tears threatened, but she squeezed her eyelids tight. Listen to yourself on your little pity-pot. You don't have time for that. She took a deep breath, opened her eyes and went to the table, pulled out a chair and sat down, resting her cast in her lap, her right elbow on the table, and propped her head on her hand. God, but she hurt. It seemed like every bone in her body ached, and her hip was sore where she landed, probably bruised. Her head throbbed in time with her arm. She just wanted to go back to bed and pull the covers over her head.

"Mama. Can I come out now?" Scarlett's voice was slightly muffled behind the closed door.

Scarlett! How could she have forgotten? "Of course, honey."

The bedroom door opened a crack, then wider and Scarlett tiptoed across the hall into the kitchen, looking around. "Did everybody go away?" Myrna nodded. "Was that nice man here? I heard Mrs. Ada, too. Does she know the nice man?"

Myrna smiled. "Yes. Everybody went away. Yes. Mr. Weston was here. Yes. Mrs. Ada was here. No. She does not know Mr. Weston."

"Why did Mr. Weston come here?"

"He wanted to tell me he would take me to the doctor this afternoon."

"Can I go along?"

"You wouldn't want to sit and wait while I saw the doctor. It wouldn't be any fun."

Yes, it would," Scarlett said.

"It's nice out. It would really be fun to go outside and play. That's much better than sitting in a boring old doctor's office."

"But I want to see that nice man again."

"I'm glad you like him, but we probably won't see him again after today. He's a very important man, and he doesn't have time for people like you and me."

"Why?"

"That's just the way it is."

"Mama, are you hungry?"

Myrna smiled. "Come to think of it, I am." She stood. "If you'll get the Corn Flakes out of the cupboard, I'll get the bowls and the milk."

After they had eaten, Scarlett pulled a chair to the sink and climbed on it. Myrna took a small enameled dishpan from the cupboard, put it in the sink, turned on the hot water and poured in a little soap. One of the blessings of Mrs. Neumann's apartment was hot water. The last apartment they'd lived in had none. Myrna gathered up the few dirty dishes and put them in the water. Scarlett took a dishcloth off the faucet where it hung to dry. "I like to wash dishes," she said.

"I'll remind you of that in a few years," Myrna replied, picking up a towel.

Only a couple of bowls remained in the dish rack, when a heavy tread sounded on the steps. Myrna closed her eyes a moment. Not anyone else. When would people leave her alone?

"Is it Mrs. Ada?" Scarlett asked, her eyes wide.

"I sure hope not," Myrna said and stepped to the window. A large man, in overalls with a heavy tool belt around his waist, carrying two boxes, trudged up the steps. Myrna stepped back and waited until he reached the landing. He knocked, and she opened the door a few inches, painfully aware that she was still in her robe and barefoot. "Yes?"

He was, maybe, in his mid-thirties, over six feet tall and had black curly hair and a nice smile. "Hi, I'm Charlie Bent from the phone company."

"I'm Myrna Schroeder."

"I've got a couple of phones to install for you."

"Phones? I didn't order any phones," Myrna said.

Charlie Bent set the boxes on the landing floor and fished in his back pocket until he brought out a rumpled sheet of pink paper. "This is an install order, and it has your name and this address on it. It says to install two telephones."

"But I didn't order any phones," Myrna repeated.

Charlie squinted at the paper in his hand. "It says here they were ordered by Joanne Bronson, a secretary at Wesmar Industries."

"I never heard of Wesmar Industries."

"It's some kind of private company. The address is out in the country."

"Well, that's interesting, but since I didn't order the phones and I can't pay for them, you'll just have to take them back," Myrna said.

Charlie looked over the paper again. "Down here at the bottom it says to charge it to Wesmar Industries."

"I still don't know anything about it and I'm not about to take something like that without knowing more than that. I'm sorry you had to climb all the way up here, but just take them back."

"But. . ." Charlie said.

"No."

"O.K., ma'am." He wrote something on the paper and stuffed it back into his pocket. The tools clanked as he bent over to pick up the boxes. "Sorry, it didn't work out."

He turned and started down the steps just as Myrna heard a car door slam. She closed her eyes, suddenly woozy. What were they doing back here?

Charlie was halfway down the steps when Ada heaved herself up to the bottom step. She stared at him like he had eight arms, and he flattened against the wall to let her pass.

Instead, she paused. "How much you give her?"

He stared. "Huh?"

Her lips disappeared into an upside down "U", and she said, "You know what I mean," then turned and struggled up the steps.

He shook his head and continued down to the ground and across the lawn to his truck. Strangest call he'd ever made.

Ada reached the landing, her face bright red and shiny with sweat. Rivulets of perspiration ran along her hairline. She clung to the porch rail, bent over, gasping for air.

"What are you doing back here?" Myrna demanded, ignoring Ada's distress. "Mr. Weston told you not to come back."

Ada heaved a huge sigh, straightened and reached for the screen door handle. Myrna quickly lifted the hook and put it in the eye, locking the door. It banged as Ada yanked on it. "Let me in," she spat, her breath recovered. "Mr. High Muckety-muck ain't got no place tellin' me what to do about my own kin. Besides, I don't expect you want to be discussin' your business for all the neighbors." She gave the door another yank.

"Quit pulling on the door. You'll break it, and Mrs. Neumann won't like that very much. Besides, we have nothing to discuss."

"Hmph! Two of 'em in an hour and a half. Must be makin' money hand over fist."

"What are you talking about?"

"Don't act all Little Miss Innocent with me. I been around the block a time or two. First your ma and then you. Next, it'll be that kid. Born whores."

Myrna's head felt like it would explode. "Get out of here," she hissed.

Ada's expression suddenly softened and she made what passed for a smile. "Now, I won't say nothin' about it to nobody."

"There's nothing to say about me to anybody," Myrna snapped.

"Don't be so hasty." Ada leaned close to the screen. "I'll make you a deal that'll make both of us a lot of bucks. And don't be in a hurry to turn it down." She lowered her voice. "Men come on to you like flies to horseshit. You must be makin' a mint, and I want some of it for all the years I had to put up with you and all the money I had to spend on you. You owe it to me. You give me twenty per cent of everything you get from the johns and I won't say a word, not even to Ernie. I can even drum up some trade for you. How does that sound?"

The world around Myrna turned red. "Get your filthy mouth out of here, and don't you ever come near me again. If you do, I'll call the cops."

Ada stood, still smiling.

"I said, 'get out,' and I mean now. Turn that lard around and get down those stairs before I push you down."

Ada finally looked startled, then her small dark eyes, turned to slits. "You'll regret this. All I done for you. Just you wait." She turned, and the building shook as she took the first step down.

Myrna slammed the inside door and found her way to the nearest chair, shaking and weak.

"Mama, are you okay?" Scarlett peered around the bedroom door, eyes wide.

"It's all right, honey. It was Mrs. Ada. She said some things that I didn't like. Now, you get dressed."

She had just put her head on the table when the steps began to shake again. Ada was coming back? It would be just like her. She ignored the pounding on the door. If it was Ada, she didn't trust herself not to push her down the steps.

Scarlett appeared, wearing only a pair of red shorts. "Mama. Aren't you gonna answer the door?" She went to the window. "It's only Uncle Ernie."

"Get away from the window and get the rest of your clothes on."

"Okay." Scarlett disappeared into the bathroom.

Myrna struggled to her feet, went to the door and opened it.

Since she stood on the kitchen floor, a couple of inches higher than the landing, she looked down on Ernie's bald head. His eyes were squinted half shut, trying to see into the room. She'd never noticed how much he looked like a weasel, with his pointy chin and pointy nose. Still, he had been good to her, sometimes even protected her from Ada. Thinking of Ada, Myrna looked over Ernie's shoulder, expecting to see her. The passenger door was open and Myrna could see Ada's dress. At least, she was staying in the car.

"Yes?"

"What happened with Ada?"

"Her foul mouth is what happened."

"Aw, honey. You know better than to mind what Ada says."

"I do mind what Ada says. I've always minded what she says, especially since she never says anything nice to me. I don't ever want to see her again. You're welcome any time you want, but don't ever bring her anywhere near me or Scarlett again."

Ernie reached for the door handle. "Let me in. We can talk about this."

"There's nothing to talk about. My arm hurts and I don't feel good. Ada made me sick. Just go away."

"That ain't no way to talk to the only folks you ever had. Why, if it wasn't for us, you'd growed up in the orphan's home."

Myrna sucked air to the bottom of her lungs. "You know, Uncle Ernie, ever since you first told me that, I wished you had taken me to the orphan's home. I was just a baby. People adopt babies. I probably would have had a real mother and father who wanted me and cared about me, not somebody who begrudged every mouthful of food I ate and every cent it cost to bring me up."

Ernie's eyes widened into dark blue marbles, and his mouth opened and stayed open, as if words wouldn't come out. Finally, he stammered, "Y-You'd rather have been adopted out? I wouldn't send you to the orphanage because you was my only sister's baby, and I don't give away my blood kin. I was doin' right by Lillie, not givin' away her baby. An' you're tellin' me, you wanted to be give away?"

"Yes."

He rubbed a hand across his face and said, almost to himself, "You wanted to be adopted out. If I'd of listened to Ada, I'd a done right and she wouldn't a changed. She'd of been her old self."

He looked at Myrna as if he'd never seen her, stepped away from the door, turned and went down the steps, heavily, slowly.

Myrna closed the inside door and locked it. She went to the sink and drew a glass of water. She was so thirsty. When the glass was empty, she put it on the sink and leaned against the porcelain. What have I done? That's my whole family. She shook her head. No, they never were a family. She and Scarlett were family.

"Do I look all right, mama?" Scarlett now wore a white sleeveless blouse over the red shorts and no shoes. She loved going barefoot in the summer.

"You look fine. Come here, give me a kiss. I really need one." Scarlett giggled, ran to Myrna, who stooped and put her good arm around the small body and kissed the firm round cheek. Scarlett kissed her back.

The outside steps rattled again. This place is a regular Grand Central Station, Myrna thought. Almost like those cartoons in the movies with one row of people going upstairs and another row going down. She looked through the window in the door. A little blonde girl climbed the big steps. Myrna opened the door.

"Hi, Mrs. Schroeder," the child said. "Can Scarlett come out and play? My mama's makin' cookies and she said we could help."

Scarlett was already at the door. "Hi, Marilyn. Can I, mama?"

"That sounds like fun and it's real nice of your mama to let Scarlett help," Myrna said to Marilyn, and to Scarlett, "Yes, and be real good for Mrs. Hartman. I don't feel good and I'm going to lie down."

Myrna unlocked the screen door and Scarlett joined her friend, and the two thumped down the steps. Myrna closed the inside door and slid a chair in front of it, so when Scarlett tried to get in, the noise would wake her. She was so tired, and she hurt everywhere. Oh, the pain pills. She shuffled into the bathroom, filled a glass with water, took a pill out of the small bottle and popped it into her mouth, then went into the bedroom and lay down.

Mournful organ music floated out of Mrs. Neumann's kitchen window just below, interrupted by a mellow baritone that announced, "Mary Noble, Backstage Wife." Myrna followed along about a beautiful girl raised in poverty who married a handsome and rich Broadway star. The music returned briefly and a woman's voice faded out as Myrna fell asleep.

Chapter 7

Myrna woke when Scarlett came home. She made lunch, washed the dishes, took a sponge bath and struggled into a red sleeveless dress, working the cast through one armhole, and then called Scarlett to take a bath.

"I don't want a bath. I'm not dirty."

"Your feet are dirty and you have to put on socks and shoes."

"I don't want to wear shoes." Scarlett's lower lip poked out and she stood flat-footed, legs spread and her arms crossed over her chest.

Myrna sighed. Scarlett hardly ever had tantrums. Why did she decide to throw one now? "You know Mrs. Neumann doesn't want you to be barefoot when she takes care of you. She's afraid you might hurt yourself and she wouldn't know what to do."

"I don't want to go to Mrs. Neumann's. She's boring. I want to go with you and that nice man."

"How many times have I told you that you can't go with me?"

"That nice man might buy me an ice cream cone."

"I don't think so." Myrna peeled one of Scarlett's arms off her chest and pulled her into the bathroom. "I've about had enough of this. Take off your clothes and get into the tub before the water gets cold. You won't like taking a bath in cold water."

Scarlett glared, but pulled off her clothes and got into the tub. She washed herself fairly well under Myrna's supervision, but Myrna had to scrub her dirty feet, awkward with one hand.

Scarlett was finally dressed and Myrna led her, still pouting, down the steps to Mrs. Neumann's apartment. When Mrs. Neumann opened the door, Scarlett beamed and said, "Guess what! I went over to Marilyn's house this morning and her mom let us help make cookies."

"Well, that must have been nice," Mrs. Neumann replied as she stepped aside. "What should we do this afternoon? Maybe we can walk to the store and get some ice cream. Would that be all right?" She looked at Myrna when she asked. Myrna raised her eyebrows, but nodded her head.

"That would be very nice. Thank you," she said, thinking, what a quick turnaround. Scarlett turned her moods on and off like a light switch.

A gleaming black car glided to a stop at the curb. "That must be Mr. Weston," Myrna said. "I shouldn't be more than an hour and a half."

She turned and went down the porch steps to meet Mr. Weston halfway to the car.

"Hey, aren't you pretty," he said. "Red becomes you." He greeted Mrs. Neumann and Scarlett.

Scarlett broke away from Mrs. Neumann and ran to Myrna. "I want to go along."

"Scarlett. I told you that you couldn't go with me," Myrna said, praying the ground would open and swallow her.

"But I want a ice cream cone," Scarlett insisted, her lower lip poked out an inch.

Myrna took a deep breath, gripped Scarlett's arm and led her back to Mrs. Neumann. She knelt to Scarlett's level and said, "You cannot go with me. Now, not another word. You go to Mrs. Neumann. Remember, Mrs. Neumann said she'd buy you some ice cream?"

Scarlett glared, the green eyes snapping and the lip poked out a little further. She turned on her heel, her back to her mother.

"Come, Scarlett," Mrs. Neumann said. "Come here. I go get my purse and we walk to the store." Scarlett went to the porch, her head high, pointedly ignoring Myrna.

Myrna sighed and stood. "I'm sorry," she said to Mr. Weston, who stood on the sidewalk, watching the scene, a crooked grin on his face. "I don't know what got into her."

"She's asserting her independence," he replied.

"She's acting like a brat," Myrna said.

"Just a little girl," he said, opening the car door. Myrna settled into the soft seat, inhaling the smell of leather. Mr. Weston slid behind the wheel and started the car. "How are you feeling? Did you get any rest after that scene this morning?"

"Yes. After a man from the phone company came, and Ada came and Ernie came and a friend of Scarlett's came to take her to her house."

"Your aunt and uncle came back? After I told them to stay away?"

"They seemed to think that being family gave them special privileges or something. I don't think they'll be back. At least, not Ada. Uncle Ernie means well."

His mouth was set in a hard line. "Maybe I'll get a guard to keep them away."

Myrna turned to stare at him. "Why on earth would you do that?"

"They're obviously threatening you."

"Well, I don't need a guard. I can take care of Scarlett and myself just fine."

"Sorry. I didn't mean to imply you couldn't." They had reached downtown and he slowed, looking for a parking place. "You said somebody from the phone company came. Did they install the phones?"

"You know about the phones?"

"I ordered them. I didn't think you should be here injured and alone without a phone. I ordered two because then you could have one by your bed and one wherever else you wanted it."

"I didn't know where they came from, so I sent them back. I've gotten along without a phone this long. What are you trying to do? Get me a guard and have phones put in without even asking me if I can pay for them?"

"Look, I was just trying to help."

"That's nice of you, but I've been on my own for a long time. I don't need help." She looked out the window. "There's a parking place, just two cars down."

Mr. Weston parked the car a half block from the doctor's office building and opened Myrna's door. She looked up, right into an oversized picture of David Holman's face. She smothered a gasp.

Mr. Weston followed her look. "Looks like old Dave has his headquarters set up already. Good location."

Myrna read the caption on the black and white photograph that was pasted on the plate glass window of the office. "Holman, Republican, Your Next Representative in Washington." She swallowed and asked, "Do you know him?"

Mr. Weston locked the car and walked beside her, on the outside like a gentleman. "I see him and his wife at the club and I played golf with him in a foursome a couple of times. He's a good lawyer, I hear, and seems like a nice guy."

Myrna couldn't think of anything to reply.

"Here we are," Mr. Weston said, opening the heavy door into the building that housed a bank on the first two floors.

The examination showed Myrna's arm beginning to heal, and when they left the office, Mr. Weston asked, "May I buy you a cup of coffee?"

Myrna caught her breath. What should she say? She'd have to talk to him, more than in the car, and her mind was completely blank. He wouldn't be interested in anything about her, and she didn't know anything about him.

"Well?"

"Yes. That would be nice."

Later, seated at a table in Oscar's, Newport City's best restaurant, where David had once taken her, Mr. Weston ordered and after the waiter left, leaned back in his chair. "Tell me about Myrna Schroeder."

Myrna stared at the white linen tablecloth and absently moved the silverware around with her right hand. "Oh, there isn't that much to tell. I just take care of Scarlett and work."

"Don't you do anything for fun?"

"I used to go to movies, and I get books from the library."

"Used to go to the movies? Why don't you go any more?"

Myrna took a deep breath. "Scarlett's a little too young." She wasn't about to tell him she couldn't afford it.

"Do you know David Holman?"

Myrna's head snapped up and her eyes went wide. Why did he ask that? "How would I know somebody like that?"

"When you got out of the car and saw his picture on the window, you seemed like you were unpleasantly surprised."

"Really? I must have been thinking about Scarlett's tantrum. Everybody in town knows who David Holman is, just like they know who his father and grandfather are. They're rich and famous. I'm nobody."

"I'm rich and everybody knows me, and I know you. I don't think you're a nobody."

"You didn't know me before yesterday when I fell off the steps. You've been very nice to me, and I appreciate it, but I'm not somebody you'd even look at ordinarily."

"Oh, I'd look at you."

Myrna sat up straight, set her jaw and stared into those sapphire eyes. "What do you mean by that?"

"Don't you like men to look at you?"

"No."

The waiter arrived with the coffee and pastry and set them on the table. "That's all," Mr. Weston said. Myrna sipped the scalding drink. She wanted to throw it in Mr. Weston's face. He was just what everyone said he was, a chaser. His poor wife.

"Did I say something to make you angry?" he asked.

Now, what could she say? Well, why not the truth. "Yes, you did. I'm really tired of men looking at me like I'm some kind of *thing*, and I'm sick and tired of men who talk dirty to me. I stay away from men as much as I can."

Mr. Weston smiled his lopsided grin. "You seem to have gotten close to at least one man."

Myrna felt like she'd been shot in the face. She couldn't breathe. She couldn't move. She clenched her fists to keep from hitting him. She shoved back her chair, stood, turned and walked quickly toward the door.

"Hey, wait a minute." Mark tossed some money on the table and went after her. She was a half-block away toward the bus stop before he caught up with her. "I'm sorry. I was out of line."

Myrna didn't reply. She kept on walking, looking straight ahead. Mark walked beside her, trying to think of something to say. Finally, as they rounded the corner to the bus stop, he said, "I'll come by tomorrow. . . to see how your arm is."

A bus wheezed to a stop at the curb. She went up the step, dropped her dime in the coin holder, found a seat on the side away from the sidewalk and looked out the window.

Mark stood next to the bus, ready to explode. How dare she? A little twit of a factory hand. Nobody, but nobody, treated Mark Weston like that. He owned the town. He owned her.

"Hey, mister, you gettin' on?"

Mark blinked. The bus driver was looking at him, his hand on the handle that closed the doors. Mark shook his head. "No. Sorry to hold you up." The door flapped shut and the bus eased away from the curb.

Mark turned on his heel and strode to the corner, head down. He stepped out into the intersection without looking up, ignoring the green light for oncoming traffic, and the honking horns, screeching brakes and obscene remarks from drivers of a half-dozen cars. When he reached the other side, he turned right toward where his car was parked. He'd pay Karl and the hospital for her treatment, then put her out of his mind. Stupid to get involved with an employee.

He saw his car and turned toward the curb, pulling his keys from his pocket.

"Mark. Mark Weston. Just the man I want to see."

Mark turned and looked into the weird green eyes of Dave Holman. Dave would never have an identity problem with voters with that fire red hair, the strangely handsome face, slightly triangular with its high-planed cheeks that sloped to a wide mouth and pointed chin. Always made him feel like he was looking at a redheaded snake. He shuddered, but pasted a smile on his face and said, "Dave," and waved his free hand toward the storefront with Dave's picture on it. "Looks like your campaign is off to a great start."

"It's a good location for a headquarters. Actually, the campaign should be duck soup. Giorgi's just been holding the seat until I was 'seasoned', as my dad says. Of course, that doesn't mean I don't need help. Lucky I ran into you. You were on my list to call to invite you to be part of our team."

"Thanks for the offer, Dave, but I've made it a practice never to get involved in politics. Bad for business."

Holman's smile didn't waver. "Hey, I could be really good for your business in Washington, be in a position to do you some big favors."

"We already have a team of lobbyists there and they seem to be doing quite well for us." Mark jingled his keys. "Sorry, but I'm already late for a meeting. Good luck."

"We'll talk again," Holman said, and turned to walk down the street.

"Not if I can help it," Mark muttered to himself as he got into the car and pulled into the street. He was in no mood to go back to the office. Besides, he had to prepare for that meeting with Alex McLaughlin in Denver and the fewer people who knew about that the better. He turned right toward the road that led to Pleasant Meadow.

Mark parked the Mercedes in the garage at the farm and went to the back door. Inge and Christer were not home, and he unlocked the door and let himself in. The kitchen was Mark's favorite room at Pleasant Meadow. It was spotless as usual, with the appliances and hard maple countertops gleaming. The sun shining through the sparkling windows turned the maple cabinets golden. Small touches of red in towels and other items turned it into the kind of place where one could imagine a stout gray-haired grandmother, rather than a six-foot three man with the physique of a wrestler, thick blond hair and ice blue eyes.

Mark went to the refrigerator, removed a bottle of milk and discovered a piece of apple pie on a shelf. He hoped he wasn't ruining Christer's menu, but he put the pie on the island, filled a glass with milk and pulled up a stool. After a bite of pie, washed down with a long swallow of milk, Mark sighed. Now, he could almost forget the disastrous afternoon.

When he finished his snack, he rinsed the dishes and put them in the dishwasher and went into the study where he'd met with Miles Endicott. He called Joanne to tell her where he was and that he wouldn't be back in the office unless there was an emergency. He slid a painting above his desk to one side on nearly invisible wires and opened a door that was flush with the paneled wall to reveal a safe. Mark tapped in a code and the safe opened. He removed a stack of thick manila file folders, closed the safe and placed the folders on his desk, sat down and opened the top folder.

Myrna still burned inside as the bus pulled into the street. How could she think Mr. Weston was different from other men? All the smiles and polite words and supposed helping didn't mean diddly. He was just like all the rest as soon as they found out she had a child but wasn't married, they thought she'd be easy to have sex with. From the talk in the break room she learned that guys didn't care about you as a person. They'd let you think they loved you, but it was all just a game to get sex, and after the sex they'd throw you out like garbage. She certainly knew that for a fact. She hadn't let any man get near her since . . . .. She wouldn't even think his name.

Maybe Mr. Weston would have her fired now. A chill went down her back, but she made herself sit straighter. If he did, he did. She could always go back to The Grill. The work was harder and the pay wasn't as good, but it was a job and it would take care of her and Scarlett.

The scene outside the bus window registered again, and Myrna realized hers was the next stop. She reached over her cast to pull the cord, but Bill, the driver, knew where she got off and eased to the curb. She stood and grabbed the seat backs to steady herself until she reached the door. "Thanks, Bill," she said, smiling.

"You take care of yourself, and watch that step," he replied

There were some nice men in the world, she thought, as she walked the half block to her building. It would be good to get home. She was really tired, and it was good not to have to think about going to work tonight. She hardly ever felt tired during the day, but the doctor said that was to be expected. Her system had had a big shock from the fall.

As soon as she turned into the walk to Mrs. Neumann's front porch, Scarlett burst through the door and ran to meet her. "Mama! Mrs. Neumann took me to the store and we got an ice cream cone. I had chocolate. It was so good, but it was gone so fast. I'd like another one."

Myrna laughed as she put her good arm around Scarlett. "I don't think so."

Mrs. Neumann came out onto the porch as Myrna went up the three steps. "You came home on the bus? Where did that Mr. Weston go? What did the doctor say?"

"Mr. Weston had business to take care of, so I took the bus home. The doctor said everything was fine and that I had to rest for a while. I have to go back in a week. Thank you for watching Scarlett and buying her an ice cream." She smiled. "Now, she wants another one."

"Scarlett, you would get a tummy ache from another ice cream," Mrs. Neumann said with a laugh.

Myrna took Scarlett's hand and turned back to the steps. "Thank you again. I don't know what I would do without you."

"Ach! You are like family. It lightens my day when she is here."

Myrna smiled down at Scarlett. "You lighten my day all the time," she said.

Later that day, Ada Schroeder stepped off the bus with a grunt and turned left toward the intersection of Holman Boulevard and Lincoln Avenue. She rocked from one stiff leg to the other. Her blue flowered cotton sleeveless dress hung over her body like a sack. She stood on the curb with three others, waiting for the light to change. When it did, she was still only halfway across Holman Boulevard by the time the others were on the opposite curb. She finally hoisted herself to the curb and stood a moment, panting and wiping her face with a large, white handkerchief, then turned right and struggled along the sidewalk, cursing the heat and the necessity to go to the drug store for a prescription. She had almost reached Herbert's Pharmacy at the opposite corner, when a large picture caught her eye and she turned to look. It was a political poster of a man who looked strangely familiar.

Ada stopped and turned to study the poster, causing a tall, well-dressed man to make a quick shuffle to avoid running into her. He strode past her on the right and shot her a disgusted glare before lengthening his stride. Ada was oblivious. She saw only the poster. If the picture was in color, the tight curls would be bright red and the eyes that looked weird even in black and white would be green. Scarlett's face was more heart-shaped, like Myrna's, but there was no doubt in Ada's mind. She was looking at Scarlett's father. A six-year mystery had been solved, and to Ada's benefit.

She finally paid attention to the printing on the poster. David Holman was the Republican candidate for Congress. She was standing on a street that was named for his family. Where had Myrna crossed a Holman's path? It really didn't matter. David Holman probably wouldn't be too happy to know he had a bastard, especially now, running for national office. Newport City voters weren't too understanding about their politicians' lapses in morality. He'd probably be willing to pay well to keep it a secret, and Ada Schroeder was going to be the beneficiary of that pay. She turned, smiling, and went into the drug store next door. She could almost see herself getting on that train to California.

Chapter 8

Several miles on the right side of the railroad tracks, David Holman drove his white Cadillac convertible up the long driveway and into the two-car garage behind his large, brick two-story home. He pulled off his tie, opened his collar and slung his suit jacket over his arm as he strode toward the connecting back door. Carol Holman stood at the kitchen sink, washing greens. David put his arm around her and kissed the top of her curly blonde head. She fit neatly into his arm. "Hi, sweetheart." He let her go and said, "God, but I'm glad to be out of that office. Nobody should have to work in this heat."

She emptied the basket of greens into a large bowl. "Hi, honey. I'm glad you said that about the heat, because we're having only a chicken salad for dinner. Okay?"

"Sure. Cooking on a day like this is masochistic."

"We're on the terrace. It'll be on the table when you're changed," she said.

David gave her shoulder a squeeze, left the kitchen and went upstairs, where he changed into a white polo shirt and beige shorts. Back in the kitchen, David took a bottle of Chardonnay from the refrigerator and went out to the terrace. A glass-topped table with in a polished aluminum frame, was already set with two plates, silverware and wine glasses. He poured the wine into the glasses as Carol came from the kitchen and set the salad in the center of the table and sat opposite him.

The terrace was shaded with a black and white striped roll-up awning. Rock steps led down to a free-form decorative pool, bordered with rocks, with bright pink moss roses tucked in the cracks of the rocks. A dozen water lilies floated in the pool, their fragrance perfuming the air. An eight-foot tall neatly trimmed boxwood hedge bordered the two-acre property, sealing in privacy. In the far left corner, a huge oak tree filtered the late afternoon sun's angry rays. Flowers in many colors, dominated by Carol's favorite white Alaska daisies, made a base for the hedge. The only extraneous noise was a dog barking in the distance and the faint buzz of a lawnmower.

When their meal was finished, Carol cleared the table and carried the dishes into the kitchen. A hint of classical music floated onto the terrace and she returned to the table with two glasses of white wine. "It's much too quiet," she said, explaining the music.

David recognized the cue. "What did Jim Beaton have to say?"

Carol sipped her wine and set the glass on the table. "He said there's a man at the University of Chicago who's doing some promising research into infertility and said he could make an appointment for us." David sighed. More tests. It seemed like they'd had endless tests to discover why Carol couldn't get pregnant. Six years of marriage and no babies was beginning to change Carol from a bubbly, cheerful young woman into one who was depressed and brooding. All the previous tests had shown that David was fertile, but doctors could not discover why Carol couldn't conceive. She wouldn't hear of adoption. She wanted a baby inside her, to give birth, to nurse it. Dave didn't care. He was happy just the way they were, but what was one more test if it gave her hope? "Sure. Tell Jim to make the appointment."

Carol smiled and reached across the table and took his hand.

To change the subject, David said, "I ran into Mark Weston today right outside my headquarters."

"Oh, what did he want?"

"He didn't want anything. He'd parked there. I invited him to join our contributors club, but he just said he didn't get involved in politics. When I suggested I could do a lot for his company in Washington he said he had all the help he needed in Washington. Strange encounter."

"He and Noreen have really never been friendly. I've never understood it."

David shook his head. "Nor I. He's a driven kind of guy, but then so am I, but I guess our interests don't match."

"Well, from what I hear, he's not too driven to find attractive women with which to cheat on Noreen. Not that she's entirely faithful either." Carol shuddered. "I can't imagine how heartbreaking it must be to know the person you love doesn't love you."

"Honey, you'll never have to worry about that. There's never been another woman that interested me – ever."

Carol leaned over and kissed him. He put his arm around her waist to pull her into his lap, when the phone rang. He kissed Carol hard and her tongue found his, and the phone continued to ring. Carol sat up, but David pulled her back. "The phone can wait," he said.

"No, it can't. It might be something important." Carol slid off his lap and ran into the kitchen. She was back in seconds. "It's some woman who wants to speak to you, only you and now, that you'd better talk to her if you want to get elected."

David frowned. "Who is she?"

"She wouldn't give her name, just insisted on talking to you right now. She sounded kind of old, you know, with a gravelly sort of voice."

David sighed and pushed himself out of the chair. The problem with running for public office, you couldn't turn away anyone who might vote for you. He went into his den and picked up the phone. "This is David Holman," he said in his best candidate voice.

"It better be," replied a voice, as Carol had described, harsh, hoarse. "I got some information for you that you'll be real interested in."

"Who is this?"

"My name don't matter. What I got to say, does, so you listen real good."

"I don't listen to anyone who won't identify themselves," David replied.

"Well, then, call me Mrs. Jones," she said pleasantly. "That's a real good name, don't you think? Easy to remember." She paused, and her tone returned to its original vague threat. "I seen a pitcher of you today and it looks just like somebody I know, only she's a little girl, five years old. She's got the same curly hair as in the pitcher and the same funny eyes that I bet are green if people look at you. Folks say those are sort of the trademarks of the Holman blood. Her face is shaped more like her mama's, who is a real pretty girl, but otherwise, she looks just like you."

"I'm sure there are many curly-haired children in Newport City. What does this have to do with me?"

"Funny thing. This little girl ain't got a daddy. Her mama turned up in the family way one day about six years ago, but she wouldn't tell

68

nobody who got her that way. Especially, she wouldn't tell him. She didn't want him to know. But I think a man's got a right to know he's got a kid, don't you? Especially when he's runnin' for high office."

David wanted to slam the phone in her ear, but he took a deep breath and replied softly, as Dad had told him. "I don't know why you called me. Goodbye." He replaced the phone gently in its cradle, and shook his head. Why do political campaigns bring out all the nuts?

He walked into the kitchen where Carol was cleaning up the remnants of their dinner.

"Was it important?" she asked.

"No. Just some crackpot. Dad warned me about them. I unplugged the phone, and I'm going to have our home phone number unlisted tomorrow."

Chapter 9

Myrna climbed the steps to the second floor at Weston Automatic Switch ten days after her accident, surprised that she was happy to see the ugly green walls and machines, have the tang from the oil catch in her throat, and hear the clang of the time clock as she punched her card. Every day after she'd told off Mr. Weston, she picked up her mail with shaking hands, expecting a letter telling her not to come back to work.

She heard scraps of conversation as she walked slowly down the hallway to the break room.

Betty's raspy contralto. Who else?

". . . nigger in those fancy clothes. Thinks she's so high and mighty. We oughta complain to the company. No nigger should be takin' a white man's job."

"You're right, Betty."

"Wonder how come they hired her?"

"Yeah. My sister-in-law come here lookin' for a job and she didn't get hired. She was pretty peeved when I told her about that nigger girl."

Myrna stood outside the door, listening. What were they talking about? Then she remembered the colored girl who started the day she was hurt. What was her name? Lydia. Lydia McIntire. She seemed like a nice girl. Well, it was strange for the company to hire a colored girl for Department 21. Any colored people who worked at the plant were always janitors. Colored people worked in the factories during the war, but just like the women, they were let go when the men came back from the service. Whatever the reason, it didn't sound like the women of Department 21 were real happy about the whole thing. Would they do something?

"Maybe we could be mean to her," said Sadie. "She'll get tired of it and quit."

"Naw. She'd tell Jack, and he'd light into us," Betty replied.

"Accidents happen." The voice sounded like Susie, a huge bull of a woman who hardly ever said anything, but when she did people listened.

"Like what?" Betty sounded interested.

"I dunno. Maybe one of the guys could fix a machine that didn't work. You know. The trips missed and the hammer came down on a finger or something?"

Myrna tried to slip through the door quietly so no one would see her.

"Speakin' of accidents, look who's back," Betty bellowed. She sat in her usual chair, backlit by the grimy window. Susie sat catty-corner from her. "Myrn! How y'doin'?"

Myrna gritted her teeth and said, "I told you. My name is Myrn-*ah*."

Betty grinned. "Oh, yeah. I remember. Like the movie star."

"That's right, and please don't forget it."

Betty's grin broadened and she checked out her companions, who grinned back.

"Oh, I won't forget. It's just that I like *Myrn*. It suits you better than a fancy movie star name."

Myrna shrugged. Might as well argue with a block of cement. She turned to the lockers and put away her lunch sack, saw a vacant chair near the end of the row and sat down.

Betty wasn't finished. "Heard the big boss knocked you down some steps." She turned to her friends on either side and grinned. "Maybe he knocked you up." There were a few embarrassed giggles. "How'd that happen?"

"Ask him," Myrna said.

"O-oh! Getting feisty, are we? They give you some kind of drug to smarten your mouth?" Betty's grin disappeared and she looked at the other women. "I bet you don't mind workin' aside a nigger." All conversation stopped and all eyes aimed at Myrna.

"Why not," she retorted. "I work alongside you."

There was a communal gasp.

Betty leaned forward, her hands in fists, her small eyes narrowed to slits. "You callin' me a nigger?"

"Why would I want to insult a whole race of people," Myrna said.

71

Betty lunged, half out of her chair before Susie grabbed her arm and held her back. She sat back in the chair, legs splayed out in front of her, hands still knotted into fists, her face flushed bright red, breathing hard. She shook one meaty fist at Myrna. "I'll get you for that, you little 'hore. You better watch your back, you and that black slut."

"Who you callin' a black slut?" Lydia McIntire stood in the doorway, wearing a neat, blue and white striped seersucker sleeveless dress. Her face was a mask, except for the dark eyes, narrowed to menacing slits.

Just then, the klaxon honked and everyone stood up at once, nearly knocking Lydia down in their rush to leave the room. Lydia turned on her heel and got in line behind Rosie, who inched a little closer to Alice in front of her. Myrna found herself behind Lydia.

"What was that all about?" Lydia asked. "By the way, I'm Lydia McIntire. I don't know if you remember me. I started the day you got hurt."

"I remember who you are." Myrna tilted her head toward the room. "Betty and I had a little disagreement. That's all."

"A disagreement that obviously involved me," Lydia said.

"Not exactly, but I'd watch my back – and all around—for a while, if I was you. Be careful on the machines. Something might accidentally break and you could get hurt."

Lydia looked at Myrna, hard, then turned back to Tim Forrester and his clipboard for her night's assignment. She nodded and walked into the department with her head high and her back straight.

"Glad to see you back, Myrna," Tim said. "The boss tells me you can't work the machines. Go on the bench, and I'll show you what I want you to do." Myrna nodded.

He checked her name, and she went into the department, to the big workbench against the far wall, climbed onto a stool and rested her bad arm on the bench top. It ached, but she'd get used to it.

She looked over at the machines. Lydia McIntire had inherited Myrna's place at the kick press. Myrna turned back to the table. A tray, which looked like a long, narrow cookie sheet with sides, was filled with black Bakelite boxes, the length of her index finger and three-quarters of an inch wide, empty switch cases, and a box of shiny copper springs sat in front of her.

She'd done the job before, so she pulled the tray close with her good arm. She could do it if she snugged the small case between her left thumb and forefinger against the cast, and used her good right hand to pick up the square, paper-thin copper spring with a tweezers, settle the hole in the top over a small raised place in the case and place the case in the tray. It was slow, but once she got into the swing of it, she'd pick up speed.

"Okay?" Jack Sweeney stood beside her, tall, blond and handsome, just like a movie star, his white shirt crisp, the red and blue striped tie tucked into the opening between the middle buttonholes. His aftershave smelled good. Myrna nodded. "Don't worry about rate tonight," he said. "If it hurts too much, let me know and I'll give you a break."

"You don't have to. I'll be all right."

"Just remember," he said and turned away.

The klaxon blatted, the riveters came to life with a roar that would last until eleven o'clock.

In his office, five floors up from Department 21, Mark Weston placed the phone on its cradle gently and leaned back in his chair, grinning. He made a jab at the air. Seattle was a done deal, and a big surprise for "Daddy" Best. He shoved back the chair and stood; he had to move, do handsprings, tap dance down the steps like Fred Astaire, bellow a Tarzan yell and swing through the jungle on a vine.

Christ, he needed a good fuck. He sure wouldn't get it from Noreen. Especially if she knew what he just did. A dozen long strides took him to the door, and he wiped the grin off his face before he opened it.

"Joanne, I'm going downstairs for a few minutes. I'll be right back."

Joanne looked up from her typewriter, nodded and turned back without missing a keystroke.

Mark strode down the hallway, the heel clips in his brown wingtips clacking heavily on the floor. He grabbed the stair rail and ran down the steps. Maybe not like Fred Astaire, but under the circumstances he could pretend. Where could he get a good fuck? Somebody in The

Sorority, of course. Kathleen Grigson, or Kipper Jaynes or Elaine. Yeah, Elaine was it. Her husband was in California on business this week. He'd call her as soon as he got back upstairs.

He didn't notice the heads glance up from machines as he strode past, didn't really know where he was until he stopped in the wide doorway, the entrance to Department 21. Myrna Schroeder's department. Suddenly, he forgot all about The Sorority.

And there she was, directly opposite where he stood, sitting at a workbench, the black silk of her hair hiding her face. She'd managed to get the cast through a white sleeveless blouse, her feet, in worn white sandals, were hooked over the rung of the stool. He remembered small white bare feet under a pink bathrobe.

From the corner of his eye, Mark saw Jack Sweeney look up from his desk, catch sight of him and catapult out of his chair. Mark raised a hand to stop him and went directly to Myrna.

Conversations, carried on at the top of each voice, stopped abruptly. Heads bent over trays of parts, and hands flew. Production increased dramatically. Mark didn't notice. He stood behind Myrna, allowing her clean, soap smell, slightly tinged with sweat, to freshen the tang of oil and metal and cigarette smoke. He spoke low, beneath the heavy thump and machine gun rattle of the machinery. "Hello, Myrna."

The switch case dropped from her hand and the spring fell to the floor where it bounced a few times before Mark could pick it up. He faced her and put the spring on the bench. "Sorry. I didn't mean to startle you."

"Mr. Weston? What are you doing here?" A fine coat of sweat veiled her face, giving it an ethereal look. Mark realized sweat was running down his own face. God, it was hot in here. Her eyes widened and she covered her mouth with her right hand. "Oh. I'm sorry. I didn't mean . . ."

Mark touched her arm lightly, and it seemed that sparks sizzled from her arm through his fingers and up his arm. "It's all right. I heard you were back and I wanted to see how you are."

"I'm fine," she said.

"That's good." He looked around at the busy machines and their operators. "I need to talk to you, but I can't hear myself think in here. How do you stand it?"

"You get used to it."

"Just a minute. I have to talk to Jack. I'll be right back," Mark said and went to the foreman's cubicle and stuck his head in the door. "I'd like to talk with Myrna in private. Excuse her for a while, will you?"

Jack's eyes widened, but he said, "Sure. She's not working on a rush job."

Mark touched Myrna's elbow. "Come with me." She looked toward the office, but Jack had his head down, concentrating on a paper on his desk. "I told Jack."

Myrna slid off the stool and followed Mark out of the department, feeling the eyes on her back. They crossed to the far wall in Department 35 to an elevator door next to the corner. Mark inserted a small key into a keyhole in the door, and it slid open. He ushered her inside the small elevator. It would hold maybe four people. It had paneled walls, a bench. upholstered in gray wool. around three walls, and a parquet floor. It hummed a few minutes, then stopped.

The door slid open to a huge room, also wood paneled, with a bright red rug with patterns of other colors. Against one long wall a pair of black leather sofas flanked a big glass coffee table. A large, round glass-topped table with a half-dozen chrome and black chairs around it was on the other wall, next to a fancy buffet or bar or something. Strangely, a big grandfather clock stood in the corner. An enormous glass and chrome desk with a black leather chair behind it, a few steps from the elevator, dominated the room. The subtle scent of leather underlay everything.

"Oh, it's cool in here," Myrna exclaimed.

"Air conditioning does have its advantages. And it's quiet. Have a seat." Mark gestured toward the black leather sofa against the wall, and then went to the desk and touched a button on a box on his desk. "Joanne," he said. "I'd like a couple of iced teas and some cookies."

"Yes, sir," came the disembodied reply.

Mark sat on the sofa opposite Myrna, leaned back and propped his left ankle on his right knee. "Now, I can hear what you say. What did Karl say about your arm?"

"Dr. Steinhart said it's healing fine and I should be able to get rid of the cast in about a month. Then, I'll have to have physical therapy to get the muscles strong again. After that, it should be perfectly normal."

"That's good news." The door at the far end of the room opened and a pretty, dark-haired woman, neatly dressed in a dark blue suit, a white blouse with a big bow at the collar, nylons and dark blue pumps came in, carrying a tray. She set the tray, which had a large insulated pitcher, two tall, sweating glasses of iced tea and a pretty dish of chocolate chip cookies, on the coffee table and smiled at Myrna.

"Joanne, I'd like you to meet Myrna Schroeder," Mark said. "Myrna, this is Joanne Bronson, who really runs Weston Switch."

"How nice to meet you, Myrna," Joanne said, with a warm smile. "I'm so sorry about your injury. How are you feeling now?"

"I'm fine, thank you," Myrna replied.

"It's good to have you back at work," Joanne said. "Well, I have to get back to my typewriter before this slave driver cracks the whip." She smiled at Mark and left.

"She's nice," Myrna said.

"Nice and smart and efficient. I don't know what I'd do without her."

"It must be nice to have a job like that."

"Would you like to be a secretary?"

"It's better than pounding a press."

"I'm sure." Mark took a swallow of tea, then set the glass on the table. "What I really wanted to talk to you about was the stupid remark I made."

"What's there to talk about?"

"I want to apologize. I really don't know why I said it. It just came out."

"People usually say what they mean," Myrna said.

Mark looked into her eyes. "Not always. Sometimes, they get into a habit of saying or doing certain things and it happens without thinking." Myrna sipped her tea but didn't reply. Mark cleared his throat and soldiered on. "Well, you didn't deserve a remark like that. From what I've observed and heard, you're a good woman, a good mother, a hard worker, quiet, but efficient and pleasant to be around. Please accept my apology."

Her breasts rose, held, and fell as she took a deep breath. He had checked up on her. Well, that was only natural, and she really had only one question. "If I don't, will you fire me?"

Mark was speechless for a moment. "Why would you ask that?"

"I supposed you wouldn't like it if I didn't forgive you, and when the boss doesn't like something a person does, he fires them," she said.

Mark heard his voice, so he must have replied, but he had no idea what he said. Did all his employees look at him that way? Actually, there were times when he got into some pretty loud shouting matches with his execs. Of course, he'd never really talked to anyone on Myrna's level. Maybe that's what the rank and file thought. It had never occurred to him.

The face opposite him suddenly changed from the flat one-dimensional way in which he saw women into a something quite different. The sapphire-blue eyes were narrowed: predator's eyes, taking aim, waiting. The pretty, soft pink mouth was tight. Muscles bunched at her jaw line. He shivered. Her breasts rose and fell rapidly. Myna Schroeder was one angry woman. Mark smiled.

"You think it's funny?"

"Uh-h, no. Sorry, I don't remember what I said. 'Fraid my brain just took a short detour."

She frowned, activating a dimple in her right cheek. "Your brain seems to take a lot of detours."

Mark's blood pressure spiked, and he waited a beat until it ebbed. "A serious flaw in my character. What did you say?"

"You said you were used to people telling you things they didn't like, and I asked what you did about it. You smiled."

Mark picked up his glass and swallowed. "If I smiled it was because I was thinking about something else. What I do about negative comments depends on the person, the subject and the circumstances. If you don't accept my apology, I'll accept that as your right since I did insult you rather seriously, and I won't bother you again. I certainly wouldn't fire you."

She sighed. "I get so tired of it. Sometimes, I wish I had zits all over my face and was cross-eyed."

Mark chuckled. "In other words, you're telling me I'm an educated, rich jerk. I had it coming. Incidentally, you're the first beautiful woman I've ever met who didn't flaunt it at every man she met." He paused. "Would you like to work up here in the executive suite?

Myrna's head snapped up, and she remembered the guy on the bus back a few weeks. "What would I do? I can't type. I had to quit school."

He almost said that with her looks, all she had to do was sit at a desk and smile, but stopped himself in time. "You could be a receptionist, answer phones, talk to people who come here. Those are all things you can learn. If you wanted, we'd even send you to school to learn to type and take shorthand so you could be a secretary. A secretary like Joanne makes good money and is a really important part of the company."

Myrna shook her head. "I don't think so. I'd feel funny. It's okay to work in Department 21."

"Well, think about it. I'll keep the offer open."

When she didn't reply, Mark continued. "I wish you'd reconsider the phones, though. You really need one for emergencies. Besides, I'd like to talk to you once in a while and I can't keep dragging you away from your job. Jack would get pretty mad at me for cutting into his production."

Myna frowned, narrow tracks between her eyes, then nodded. "It would be nice to have a phone for emergencies. Sometimes I worry about Scarlett getting sick or hurt and Mrs. Neumann not being home so I could use her phone." She paused. "But why on earth would you want to call me?"

Mark laughed. 'Oh, lady. You have no idea of what you are! I like you. You are as refreshing as an ocean breeze. Sometimes, when things get crazy around here, I like to shift gears to clear my head. Talking to you would help a lot."

"Can't you talk to your wife?"

"U-uh! In a word, no. We don't like each other much."

"Oh." Myrna reached for her tea.

"Wait. That's warm. The ice cubes have melted. The thermos keeps it cold. I'll pour you a fresh one.' He picked up both glasses, went to the bar across the room, emptied the stale tea into the sink and rinsed the glasses. When he came back, he poured fresh brew into them. "That should be better."

Myrna swallowed. "It's good. Thank you."

They drank the tea in silence and Mark munched on a cookie. Joanne had them made fresh for him every day. The rest of the office appreciated the leftovers.

Myrna put down her glass. "I accept your apology for what you said to me, but I won't forget it right away." She paused. "Thanks for the offer of the phones, but I just can't."

Mark felt like a light had just gone on inside him. "Thank you for accepting my apology, but I'm disappointed that you won't take the phones."

"It just wouldn't feel right. Is there anything else?" she asked.

Oh, a lot, he thought, but said, "For now, I feel a hundred per cent better."

She stood. "Well, I guess I'd better be getting back downstairs."

He walked her to the elevator and told her which button to push and waited until the door whispered shut and the motor made a genteel hum. His brain gave all the right commands to move from the elevator to his desk chair. He opened the Glen Livet drawer, removed the bottle and glass, set them on the desk, and leaned back, his clasped fingers touching his chin. Tiny rainbows simmered in the designs carved into the crystal. Funny, he'd never noticed that before. He'd never really noticed a woman before, either.

He certainly hadn't lived in a cloister. There'd always been women, but they were always on the edge of his life, there for him when he needed them, ignored when he didn't. Gran took care of him when he was small. In prep school, girls were something you took to dances, and, if they let you, feel up or screw. Noreen was the money spigot for his dream. Joanne was part of the officer machinery. The women in The Sorority were like the high school girls, handy for screwing when necessary.

When they weren't catering to him, the women Mark knew spent a lot of time and money on clothes and looking beautiful. In summer, they all spent their days around the pool at the country club, drinking and gossiping. In winter, they spent their days at each other's homes playing bridge, drinking and gossiping. Most of them had degrees from prestigious women's colleges like Vassar, Radcliffe, Smith or Mount Holyoke. The degrees were packed away in the attic and only mentioned when it was socially or politically mandated. Most of them had children who were turned over to nannies at birth and sent away to school as adolescents. Mark knew he had a reputation with women as a charming man and smooth talker, but he never considered having a serious conversation with any of them.

And he'd just had a fairly serious conversation with a young woman who hadn't even graduated from high school, who wore her beauty like a comfortable old coat, who had a life most people scorned, who made him look at himself as he never had. Myrna Schroeder was real; strong, quiet and more dignified than any old dowager he'd ever met, and a fierce protector of her independence and her illegitimate child. At the same time, she had a vulnerability that made him want to don armor and run a sword through anyone who hurt her.

Chapter 10

Myrna stepped out of the small elevator into Department 43 just as the klaxon blared for supper break. She walked toward the break room, trying to figure out the strange conversation she'd just had. Mark Weston didn't seem like a real person, more like a movie star, someone you see close up but don't really know. Why would he want her to forgive him for a nasty remark? He could do or say anything he wanted and most people would say "yes sir," and go on. She was nobody. Most people thought she was a whore because she wasn't married and had Scarlett, they didn't care what they said to her. She was fair game. If she complained, they did it all the more, just like Betty. She'd really been nasty to Mr. Weston and he apologized. He even offered her a better job. Made no sense.

She detoured into the break room, took her sack lunch from the locker and continued down the hall to the cafeteria. A pair of heels clattered behind her, like somebody trying to catch up, and she turned to see who it was.

"Hi," Lydia McIntire said, breathless. "Are you going to eat in the cafeteria?"

"I'm sure not going to go out to the boss's private stairs again," Myrna replied.

Lydia laughed. "I wonder why."

"One broken arm is enough."

"How are you getting along? Do you need any help at home?"

Myrna smiled. "That's nice of you. Scarlett and I are doing just fine. For a five-year-old, she's a big help."

The cafeteria was a big square room, blessedly cool, filled with long tables flanked by metal folding chairs and a food serving station across the far end, just like her high school cafeteria. Betty Brown and her crowd plunked purses on one table, reserving it for themselves before they got into the food line. Lydia joined the line. "Watch out for Betty and her crew. They might try something," Myrna cautioned.

"You think that hasn't happened to me before?" Lydia smiled and moved up in line.

Myrna went to a table near the far wall by one of the room's four windows. Large posters of Norman Rockwell's "Four Freedoms," left over from the war, hung between the windows. "Freedom from Want," closest to Myrna showed a family sitting down to a Thanksgiving dinner with tons of food on the table and an enormous turkey that Grandpa was about to carve. Myrna thought it was ridiculous. Nobody had that much food during the war, unless everybody chipped in their ration coupons for it, and she'd never seen a turkey that big. Well, she'd only seen one turkey, period, and it was about half that size. She shifted her gaze to the window, with its view of the railroad tracks a half-block away and the row of paintless buildings across the street.

Lydia returned carrying a tray with a bowl of soup, a sandwich and a cup of coffee, and sat down opposite Myrna, who took the peanut butter sandwich out of her sack. "Scarlett made the sandwich," she said, as she took a bite. "She loves peanut butter."

"Do you?" Lydia asked. She sipped a spoonful of soup and made a face. "They charge money for this? It's supposed to be beef vegetable, but if any beef got near it, it was just passin' through."

Myrna laughed. "That's one reason I bring my own food."

After a few more spoonsful, Lydia pushed her tray aside, picking up the coffee cup. "That's enough of that." She took a sip of the coffee and set it on the table. "How come you let Betty get away with bullying you like that?"

"Did she do anything to you in the line?"

"She won't bother me. I won't let her. She's a wimp, like most bullies. All you have to do is talk back to her and she shuts up."

"But then, she can do something bad," Myrna said.

"Like what?"

"Get somebody fired."

"You're joking?"

"She's been here longer than anybody, all through the war, which means she has a lot of seniority and a lot of pull with the bosses. They don't want to lose her, so they listen when she complains."

Lydia took another sip of coffee. "She ought to be fired."

"Yeah. Sure. When pigs fly."

"Do you know anything about the mercury switch department?"

"Not much, except that I'm glad I don't work there."

"Why?"

"It's dangerous." Myrna folded the waxed paper that had wrapped her sandwich and put it into the sack.

"How is it dangerous?"

"Well. Mercury is dangerous and those girls have to handle it. Why do you want to know?"

"Just curious."

They sat in silence for a few moments, Lydia slowly drinking her coffee.

"You live in Newport City all your life?" Myrna asked.

Lydia set the cup down. "I just came here, to Newport, a month ago. My mama retired from her job in Chicago and moved here. Why, I'll never know. I graduated from college the fourth of June. I came here to be with her and to help out, since she did so much to be sure I got a good education."

"You went to college?" Myrna stared. "What are you doing here?"

"I just told you."

"No. I mean, why are you working in a factory when you have a college education?"

"Well. I'm trained to teach high school science, mainly physics, and there's no place for a high school physics teacher in Newport City. Especially, there's no place for a colored physics teacher anywhere but in a colored school down south, and that doesn't appeal to me."

"Oh. I didn't think about that. I thought if you had a college education you could get a job anywhere."

Lydia made a derisive snort. "Hardly." She leaned across the table. "To change the subject, are you all right? I mean financially? I mean, you were off work a week and we don't get sick pay."

"It's okay. Mr. Weston is paying for everything and he saw to it that I didn't lose any pay."

Lydia took another swallow of coffee. "That's nice. Wonder if he'd do that for somebody like me or Betty." She tilted her head toward the table where Betty and her friends were laughing.

"I don't know why not."

"We don't look like you."

Myrna managed to swallow her mouthful of sandwich without choking, but she couldn't speak. "Is something wrong?" Lydia asked. "You look funny."

Myrna cleared her throat and swallowed. "One minute I get my expenses paid because I don't look like you and Betty, and the next minute I look funny. Which is it?"

Lydia shrugged. "In the first place, I meant that you are a good-looking woman and from what I hear, Mark Weston likes good-looking women. Second, I meant, you looked like you were sick or in pain or something. I meant 'funny' like 'strange, unusual.'"

"I'm really tired of people thinking I get special favors or that I put out for men because I'm supposed to be pretty, especially since I have a little girl and no husband. For your information, I don't think I'm pretty. I'm just ordinary. I didn't even finish high school. What good is it being pretty if you're dumb?"

"Hey, wait a minute. I didn't mean to insult you. And whether you think so or not, you are a very beautiful woman. And whether you finished high school or not, you are *not* dumb. Put that out of your head right this minute." Lydia leaned forward and folded her hands on the table. "It was a stupid attempt to get around to the subject I'm really interested in, the working conditions in this place."

"What do you mean, working conditions?"

"Well, the big boss wants to talk to you, but it's too noisy in the department. Did it ever occur to him that those of us who have to work in it don't like it any more than he does? He causes an accident that injures you, so he picks up the bill and pays your salary when you're off. If you had fallen down somewhere else and he had never set eyes on you, our wonderful insurance would have only paid part of the medical bills and you wouldn't get one cent in sick pay. From what I hear, the women who work in the mercury switch department are sent to the company doctor when they complain about rashes and not feeling good, and he tells them there's nothing dangerous about mercury, that the rashes or their feeling bad is from something else. Then he tells the company that person is just trying to get some time off. The machines we work on are dangerous. Are there any safety controls on them?"

"You have to hit both trips on the presses before the hammer comes down," Myrna said. "You can't have your hands under the hammer that way."

"And if something goes wrong and the hammer accidentally comes down?"

Myrna shrugged. "You'd get hurt. But what can you do about it?"

Lydia leaned even closer, and spoke softly. "Did you ever think about a union?"

Myrna's eyes widened and she caught her breath. "A union," she whispered, and looked around. "Don't say that where anybody can hear you. You can get fired for talking about a union. Besides, what can a union do? You just have to pay a lot of money in dues and then they go on strike and you don't get paid, and if you lose the strike, you lose your job. No. Unions are not good things."

"Unions let people like you and me get together with other people just like us and make the company do right by us. They give us power."

Myrna looked hard at the woman with the brown skin and black eyes sitting across from her. "Who are you?"

Lydia pushed back her chair, stood, and picked up her tray. "Well, honey," she drawled. "I'm just a li'l ole colored girl workin' in this here factory to help out her mama." She grinned "Back to the salt mines," she said, picking up her tray and walking toward the empty tray rack.

Late afternoon sunlight blazed through the window behind the old desk. A sunbeam danced across the top of tightly curled red hair, spotlighting a portrait of a black clad, white whiskered patriarch framed in ornate gold frame. "David Holman" read the gold plate engraved on the frame, the founder of Holman, Holman and Holman, Attorneys at Law. David Holman III, his great-grandson, pushed back the big leather chair, stood and stretched.

He went to the bar beside the window, slid open a door and took a bottle of Johnnie Walker Black Label from a shelf under the bar. The cheap stuff in the Steuben glass decanter was for clients. He poured a couple of fingers into a glass and tossed it down. He poured another measure into the glass and took it back to the desk, sat down, elbows on the desk and rubbed his eyes. His yellow legal pad lay blank on the desktop and he sighed. Times like this he questioned his decision to run for Congress. He hated to write speeches, and this one was important. Tomorrow night he was speaking to the Rosecrans County Grange on farm subsidies, top priority to his large rural constituency. At least, after he was elected, he'd have a speechwriter.

It was quiet in the office, the way David liked it. No clattering typewriters, no ringing phones, no people talking, He could think better when it was quiet. He bent his head over the yellow pad and began to write. The phone on his desk shrilled, startling him into making a squiggly line across his paper. Who the hell could be calling him now?

"Holman, Holman and Holman," he said.

"Sounds like it's David Holman," was the reply in a coarse, low-pitched female voice, vaguely familiar.

"Which David Holman did you wish to speak with?"

"Don't give me that snobbery stuff Davey-boy. It's been over a month and I ain't heard nothin' from you."

David frowned. "I beg your pardon?"

"Don't get high and might with me, Davey-boy."

"I'm sorry. There's no reason to continue this conversation." He moved the phone from his ear, but not fast enough to miss the threatening tone coming from the receiver. "Remember the little girl that looks like you and the fifty thousand bucks I need to keep shut about it?"

David took a deep breath. That call at home, the one he dismissed as a crank. He replaced the phone on the cradle.

What could she be talking about? He'd been totally faithful to Carol since their marriage. Of course, there'd been girls before he proposed to Carol, like any red-blooded young guy, but that was a long time ago. What could a little one-night-stand when he was single do to him now? In fact, there were so many from the time he was sixteen until he asked Carol to marry him he couldn't possibly remember just one. He shrugged and bent over his work again.

The phone rang again an hour later. David stared at it as if it was a cobra about to strike, and finally picked it up on the third ring. "Yes."

"David? Are you still working? Dinner is getting cold."

He let out the breath he had been holding. "Honey. I'm sorry. I should have called, but I got caught up in trying to finish this speech for tomorrow night. When did you get back from Chicago? I didn't think you'd be cooking tonight."

"Oh, David. I'm so excited. Dr. Cornwell diagnosed my problem as endometriosis. He's starting a study on endometriosis and he wants me to be part of it. He thinks he can clear the tubes by medication instead of with surgery. I told him I'd discuss it with you."

"Wait a minute. We want a baby, not for you to be a guinea pig in an experiment that might not work. You know that not everyone gets the treatment. Some get what they call a placebo, sugar pills, and you're certainly not going to have experimental surgery."

"But David, what if it does work?"

"Then, we'll have a baby. If it doesn't, we'll adopt a baby."

"No, David. I want a baby of my own. I want to be pregnant and to give birth and hold the baby you and I made, not somebody else's."

David sighed and ran his free hand through his tight red curls. "This is not the time to talk about it." His voice softened. "I know how much you want a baby of your own and so do I, but I'm not about to allow you to risk your life or another disappointment on an experiment. I love you too much. Can you put the dinner in the refrigerator? I'll be home in about a half hour and we can go out."

"All right."

David hung up and leaned back in his chair. Carol. Oh, my god. A shudder went through him. What if what that old lady said was true? Carol would strip off his hide one small piece at a time and she certainly wouldn't stick around.

He propped his elbows on the desk and buried his face in his hands. From in the deep recesses of his memory a bubble slowly rose to the surface and projected a picture of a girl with silky dark hair, the face of an angel and a body to die for. As he watched, the angelic face twisted in pain, fear and disgust.

The breath went out of him as the entire memory came back. The sexy waitress who brushed off Keith's crude remarks in that crummy diner just after law school. I bet Keith a hundred dollars I could get inside the waitress's pants with charm. Charm hadn't worked. She didn't want sex. She even tried to get out of the car, but I was too fast for her and grabbed her before she could get out. I got her cherry, too, and Keith coughed up another fifty bucks. After Keith paid off, he'd totally forgotten the incident.

David's face burned. He hadn't used any protection that night. The time was about right. My god. The old lady could be right. He could have a kid out there somewhere. What was that girl's name? Why hadn't she said anything? Maybe she gave it up for adoption, maybe she didn't even live in Newport City any more. But the old lady sounded like she was right here, that she had pictures. He sat up. The girl had kept it a secret all this time. Maybe she didn't want it known any more than he did. Forget it.

David bent over his legal pad and returned to his writing.

Chapter 11

A soft rap on Mark's office door was followed by the door opening a crack and Joanne's face peering through it. "Mr. Best is here to see you," she said.

Mark looked over the top of his frameless reading glasses. "What the hell does he want?" He shook his head and waved a hand. "Sorry. Give me five minutes, then send him in." As soon as the door closed, Mark shuffled the papers on the desk's glass top into a neat pile and slipped them into a file folder. He swiveled the big leather chair around to an open file drawer behind him and fit the file into place, then removed another, closed the drawer and turned back to face the door. He opened the file folder, read the top paper, and grinned. It was a two-year-old letter of appreciation for some donation or other. Nice to know he was appreciated for something. He pressed the intercom button. "You can send Mr. Best in now, Joanne."

The door opened again and Ed Best entered. He was casually dressed in khakis, carefully tailored to fit over his paunch and held up with plaid suspenders, a white, short-sleeved polo shirt with the neck open, and loafers. The aroma of cigar smoke grew as he came closer. He nodded his head, displaying the bare skin centered in the tonsure of white hair and looked left toward the sofa grouping against the wall.

Mark saw the look and carefully folded his hands across the file folder, indicating that he planned to stay where he was. "Ed. What brings you to the wrong side of the tracks?"

"Board meeting next week and I came to get some stuff." Ed eased himself into a chair in front of Mark's desk.

"I certainly don't have your 'stuff,' and I thought you always had it couriered to your house."

"Thought I'd come see how things are. Haven't seen you for a while. Noreen says you're too busy for dinner with the old folks."

"After the last dinner with 'the old folks,' I saw no reason to subject myself to that empty ritual any longer. Frankly, those dinners have bored the hell out of me for fifteen years."

"You still mad about that mix-up with Miles Endicott?"

"Why would I be mad that you tried to cheat me out of my patent and make a deal to sell the company without my knowing anything about it until it was all but signed?"

"We'd've made a bundle," Ed replied.

"We'd've made a bundle more if I'd been consulted."

"You gonna say anything about it at the board meeting?"

"You're the chairman. You made all the deals. I'll let you give them the good news. They're used to your machinations."

"That's no way to talk after all I've done for you." Ed patted the pocket on his shirt, reached inside and pulled out a cigar. He started to unwrap it.

Mark raised a hand. "Not in here. You know that. I can't stand the stink of those things."

"Real men like the smell of a good cigar," Ed muttered as he replaced the cigar. "Like I said, you ought to be more grateful after all I've done for you."

Mark leaned forward across the file folder. "You know, Ed, I'm really sick of that old song. You made an investment fifteen years ago. That investment made you a lot richer than you were then. My brains and my work made that possible. I owe you nothing. If you need money, I'll buy you out."

Ed was silent for a moment, his face turning red with the effort. "I don't need money, but I like to make it. We'll never get as good an offer again. Might as well sell it. Doesn't look like there'll be any grandchildren to carry it on."

Mark leaned back in his chair. "Talk to your daughter about that. She's revolted by the idea of pregnancy, childbirth and caring for children. It would spoil her fun."

Ed Best didn't reply and looked out the nearest window.

"Tell you what, Ed. I'll give the business, minus the patent, to Noreen as a divorce settlement."

Ed sat up as if someone had poked a hot knife into his back. "A divorce settlement. What are you talking about? Noreen's been a damn good wife to you. She puts up with all your running around."

"As I put up with hers."

"Don't you talk about my daughter like that."

"We have an agreement. Since she won't fuck me, I don't ask her where she gets hers and she doesn't ask me where I get mine. Simple.

"Ed, you know as well as I do, that I didn't marry Noreen for love. If I had, it sure would have cooled in a hurry, because she made it quite clear that despite my heavy-duty ancestors and my grandfather's money, I was dirt under her feet. Her only ambition is to be the social queen bee in a tiny hive, and to find her pleasures with the gigolos at the country club."

Ed stood up, pushing the chair back. His face was nearly purple as he leaned over the desk and planted his hands on the top. "Don't you dare talk about my daughter like that. I'll ruin you in this town if you ever say another word against her." He straightened, made an about-face, stalked across the carpet, opened the door and slammed it hard after himself. The old clock in the corner sounded a bass chime from the vibration.

Mark leaned back in his chair and smiled.

Back in Department 21 Myrna slid on to the high stool, bracing herself against the workbench to balance her cast. Suddenly an arm went around her arm and squeezed the injured place. "How's the arm, Myrn? Hurt much? Or did the visit from the big boss make it all better?"

Myrna gasped and clenched her teeth to keep from crying out. When she could speak, she said, "Yes, it hurts. Now take your hands off me."

Betty gave the arm another squeeze. "Gonna tell the big man to fire me? Why, he handed me my 'E' pin, hisself. He won't fire a good worker like me," she sneered, then walked to her riveter a few feet away, laughing. She climbed on her chair and switched on the machine, which roared to life, drowning her laughter.

Myrna picked up a switch case and pushed it into her left hand. Her right hand shook as she squeezed the tweezers to pick a spring out of the box, and the tweezers fell to the floor. Her arm throbbed after Betty's ministrations, and she felt a little nauseous. Just the thought of getting down off the stool, stooping to pick up the tweezers, then getting back up was more than she could do. She sat quietly, breathing down the nausea, the pain pounding through her whole body. In a minute, she'd have enough strength to get the tweezers.

Jack's voice made her jump. "Myrna, you OK? I saw Betty put her arm around you. Did she hurt you?" He stood beside her, looking at her closely.

"I do feel kind of woozy and my arm hurts more than it did. I dropped the tweezers. Give me a minute and I'll pick it up." No way was she going to tell him what Betty did.

"Forget that. I'm calling a cab and you're going home. Can your babysitter keep Scarlett all night?"

She hesitated a moment, thinking about the lost pay, but she felt so bad, she didn't know how she could get through the rest of the shift. "I'll call her. I guess it would be all right."

Jack stooped, picked up the tweezers, then held her right elbow gently and helped her off the stool. "Use the phone in my office."

The chair in Jack's glass cubicle was more comfortable than the stool and the pain subsided a bit. Jack dialed the number and handed the phone to Myrna. Mrs. Neumann was happy to keep Scarlett in her apartment. Jack called the cab company and went downstairs with her to wait.

They sat on the bench just inside the glass entrance door. The darkness made a mirror of the glass, reflecting the images of a tall, neat man with blond hair and a dark-haired woman. For a minute, they didn't look like Jack Sweeney and Myrna Schroeder.

"Mark Weston feels real bad about hurting you. He's not all bad for a rich guy," Jack said.

"He has been nice."

"You know he's married?"

"Yes."

"No kids, though."

"That's too bad, I guess."

"You gonna be all right alone? Is there somebody I can call to stay with you?"

"I'd rather be alone."

"OK." Jack stood. "Well, here's your cab. Here, let me help you."

Myrna saw the dim shape of the battered Yellow Cab through the glass, its dome light casting a weird glow on the driver's face. No Robert Taylor there. Superimposed over the cab in the reflection, like a double exposure, she saw Jack take her hand to help her stand and put his hand on her right arm. She wanted to giggle, but the image disappeared when Jack opened the door. He helped her into the grimy back seat and gave the driver her address. "And you wait until she gets into the house." Myrna noticed he slipped a bill into the driver's hand.

"OK, buddy," the driver replied.

Jack looked back at Myrna. "Take care of yourself, and don't come in tomorrow unless you feel a whole lot better. Weston said you'd be paid for any time you were off."

Myrna managed a smile. "Thanks for all your help. I'll try to come in."

Jack shook his head and stepped back on the sidewalk. The cabbie ground the gears, spun the steering wheel, made a U-turn in the deserted street and headed west. Jack waved.

Myrna rested her head against the back of the taxicab's seat, which stank of unwashed hair and old cigarette smoke. Up front the driver created a cloud of fresh smoke, which didn't smell any better and made her want to cough. She didn't. Coughing made her arm hurt; everything made her arm hurt. It was a good fifteen-minute trip to her apartment, so she closed her eyes and tried to settle her arm into a comfortable spot. The cab's springs squawked as it bounced over the patches in last winter's potholes, but Myrna shut out the jarring and the noise. For the first time in the five days since Mr. Weston had knocked her off the steps she had time to think.

She felt like two people at the same time. One Myrna Schroeder went Scarlett, cooking, doing the wash, cleaning the apartment, putting parts of switches together every night at Weston Switch. Then, there was the other Myrna, the one nobody knew, the Myrna who wanted somebody to love her and take care of her, a man, a nice man. She would take care of him and keep house and cook and have other babies. They'd live in a nice house like those new ones Charlie Summers was building out on the west side.

What's the matter with me, she thought. I haven't thought about things like this for years.

With a sound of metal grinding against metal, the cab stopped. "This your place?"

Myrna looked out the window. Her outside light was on and she could see a yellow glow behind Mrs. Neumann's drawn shades. "Yes. This is it. I live upstairs."

She eased herself out of the cab, said good night to the cabbie, and crossed the grass strip to the stairway. She gripped the railing and went up the steps as lightly as possible so Mrs. Neumann and Scarlett wouldn't hear. A sliver ran into the heel of her hand and she stifled an "ouch." The cab waited, just the way Jack said he should. She got the screen door open and let it rest against her back while she fumbled through her purse for the house key. There it was, on the bottom. She unlocked the door and opened it to a gust of air as hot and stuffy as at the plant. She stepped inside and flipped on the light. Outside, the cab roared away. She closed and locked the door, glanced at the clock on the wall above the sink. Nine o'clock, and she was as tired as if it were six in the morning.

Everything was just as she'd left it; the kitchen spotless, overlaid with a faint odor of Clorox bleach. Nothing was out of place in the living room and she opened the window. The outside air was almost as hot as inside. In the bedroom, she nearly succumbed to the invitation of the smooth sheets and pillows, but she couldn't leave her purse on the kitchen table. Newspapers said the first place burglars looked for pocketbooks was on the kitchen table. She returned to the kitchen and put the purse in a cupboard drawer. She was so hot and sweaty, so thirsty. She took a pitcher of water from the refrigerator, filled a glass and drank it without putting the glass down.

The bedroom window stuck halfway open and Myrna didn't have the strength to work it loose. Maybe a stray breeze or two might make its way through the opening. She turned down the top sheet and sat on the edge of the bed to struggle out of her clothes. Whoever would think that just putting on your clothes and taking them off would be so hard. Finally, she slid between the smooth sheets and pulled Scarlett's pillow down so she could rest her arm on it.

The bed was empty without Scarlett, without her sweet little girl smell and the way she tucked her hand under her cheek when she went to sleep. Myrna blinked back sudden tears. Scarlett was a lot better off with Mrs. Neumann. It wasn't nearly as hot in Mrs. Neumann's apartment downstairs, and she would probably let Scarlett sleep on the living room floor. That was Scarlett's favorite summer thing to do. Myrna smiled as she settled her cast and burrowed into the pillow, but as soon as she tried to relax into sleep a mosquito began its thin, tinny song. At first, it was far away, across the room, then it picked up volume as it swirled around her left ear. She waved her hand and the sound went away, only to repeat its routine a moment later.

Myrna pulled the sheet over her head until she couldn't hear the mosquito, but just as she was drifting off, guilt flooded her and she jerked awake. She tried to think of Scarlett, of how Mr. Weston's car smelled, of how she could get a good rate on the bench with her arm in a cast, anything to kill the memory of that summer night in Mercer Park Even after all this time, she cringed, repeating the same old tune that stuck in her head like the whining of the mosquito. Why didn't she go back into the restaurant when he surprised her? Harry would have taken her home, she even was stupid enough to let him walk her home. If only she'd used her brain, nothing else would have happened. She twisted and turned, winding the sheet around her trying to escape the pictures that had already begun to roll across her mind.

The summer all Myrna's dreams died. The summer she was sixteen. "Sweet sixteen and never been kissed," certainly applied to her. Aunt Ada never let her go out with any boy at school. She said it was chasing after boys that got her mother in trouble, and saddled her and Ernie with Myrna at six months, and she wasn't about to do that again.

Aunt Ada said it was time Myrna got a job and started paying back all the money she and Uncle Ernie had spent to bring her up. Uncle Ernie said his friend, Harry, who owned a restaurant, needed a waitress, so as soon as school was out, she'd gone to work at Harry's All Nite Eatery. She'd worked nights then, too, and it was hot, just like Department 21.

In September, Uncle Ernie broke the news that she wouldn't be going back to school. The money was too good for her to waste her time in school. When she went to work she walked along streets where she wouldn't see kids coming home from school. It hurt too much. She gave all her salary to Ada and lied that the money included her tips. She took an old history book from school, glued the edges of the pages together and cut a big square hole in the middle. She put most of her tip money in the hole and set the book in plain sight on her dresser. Ada would never think to look in a book for money. Ada didn't have much use for books. When Myrna had a hundred dollars, she opened a savings account in the bank. As soon as she had two hundred dollars in the bank, she could get away from Ernie and Ada.

After only six months, Myrna had her two hundred dollars. She saw an ad in the paper for a room for rent and she went to see it. It was about the size of Ada's bathroom, and the furniture was old and scratched, but it was clean, and the landlady even cooked meals. She gave the woman, Mrs. Bobb, twenty dollars for the first month's rent. She could still see Ada's face when she told them she was moving out. It turned red, then darker red, then purple as she screamed. "No, you won't. You owe me money, thousands and thousands for everything I done for you. I'll go to the law to get it back."

Myrna's knees turned to water, but she stood tall. "I don't owe you a thing. You decided to raise me. You won't let me finish school, so I guess I'm ready to be on my own."

The small room she'd rented in a boarding house six blocks from the restaurant had a bed covered with a tattered old quilt, a scratched dresser and a chair, but to Myrna it was a palace. She went to the library every week to get books that would help her learn what she was missing in school.

Two years later, her life had settled into a pattern: sleep in the morning, the library and study in the afternoon and Harry's all night. On a hot, muggy June night at Harry's, the night she should have graduated from high school, the smell of grease was thicker than usual. The jukebox blasted Patty Page singing a duet with herself about a doggie in the window, the cook slammed pots and pans around and cussed a blue streak, the customers all snapped their orders and left measly tips. Myrna was counting the minutes until her shift ended at midnight, when four young men came in and sat in one of her booths.

"Slummers." Myrna ground her teeth behind her smile. They all wore dark, neatly pressed trousers, wrinkled white shirts unbuttoned at the collar. Myrna bet the neckties and the jackets that matched the pants were in a car somewhere. They probably thought they looked like the rest of the "riff-raff" that patronized Harry's.

Myrna made the smile and walked to the table with her order pad, pencil poised, praying they'd just want coffee. "How can I help you this evening?" she said.

The tall blond, his hair carefully combed back into a slight pompadour, grinned. "I've got a Buick Electra just outside with a big back seat. You can help me there."

Myrna ignored him.

Beside him, next to the wall, the one with the dark, tightly curled hair and eyes so dark they looked black, shoved a nickel into the jukebox and made a selection. He flashed white teeth at Myrna. "I'll have a cheeseburger with lettuce and tomato."

She wrote the order on her pad and looked at the one across the table. His brown hair was shaved almost bald. Home on leave, Myrna thought. That was a surprise. The war was over but the draft wasn't and the rich ones, like these, managed to escape.

"I'll have the same thing and black coffee."

Myrna noted it and turned to the next man, seated right in front of her. His bright orange hair fit his head in tight curls, and he looked older than the others. Maybe he'd been in the army or something. Eyes the color of limes looked back at her and he smiled. "I'll have a burger with ketchup and fries and black coffee."

After writing the order, Myrna turned back to the first man. "Are you ready to order now, sir?"

His ice blue eyes narrowed as he looked at her, then down at his menu. "A burger, fries, coffee with cream and sugar."

No tip there, Myrna thought. "Thank you," she said.

"Slut," she heard him say as she turned away toward the kitchen.

"Oh, grow up, Randy," said another voice. It sounded like the redhead. "Just because a girl doesn't go for your corny line, doesn't make her a slut."

As Myrna slid the order slip through the high opening into the kitchen, a shout of laughter came from the booth with the four slummers. Wonder what's so funny, she thought, and went to the next table where two women and two men, all wearing jeans and T-shirts, just off the night shift at Weston Automatic Switch, waited to order.

When the slummers' order was ready, she took it to the booth and smiled until her cheeks ached, especially at the blond. She'd get a tip out of him yet. They each looked up and smiled back as she set the plates in front of them. The redhead's smile was real, went all the way to his eyes, and he said, "Thank you."

"You're welcome."

After the four left, as she wiped off their table and pocketed the tips, nothing from the blond, she wondered what it would be like to have so much money, to have nice clothes and a big car. She sighed. That was something she'd never have to worry about.

Harry flipped the "OPEN" sign in the front door to "CLOSED" and Myrna let herself out the back door of the restaurant. She let the screen slam behind her and took a step into the alley, between the overflowing garbage cans, in the anemic light of a bulb over the door. A hand grasped her arm. She jumped and yelped.

"Sh-h. It's okay." The hand dropped from her arm, and she turned. It was the red-haired slummer.

"You scared me out of ten years growth. What are you doing here?"

"I'm sorry. I couldn't let a girl as beautiful as you just walk out of my life, so I asked the cashier when you'd be off and she told me you always came out this door."

I'll have a few strong words with Elsa, Myrna thought. "She had no business telling you that. I don't go out with guys who come to the restaurant."

"Why not? It looks like a good place to get dates."

"Some people have to work to pay the rent," she snapped.

He ducked his head and spread his arms, palms open. "Sorry. My name's Dave, by the way. What's yours?"

"Alice," Myrna replied.

"That's pretty name. I like the song, Alice Blue Gown. Hey, can I walk you home? You shouldn't be out alone this late at night."

"I'm out this late alone every night and I get home just fine, thank you. Where's your friend's fancy Buick?"

"They went on to a bar out of town that stays open late."

"How will you get home? I'm sure you don't live in this neighborhood."

"They said they'd come back for me in an hour if I didn't scor. . ., if you wouldn't let me walk you home."

"If you didn't score, isn't it? Well, Dave, you won't score. You can go find a phone and call your buddy and tell him to pick you up." Myrna turned and started down the alley.

"Wait a minute," Dave called. He ran to catch up with her. "Look, Alice. I'm sorry. I sounded like the worst kind of clod. I truly like you and I'd like to take you to a movie sometime." He grinned, a cute, lopsided sort of grin. "That is, in the next two weeks. I'm on leave."

Myrna looked at him in the dim light from the doorway. He was good looking and he seemed nice, polite. Then, rich guys were always polite. She hadn't told anybody she'd never had a date. Ada would never let her go out with boys from school, and she didn't like the ones she met here at Harry's. But this David seemed different.

"All right. When do you want to go? I work every night but Mondays."

"Next Monday night it is, then. Now, I'll have to walk you home to see where you live."

On Monday night, she stood in front of the murky mirror in her room, turning around to see how she looked in her new dress. She'd taken money from her precious savings and gone to Sears. There were so many pretty dresses on the racks, she had a hard time making up her mind. Then she saw the blue one. The salesgirl said it just matched her eyes, but then salesgirls were paid to tell people things like that. It was made from shiny material that shaped itself to her body, but not too tight. It had a modestly scooped neckline and no sleeves, but the edges of the neck and the armholes were trimmed with dainty white lace. After she bought the dress, she realized she had to have some pretty shoes to go with it, and since she was already in the store, she found a pair of white sandals in the shoe department.

David had said he would be here at seven o'clock and it was already five minutes to. What if he didn't come? Her stomach got fluttery. Why would somebody like him go out with a girl like her? Maybe it was just a way to get her to have sex with him. Well, she'd made herself clear on that subject. She took one last turn in front of the mirror. It would have to do. She picked up the little white purse she'd also bought, and went downstairs to the parlor. All the roomers could use the parlor, and Myrna gave a sigh of relief that nobody else was there. She sat down on the edge of the couch, knees tight together, clutching the handbag with both hands. The clock on a nearby table struck seven. Myrna's stomach was in knots.

He won't come. Don't be silly, it only just struck seven. Maybe the clock was fast. He still had a couple of minutes. Try as she might, she couldn't take her eyes off the minute hand, which seemed like it didn't move at all. Five minutes past seven, ten, fifteen. Myrna swallowed hard. He wasn't coming. She stood up to go back to her room, then heard someone running up the porch steps. In a second, the doorbell rang.

Myrna made herself walk slowly to the door and open it. David stood there, his red curls slicked back, wearing a tan suit with a white shirt and a brown and gold striped tie.

"Sorry I'm late. I got lost." He sounded a little breathless.

"That's all right." Suddenly, she smelled fried onions and grease from whatever the landlady had cooked for supper. She hoped he didn't notice. "I'm ready. Let's go."

A big smile lit his face. "Hey, an Alice Blue gown. Just matches your eyes."

Myrna looked at the floor. "I-uh" She took a deep breath and let it all out in a rush. "My name isn't Alice. I just said that so you wouldn't know my real name. It's Myrna. Myrna Schroeder."

His smile faded and Myrna found it hard to breathe. Now, he'd turn around and walk out the door. The smile came back. "Well, that's a surprise, but what's in a name? Myrna's a nice name. Come on. The movie starts in ten minutes, thanks to me being so late."

Two weeks later, after another movie, David parked the car in Everson Park, "Why did you come here?" Myrna asked.

"We've gone out for a couple of weeks. It's about time I got a little of what you give to the guys who come to that greasy spoon where you work." He slid out from under the steering wheel, put his arm around Myrna and pulled her close. She tried to move away, but he pulled her closer, then kissed her, hard.

Myrna turned her head away. "Don't do that. I don't like it."

"Don't give me that line. Come on. Give." He gripped her chin to turn her head around and forced his tongue into her mouth and worked it around inside. She gagged, and he sat back. "You little tease. I'll show you. I'm not playing any games." Before she knew it, he put his hand down the front of her dress and inside her bra and started rubbing her breast.

"Stop it. That hurts." She felt for the door handle and had the door partly open when he caught the arm rest and slammed it shut.

"Oh, no, you don't," he growled and yanked her hand away from the door handle. David fumbled with his pants until he had the zipper down and pulled them over his hips, along with his tight white underpants. Then, he struggled with her dress, and finally ripped it down the front and pulled her bra straps down over her arms. He reached under what was left of her dress and slid her panties off.

"Let me go," she screamed.

In answer, he slapped his hand across her mouth. "Shut up," he growled. She twisted her head back and forth, but he just held her more tightly. She tried to bite his hand, but her squeezed her cheeks until she thought his hands would make holes in them. "Not another sound out of you," he said, and removed his hands to grab her thighs and then yanked her to her back, striking her head against the window crank.

Myrna screamed. "Help me, somebody. Help."

David clamped his hand over her mouth again. "Shut up, I said." he snarled as he slid down until he was between her legs, pushing against her then until they were wide apart. She tried to pull them back, but he pushed harder, then took his hand from her mouth, "Don't you dare scream again. Now, we're going to have some fun. I'll bet you've never had it so good. Actually, I like it if you fight me. Makes it more exciting."

He lay down on top of her and she felt something hard rubbing against her bush. She squirmed to get away, but he just rubbed harder. Tears ran down her face. The rubbing stopped and suddenly the hardness was pushed inside of her. She screamed again, this time with pain.

"What the hell," he said. "What have you got in there?" Suddenly, he laughed. "My God, you are a virgin. That's great. Wait 'til I tell Randy." He began to pump inside her until she felt something wet and he flopped on her, breathing hard. "Wow! A virgin. I've never taken a girl's cherry before."

David lay quietly for a few minutes. Myrna held her breath. He was so heavy. Finally, he sat up and reached to the floor to pick up his underwear. As soon as he moved off her, she sat up, watching him carefully, and slid slowly toward the door. While he was trying to put on his pants under the steering wheel, she slowly pressed down on the door opener. He arched his back to get the pants over his rump, and Myrna pushed open the door and ran, not even trying to close her torn dress.

Sobbing, she ran toward the next street light. To her left, down the road, she saw the yellow square sign that meant a bus stop. A life saver. She ran to it and held it, gasping for air. Safe. Then she looked at her torn dress, her breast still outside her bra. She pulled the straps over her shoulders, and tried to close the tear in her dress. Then, she remembered. Her purse was in the car. She had no money for the bus. What would she do now? Where could she go? It was a long way to her rooming house. She looked back at the car. The headlights came on and the motor started. There was a crunch as the tires bit the asphalt when they turned and the headlights speared her. She clung to the bus stop sign, but the car stopped opposite her. The window rolled down.

"Get out of here. I never want to see you again."

A pair of headlights appeared coming slowly toward them from the opposite direction. ROSECRANS COUNTY SHERIFF written in white across the side of the black car. Myrna hid behind a nearby bush. The patrol car stopped beside David. "Everything all right?" the officer asked from his vehicle.

"Sure," David replied. "Just a little misunderstanding with my girlfriend. You know how that goes."

The officer chuckled. "I did a couple hundred years ago. Then, I got married and I live with it." He looked harder into David's car. "Where is she?"

"She had to pee and she went behind the bushes."

"That's against the law," the officer said.

"What are you supposed to do? There are no rest rooms open."

"OK for now. Just don't let it happen again." The officer squinted at David. "Ain't you a Holman? That red hair sure looks like a Holman."

"Story of my life, officer. I can't get away with a thing. That makes me the most honest guy in town," David said with a laugh.

"Well, get things straightened out with your girl. She don't know how lucky she is," the officer said as he put the cruiser in gear and pulled away.

When the patrol car was out of sight, David called. "I know you're in those bushes. Get in the car."

Myrna said nothing. David got out of the car and came toward where she hid, and she tried to move back into the bushes, but they gave way.

"Come on. I'll take you home. I'm tired of fighting you. If you don't want to play, I won't."

Myrna stood, her hands gripping the tear in her dress. "I don't believe you."

"Believe me. I got more than I came for. I won the bet, plus your cherry. That's a lot more than I expected."

Myrna felt as if her feet had grown into the ground. "You did all that for a bet?"

"Sure. You wouldn't give Randy the time of day, so I bet him I could score with you. A hundred bucks."

"You hurt me just so you could win a bet?" Myrna felt as if she were covered in dirt, like she wasn't even human.

"I'd like some more of that, especially with the fighting, bur my girlfriend is coming home in a couple of days, so . . ."

"You PIG," Myrna spat.

"Come on," David said. 'You can't go on the bus like that and your purse is in my car."

Myrna got back into the car and sat as close to the door as she could. David drove her to her rooming house without another word. She got out as soon as he stopped, and the tires chirped as he drove away. The last thing she saw of him were the tail lights as he turned the corner. It was another two months before the doctor told her she didn't have the flu. She was sick to her stomach because she was pregnant.

Chapter 12

June melted into July. Myrna's arm no longer ached, but it itched under the cast until she wanted to take a hammer to the plaster and smash it, and scratch and scratch and scratch. One more week, the doctor said, and she'd be rid of the hot, heavy chunk of plaster that imprisoned her left arm for six long weeks. She still worked the bench, but only because it took both hands to operate the machines.

Betty grew bored with Myrna; another juicier topic of gossip took her place. Esther Morrow, a thirtyish divorced mother of three school-aged children, had a sizzling affair with a married setup man from another department and got pregnant. The setup man took Esther across the Mississippi to Dubuque, Iowa, where she had an abortion by some back-alley nurse. Except that the abortion didn't work until four days after she got home. She hemorrhaged and ended up in the hospital with a nasty infection. Myrna couldn't understand why Esther had gone that far. Abortions could kill you. Then, what would become of her kids? conversation with one or another of the Department 21 women in a quiet place outside the break room or the department. Talking about a union, probably. Lydia hadn't said much more about a union to Myrna, but what she had said stuck in Myrna's mind. A union might not be so bad. Especially if it did something about the girls in the mercury switch department.

She'd seen little of Mark Weston since that day in his office, which didn't surprise her. Why should she bother herself with him, especially since he had a wife? From the rumors, he had no problem finding women to take care of him. But every once in a while, Myrna would look up from the bench and catch a glimpse of him by the wall outside Department 43 right in her line of vision, just standing there, looking at her. It felt creepy.

The Fourth of July was typically hot and sunny, and Myrna packed Scarlett's favorite peanut butter and strawberry jam sandwiches, a large bag of potato chips, a couple of bananas and a Thermos of lemonade into a grocery sack and folded a light blanket on top of the food. They caught the bus to Lincoln Park, where the fireworks started when it was dark, about nine o'clock. They were early enough to get a good place to sit on the grass and Scarlett helped Myrna spread the blanket.

"Can I go swing, Mama?" she begged, dancing with excitement until the skirt of her red, white and blue dress twirled around her legs.

Myrna had a clear view of the swing set from the blanket, so she could see Scarlett easily on them. "Okay, honey. Just don't swing too high."

"Can't you push me?"

"You know I can't with this cast, I'd push you all crooked and you wouldn't like that. Besides, I can't leave the food here. I'll watch and you can pump yourself up. You can do it. I've seen you."

Scarlett frowned, just a little, then ran off toward the swings and soon Myrna saw the red skirt of her dress fly out behind the swing as she pushed it higher and higher. Myrna smiled. There was nothing better than watching her baby. Soon, the empty spaces around their blanket began to fill with other picnickers, and Scarlett ran back and flopped on the blanket, her face almost as red as her hair.

"I'm hot," she announced.

"How about some lemonade? You'll have to take the cup off the Thermos bottle. I can pour it."

Scarlett removed the metal cup and Myrna poured it half full of lemonade, which Scarlett gulped down in two swallows. "I'm thirsty. Can I have some more?" This time, Myrna filled the cup and Scarlett drank more slowly. She handed the cup to Myrna. "Now, it's your turn."

"Thank you."

"Mama. There's an ice cream stand over there. Can I have some ice cream?"

"Maybe after you eat your supper."

"Can we eat now?"

Other families were beginning to eat, so Myrna took the food from the bag. The potato chips made Scarlett thirsty again, and Myrna poured more lemonade. After Scarlett ate her banana, Myrna gave her a nickel and told her she could get an ice cream cone. She ran off into the crowd toward the nearby refreshment stand and returned slowly, licking a large dollop of chocolate ice cream that was about to fall off the cone.

"Is it good?" Myrna asked.

"M-hm," Scarlett replied. A chocolate ring circled her mouth and her pink tongue made a point to scoop the heavenly stuff into her mouth. She sat carefully, facing Myrna, and then looked up at something behind Myrna, and said, "Hi." Myrna turned her head and was shocked speechless to see Mark Weston standing right behind her.

"Hi, yourself," Mark said to Scarlett, then to Myrna, "May I sit down?"

Myrna slid a little to one side and nodded. "What are you doing here?" she asked when her vocal cords recovered.

Mark folded his long legs, encased in khaki slacks, and lowered himself beside her. He wore a sky blue knit shirt with short sleeves; the three buttons at the neck open, letting a generous thatch of black curly hair escape. His arms had a light covering of black hair, too. White canvas shoes were on his sockless feet. "Thought I'd come to see the fireworks."

"Don't you have better ones at the country club?"

He made a face. "No. And I don't know anybody there with children. Fireworks need kids to be enjoyed. I took a chance that I might find you and Scarlett here. I hope you don't mind."

"I don't mind. I'm just surprised." The bag of potato chips was still half full, and she held it open toward him.

He shook his head. "No, thanks. I just had a hot dog and some potato salad. You know, Scarlett, that ice cream cone looks good. Myrna, did you have one?"

"No," she said.

"What flavor do you like?" he asked.

"Vanilla."

He unfolded from the blanket and spoke to Scarlett. "Want to come along? Maybe we can find something else to go with your ice cream."

"Can I, Mama?"

"Yes, but you don't need anything more to eat. That cone was enough for two little girls."

107

Mark laughed, and held out his hand to Scarlett, who took it and bounced along beside him. When they returned, Mark walked slowly, carrying two cones, and Scarlett held up her arm so Myrna could see a small beaded bracelet on her wrist.

"You shouldn't have," she said to Mark. "You'll spoil her."

"Little girls need to be spoiled sometimes, especially on the Fourth of July. Besides, it only cost a quarter. She needs to practice for someday when a man buys her a diamond bracelet."

"Oh, sure," Myrna replied, laughing.

A bright light made its way overhead, trailing a wiggly black tail, then exploded with a boom that erupted into a shower of red, white and blue shimmering stars. The fireworks had begun. The display ended an hour later with a waterfall of the Stars and Stripes, and Myrna put the remains of the picnic into the grocery bag while Mark and Scarlett folded the blanket.

"What time is it?" she asked Mark.

He glanced at his watch. "Nine forty-five."

"Oh, we only have five minutes to get to the bus. Come on, Scarlett," she said, then covered her mouth and turned to Mark. "I'm sorry. I hope you liked the fireworks. It was nice to have you sit with us." She reached her good hand for Scarlett. "Come on, honey. Don't let go of my hand. I don't want you getting lost in this crowd."

Mark took the sack from her. "You're certainly not going home on the bus. The least I can do to thank you for a wonderful evening is to take you home. My car is a couple of blocks from here, I'm afraid. I didn't think about parking when I decided to come. Take my hand, too, Scarlett. Then, you can't possibly get lost."

When they reached the car, Myrna noticed it was the black car he'd taken her to the doctor in. Mark opened the back door and helped Scarlett into the back seat, then opened the passenger door for Myrna. By the time they reached Myrna's apartment, Scarlett was asleep. "What's prettier than a sleeping child," he said, as he carefully picked her up. "I'll carry her up, if you can handle the bag."

"I carried it to the park on the bus," she said. "And thanks for taking Scarlett."

She led the way up the steps, unlocked the door and led Mark into the bedroom and directed him to lay Scarlett on the bed. She removed Scarlett's shoes, then they tiptoed out and she closed the door. They walked out onto the small landing, and Mark leaned on the railing and raised his head, his back to Myrna.

"What a night," he said. "Look at the stars. They're having their own fireworks display. And smell the grass. Somebody must have just mown it. And the heavenly fragrance of whatever flowers are out there."

"Mrs. Neumann has rose bushes in the back," Myrna said.

"They smell better than any from the very best florist." He paused. "You know, I almost hate to go home."

Myrna tensed. Was he waiting for an invitation? She said, quietly, "Isn't your home beautiful?"

His back was still to her, and his voice changed, lower, harder, edged with cynicism. "Oh, yes. It's very beautiful. It's even been photographed for a couple of those 'how to decorate your home' magazines. Not a pillow out of place. Not a dent in the carpet. Old silver polished to a perfect patina. Like Noreen, it's an icicle hanging from the eave, spectacularly beautiful until you touch it and discover that it's hard and cold and has a very sharp point."

What could she say? Suddenly, she sensed an overtone to his words. "You must be very lonely."

He turned at that, and it was like one of those creatures in sci fi, a shape-shifter. It was as if he'd pulled a mask from his face. The dark eyes glistened. Tears? From a man? From this man? His features softened. His hands were still on the railing behind him, the knuckles white where he clenched the boards. He cleared his throat and smiled, the mask firmly back in place.

"Lonely? Me? Hardly. I don't have time." He straightened. "Thank you for the most pleasant afternoon and evening I've spent in a long time. I feel almost human." He bent and quickly touched his lips to her cheek, then ran down the steps, strode to his car and opened the door. Before he got inside, he waved to Myrna. In a moment, the motor purred, the lights flashed on and the car glided from the curb.

Mark's face burned and he swore under his breath as he drove out of Myrna's neighborhood. What made her think I'm lonely? She's a fine one to talk. She's got nothing, and I've got the world on a string— except for Noreen and Ed and a few more like that. I've got money and power and brains. That's all anyone needs in this world. Okay, then, when she made that comment why did it feel like a hot needle on a ripe boil? And why did I go haring off to the public fireworks just to find her? Why did it feel so good just to sit there and do nothing, but play with the kid and feel the warmth from Myrna's body so close and yet so far?

CHAPTER 13

Mark turned into the country club drive and started for the parking lot. Jeez. Where was Noreen supposed to be tonight, he thought, Sure as hell don't want to run into her.

A tap on the window brought him to attention. The parking attendant. "Can I park your car, Mr. Weston?" Mark got out of the car, fumbled around in his pants pocket and stuffed a five into the kid's hand. The kid got in and headed for the parking lot. Mark took the wide steps two at a time as the doorman opened the door. "Good evening, Mr. Weston.",

"Evening, George. Busy night?"

"The Fourth is always busy, sir. Fireworks, you know." Mark nodded, and George stepped aside to let him enter. At the end of the hall he could see into the ballroom, where the loud music was coming from. A long table, covered in white, with a bride and tuxedo-clad man beside her. A wedding. On the Fourth of July? It takes all kinds. Poor suckers.

He turned a sharp right into the darkened bar. The door shut softly behind him, and the music disappeared. Never before had he so appreciated donating the money to soundproof the bar. The room smelled like wax and good booze. He nodded to the bartender. "My usual, but double this time."

"Coming right up, Mr. Weston."

Mark walked to a dark corner table and sat down, facing the bar, a good place to get seriously drunk.

Two hours later, Mark drove up Walnut Hill, which was bathed in the discreet glow of twentieth century streetlights disguised as Victorian gaslights. Light fog reflected the Mercedes' headlights back at him, or was it the fog in his brain from all the Glen Livet.

The ten-foot-high iron gate materialized through the fog like a medieval portcullis, its sides permanently set into a pair of flanking square pillars made from smooth silver-gray granite river stones. Damn! He opened the car door and levered himself to his feet, grasping the top of the door frame for balance. He squinted, contemplating the vast expanse of five feet of empty space to reach the gate He straightened his arms and took an unsteady step away from the safety of the car and placed one foot carefully ahead of the other, running his right hand along the car's hood and fender until his left hand touched the safety of a cool iron bar. He gripped a bar, steadied himself, took a couple of steps to the next bar, gripped it and next across the gate until he reached the pillar, pushed the release button and propped himself against the stone with the other hand as the gate separated in the center and gracefully, silently swung wide. Now, to get back to the car.

The cool night air and the concentration had sobered him a little, and he didn't weave quite as much before he reached the car. He lowered himself into the seat with a huge sigh of relief. Have to figure out some way to open the fucking gate without getting out of the car. He pulled the door closed, started the car and, concentrating on the open space between the gate wings, drove the car through and toward the garage. Damned if he'd get out again to close the fool thing. The garage doors loomed as a huge wall of white.

He fumbled over the visor and the garage door opener fell on the floor. When he leaned over to look for it, his head spun and nausea threatened. He sat up fast. Well, the car can just stay out. He got out, found the lock and remembered to turn the key when it slipped into the hole. He squinted at the door and gave a sigh of relief. He hadn't scratched the paint. He turned toward the house and a light at the corner of the second floor caught his eye. Double god-damn! Noreen was up. Now there'd be hell to pay. If I'm real quiet, she may not hear me.

Mark negotiated two of the three steps to the back door, but caught his toe on the top and crashed into the door. The sound seemed loud enough to wake the entire neighborhood. So much for stealth. He fumbled with the door lock until it clicked, and swung it open where it banged into the iron doorstop that Martha, the cook, used to prop it open in hot weather. He got through the kitchen, only bumping into one chair, and into the foyer and the foot of the stairs. Noreen stood at the top wearing a floor-length ice blue satin robe, arms crossed over her breasts, backlit, the image of the Avenging Angel.

Mark grabbed the banister and hauled one foot to the bottom step.

"Where have you been?" The words were old, but something about her voice was wrong

"What difference does it make to you?" He climbed the stairs, making sure each foot was firmly on a step, gripping the bannister like a lifeline.

"I've been calling everywhere. I even got Jim Forsythe to drive around looking for you."

"I was enjoying some fireworks," he said.

"You were enjoying fireworks." Her tone could have cut glass. "I hope you had a good time." She sniffed and pulled a handkerchief from her pocket. "While you were having a good time, I was frantically trying to find you to tell you Daddy had died." She blew her nose.

"Ed? Died? How? When? I talked to him on the phone just this afternoon." Mark was suddenly sober.

Noreen made another delicate snort into the handkerchief, but tears started down her face again. "We had just finished dinner. He got up to go into his den. He got a strange look on his face." She hiccupped. "And he collapsed. He just dropped. Like a stone. Right where he was standing. Mother called his name and ran over to him. I guess it was Leo who called the ambulance. When it came, they couldn't revive him."

She threw herself against Mark and wrapped her arms around him, sobbing on his arm. He found his arms going around her, holding her, stroking her back. She whimpered like a small child. "Mark. What am I going to do?"

"It's all right. Don't worry," he murmured. Her hair smelled sour, like it hadn't been washed for days. He swallowed hard. He'd almost said, "I'll take care of you."

Her arms tightened around him, and suddenly she ground her groin into his. "Take me, Mark. Take me. Right now. Please. I need you."

Her mouth was on his, her tongue tasting the inside of his mouth. Her tongue tasted like gin. She backed away slightly and worked his belt loose, pulled down the zipper, and yanked his pants down around his hips. She gripped his lapels and lowered herself to the floor, pulling him with her. She lay back and her robe opened. She was naked.

Mark fumbled to get his jockey shorts over his hard penis and kicked free of his trousers. His tongue was in her mouth. The gin flavor tasted good. One hand found her breast and stroked the hard nipple. He pulled away from her mouth and circled the nipple with his tongue. She groaned and arched against him, squeezing her legs around his penis, rubbing it against her wet labia, until it found the clitoris. She spread her legs, moaning, begging for him to rub harder. She opened wider, and he slipped inside, the slick warm tunnel that gripped and released, gripped and released until he was in an agony of pleasure, ready to explode but holding, holding, holding for the sheer joy of the restraint. She thrust up hard, and he lost the restraint, and shouted "MYRNA" as he came hard.

Noreen suddenly collapsed without climaxing, and turned to face him. "What was that name?"

"What name?"

"When you came, you shouted a name—and it wasn't 'Noreen.'"

He squeezed a nipple and bent to tease it with his tongue. "I don't remember shouting anything." He grinned. "That was so good, I probably yelled 'Hallelujah!'"

"Get off of me," she snapped and rolled away as he raised himself and stood. She sat up, and he held out his hand to help her to her feet. He wrapped her robe around her and bent to kiss the back of her neck, but she twisted out of his grasp.

She clapped her hand over her mouth and began to laugh, just a beat short of hysteria. She gasped for breath and backed up, pointing at his naked lower half. "You look so funny. Handsome, elegant, debonair Mark Weston, all dressed up from his collar to his . . .his . . . little . . ." She doubled over, limp with laughter. Mark staggered as if she'd hit him and stood still for the space between two breaths. He clenched his jaw, snatched up his clothing to keep his hands from fastening around Noreen's neck, and pulled on his underwear. Keeping his eyes straight ahead, he walked around her, down the hall and into his bedroom.

He slammed the door behind him and snapped on the overhead light. A silver backed hairbrush made a soft thud on the carpet. He stared at it, then stooped, picked it up and hurled it into the mirror above the dresser. In slow motion, cracks spread across the two-hundred-year-old glass that had survived the three-month voyage across the Atlantic on a sailing ship, A mirror that had been polished and silvered to perfection; no bubbles on this glass; the edges beveled smooth and shaped to fit inside the oval bent oak frame that had been made for it. The cracks spread into a thousand tributaries and fell from the frame in a shimmering shower of light.

Mark stared at the shattered mirror, fists clenched at his sides, breathing hard.

From far away he heard pounding and Noreen shouting: "Mark! What are you doing?" The door latch released with a click, and he took one long stride and pressed the lock button.

The pounding resumed. "Mark! Open this door! Right now!"

Mark turned toward the window that faced east, pulling off his shirt as he went, tossing it into the big leather chair. The pounding and screaming went on, but he tuned her out. He pushed up the window and stood in front of it, naked to the waist. A storm had moved in, and the air reeked of ozone and washed over him like a cold shower. A door slammed somewhere downstairs. Moments later, the garage door rose and Noreen's white Mercedes backed out, turned, and with a chirp of tires, sped out of the drive. Mark thought briefly he should go down and close the door, but shrugged. If somebody wanted to steal the cars, let them. Noreen was gone. He had a feeling she wouldn't be back.

Lightning split the dark, creating a surreal still life of the rose border along the garden wall, painting them electric shades of red, pink and white against a dark green so intense it shimmered. A tremendous crash of thunder followed. Rain lashed the window, showering Mark, and he closed it, but stood watching the storm, until the rain curtained the window throwing back his reflection. That, he could do without. He sat on the edge of the bed and took off his shoes and socks, flipped the heavy quilted silk spread to the foot of the bed, pulled the sheets aside and lay down. Rain still sluiced down the window and thunder beat like kettledrums, followed by lightning, dim through the curtain of water.

Die Götterdämmerung, he thought. The twilight of the gods in his life had arrived.

Two days later, in his fifth floor office, Mark sprawled on the sofa, his feet propped on the coffee table, black custom-made loafers dangling from his toes, the collar button of his white Egyptian cotton shirt unfastened, the knot of his navy silk tie with its pattern of small red anchors, askew. His navy suit coat was draped over the chair across the coffee table. He had turned off the intercom, told Joanne not to allow phone calls from anyone, short of Ike, and locked the door. His reading glasses rested on the tip of his nose as he stared at the thick document in his hands, Ed Best's argument to the Board for a sale to American Electric. With Ed dead and Noreen chairman of the board, he had to read and digest every twist and turn of the convoluted legal language. Mike Anderson would cut through the legal mumbo jumbo later, but Mark wanted to read and understand it first. Given Ed's shenanigans before he died, he didn't want to rely totally on the lawyer's report. Mike didn't know Ed Best's devious mind, nor, for that matter, Noreen's.

After an hour, the miniscule print and legalese of the document blurred and for the last fifteen minutes he'd stared at the same page without reading a thing. He sure didn't grieve for Ed Best. Good riddance, was his dominant reaction, except for the fact of the "family ownership rule" that Ed had insisted on. Mark had been too young and too hungry for the money to think beyond the dollar signs that would make his dream a reality.

CHAPTER 14

Monday afternoon, Myrna pushed open the door to the second floor at Weston Switch and almost ran into Lydia McIntire, who stood right in front of it, blocking her way.

"Punch in and then come with me," Lydia said, stepping aside.

Myrna punched her time card, and Lydia took her arm, guiding her along the hallway, away from the Department 21 break room toward the cafeteria. They stopped beside the large employee bulletin board on the wall. All the little notes, pictures and notices were gone, leaving a single sheet of paper tacked to a sheet of black construction paper.

"Read it," Lydia said. It was typed on company letterhead.

"To the Employees of Weston Automatic Switch Company:
It is with great sorrow that I inform you of the death of my father, Edward Otto Best, Co-founder and Chairman of the Board of Weston Automatic Switch Company. He died unexpectedly Friday, July 4 in his home from a massive heart attack.
Private funeral services will be Wednesday, July 9 in St. Mark's Episcopal Church. A public memorial service will be at 10:00 a.m., Thursday, July 10 in the Edward O. Best Auditorium, 220 North Best Avenue.
In respect to Mr. Best, Weston Automatic Switch Company will be closed all day July 9 and two hours for the memorial service on July 10.
The family of Edward O. Best is grateful for the donation of time by the employees in respect to him.
Sincerely,
Noreen Best Weston
Chairman of the Board
Weston Automatic Switch Company"

Myrna frowned and read the letter a second time, then turned to Lydia. "Other than the man died, what does it mean to us?"

"First, it means that Mark Weston's wife is now chairman of the board of this company. I read up on it. Old man Best held the controlling number of shares in the company and was chairman of the board in perpetuity. Upon his death, his daughter or if she dies, the grandchildren automatically became chairman."

"You mean that Mrs. Weston is now Mr. Weston's boss?"

Lydia smiled like a cat with feathers on its face. "No," she said. "But that isn't what's most important about that letter. It's the last paragraph. It's in double-talk so peons like you and me and everybody else in the factory can't understand it. You see where it says 'donation of time' by the employees?" Myrna nodded. "Well, that means we won't be paid when the plant closes for the services. In short, we'll lose more than a day's pay, and the company will make a killing."

"Can they do that?"

"You bet your sweet life they can," Lydia said. She took Myrna's arm and turned her toward the cafeteria. "I called everybody in the department as soon as I heard about this. You don't have a phone I couldn't reach you. Let's get a cup of coffee and I'll fill you in."

Only a handful of people sat at the tables in the cafeteria, and it was quiet in the big room, usually full of conversation, the rattle of dishes and clang of pots and pans. "Go over to the far corner and I'll get us some coffee," Lydia said, dropping Myrna's arm and going to the fifty-cup aluminum coffee urns on a table with cups and accessories. She brought the coffee to where Myrna waited, set it on the table and sat down.

"What's all the mystery?" Myrna asked. "We'll be late."

"Just listen. Everybody's hopping mad about this, so we're going to do what is called a little 'job action.' In this case, a sit-down strike."

At the word 'strike,' Myrna suddenly went cold. She took a sip of the scalding coffee and welcomed the burn all the way to her stomach. "What do you mean, sit-down strike?"

"We'll all go to work as usual until after supper. Then, when we go back into the department, instead of turning on the machines, we'll just sit down and do nothing. That will get management's attention real fast. And we'll stay there until they agree to pay us for the forced days off."

"They'll fire us."

"Not the whole department."

"What about Betty and her bunch? They'll run right to management."

Lydia smiled again. "This hits Betty in the pocketbook. She is mad as hell, ready to tear Mark Weston's head from his shoulders."

"Why Mark? He didn't do anything?"

"That's just it. He didn't do a damn thing. Just sat back and let his wife do the dirty work for him. Get the stars out of your eyes, girl. Money is all those folks care about." Lydia glanced at her watch. "It's almost time to go. Are you with us?"

Myrna took another sip of the coffee and said, her voice shaking, "Yes."

Lydia's smile was real this time. She reached across the table and patted Myrna's hand. "I knew you would. Remember. After supper, just go to the bench and sit there. Don't do a thing. OK?"

"OK."

The klaxon sounded after supper and the women of Department 21 straggled into the room and sat at their workplaces, their backs to the machines. Myrna couldn't keep her eyes off Betty, a few feet away at the riveter. She didn't trust Betty not to cause some sort of trouble. It just wasn't like her to go along with a plan like this, especially when it came from someone like Lydia. Betty carried a large cloth bag with a wood handle and set it on the floor beside her chair, then bent over and removed what looked like a large white cloth from it. Betty deftly twisted a thin thread through the sausage-sized fingers on her left hand, the same hand that held the cloth. Her right hand nearly buried a slim silver crochet hook that she dipped into the white object, which Myrna now could see would be one of those beautiful doilies with big ruffles. Tough, hardboiled Betty Brown crocheting? A ruffled doily, no less. Myrna would have been less surprised if a fairy godmother appeared and turned Betty into a slim, beautiful glamour girl.

Everyone else had their eyes on Jack Sweeney, shuffling papers at his desk. He looked up, glanced at the big clock on the wall, then at his watch. It had been five minutes since the klaxon sounded. Finally, he realized there was no noise, and every woman sat with her back to her machine. The two set-up men leaned against the far wall. He was up and out into the center of the room, beside the entry in three strides. "Gather round," he said, a frown on his usually genial face, a deep crease between his eyes. The fire from his blue eyes could have scorched the room.

All eyes turned to Lydia. She shook her head. Nobody moved. Betty put her crocheting back into the bag, but stayed at her machine.

"What in the hell is going on here?" Jack said, quietly, too quietly. "It's way past the time you should be working. Now, get back to your places and start up those machines."

Lydia stepped forward. "Nobody in this department is going to put out one more part until there's a change in that letter on the bulletin board. This is a 'job action' to protest being forced to give up a day and a half of pay to memorialize somebody nobody here ever heard of."

"You mean a wildcat strike?" Jack said, cocking his head as if he hadn't heard Lydia, and turned to face the others. "You mean you're willing to risk your jobs because of the death of a man you never knew? Even if you didn't know him, you should show respect. If it wasn't for him, you wouldn't have your jobs. He started this business."

Lydia's mouth twisted into an ironic smile. "You know better than that," she said. "From what I've heard of Ed Best, he's probably toasting his toes on the shores of the lake of fire with the devil. If his daughter wants to shut down the plant to memorialize him, let her. But not at the expense of all the people who work here. Nobody here is willing to do without a day and a half pay just because the old reprobate kicked off. If they're so eager to memorialize him by closing the plant and not paying anybody, we'll close it a little early for our benefit, but we'll stay here. This is what's called a sit-down strike. We stay here as we are until we can talk face-to-face with management. Except, that is, when we all show up at the memorial service. That should be a really memorable memorial, especially since we won't have had baths or anything in all that time."

Jack looked like he was about to explode. "You're out of your mind." He turned to the others. "You don't want to go along with this craziness. It can get you fired. Go on. Get back to work before this goes any further."

"Nope. I ain't donatin' any money to the Best family. They pay us for the days off or we just sit here," said Betty, her little eyes nearly closed and her mouth thinned to invisibility.

Jack stood, silent, his eyes moving from one person to another, waiting, then moving on. Nobody spoke or moved. He ran his hand over his head, mussing his perfectly groomed hair. "I never thought people in this department would pull a stunt like this," he said, and turned on his heel and strode back to his desk where he picked up the phone.

Lydia made a small movement with her hand and the workers all returned to their places. She stayed where she was. Betty took out her crocheting. Myrna realized she was shaking and wished she had some crocheting to keep her own hands busy. What if management did fire them? What would she do? How could she pay the rent and buy food and school stuff for Scarlett? Would anybody hire her if she was fired for taking part in this 'job action,' as Lydia called it?

All eyes were on Jack in the office. He was nodding his head and still mussing his hair as he spoke to someone on the phone. Probably the night manager reading him the riot act. Nobody made a sound. It was as if they were all holding their breath. Myrna knew she was.

The silence from Department 21 drifted through the large opening into Department 43, as did Jack's harangue. More people than usual found reasons to wander close to the door and peer at the silent employees of Department 21, who sat with their backs to their machines. Ruth Kimball, a drill press operator in Department 43, sat at her machine at the edge of the door. Myrna saw her motion to Lydia, who stood and sauntered toward her. They talked briefly and Lydia returned to her seat. Jack was still on the phone, then hung up and stood. He came out into the department.

"Chuck Richter will be here in a minute," he said, then returned to the office. Chuck Richter was the night plant manager.

The time dragged on. Richter's office wasn't that far, Myrna thought. She also realized Department 43 had gone silent. She couldn't see the machines, except for Ruth Kimball's, and she was sitting with her back to her machine. Suddenly, Tony Schultz, the night foreman for Department 43, a short box of a man with a graying buzz cut, appeared in the center of the room, waving his arms and yelling: "What in hell is going on here? Get those goddamn machines started. Now! Or you're all out of here for good."

At that moment, Chuck Richter appeared, a tall, slim man, his brown hair combed neatly from a right side part, wearing a navy blue suit, a white shirt and red printed tie. His mouth was set in a tight line. He stopped to speak to Tony, and Tony joined him as they both entered

121

Department 21 and went into Jack's office. Jack closed the door. Myrna wished she could read lips, but the way they stood and moved told her a lot. Richter listened as both assistants apparently related their experiences, and then Jack went to the door and called for Lydia. Lydia stood tall and calm, speaking to the men. Tony's face was red as a firecracker. Jack picked up the phone, and all three watched as he spoke briefly and then hung up. It seemed like the air went out of all the people in the office. What on earth was going on?

Myrna didn't have long to wait.

Moments later, Mark Weston strode down the aisle through Department 43 into Department 21. Chairs creaked and scraped the floor as people shifted when they saw him. This was serious. He looked directly at Myrna, whose workplace was in his line of sight, and frowned, then went into the office. Myrna shivered. For a moment, she was embarrassed, but quickly remembered why they were all doing this.

After another five minutes of intense conversation, the men came out of the office and stood in the empty space by the doorway. Mark Weston spoke. "Miss McIntire says you all agreed to this 'sit-down strike' to protest not being paid for the time the plant is closed for Mr. Best's services. Is that true?" Nobody spoke. He looked directly at Betty. "Mrs. Brown. Do you agree with this?"

Betty straightened in her chair. "You bet I do. You got no right to close the plant for no reason and not pay us."

"I'm afraid we do," Mark replied.

Betty looked at Lydia. "In a way," Lydia   replied. "It's called a lockout, but it usually goes along with bargaining."

"This company is not unionized; therefore, collective bargaining law doesn't apply," Mark said. "What you're doing here is a wildcat strike, which does not have protection under the law, even if you were organized."

"It's not a strike," Lydia said. "It's a job action in protest over unfair treatment by the company. Nobody asked us if we wanted to 'donate' a day and a half of our income to memorialize Ed Best."

Mark didn't reply at once. He looked around at the employees in both departments. The anger drained from his face and he looked exhausted. "You have a point," he said. "It is unfair." He made a twisted smile. "If we close the plant, we lose the money that could be made from the products produced. If we close the plant and pay the employees for doing nothing, we lose more money in the salaries paid to those employees. It adds up to something close to $100,000."

"You won't go broke on that amount, will you?" Betty asked.

"Hardly."

"Well. Is it worth a hundred grand in your pocket to keep the plant open and pay us or lose that much just to make some kind of statement about somebody none of us even knew?" Betty said. "Sounds like a no-brainer to me."

Mark sighed. "You're right. I don't know about keeping the plant open. Mrs. Weston is pretty adamant about that. But I promise you will be paid whether it's open or not."

"Mr. Weston," Lydia said. "Will you please explain what is going on with the management of this company? Is that letter on the bulletin board an indication of what we can expect in the future?"

"Of course. I'll explain it to you now and post a letter for the entire plant tomorrow. According to Mr. Best's will, upon his death, the stock and the chairmanship would go to his daughter, and/or any grandchildren." His mouth twisted in a wry smile. "There are no grandchildren, so Mrs. Weston is now chairman of the board and majority stock holder. I am still president of the company and run it on a day-to-day basis. She is in charge of board business."

"Does that mean things will stay the same or will there be changes?" Lydia asked.

"For the time being, things will remain the same. I can't say what the future will bring. Mr. Best's death was so sudden and shocking, it has us all scrambling."

"I'll take you at your word, but if we are locked out and not paid, there will be trouble," Lydia said. She turned to the employees. "I guess we made our point. We can get back to work." She turned back to Mark. "All right, Mr. Weston?"

He nodded. "All right," and then turned on his heel and strode through Department 43 to his private elevator.

As soon as he reached his desk, Mark picked up the phone and gave the Best's number. A maid answered. "This is Mr. Weston, Lucy. I'd like to speak to Mrs. Weston. Thank you."

After a long silence, Noreen's voice said, "What do you want?"

"I want to talk to you, here in my office. Be here in fifteen minutes."

"I can't leave Mother. She's devastated."

"If you want this company to continue, your mother can be devastated without you. Get your ass down here." He slammed the receiver into the cradle before Noreen could answer.

A half hour later, the elevator hummed and when the door opened, Noreen stepped out, dressed all in black. A small hat held a black veil that fell to her chin. Her earrings were black pearl drops. The long sleeves of her knee-length black silk dress were sheer; a concession to the heat, black silk stockings and medium heel black calf pumps completed the ensemble.

"How'd you get that outfit put together so fast?" Mark said.

"Is that why you swore at me and ordered me to come here immediately, at this hour?" She glanced at her watch, a small tasteful gold with a black velvet wristband. "It's past seven."

Mark didn't invite her to sit, but she flowed into one of the chairs in front of the desk. He put both arms on the desk, folded his hands and spoke softly.

"That letter you posted on the bulletin boards created the first labor trouble this company has had in the fifteen years of its existence. What the hell were you thinking?"

"I thought it only fitting that the people who owe their living to my father should honor his memory."

"Owe their living to your father! Jesus H. Christ! That's the biggest load of bullshit I've ever heard."

"Will you please stop swearing? It doesn't help. You, of all people should be aware of the debt of gratitude owed my father."

Mark hammered his fist on the desktop. "If I hear that comment one more time, I'll walk out of here immediately—with my patents—and let you try to run this company. I'd love to see how you'd handle the situation that occurred here an hour and a half ago."

"What happened?"

"Two departments refused to work. They sat with their backs to their machines and did nothing. They were protesting being forced to give up a day and a half pay to honor your father, someone few people in the plant ever heard of. That money means food and rent or mortgage payments, medicine, clothing and all the necessities of life, not country club dues or thousand-dollar designer mourning clothes."

Noreen kept her hands folded in her lap. "Those people," and she said it as if she were discussing a pile of old garbage, "don't have appearances to keep up. What would they do at the club or with expensive clothes?"

"The same thing you do. Nothing."

She sat up straighter. "More to the point, what did YOU do about this insubordination?"

"I wouldn't call it insubordination. They had a legitimate complaint, and like the good employer I've tried to be all these years, I agreed to close the plant in respect to your father, but I promised them they would be paid."

Noreen gasped, as if she'd been stabbed. "Do you have any idea what that will cost?"

"To the penny."

"The company can't afford it."

"Bullshit. Our profit margin is one of the highest in the country. We share some of it with the people who make it possible." Mark paused. "What you would have done in a similar situation?"

"I'd have fired them all on the spot."

"And who would make the products that paid for that outfit?"

"It's not hard to hire riff-raff off the street."

"If you want to employ riff-raff. If you want intelligent, honest, hardworking people who take pride in their work, it will take at least a year to get back up to speed. That's a lot of money lost."

Noreen sniffed. "What's so difficult about what they do that can't be learned in fifteen minutes?"

Mark grinned. "Would you like to try? I can take you down to Department 21 right now and put you on a kick press and see how close you come to the night's rate." His grin grew wider. "Actually, part of that's a good idea. I wouldn't put you on a machine and mess up Jack's quota, but it would give the employees an opportunity to express their condolences personally."

Noreen stood. "You are not funny." She stood and took two steps toward the elevator, then turned to look at him. "You should know, as soon as the memorials are over, I'm flying to Reno to take up residence to get a divorce. I want you and your things out of the house before I get back. I suggest you see a lawyer."

Mark leaned back in his chair. "That's the best news I've had in fifteen years. Thank you.

Chapter 15

Weeks had passed since the Fourth of July and the death of Ed Best, and Mark Weston had disappeared from Myrna's life. She saw him occasionally as he walked through Department 43 toward his private elevator. By the time August's heat wave rolled in, she had put the incident from her mind. She'd been his latest experiment in womanizing, romancing a factory girl, and he'd moved on. Her arm was healing. Life resumed its usual pattern.

"Mama. Mama. Mama." Scarlett's voice filtered through Myrna's dream, and she slowly opened her eyes, blinking at the sunlight streaming through the sheer curtains in the living room. What was she doing in the living room? Before she could move, Scarlett bounded into the room and onto the sofa at Myrna's feet. "How come you're sleeping on the couch?"

Myrna struggled to a sitting position. "I was hot," she said. "Come here. Let me give you a hug," she said, and Scarlett slid under her arm. Myrna squeezed the small body close, and dropped a kiss onto the wild tangle of red curls. "I slept on the couch because it was too hot in the bedroom."

Scarlett turned her face up, and the freckles seemed to bounce and her green eyes danced. "I got to sleep on the floor in Mrs. Neumann's living room 'cause it was so hot. Mrs. Neumann let the door open and it was real nice. She put sheets on the floor so it would be smooth. It was fun. Can I sleep on the floor here?"

"Good morning," said Mrs. Neumann in her heavy German accent. She looked the part of a German hausfrau, a square, stocky body dressed in a yellow print housedress, heavy cotton stockings over thick legs and sturdy black shoes with solid square heels. Her gray hair was cinched back from her square face and knotted into a tight bun. Round, gold-framed glasses magnified her ice blue eyes. Her thin lips were parted in a smile. "How is your arm feeling today?"

"I'm fine," Myrna replied. "Thank you for letting Scarlett stay over. I really needed the rest." She gave Scarlett a squeeze and stood up. "Let me get some coffee."

"Nein. I will make the coffee, and I brought some cinnamon rolls I made yesterday. You rest."

"Mama, can I go out and play?"

"We have to eat breakfast first," Myrna said. "My, you look so pretty in that red dress."

"Can I go barefooted?"

"If you're careful."

Mrs. Neumann had filled the coffee pot and set it on the stove, and in minutes the rich fragrance filled the room. She set the table with dishes from the cupboard and placed the plate filled with frosted cinnamon rolls the size of coffee cups in the center. "Come, sit," she said.

Myrna placed a cinnamon roll on Scarlett's plate and cut it in half, and then picked up her cup, inhaled the coffee aroma and sipped a mouthful. The strong, hot brew eased Myrna's tension. Scarlett took a big bite of her roll, getting a bit of frosting on the tip of her nose.

Myrna laughed. "You look like a cinnamon roll with frosting on you." Scarlett grinned and took an even bigger bite, tipping her nose to get more frosting on it. Myrna tousled her hair and shook her head. "You're a silly-billy."

Mrs. Neumann set a glass of milk in front of Scarlett and wiped the frosting off her nose with a napkin, then sat opposite Myrna. Myrna cut a piece of roll for herself and took a bit. The buttery sweetness seemed to melt in her mouth. "M-m-m. This is good. You'll have to teach me how to make them."

"Ja. I would like that." Mrs. Neumann said.

Myrna's feet felt like they were encased in deep-sea divers' lead boots as she climbed the dented concrete steps to the second floor at Weston Switch. Would this heat never let up? It was already late August and it had been ninety or a hundred degrees since June. It wore her out. At least, the cast was gone. Right now, she felt like she was swimming in sweat. Scarlett had been grouchy and whiny for days. Ordinarily reasonable people snapped at each other, at store clerks, at waitresses and factory workers. The three fans in Department 21 just moved the hot air around, and now she faced another eight hours of it.

The first breath of acrid air scraped against her throat and she coughed. As she turned to pull her time card from the slot she saw Mark Weston at the far end of the hall, next to the window waiting for his elevator.

Her heart thumped for a couple of beats. He had disappeared from her life as suddenly as he'd entered it, and she told herself not to be surprised. Her arm was healed. There was no reason for him to remember her. Except for the way he had looked at her sometimes, and that strange Fourth of July. Ed Best had died that night, and she hadn't seen or heard from Mark since then, except at that "sit-down strike" to protest the plant closing. He had looked at her as if he were surprised that she was part of it. Maybe he felt like she'd turned on him after he had been so good to her. As she watched, he stepped forward and disappeared. Well, time to put Mark Weston in the "forget it" section of her brain.

Myrna punched her time card "IN". She approached the break room; something had changed. It was quiet. You could always hear people talking from twenty feet away, especially Betty. When she turned toward the door, she almost ran into it. The door was closed. What was going on? That door was never closed.

Myrna opened it a few inches and peered inside.

The women of Department 21 sat in their chairs along the walls as if assigned; nobody looked toward the door. They were all turned toward Lydia, who sat in a metal folding chair facing the others, legs spread in front of her, elbows on knees, leaning forward. The department's attitude toward Lydia had shifted three hundred sixty degrees since the showdown with Mark Weston. Now, everyone looked to her for advice and information.

Betty was talking. Well, that wasn't any different, Myrna thought as she eased through the door and found an empty chair next to it.

"I know it's true," Betty expounded. "Joe heard it from George, who's the foreman over at Plant 2, and his wife works in the office right outside Mr. Muckety-muck's. And his secretary told George's wife that Mr. Muckety-muck is going to sell the company."

Alice, her gray hair skinned back into a bun at the nape of her neck, folded her arms across her spare chest and stuck out her chin. "I don't believe you."

"It's his company. Makes no sense that he would sell it."

Betty sat in her usual place, haloed in the gray light from the grimy window, thick legs in their crisply pressed brown pants, splayed out in front of her. "These big wheels don't give a damn about who owns it. Just so they get a bundle of money. I hear Mr. Big Shot wants to get rid of his wife. Might take that much for a settlement."

A chill went down Myrna's spine. Sell the company? Did that mean everybody would be laid off? Scarlett would start kindergarten in a couple of weeks. Where could she find another job? Another thought crept into her mind: *I'll never see Mark again.* She quickly shut it down.

"What's going on?" she whispered to Dorothy, who sat beside her.

"You just heard Betty."

"That's all? Just a bunch of rumors?"

Dorothy shrugged and turned her attention to Lydia.

"I'll find out as much as I can," Lydia said. "We'll talk about it at the meeting on Sunday. Remember, Sunday at two o'clock in the Labor Hall. Do you all know where that is?"

Most shook their heads or said, "No," so Lydia gave detailed directions. The klaxon blared, the women struggled to their feet and shuffled toward the door.

In his office, Mark Weston leaned back in his desk chair. Seeing Myrna at the other end of the hallway downstairs had given him a jolt. He hadn't seen her in weeks. Actually, he'd almost forgotten her, especially after that little set-to in Department 21 about Ed Best's funeral. After all he had done for her, she should have had more loyalty to him and the company. Karl had told him her arm was healed and she was receiving physical therapy. Soon, her arm would be completely normal. Besides, she made it clear she wasn't interested in him as a man. Why pursue failure? It wasn't his style.

He took his reading glasses from his pocket, slipped them on and opened the folder on his desk. It contained the latest letter from Noreen's lawyer in Reno. It looked like freedom for both of them was only three weeks away, if he met her demands. He already knew she wanted the house and everything in it, her car, and various other items. She also wanted the patent for the Weston switch and one million in cash. And, of course, attorney's fees, travel and residence expenses in order to get the divorce.

He slapped the folder shut and tossed it back into the in-box. She wasn't about to get either the patent or the cash. She already had a majority of the stock shares, thanks to Ed's will. That was worth a cool ten million. What did she need the cash for? As for the attorney's fees, she filed for the divorce. She could pay for it.

The next folder was more rewarding, the deed to a small building in Bellevue, Washington. He could hardly wait to get started on the switch for the new jumbo jet plane Boeing was planning. It was a beautiful city in a beautiful part of the country, and opportunity was there just waiting to be caught. And there were some pretty women in Seattle.

Only none of them looked like Snow White.

Chapter 16

The hinges creaked as David Holman opened the door to his political headquarters. Inside, a thin veil of cigarette smoke hovered over a dozen women who sat at three card tables folding, stuffing and sealing envelopes. Ashtrays on each table overflowed with the remains of lipstick-ringed dead cigarettes. His face smiled at him from a half-dozen large posters on the walls. An extra card table held boxes of campaign buttons and literature.

"Good afternoon, ladies. Sorry to be so late, but a long, drawn-out legal case was finally settled this afternoon. Now, I can concentrate on my campaign."

His part-time secretary sorted a pile of mail at her desk beside the door. "I'll take my mail in a minute, Barbara."

He made the rounds of the tables: To a carefully coiffed and dyed blonde, well past middle age, he said, "Thank you for coming Mrs. Schmich. I know how busy you are with the League of Women Voters." To a pretty young redhead, it was, "Hello, Connie. How's little Anthony?" To a fiftyish woman who sat ramrod straight in her chair, her short salt-and-pepper hair crimped in tight curls, he offered, "Miss Hazelton. How good of you to take your day off from the hospital to help us."

As David worked the tables, he recalled his father's lesson on how to remember names and faces. He was only six at the time, barely able to see above the big desk in his father's home office. Father would place faces cut from newspapers and magazines on the desk and give each face a name. David wasn't allowed to leave the desk until he got them all right. Now, he never forgot a face nor a name.

When David finished greeting the volunteers, he went into his private office, with its bare, dingy cream-colored walls. The room was just big enough for a battered gray metal desk, an office chair on rollers and a two-drawer filing cabinet. Barbara followed him inside and handed him a packet of letters.

"You said to pay attention to unusual ones," she said. "The one on top looks really funny."

The address was printed in block letters, in wobbly, uneven script. "Probably some kid." He smiled. "Gives them a thrill to get a letter back. It's OK, but thanks for being careful." Barbara nodded and closed the door as she left.

He slit the strange envelope, but instead of lined tablet paper from a child, a single sheet of plain paper folded around two photographs fell to the desktop. He picked up the pictures first. One was a professional black and white portrait of a curly-haired baby girl about a year old. The other was apparently a snapshot of the same child, maybe three, standing in somebody's yard. He frowned and turned to the paper.

"I TOLD YOU I HAD PITCHERS. TAKE A GOOD LOOK. YOU CAN'T SAY SHE AN'T YOUR KID. I WANT MY $50 THOUSAND IN $20'S, $50'S AND $100'S. CALL RED 712 AND FIND OUT WHERE TO TAKE IT. IF IT AN'T THEIR 24 HOURS AFTER I TELL YOU WHERE, I SEND THE PITCHERS TO THE PAPER".

He raised the pictures with a shaky hand. The baby was smiling, showing her two teeth, and her baby hair curled tightly against her head. In the black and white photo, it looked light. It could have been blonde or red. Her eyes were unusually light, too. Probably, light blue. The other picture was a small snapshot and it was hard to see the features clearly. He went to the door, opened it and called to Barbara. "Do you have a magnifying glass?" The volunteers all looked up, surprised at his shout.

"There was one around here somewhere," Barbara replied. "I'll try to find it and bring it to you."

David ignored the volunteers, shut the door and squinted at the black and white picture of the older child. Her face had lost some of its baby fat and was more defined, more heart-shaped than round. That left him out. His face was triangular. The hair was longer, but still in tight ringlets. He ran his hand through his own tightly curled hair.

There was a light rap on the door before Barbara opened it. "I found the magnifying glass," she said, handing him the small object.

David didn't look up. He took the glass and raised it to the small photo. "Oh, thanks, Barbara." She nodded and closed the door.

The picture was slightly out of focus, but when he squinted, he could make out the eyes, but not clearly enough to tell whether they were light or dark. She was facing the camera straight on, so it was hard to see the shape of her nose, but it appeared to be straight and well proportioned. Her mouth was wide, with well-shaped lips, much like his, only more feminine. He took one last look and returned the note and pictures to the envelope. Cute kid, but not mine, he thought, before he tossed it into the wastebasket. On second thought, he retrieved it. Never do to leave it there. Somebody might find it. He took a manila folder from the filing cabinet, scrawled "Pro Bono 1948" on it and put it in among other unimportant files. Nobody ever looked in that part of the filing cabinet and if someone did find it, it would look like an old case. He sighed in relief, turned back to his desk and opened another letter. This one had a check in it for a thousand dollars. All thought of photographs of a little girl and a threatening letter vanished.

An hour later, back in his law office, David turned his chair around so it faced the portrait of his grandfather, David Holman, chief justice of the Illinois Supreme Court, founder of the Holman dynasty, ultimate role model. Could he live up to all that hope.

As he sat there, a hazy memory invaded his brain. A hot June night. Carol was visiting an aunt in California and he was riding around with a bunch of guys, looking for some action in this boring little town. It was just dumb luck that they had dropped in to that greasy spoon and met that gorgeous waitress. And the bet with Randy. It should have been easy to make that score, win that bet. A girl who worked in a place like that was bound to be easy pickings. How was he supposed to know she was a virgin? Why didn't he just take her home when she said she didn't want any? He wasn't even drunk. Just because Randy made a bet. What was that girl's name? All he could remember was that she'd been a stunning little thing.

Carol came home the next day and he never saw or heard from the girl again. He did win his bet with Randy. Even got an extra fifty bucks because she was a virgin, and forgot all about her.

Chapter 16

Sunday afternoon Myrna lifted Scarlett off the bottom step of the bus, and waited to cross the street as it wheezed around the corner. She grasped Scarlett's hand and crossed the street. The Labor Hall was a two-story square frame building halfway down the block, nudging similar constructions on either side. She pushed open a wood double door with flaking brown paint that led to a small entry and a narrow enclosed stairway. Lydia's directions had said the meeting room was upstairs, so, with Scarlett trailing, Myrna climbed the steps. The air in the stuffy stairwell smelled like hot dust overlaid with coffee and the ghosts of sweaty bodies. The stairs opened into a large room, furnished with two sections of scratched and dented brown metal folding chairs facing a card table and another chair. Susie, Lou, Emma and Katie from the department stood on the other side of the chairs, leaning on a counter that held a fifty-cup coffee urn, a couple of trays filled with assorted sweets, three stacks of paper cups, a pile of paper napkins, a carton of cream and a sugar bowl. The coffee pot's small round light glowed red. The coffee wasn't quite ready. A dingy window let in a dim light, and a small rotating electric fan brushed air back and forth in front of the rows of chairs.

A pair of windows at the back of the room flanked four wall shelves filled with stacks of papers and large loose-leaf notebooks. Lydia sat at a wood desk under the windows, looking through some papers, her back to the room. Myrna threaded her way through two rows of chairs, Scarlett close behind, and stood beside the coffee pot.

"Hi, Myrna," said Susie. "Is that Scarlett?"

Myrna felt Scarlett's hand fold into hers. Myrna squeezed the hand and looked down. "These ladies are Susie, Lou, Emma and Katie. I work with them and I've told them about you." She turned to Susie. "Yes, this is Scarlett. Scarlett, this is Susie."

"Hello," Scarlett said, half behind Myrna's skirt.

"My. My. Look at that hair," Lou exclaimed. "Ain't you pretty."

"Do people call you Red?" Emma asked.

Scarlett shook her head, the red curls bouncing.

"Hey, the coffee light's turned green," Emma announced. "Scarlett, would you like a doughnut?"

135

Scarlett looked up at Myrna, who nodded permission.

"I'd like a pink one," Scarlett said softly. Emma handed her a napkin and a doughnut covered with pink frosting and sprinkles. "Thank you," Scarlett said.

"Why don't you find a chair and sit down and eat your doughnut, honey," Myrna said. Scarlett held her doughnut carefully in the napkin and walked to a chair in the middle of the third row.

Katie took a paper cup, filled it with coffee and handed it to Susie. She repeated the process until all were served. "I shoulda brought cookies, too," she said, shaking her head.

"This all that's comin'?" asked Lou.

"I think Betty said she was," Emma said. Heavy tread sounded from the stairwell, followed by lighter footsteps. "Speak of the devil."

Betty Brown's stomach hove into view in the doorway, like a ship's prow. The rest heaved itself over the top step into the room. Myrna stared. Betty wore a dress. Not only a dress, but also nylons and pumps with one-inch heels. Sadie Jonas, her shadow, followed.

"Whatcha all starin' at," Betty bellowed.

Lydia turned around in her chair, her eyebrows arched in surprise.

"I guess the dress," Lou stammered.

Betty scowled. "What's wrong with the dress?"

"Nothin'. It's a nice dress." Lou struggled on. "It's just that we never seen you—uh—wear a dress before."

"You don't think I'd wear a dress to that garbage pit?"

"No," Lou said. "It looks good on you. That light blue with all the pink and yellow flowers is real pretty."

Betty nodded thanks and stumped to the coffee pot in her heels. Emma quickly filled a paper cup with coffee and handed it to Betty.

Apparently, one thank you was enough, Myrna thought.

Betty moved to the pastry trays and studied the contents for a few moments, then picked up a large cheese Danish with her bare fingers. "When's this meeting start?" she barked.

Lydia, still at the desk, turned around, and then consulted her wrist. "In ten minutes," she replied. "Thanks for the treats, Emma." She turned to Myrna. "Joan brought her two kids, so Scarlett can have somebody to play with. They told me there's a playroom downstairs the kids can use."

"My oldest girl's down there. She'll watch the little ones. She's fourteen and she baby-sits all the time," Susie said.

Myrna took Scarlett's hand and they went downstairs to a large room where two girls Scarlett's age were sat at a table playing with puzzles and a young teenager helped them.

Lydia got up from the desk, pushed the chair under it and walked to the counter. Emma held a cup of coffee toward her, and she took it with a smile. "Thank you, Emma." She sipped from the cup. "That's good. I was ready for coffee."

More thuds announced new arrivals. By two o'clock, twelve women and Tim Forrester sat in the first two rows of folding chairs. Lydia faced them, standing behind the card table.

"Thanks for coming," Lydia said. "I know you have a lot of questions that can't be answered at the plant. I'm not a union member, but I have some friends who are, and they let me use this place."

"If you ain't a union organizer, why do you keep talkin' union to everybody?" Tim asked.

"I believe in unions, and this town really needs them. A handful of millionaires own all the big companies that employ almost everybody in town and pay them dirt. They threatened the Chamber of Commerce to keep new business out, so they can keep control of things."

"If you ain't no official organizer, and I never heard of a union that has ni—uh—Negroes as members, much less organizers, what makes you think you can change what the owners do?" Betty asked.

"You're *right*. Most unions do keep out colored people, but some organize them, like people who work in hotels and other similar industries. I know that I can't do anything by myself. After all, I'm not only colored, but I'm just a kid fresh out of college. No big shot in his right mind would give the time of day to me, even if I were white. It's you, together, who can do it. All I can do is give you information."

"You talk about the big boys," Susie said. "We start talkin' union and they'll fire every last one of us and hire a whole new outfit, and blackball us at the same time. We'd never get decent jobs in Newport City again."

"If you go about it the right way, they can't fire you," Lydia replied. "There are laws that allow people to decide to join a union. They fire you, and they've got a big lawsuit on their hands."

"Why the hell should I pay out good money for union dues and take a chance on goin' on strike and gettin' blackballed all over town? What's a union gonna do for me?" Betty demanded.

Lydia took a deep breath. "First, you negotiate a contract that will get you better pay and better working conditions, and protections against what Weston's wife tried to do. If we'd had a union, that never would have happened."

"Can we get more fans?" Elvera asked from the back row.

"That would be called 'working conditions.' It's something to negotiate."

"What's 'negotiate' mean?" Elvera added.

"People from the union and people from the company get together and talk. The company says what they're willing to do, and the union says what it wants. They meet and talk about it until both sides agree on what they are willing to accept. The union tells its members what the decision is, and the members vote whether they accept it or not. If they accept, a contract is written and both the company and the union sign it. If the union members don't accept the offer, they go back to the table and talk some more."

"Sounds like it takes a long time," Katie commented.

"Sometimes it does," Lydia replied.

"I don't want to go on strike," Sadie spoke from the back row, looking down as if she had shocked herself by speaking.

"Nobody's going on a strike. Strikes usually happen during contract negotiations when they reach an impasse, and it takes voting by the members and permission from the international headquarters and all sorts of legal stuff before a union goes on strike."

Tim, the only set-up man there, spoke up. "Well, Thomas Trucks went on strike a few years ago and the company brought in a bunch of people to take their place. There were ugly fights and people ended up in jail and the hospital, and when it was over, the company fired everybody who went on strike. I worked there then, and I swore I'd never get involved in a union again."

"Then, why are you here?" Lydia asked, her face suddenly an expressionless mask.

"I wanted to hear what you had to say."

"And are you going back to the bosses and tell them what you heard? Is that why you're the only set-up man here?"

Tim's face turned red. "Hell, no. I ain't no stool pigeon. I just don't hold with unions after that business at Thomas, and I thought somebody oughta give the other side of the story."

"That's nice and intelligent, Tim," Lydia said. "And if anyone here gets in trouble because of this meeting, I'll know just who spilled the beans, won't I?"

"Shit. Nobody's gonna listen to a nigger girl. Just 'cause you went to college don't mean you're as good as a white man, and don't you forget it." His chair screeched as he stood and shook his finger at Lydia. "I ain't about to say nothin' to the bosses, but you bet your biffie there's others that will. You mind your business, girl, and remember your place." He strode down the aisle between the rows of chairs and stomped down the stairs. They heard the doors squeak open and slam shut before anyone spoke.

"I'm scared," said Sadie, a tremor in her weak voice.

"That's just what he wanted," Lydia said. "For us to be scared. In some ways, he's right. Somebody will go to the bosses. We just have to be ready for them."

"If anybody goes to the bosses, it would be our little movie star," said Betty. "She's the one that's been tight with the big man. I bet she runs from this room right to a phone and tells him every word we said."

Myrna's blood rushed to her head and she started to stand. "I'll do no such . . .," she said, when Lydia waved her to her seat.

139

"That kind of comment and that attitude won't help us one bit. The word is union. It means all as one. We work together. No insults. No name calling. We will be polite to each other."

"What's the point of this? You got us all here. We done a lot of talkin'. What are we supposed to do? I'm like everybody else. I'm scared of unions. Weston Switch has the best jobs in town. I don't want to mess with that."

"You've heard the rumors," Lydia replied. "Weston is getting a divorce and he's pulling out. Going somewhere else. Then, you get his ex and the stunt she pulled about her old man's funeral. There won't be any Mark Weston to overrule her. We need to be ready for that. Just think about it."

Half an hour later, all of the questions had been asked and answered, and chairs scraped the floor as people pushed them back to get up. Scarlett and Joan's two little girls came up the stairs, holding papers. Scarlett showed Myrna her picture, a big bird, colored with brown crayon and a bright red eye. "You did real good, Scarlett. There's hardly any color outside the lines. That's a wonderful bird." Scarlett beamed.

All but Emma and Susie left, and they both carried the heavy coffee urn into a kitchen next to the meeting room, and Myrna heard running water. "I ought to go help them wash up," she said.

"You'd ruin Emma's day," Lydia replied.

"What?"

"Emma loves to do stuff like that. I think she works in the kitchen at her church all the time."

The two women returned to the meeting room, Susie carrying the coffee pot. She set it on the counter, wiped the counter with a damp dishrag and returned it to the kitchen.

"Anything else?" Emma asked.

Lydia shook her head, and Emma said, "Then, I guess I'll head out. Susie, you coming?"

"I'm right behind you," Susie said, and followed Emma down the steps, her rubber soled shoes barely making a sound.

"Are you in a hurry to get home?" Lydia asked.

"I'm in no rush," Myrna replied.

"I'll give you a lift, but first, I'd like to take you and Scarlett by my house to meet my mother."

"Why, that's real nice of you. I'd love to meet your mother."

Lydia looked around the room one more time. "Well, I guess everything's all right. Let's go." She switched off the lights and they went downstairs, where she turned off the stair light and locked the outer door after them.

Lydia's house was on the wrong side of the river, where all the colored people lived. The street was blacktopped, but the sidewalk stopped at the second house on the left side of the street and didn't exist on the 'side. There were no curbs or gutters. Most of the small houses had sagging front porches, lacked paint, and had yards that were unmowed or consisted of weeds. Several were neatly painted, some had screened porches and small, neat squares of grass in front and Myrna could see larger expanses of lawn in the back with splashes of color where flowers grew.

Lydia's home was a small two-story cottage painted a fresh crisp white, trimmed in black, with a porch across the front and a large television antenna on the roof. The house was set back the required twenty feet from the street, the space covered by neatly mown grass. Bright zinnias in many colors snugged up to the lattice that hid the underside of the porch. Flower boxes filled to overflowing with red impatiens were fastened to the porch railings on either side of the four black-painted wood steps to the porch. An old rocking chair sat on the right side, and a wood porch swing, painted deep green, hung from the ceiling of the left. Lydia wiped her shoes on a brush mat in front of the screen door. Myrna rubbed her shoes on the mat and told Scarlett, who did so with enthusiasm.

Lydia held open the screen door. "Come in. I'll bet Mama has iced tea made."

They walked into a small dining room with a square oak table in the center, set with a ruffled crocheted doily around a tall, clear glass vase of red zinnias in the center. Myrna wasn't sure what kind. Four tall-backed chairs sat one to a side. A sideboard was placed against the outside wall with a pair of silver candleholders at the ends, each holding white tapers. A wide mirror hung above it. A large window looked over the porch.

A tall, slender woman, with silver shot through her black pressed hair, came through a door that revealed a kitchen counter as it opened, releasing the rich aroma of roasting meat. Myrna's mouth watered. The woman's skin was the same coffee-with-cream shade as Lydia's and she had the same smile and the same cool poise.

"Mama. This is Myrna Schroeder and her daughter, Scarlett. Myrna, my mother, Sarah McIntire."

Sarah smiled and extended her hand. Myrna clasped it, finding it warm and gentle. "Welcome to our home, Myrna and Scarlett." She knelt to Scarlett's level. "I'm so pleased to have such a nice little girl in my house. You know," she said, in a conspiratorial tone, "this tall, grown-up lady was once just as small and just as pretty as you are. I miss having a little girl in the house." Scarlett made a shy smile, and Sarah straightened. "Won't you come into the living room and have some tea and cookies? I'll bet Scarlett would like some chocolate milk with her cookies."

Lydia led the way through the kitchen, which had beautiful oak cupboards, ceramic tile counter tops and backsplash, a large sink with faucets for hot and cold water, a gleaming white stove and refrigerator. Green glass containers that looked like old-fashioned candy jars that held flour, sugar, coffee and tea, sat on the counter between the sink and the stove. A bright red geranium plant was on the window sill above the sink.

The living room was large and dominated by a huge picture window that framed the view of the back yard and garden and a television set against the opposite wall, the mechanism for the antenna on top. An upright piano and stool filled a corner. Myrna's feet sank into the beige carpet.

"Please sit down," Sarah said, indicating the big, dark green sofa. Myrna sat on the deep cushions at one end and Lydia sat at the other, leaning back. "If you'll excuse me, I'll get the tea and cookies. Scarlett, would you like to come into the kitchen and help me get them ready?"

Scarlett looked at Myrna, who smiled. She turned to Sarah and nodded, her red curls bouncing.

When Sarah and Scarlett disappeared into the kitchen, Lydia asked, "What did you think of the meeting?"

"I learned a lot. I didn't know much about unions before. Of course, I don't know a whole lot more now. All I ever heard was that they take a big chunk out of your pay for dues and make you go on strike and you won't have any money."

"You do pay dues, but it isn't all that much. For you, about seventy-five cents a month. Strikes don't just happen. Like I said at the meeting, they usually happen during contract negotiations when the company and the union are deadlocked, and you need permission from the national headquarters in Washington."

"That wasn't a strike. Besides, we don't have a union and so there's no headquarters. It was a 'work stoppage' to protest something the company did wrong. Weston agreed it was wrong, if you remember."

"I was really scared we might all get fired," Myrna said.

"In some cases, we could have been, but that was such an egregious situation it wasn't likely."

"Eg. . . what?"

"Egregious," Lydia said. "It means something really bad."

"Oh. Why didn't he fire us, then?"

"What we did wasn't the thing that was the most egregious, although it came close. In fact, it was the result of the egregious act, which was the letter his wife wrote ordering the plant shut down and the employees not paid. She had no business writing the letter. Her husband is in charge of the plant and the employees. At that point, she was just a board member, whose business is to figure out how to make more money."

"How do you know so much about all this?" Myrna asked.

"I've been interested in the labor movement for a long time. You know Mama worked in hotels as a maid for a long time. Because the maids were Negroes and women, they were paid really bad. Finally, the maids in one Chicago hotel asked the Building Service Employees Union about joining. After the maids voted the union in, the janitors and some other workers joined. The union negotiated a contract with the hotel and they got a nice raise and better hours and working conditions, such as break time. After fifteen years, the hotel promoted Mama to head housekeeper, which made her a member of management so she had to quit the union. But because of the union, she made enough money to buy this house and to send me to college. I got some scholarships, which helped, but she saved enough to get me there in the first place.

"I've always noticed people who do the dirty work, how hard they work and how little they get paid. So, I decided I wanted to work for a union. I'd go to law school, but law schools don't take Negroes or women. Meanwhile, I work at Weston Switch and study on my own how to organize a union."

Myrna didn't know how to answer. Finally, she said, "This is a nice house. You have really nice things."

"They're Mama's things. Just because we're forced to live in a poor part of town doesn't mean we can't live comfortably."

"I didn't mean that I thought you would live in a shack," Myrna stammered. "It just looks and feels so nice and homey."

"That's okay. People usually think that's how everybody who lives in this part of town is, especially us colored folk."

"Mama. Look." Scarlett proudly carried a silver tray with cookies arranged in three neat rows, chocolate, sugar, and Toll House. Sarah followed with a large crystal pitcher of iced tea. Scarlett set the tray on the coffee table in front of the sofa with great care.

"Lydia, will you please bring the glasses and some plates?"

Lydia went into the kitchen and returned with a black tin tray decorated with painted pink roses and filled with tall glasses, long-handled spoons and small glass plates and placed it on the coffee table. Sarah disappeared into the kitchen and returned with a tall glass of chocolate milk. She took a large pillow from the big chair beside the sofa and placed it on the floor in front of the coffee table. "You can sit here, Scarlett. It's just the right height for you."

After the tea and cookies, Sarah invited them to visit the garden. Myrna's stomach did a flip-flop. The garden was so much like Ada's. As Sarah led them around the flower beds, explaining what each was, Myrna realized it wasn't anything like Ada's. Ada's garden was all straight lines and flowers planted so that big swathes of color were all in one place. Sarah's garden was really a lot of small round gardens with different plants in each one, and a rainbow of colors. Near the house was a neat rectangular vegetable plot.

"Mama, the flowers are so pretty," Scarlett said, kneeling on the ground and reaching out to touch one.

"No, baby. You mustn't touch them," Myrna replied.

"Of course, she must touch them," said Sarah, who knelt beside Scarlett and told her how to touch the flower. "It's called a rose, and you must be careful because the stem has sharp things called thorns on it, and they can prick your finger. But you can put your nose near the blossom and smell it. Roses have a wonderful smell as well as being beautiful."

Scarlett inhaled deeply and a big smile lit her face. "Oh, Mama. I never smelled anything so pretty."

By the time Myrna thought they should be leaving, Sarah said, "No sense in leaving now, just when the roast is done and dinner is almost on the table."

"But . . ." Myrna began.

"No 'buts.' You'll stay to dinner."

The roast lived up to its aromatic promise, as well as the mashed potatoes and gravy, fresh green beans with vinegar and bacon bits crumbled on them, a salad of crisp lettuce, tiny tomatoes and cucumber with a dressing Myrna couldn't identify. Dessert was apple pie with ice cream.

It was nearly nine o'clock when Lydia stopped outside Myrna's apartment. "That was a wonderful time, Lydia," she said, and hesitated. "Why are you so nice to me and Scarlett?"

It was too dark to see Lydia's face, but she sounded surprised. "Why not? I'm new here and I want to make new friends, and you're someone I'd like for a friend. You're a classy lady Myrna Schroeder, and that little girl . . ." she reached over to Scarlett, who was half-asleep on Myrna's lap and ruffled her hair. "That little girl is just the most precious thing."

Later, with Scarlett sound asleep beside her, Myrna lay in bed, awake. Lydia's words, "You're someone I'd like for a friend. You're a good woman, a classy lady," floated through her mind. Nobody ever said they wanted her for a friend, and for sure, nobody ever called her a good woman or "classy."

Chapter 17

Ada Schroeder grunted as she bent over the tomato plant in her garden. Fat red balls hung like Christmas ornaments among the dark leaves. She plucked two and grunted again when she straightened. From the looks of it, she'd be canning tomatoes next week. Sweet corn looked ready to pick, too. That she'd freeze, a lot less work. On second thought, why bother. She wouldn't be around to be eating either.

She pulled the husks back from two ears of corn and peered at the perfect small yellow kernels, then twisted them off the stalk. Nothing better for supper than tomato slicers, sweet corn and hamburgers. She waddled back to the house and up the steps, and almost dropped the vegetables when she heard the phone ringing. She shifted the corn and tomatoes to her left arm, pulling open the screen door with her right. She dumped the vegetables into the sink and reached for the wall phone. Her "hello" caught in her throat. She swallowed and took a deep breath and said again, "Hello."

"To whom am I speaking?" The voice was male, deep, cultured.

"Who're you callin'?"

"I'm sorry," the voice said. "I called the Schroeder residence."

"This is Ada."

"I'm trying to contact Myrna Schroeder. Do you know how I can reach her?"

A flash of anger shot through Ada. "No. I don't know how to reach her," she growled and slammed the phone back in its hook. Of all the nerve. Now, the johns were callin' here. That little slut. She turned back to the sink, still mumbling, and turned on the water to wash the tomatoes. How could she get to that lawyer? Winter wasn't that far away and she wanted to be in California before the first snow fell. The phone call reminded her. It was Thursday. She'd have to hurry with the tomatoes, so she could be downtown at the pay phone by three o'clock.

Mark Weston held his phone away from his ear and stared at it, before placing it back in its cradle. I guess I should have expected that, he thought, recalling his brief run-in with Ada Schroeder. He leaned back in the black leather desk chair. How in the hell was he going to get to Myrna? He couldn't go waltzing down to the department and ask her to dinner in front of the whole place? Why the hell didn't she let him get her a phone?

He glanced at the grandfather clock in the corner. Five past five. The night shift would have started two hours ago. It had taken him weeks since the divorce was final to work up the nerve to actually ask Myrna on a formal date. Now, she might as well be on Mars. He drummed his fingers on the arm of the chair. There had to be a way. Suddenly, he sat up. Of course. He'd show up when she got off work and take her home. The gossip mill would go into high gear, but what the hell. He owned them.

At a quarter to eleven, Mark eased the Mercedes to the curb outside Weston Switch's employee entrance. Five taxis were lined up at the curb, waiting for the night shift women. He parked in the shadow of a streetlight a couple of car lengths behind the last taxi. He got out of the car and walked to the door where Andy Jones, the chief night security guard, also waited for the shift to end.

"Evening, Andy," Mark said.

Andy turned his head and stared. "Mr. Weston. What are you—uh—evening sir."

"Do you know Myrna Schroeder?"

Andy nodded. "That pretty dark-haired girl? Yeah."

"When she comes out, will you bring her to my car? It's parked up there behind the street light."

Andy squinted to make out the shadowy car and nodded again.

"Thanks." Mark turned and strolled back to the car. He sat behind the steering wheel, staring at the door as if he could will Myrna to come out. He looked at his watch, exactly three minutes after he last had checked the time. Five more minutes.

Finally, the heavy glass door swung out and a stream of women poured through, dispersing to the waiting cabs. In the midst of the exodus, Mark saw Myrna walking beside Andy, looking at him. She nodded and turned her head to peer into the dark toward his car, then looked back to Andy. Andy stopped, and turned back, while Myrna came toward the car. Finally, she stood at the passenger door window. Mark touched the button that opened it.

She stooped to his level. "You wanted to see me?"

"I want to give you a ride home."

Myrna straightened and looked back at the line of cabs, which were beginning to move. "Why?"

"I want to talk to you. You don't have a phone and I can't keep calling you off the floor. Come on, get in."

She looked at the cabs. Only one remained and it had started to roll forward. "I guess I don't have a choice," she said and opened the door.

When she was settled, Mark pulled away from the curb and made a U-turn in the middle of the street toward Myrna's part of town. He inhaled deeply. Her "perfume," sweat overlaid with a fine layer of oil and metal, was as seductive to him as *Joy*. He couldn't think of a single thing to say.

"What do you want to talk to me about?" she asked after a moment.

Mark cleared his throat and finally said, "It's been a long time. What have you been doing all summer?"

"Mostly working."

"M-m-mm. How's Scarlett? She's a really cute little girl."

"Scarlett's fine. She starts kindergarten in a couple of weeks."

"That's a big step. Is she excited about it?"

"Yes."

He stopped for a red light and the silence lasted longer than the light. "Oh, yes. Karl told me your arm is healed."

"M-hm. I'm taking physical therapy to get the strength back.

"Good. Is it working?"

"Yes."

Mark turned a corner and drove another two blocks in silence, past darkened store windows. In Newport City, even the department store display lights were turned off at nine o'clock. Streetlights illuminated empty streets, except in front of and across the street from The City Club, the only bar on Holman Boulevard. What ailed him? He was definitely not the tongue-tied type in the presence of a beautiful woman. Just the opposite. But now his brain seemed to have turned to mush.

Myrna broke the silence. "Is that what you wanted to talk to me about? My arm?"

"Some, I guess. I really just wanted to see you." He swallowed hard, like a kid asking his first girl for a date. "I missed you." She suddenly turned to look at him, but he kept his eyes on the road. Business district lights gave way to darker residential streets, houses and trees darker shadows, occasionally relieved with a yellow rectangle glowing high off the ground. "My divorce was final three weeks ago. Now I can legally ask you for a date."

"A date?"

It all came in a rush. "We both have something to celebrate, your healed arm and my divorce. Will you have dinner with me?" There was silence from the other seat. To break the silence, he rushed on. "I-I just thought it would be nice."

"I'm sorry," she said, her voice barely above a whisper. "I just don't know what to say?"

"Yes, Mark, I would love to have dinner with you, would be a good answer," he said.

Myrna giggled.

"I didn't think going to dinner with me was a laughing matter," he commented, stung.

"I'm sorry again," she replied. "It was just the way you said it, like a robot." She giggled again. "Yes, Mark, I would like to have dinner with you," she repeated in the same flat tone, adding, "Is that better?"

He looked at her, her deep blue eyes sparkling with fun, her lovely smile, her face shining, and his heart turned over. "It's much better," he said, softly, aching to kiss her. He took his hand from the steering wheel and put his arm around her. She stiffened and pulled back. Mark removed his arm.

In the quiet cocoon of the car and the night, it was enough to have her close. Words were superfluous, but he talked about the weather, asked what food she liked, until he sensed that he was talking to himself. He looked at her as the car passed under a streetlight and saw that she was asleep, long dark lashes lying against silky skin.

He stopped the car next to the curb outside her apartment, reached through the steering wheel with his left hand and turned off the ignition. He sat there, watching her sleep and wishing the world would stop right now. He bent and kissed her lightly on the forehead.

Her eyes flew open and she sat up, sliding toward the door. "What do you think you're doing?"

"I'm sorry. I didn't mean to wake you," Mark said. She didn't answer, just stared at him, her eyes wide with fear, anger sparking like a downed power line. "You looked so sweet, I couldn't help kissing you." He took a deep breath. "I think I'm falling in love with you."

Myrna gasped, and reached for the door handle. "Oh, no. I'm not about to fall for that line. I may be a bastard and the mother of a bastard, but that's all I am. I work hard. I take care of Scarlett and myself, and that's all I do. Just because you own the company and you helped me out of a bad spot, doesn't mean I'm one of your whores. I'll pay you back, if it takes fifty years."

He tried to take her hand, but she yanked it away as if he offered her a rattlesnake and turned to the door. "Wait a minute," he said. Suddenly, he slapped his forehead with the heel of his hand. "Geez, Weston. How stupid can you get? I'm sorry, Myrna. I wasn't thinking. Of course, as lovely as you are, you've probably had men coming on to you all your life. Believe me, my intentions are purely honorable. Not that I don't want you. But that isn't what I want from you now. It may sound crazy coming from me, but I want to take care of you—and Scarlett—to keep you safe." He stopped. For the first time since Gramps died, his eyes filled with tears. He turned to stare out the windshield. "I would. . ." He cleared the lump from his throat. "I would be the happiest man in the universe if you could bring yourself to love me."

She was still as a shadow. Finally, she whispered, "Why? I'm nothing but a factory hand, a nobody. Men like you don't love girls like me. You just want us to put a notch in your belt."

A slap in the face wouldn't have hurt as much. Mark's temper flared. "I've not told a woman I loved her in more years than I care to recall. I didn't do it to put 'a notch in my belt.'"

Instantly, her expression softened. "Sorry. You're right. I've had some ugly experiences with men, especially one who told me he loved me and disappeared after making me pregnant."

"Do you want to tell me about it?"

"No. I've never told anyone and I never will."

"Okay," he said softly. "I respect that. I'd also like to throttle the guy who did that to you. Loving doesn't come easily to me, either. I just want you to think about it. Forget being a 'factory hand' and a 'bastard.' For what it's worth, I'm a bastard, too. I was lucky enough to have grandparents who loved me and took good care of me."

She stared. "You . . . didn't have a father?"

"I have no idea who my father was. My mother drank too much bathtub gin and ended her days in a mental hospital at twenty-five. My grandparents adored only child."

"I'm so sorry. Do you remember her?"

Mark shook his head. "Vaguely, a pretty blonde lady who'd pat me on the head, or maybe it was my fantasy from seeing her picture. I really can't tell."

"My mother was killed when a train hit the car she was in. I was six months old. She was sixteen. Ernie is her brother, and he made Ada take care of me. She wanted to put me in an orphanage."

"Good lord. That's awful." Mark gave a bitter laugh. "Quite a pair, aren't we? The only real difference between us is that my grandparents really loved me and they were rich." He opened the car door. "Come on. It's time you were getting your beauty sleep."

They tiptoed up the stairs, trying not to disturb Mrs. Neumann and Scarlett, presumably asleep in Mrs. Neumann's apartment.

Myrna opened the screen door, put the key in the wood door, and turned to Mark. She opened her mouth to speak, but he put his finger on her lips. "Sh-h-h. Not a word. I'll pick you up Saturday at eight for dinner."

He waited on the landing until she was inside with the door locked, then, forgetting the sleepers, did a Fred Astaire down the steps.

Chapter 18

George Kretzmer was Rosecrans County Clerk, with an "aw-shucks" style that had reelected him for thirty years. Last year he'd decided to try for higher stakes and announced his candidacy for Democratic Representative from the 24th District for the U. S. House of Representatives. He had a good, solid base and hadn't figured on serious opposition, until out of the blue, young Holman tossed his hat in the ring. With all the Holman money, the blue-blooded family history and the political clout, Kretzmer saw his support suddenly melt away. He was not a happy man when Sally, his secretary, tossed an envelope on his desk. He took a second look.

The address looked like it had been cut from a newspaper headline and pasted to the envelope. He slit it open with the letter opener on his desk blotter and a photograph fell out of a folded piece of piece of paper still inside the envelope. He picked it up and stared at the fuzzy image through the lower half of his bifocals. A little girl. Didn't look like anybody he knew. He slipped the paper out and unfolded it. It, too, was written with words cut from a newspaper. Some people sure liked melodrama. Probably saw too many bad movies.

"DEAR MR. KRETZMER,

I HEAR YOUR CAMPANE IS GOING DOWN THE TOILET. THIS PITCHER MIGHT HELP YOU PULL IT OUT. TAKE A GOOD LOOK AT THE KID. SHE LOOKS JUST LIKE HER DADDY. ONLY SHE DON'T KNOW WHO HER DADDY IS, AND HER DADDY DON'T KNOW WHO SHE IS. BUT I DO. COULD BE THE GUY YOUR RUNNIN' AGAINST. SHE JUST TURNED 5 YRS. OLD.

YOURS TRULY,

A FRIEND"

A telephone number was scribbled in pencil after the signature. Kretzmer opened the center drawer in his desk and rummaged around in it until he found a magnifying glass. He held it close to the photograph. The enlargement didn't help the graininess, but he could make out a little girl with hair curlier than Shirley Temple's. Still didn't look like anybody he knew, and besides, how the hell could a picture of a little girl help his campaign?

He read the note again. Somebody's bastard. Town the size of Newport City, somebody like Holman, the whole town would know if he had a by-blow. There'd never been a word of anything ugly about Holman. Mr. Clean. But according to the note, the father didn't know he had a kid—and the kid didn't know her father. How could somebody keep a secret like that for six years in a gossip center like Newport City? The mother surely would have come after the Holmans for money. Was the note writer the mother? Why make a stink now, disgrace the whole family, ruin their lives? Of course, if it was Holman he'd ruined her life and the kid's. People had taken revenge on less than that.

Kretzmer leaned back in his chair and studied the picture and the note some more. He'd have to get a good picture of David Holman. "Hmm. The debate is in three weeks. If I could get proof, what a bombshell I could blow on Mr. David Holman III and his whole high-falutin' outfit," he told himself. He returned the note and the picture to the envelope, stood, grimacing as his knees objected, and walked to the wall safe hidden behind a plat map of the county. He spun the combination from thirty years of practice, and locked the items inside. Only he had the combination.

He'd think about it a couple of days, then call that phone number.

A few blocks away in the walnut paneled elegance of Holman, Holman and Holman, Attorneys at Law, David Holman II peered over the top of his half-glasses at his son, David Holman III, who sat across the huge cherry-wood desk in a client's chair. "Heard any more from that woman?"

"There's no way I could hear from her," David replied. "My home phone's unlisted. Shirley headed her off here and tosses any suspicious mail, and Barb at campaign headquarters does the same."

"She could show up at your campaign headquarters."

"I doubt it. She obviously doesn't want us to know who she is."

David II pulled off the glasses and swung them by one temple. "I don't know. I have a funny feeling about this. She wants money—badly. She isn't going to quit easily. Are you sure there's no truth to her allegations?"

"How many times do I have to tell you? No. No. And no. She probably found this picture somewhere, decided it looked like me and set up her scheme."

"Somewhere out there, a shoe is going to drop," his father said. "And when it does, I have a feeling it's going to squash something. I just hope it isn't our family."

The discussion with his father left David in a foul mood all day, and when he walked into the kitchen of his home he didn't immediately notice that Carol wasn't there. He finally realized the house was silent and that no dinner preparations were underway. "Honey, I'm home," he called. There was no response.

He looked in all the downstairs rooms, ran upstairs and looked in the bedrooms and the bathrooms, but still no Carol. Where the hell was she? It wasn't like her to take off and not say anything. He was about to walk out of their bedroom when he noticed the pad on her bedside table, next to the phone. "Dr. Fritz. 5:00." A doctor's appointment at five o'clock? That was odd. Doctors didn't usually make appointments at that hour unless it was an emergency. His blood ran cold. She'd gotten sick and called the doctor? How had she gotten there? Her car was still in the garage. Her mother. He called his in-laws' number, but there was no answer after ten rings. He disconnected the call with a finger on the bar, and immediately gave the operator the doctor's number. That number rang and rang, but no one answered. He hung up and picked up the telephone directory to call the hospital, when he heard the downstairs door open.

"David," Carol called. "Are you home?"

He ran down the stairs, flung his arms around her and held her close. "You had me scared to death. I saw that note with the doctor's name and a time and I thought something terrible had happened to you." She managed a wobbly smile and he realized she had been crying. He guided her to a chair in the living room. "What is it? What's the matter? Are you seriously ill?"

Carol shook her head, and tears rolled down her cheeks. "Dr. Fritz said . . ." She gulped. "He said . . . They called from the University of Chicago. They turned me down for the study at the University of Chicago. T-They said I wasn't a good candidate for it. D-Dr. Fritz said I h-had to—to face it." She began to sob.

David knelt beside her, held her close and kissed her wet cheeks. "S-sh. What did he say you had to face?"

She buried her face against his arm and the tears soaked into his shirt. "Oh, David. I will never have a baby. My uterus is too damaged from the endometriosis." For a moment, a wave of relief washed through David, but he pushed it away to comfort Carol. "Honey, there are thousands of babies out there who need good parents. We can adopt. It's no big deal."

Carol sat up and brushed the tears from her face. "No big deal?" she threw back at him. "How can you say such a thing? After all these years of trying and praying and doctoring to have a baby of my own?"

He stood. "I'm sorry, sweetheart. That was a stupid thing to say. It is a big deal. I meant that adopting a baby wouldn't be hard for us. We're still young enough, affluent enough, well educated, prominent in our community. They'd probably pay us to take a baby."

"I don't want a baby some other woman was pregnant with and gave birth to. It's a slap in the face, a constant reminder of what a failure I am as a woman."

"You're no failure as a woman. You're a wonderful woman. A wonderful wife. We've had a good life together without children. It can continue to be good without them, better, maybe, because we've spent so much energy on trying to have them. Now, we can relax and build our lives around each other."

Carol glared at him. "I can't believe what I'm hearing. My life has just been destroyed. The one thing I wanted all my life and now I'm told I can never have it, and all you can do is say, maybe our life will be better without children." She stood and strode into the kitchen and through it to the door to the garage. The slamming door shook the house, and moments later, her turquoise T-bird backed out of the garage and into the street. The tires screeched as she turned and sped away.

David stared out the window, numb. Suddenly, he thought of the picture of the little girl. She wasn't a baby, but if she was his, that might solve all his problems. He would get custody of her and Carol would have his child. It wouldn't be exactly the same as adoption. He sighed. But, then, how could he explain the child to her. He sank down in the chair Carol had vacated and buried his face in his hands.

At the law office next morning, David yawned over a page of farm statistics in preparation for his debate with George Kretzmer. Carol had come home an hour after she left last night, contrite, and they had made lingering, tender love for hours. Now, he was mellow, but he couldn't keep his eyes open. Wading through dull statistics on the price of pork bellies didn't help. He reached toward his intercom to ask for a cup of coffee when the red light came on.

Shirley's voice crackled through the speaker. "Mr. George Kretzmer wants to speak with you."

"George Kretzmer?" David was wide-awake. "What does he want?"

"I don't know, sir. He just asked to talk with you."

"O. K. I'll take it." The red light went out and David picked up the phone.

"Morning George. What can I do for you?"

"Could be something I can do for you," said Kretzmer. "I've got a piece of mail here with a couple of pictures in it and a note pasted up from the newspaper. The note says the pictures are of your kid. I didn't know you had any kids."

David swallowed hard, but made himself speak lightly. "Oh, no. She's not gone to you with that crap, too."

"What do you mean, come to me, too? You mean you know about this. Other people have gotten the same thing?"

"Yeah. She's been after me for a couple of months. She started by calling me on the phone at home, so I changed my number, and Shirley's fielded a couple of calls from her here. She claims the child in the picture is mine by some relative of hers, and threatened to go to the newspaper if I didn't fork over fifty grand. When I didn't bite she sent me the pictures and the note."

"Her? You know who she is?"

"No. I said she called me. I spoke to her, but I don't know who she is."

"She sounds pretty sure of herself."

"She thinks she's figured out a scheme to get money. She's nuts. Carol and I don't have kids. In fact, we're considering adoption. And I sure don't have any by-blows."

Kretzmer chuckled, a deep, gravely sound. "What makes you so sure, boy? You a virgin until you got married? Never had a one-night stand since?"

David's face burned. "Never had the need for anything on the side," he said with a laugh that he hoped didn't sound forced.

"You must have quite a woman. I'd like to meet her sometime."

"Maybe you will. After the debate."

"May be," Kretzmer said. "Nice visitin' with you. See you in three weeks." A soft click and the line went dead.

David placed the phone in the cradle with a sweaty hand. That god damned bitch. If he ever got his hands on her, he'd shut her mouth permanently. No anonymous stupid extortionist was going to ruin his life. But, who in the hell was she? Maybe he should go to the cops. They could trace her fingerprints on the notes. If they did, and it turned out what she said was true, he'd be in an even bigger mess. What in the hell ever made him take that stupid bet?

He flipped the toggle on the intercom. "Shirley, can you get me a cup of coffee, fresh and strong."

"Yes, Mr. Holman."

David snapped the toggle down and turned back to the price of pork bellies, but the image of a little girl's face topped by a mass of curly hair got in the way of the statistics.

The County Clerk's big wood desk chair squawked when George Kretzmer leaned back. Interesting conversation. No way a young blueblood like Holman didn't sow his wild oats. Rich young studs like that thought they owned the world, especially all the women. He slid the photograph of the curly haired little girl across the desktop next to the campaign brochure with David Holman's picture on it. Kid's curly hair sure was a lot like Holman's. Be nice to know if it was red. Too bad the kid's features were so blurry.

The note said to call at 3:00 on Thursday afternoon. Well, it was 3:10 by the big clock on the office wall and it was Thursday. The letter writer was probably waiting for the phone to ring. He picked up his phone and gave the operator the number.

Several rings, then a second of silence quickly filled with traffic noise. A pay phone. "Hullo." The voice was almost as gruff as Kretzmer's.

Kretzmer cleared his throat. "This is the County Clerk's office returning your call."

"I never called no County Clerk. This phone's for a special call, so get off the line."

"Maybe you didn't call the County Clerk, but I'm the County Clerk and I got a note I got in the mail with a couple of pictures in it that said to call this number at this time on this day."

He could hear her breathing hard over the honking horns, a siren, and car engines. "You got a note with pitchers in it? What were the pitchers of?"

"A baby with fuzzy curly hair and an older girl with real curly hair."

Another pause. "What did the note say?"

"It said the child didn't know who her daddy was and her daddy didn't know who she was. It said the writer knew who the daddy was and that the information could help my campaign."

"What's your name?"

"Kretzmer. What's yours?"

"Oh, no. You don't ketch me up that quick."

Kretzmer smiled. "Smart lady."

"Who you runnin' against for Congress?"

"David Holman. Everybody knows that."

"What if I was to tell you I can prove that the kid in them pitchers is his bastard?"

"That would be real interesting. Can you? Prove it, that is?"

"You're the County Clerk. For fifty thousand bucks, I'll tell you the mother's name, and you can look up a birth certificate."

"Fifty thousand dollars. You're out of your ever-lovin' mind." Angie, waiting on a citizen at the counter, turned to stare at his shout, and the citizen looked up, surprised. George cleared his throat and lowered his voice. "Lady, that's extortion. In case you don't know it, it's also a crime. I can call the police right now."

A male voice came from farther from the phone. "Hey, lady. Get off the damn phone. You ain't the only one needin' to talk to somebody so's other people don't know about it. Tell your boyfriend you'll meet him at the Lazy Inn for an hour and hang up the fuckin' phone."

A police car with siren screaming, sped past the County Clerk's office, and George heard its wail through the phone as it passed the phone booth. So, she was right there on Holman Boulevard, not more than a block away. There was a soft click, and then, silence.

"Hello," he said, and then repeated, "Hello." Silence. Damn. His crack about the police, followed right away by that squad car, probably spooked her. He hung up, pushed the phone back to the corner of his desk, and leaned back in his chair, causing the spring to twang. What if there was something to what she was accusing? If somebody handed him the key to Fort Knox and told him to help himself, would he turn them down? Not by a long shot. It was past time to put an end to the Holman political dynasty. If it took a sex scandal to do it, George Kretzmer was not the politician to hold back. The chair twanged again as he bent over the desk. Let's see. The kid was five years old, the note said. Meant she was born in '47 or '48. All around him were the vital statistics of every citizen of Rosecrans County for more than a hundred years. Shouldn't be too hard to find the birth certificate of a female child with a father by the name of "UNKNOWN."

Angie," he shouted.

On Holman Boulevard, across the street from where a large poster of David Holman's face stared from his campaign office window, Ada Schroeder held the pay phone's receiver in her hand, staring at the wall of the booth. The siren had faded into the distance, but she still shook.

"Lady, you just gonna stand there with the phone in your hand?" The scrawny middle-aged guy with a three-day growth of whiskers and a scraggly fringe of graying dark hair around his naked pate, scowled at her.

She blinked, as if she had been roused from a stupor, and slammed the phone onto the hook. It slipped off, and she had to replace it more gently. "Make your stupid phone call, jerk," she said and stumped down the street toward the bus stop. At least, Kretzmer called. Maybe he'd be curious enough to pay the money.

Her face was red and her lips pursed in a thin line. She'd prove that Scarlett Schroeder's name ought to be Scarlett Holman, if it was the last thing she ever did.

Chapter 19

Myrna glanced at the round clock above the kitchen sink. Twenty-five minutes to eight. Her mouth was dry and her stomach quivered. The last time she had a date, she had the same butterflies, but that time David Holman had been late. Mark Weston wasn't due to arrive for another twenty-five minutes. She brushed an imaginary piece of lint off the skirt of her seafoam green silk dress. Lydia had loaned her the dress, and Sarah had altered it so that now it looked like something out of a high-priced store. Lydia's pearls gleamed against her skin, setting off the sweetheart neckline and short puffed sleeves. She made a little pirouette to make the ruffled skirt twirl. Did she look as nice as she had in the Alice blue dress? The thought conjured up the memory of how that evening ended, and she put a fist to her mouth to keep from crying. Stop that, she told herself. It's ancient history.

Instead, she thought of Scarlett.

"Oh, Mama. You're so pretty," Scarlett had said, her green eyes shining when she saw Myrna all dressed up. She clapped her hands and bounced on her toes when Myrna told her she was going to eat in a restaurant with Mr. Weston. "He's nice, Mama," she said.

"You have a good time with your young man," Mrs. Neumann had said, smiling. "Is good you go with a young man. You are too pretty to be shut up in a factory and in the house all the time."

Now, Scarlett was downstairs with Mrs. Neumann, who promised that they would make cookies in the morning. Nothing left but an evening with a man she hardly knew, who was miles above her in money, education and everything else. He kept telling her he loved her. It sounded nice, but that was usually just a line to get a girl to have sex. If he meant it, why would he fall in love with her, a nobody, a girl with an illegitimate child, a factory hand in the factory he ran? It made no sense.

If it made no sense, then why was she going out with him? She was out of breath, as if she'd run a mile. She stood up and walked into the living room, too antsy to sit. The street in front of the house was quiet, for a change. In a way, it was a relief. Nobody would see her take off in a fancy car, a car that no one in the neighborhood could even dream of owning. She strode back to the kitchen and looked at the clock. Five minutes to eight.

The steps began to shake against the outside wall. Myrna's heart pounded in her throat, choking her air. Her nails dug into her icy palms.

There was a knock. Myrna swallowed, took a deep breath and opened the door.

Mark stood there, a lopsided smile on his face, not saying a word. Then: "Oh, my. You take my breath away. How could you become even more beautiful?"

Myrna's face caught fire. "That's nice of you to say," she said. "You look nice, too. But then, you always look nice."

Mark laughed. "Well, shall we stand here admiring each other, or shall we go see what good things Manzullo's in Riverton can feed us?"

"Manzullo's in Riverton?" Myrna echoed. "That's supposed to be the best place in the state."

"There are a few restaurants in Chicago that are better, but Chicago was a bit far for tonight. Besides, I don't want to waste three hours driving. I've waited long enough to be alone with you."

Myrna took her key from her purse, but Mark lifted it from her fingers, locked the door and pocketed the key. "Tonight, I'm going to spoil you. I won't let you lift a finger to do anything for yourself." He took her arm and held it lightly to help her down the steps, across the sidewalk and into the gleaming Rolls Royce. Mark started to close the car door when she heard a rapping on glass and stopped him. Scarlett was peering through Mrs. Neumann's window, waving goodbye. Myrna blew her a kiss, and Mark closed the door. She waved until Scarlett's face disappeared back into Mrs. Neumann's apartment.

Mark slid behind the wheel, and turned to her with a wide smile. "I can't believe this is actually happening. You me, together, going out to have a good time. I can't stop grinning."

Myrna's smile was less enthusiastic. She looked out of the windows, up and down the street. They had to drive through downtown to reach the highway, and Myrna clenched the armrest each time with her right hand each time Mark slowed for a stop sign or a red light. She looked hard at everyone at the corners and on the sidewalks, even in cars that pulled parallel to them at each traffic signal.

"What's the matter?" Mark said.

"Nothing. What makes you think something's wrong?"

"Because you're watching everyone on the street as if you were expecting someone to attack you."

Myrna sighed. "I'm afraid someone will see me."

Mark stared. "Afraid someone will see you? Are you ashamed to be with me?"

"Oh, no. I just don't want the girls in the department gossiping about me."

Mark snorted. "Let 'em gossip. Give 'em a thrill. Come on. We're here to enjoy ourselves. Forget the department. I'm responsible for the whole place, but I make a point of putting it out of my mind when I'm out for a good time. Now, let's see a real smile."

Myrna obliged and relaxed, especially since they were now out in the country with no nosey eyes to watch. She eased back against the seat, surrounded by the scent of leather and Mark's subtle aftershave. The sun had slipped over the horizon, and the sky had put on the blue between day and dark. "I love this time of day," she said. "The color of the sky is so beautiful it makes me want to cry. I've often wondered if it had a name."

"Why?"

"Anything that beautiful needs a name. Something that when somebody says it you know exactly what they mean." She paused. "To myself, I call it 'twilight blue'."

"That's the perfect name. The color is exquisite. I'm ashamed to say, I've never paid a whole lot of attention to the sky. Too much time with the ledgers." He took his hand from the steering wheel and laid it over hers. "I'd love to see you in a dress that color."

"I don't think anyone can make a color like that. Only nature can paint like that."

"Hey, lady. You're a poet and a romantic. Great combination."

Mark's hand was warm and soft, and he gave hers a gentle squeeze. She turned her palm up and returned the pressure. It felt right. The car, its motor crafted by the most skilled hands in the business, hummed.

The grooves in the tires sang against the pavement. Myrna settled back, her head against the seat back and looked at him: his clean profile against the fading light, the thick dark waves of his hair, painted with silver at the temples, his hands strong on the steering wheel, his gleaming black shoe playing lightly on the accelerator. What was there not to trust about this man? He had been nothing but kind to her and to Scarlett since she first saw him bending over her in the parking lot. He had declared his love and showed it in so many ways, most important that he didn't push sex. He'd wait, he said, until she was ready. Would that ever be? What was wrong with her that she couldn't just accept this miraculous gift?

"Mark. I have to ask you something," she said, hardly able to get the words out.

He looked at her, one eyebrow lifted in surprise. "Sure. Ask away."

She took a deep breath "You say you love me. What does it mean? What do you feel?"

He turned his head sharply. "What? What kind of a question is that?"

She suddenly felt braver, but still scared. "I need to know. What makes you say that you love me? How do you know? I don't know what people mean when they say they love someone, except for Scarlett, of course. But that's different. I thought I was in love with her father, but I certainly missed the boat on that."

Mark grunted. "Why? He's the one who missed the boat. Because he lied to you just to use you and then abandoned you, doesn't't mean that anything was wrong with your love."

"You didn't answer my question. It's important to me."

Mark turned his attention back to the road; it was dark now and other cars passed them, following their twin streams of headlights in the opposite direction, He gave a huge sigh. Still keeping his eyes straight ahead, watching the road, he said: "When I first saw you, like any other healthy male, I was attracted by your beautiful face and body. Then, I began to see the beauty inside you, your honesty, your dignity, your courage. And the more I saw you, the more I wanted to be with you, to have you close to talk to, to share my day, tell you all the things that went wrong and all the things that went right. And I hope you'd tell me what a wonderful guy I am. Or to tell me I'm full of shit when I need to hear it. I want to do things for you that make you smile and laugh. I want to keep you safe so no one will ever hurt you again. I want to be a father to your children, the one you have now, and those that we will have together. I want you to be my best friend."

He stopped to pass a car ahead, then cleared his throat. "I want to touch you, to feel your skin, your hair. Most of all, I want to hold you close, to make love to you for hours." He paused. "That's all I can think of off the top of my head. Is that what you wanted to know?"

Myrna brushed tears from her eyes and swallowed hard. Finally, she whispered, "Do you really mean all that?"

"I wouldn't have said it if I didn't." He released her hand and passed another car. "Can you feel any of that for me?"

She sighed. "I want to. No one has ever been so good to me and to Scarlett. I'm not used to people being good to me. Men always make nasty cracks about what I look like and about having sex with me. Women turn their noses up because of Scarlett. Lydia and Sarah and Mrs. Neumann are the first people I've ever known who treat me like a person." Tears threatened, but she blinked them back and waited a minute to speak until she was sure her voice wouldn't betray her. "And then you come along, with your reputation of playing around a lot. I was so scared. If I didn't do what you wanted you could fire me. If I did, I'd be a stupid fool again." She looked out at the darkness. "I am so tired of always being afraid."

"Well, I said you could tell me when I'm full of shit. I guess you just did. And you're right. I have played around. A lot. 'Daddy's Girl' had a lot of headaches when she went to bed. Then I discovered the headaches disappeared when certain other men came along. I'm human. I found willing partners whenever I needed them. We set up separate bedrooms to 'cure' her headaches. You know something? I didn't miss her a bit. We stayed together only because of her father and the business. An epic love affair, it wasn't. Now, I'm free from all that."

Traffic was heavier as they approached Riverton and the Rolls slowed. Mark held her hand again. "My darling girl," he said. "I love you because despite your fears and silly sense of inferiority, I know you see under my skin and that you also see me as an ordinary mortal. You care about how other people feel. Even nasty old me.

"Myrna, I would walk on spikes and a bed of hot coals to keep you safe and free from fear. I think I could even kill someone who hurt you or Scarlett. You don't have to be afraid any more."

"I don't want to be." She gave a nervous giggle. "I just don't know how."

"Let go of the fear and let your heart and body just feel. They know what to do." He chuckled. "If I weren't driving right now, I'd hold you and kiss you until you couldn't breathe."

Myrna suddenly felt as if a steel shell had fallen from her. She laughed. "Okay. But right now, I'm starved."

"Well, then, let's get there." The Rolls' purr deepened and it raced down the road like a panther after prey.

Mark held the heavy glass door to Manzullo's open for Myrna, and then followed her to a tall desk where a girl stood, smiling. "Good evening Mr. Weston. How nice to see you again."

The girl's neat blonde pageboy brushed her shoulders. Her arms, as smooth as her long-sleeved, floor length black dress, its deep "V" neckline showing a hint of cleavage. Myrna wondered what it would be like to wear an evening gown every night. The girl smiled like a model, her skin was smooth and her face was made up to perfection.

"Good evening, Joyce," Mark replied. "How's Alicia?"

The girl's smile widened, turned real. Her blue eyes sparkled, her beautiful mask softened and became more human. "Oh, she's so much better. She's starting school in a couple of weeks."

"Joyce. I'd like you to meet my friend, Myrna," Mark said. "She has a daughter the same age as Alicia. Myrna, Joyce's little girl was really sick. She had to have an operation a couple of months ago."

Myrna suddenly saw someone like herself, a mother who worried about her little girl. She realized the beautiful black dress wasn't really an evening gown. It was work clothes just like the cotton skirts and blouses she wore.

"My little girl's name is Scarlett and she's starting kindergarten in a couple of weeks, too," she said. "I'm so sorry Alicia was sick. It must have been scary for you when such a little girl had to have an operation."

167

"Yes, it was, but now she's completely healthy." Joyce looked at Mark and gave him a warm smile. Myrna knew without asking that Mark had probably paid or helped to pay for the operation.

A tall man, wearing a tuxedo and a haughty expression, and carrying large menus, came to the desk. "Here's Angelo, Mr. Weston." The mask came back to her face.

"Mr. Weston. A pleasure," Angelo said. "Your banquette is ready." He turned and walked away. Myrna felt Mark's hand on her arm and followed Angelo. Like Joyce, she thought, the tuxedo was his work clothes and the snooty look on his face was a mask.

Angelo led them to a secluded corner of the restaurant to a curved booth, a 'banquette,' Angelo had said. Silver and large, snowy napkins were set for two diners on the round table. A stand holding a silver ice bucket with a bottle in it sat next to the table. Myrna slid across the dark red leather seat to the farthest place setting and Mark settled in beside her. Angelo handed Mark the menus.

"I think we'll start with the champagne," Mark said. "Then, we'll order."

Angelo lifted the bottle from the ice bucket, wrapped a white napkin around it, fit a tool that removed the wire over the opening and pierced the cork. He twisted the tool. There was a gentcel pop as the cork came off. He poured a small amount into the tulip shaped glass and handed it to Mark, who swirled the fizzy wine gently, inhaled it, then sipped it. In a moment, he swallowed and smiled. "Very good." Angelo poured champagne into Myrna's glass and then Mark's, bowed and left.

Mark allowed the bubbles to float for a moment, then raised his glass and indicated that Myrna should raise hers. He then lightly touched her glass with his. The crystal rang with a soft chime. "To us," Mark said, and took a sip. Myrna sipped and swallowed the cool, tangy wine, the bubbles making tiny pops in her mouth.

The restaurant had only about twenty-five tables and banquettes, which were nearly all filled with beautiful people in beautiful clothes. The tables, all covered in spotless white, each held a slim vase with a single deep red rose. Tea candles in ornate crystal holders were set beside the flowers. The walls had pictures painted on them. Murals, Myrna remembered from her high school art class. They were scenes of men in long white robes, holding scrolls, standing on the steps of a building with tall columns. Others depicted men standing up, pushing boats through water with long poles, usually with a man and a woman seated in the middle. Soft gold stone houses and buildings were on both sides of the water. The front of a large church was painted on another wall, with a huge flat structure in front of it with birds settled all around it.

"The murals are scenes from Italy," Mark explained. "The first one is of ancient Rome and probably the Senate. The men in the togas are probably Senators. The next one is Venice, which has canals instead of streets. The boats are called gondolas and the man with the pole is a gondolier. That's how Venetians get around much of the city. The church is San Marcos, or St. Mark's, a very famous church in Venice. The piazza and the pigeons are also very famous. The last wall is a scene at a winery. See the rows of grape vines. Next, people are stomping on the tubs of grapes to get the juice out of them. I think they have machines to do that now. The one with the rows of barrels is the winery where the juice ferments into wine."

"I've heard of some of that," Myrna said. "Especially Venice and the gondoliers. I always thought it would be fun to ride in a gondola."

Mark took her hand and squeezed it. "I'll take you there." He picked up his glass of champagne with his free hand. "Drink up. Can't let this go to waste."

Myrna hesitated. "I've never had any wine or anything like that."

"Of course. Well, don't 'drink up,' just take a few sips. It's okay."

Another wine arrived with the Veal Parmesan, this was a dark red Pinot Noir. It was heavy and silky on the tongue, but burned a little when she swallowed. Myrna took a bite of the veal. The rich tang of the cheese and the sweet veal nearly melted in her mouth. "Oh, my. This is good."

"Specialty of the house," Mark replied, digging into his own plate.

Somewhere during the meal Mark asked, "Do you have any pictures of your mother? Do you look like her?"

"Uncle Ernie keeps a picture in the room where he works on his model airplanes. Ada won't have it anywhere in the house where she can see it. She didn't like my mother. She called her a whore." Myrna said.

"She was pretty. Her hair was dark, like mine, and she had it cut short like they did back then. Uncle Ernie says I have her eyes, too, so I guess I kind of look like her. Nobody ever knew who my father was, so I don't know if I look anything like him or not."

"Does Scarlett look like her father?'

The food was suddenly tasteless and Myrna's blood froze. "She does," she said quickly and finally.

"Sorry. I shouldn't have asked that, but she certainly doesn't look anything like you, except in the shape of her face. I thought maybe someone in your family had the red hair and green eyes."

"No. Those are her own." She paused. "Tell me about your mother."

"As I told you, I vaguely remember a pretty blonde woman who smelled nice. Gramps told me once that it wasn't perfume. It was booze. She was very smart. They'd sent her to Radcliffe, which is a sort of Harvard for girls. But she got in with a crowd that was more interested in parties than education. That was during Prohibition, of course, and they drank bootleg liquor. Some of it was bad and she was poisoned with it. It destroyed her mind. They had to put her in a mental hospital and she died there. I was born just before they put her away. The doctors told my grandparents I was lucky to be alive, because of her alcoholism." He took a deep swallow of wine. "Gramps and Gram were wonderful, loving grandparents, but I always felt different from other kids because I didn't have any parents. It was a big secret, of course, that nobody knew who my father was. There was a tale made up that he'd been killed in a car accident." He took another drink of wine, emptying the glass. "What kind of story did they make up about your father?"

Myrna looked into the wineglass. "They didn't. I was six months old when my mother was killed and Ada wanted to put me in an orphanage, but Uncle Ernie wouldn't hear of it. He was fifteen years older than my mother and he adored her. He wasn't going to throw away her child, he said. He and Ada never had children of their own. I guess there was some reason they couldn't and it was Uncle Ernie's fault. Ada was really mad that he wouldn't put me in an orphan's home and forced her to take care of me. She hated me, still does. Told me all my life my mother was a whore, and that I was just like her." She took a deep breath. "She said Scarlett would be a whore just like my mother and me. That's when I told her to stay away from Scarlett and me."

"Good god. How on earth did you turn out to be such a sweet, loving person with a background like that?"

Myrna shrugged. "I don't know. I guess I didn't want to be like Ada. I pretended that my mother really loved me and would want me to be nice. That was before I knew she was just a wild teenager who wanted a good time and to not be tied down with a baby."

"And that's why you're such a good mother to Scarlett."

"Scarlett is my whole life. It isn't her fault that her father was a spoiled rich kid, who took whatever he wanted, whenever he wanted it. She's a wonderful, happy little girl and I want her to stay that way."

"If her father was—is—rich, don't you want him to support her so you don't have to work so hard?"

"No." The word was an explosion. "He doesn't know that she exists and I don't want him ever to know. He doesn't deserve her."

"Okay. I can understand that. Besides, if he did, then it would cut me out of the equation. I want to be Scarlett's only father."

Myrna went still inside. She couldn't even feel her heart beat. "You, what?"

"I keep telling you I love you. I waited until the divorce was final to ask you on a formal date because I didn't want any talk. As you said, I have a reputation for playing around and I didn't want that to rub off on you. I think I fell in love with you the first time I saw you, lying on the pavement in the parking lot. At first, it was your beauty, but the more I got to know you, the more I realized you were the woman I've been looking for all my life. Long and short of it, I want to marry you and I want to be Scarlett's father. I've always wanted children. Noreen didn't and that was that."

"But *why* do you want to marry me?"

"I don't know *why*," he said, irritation edging his voice. "I just know that I go weak in the knees whenever I see you. I think about you all the time. I wonder what you're doing when I can't see you. I was eternally frustrated that I couldn't be open about my feelings. I want you to love me." He looked at the table. "I've said all this over and over and over. What do I have to do to make you understand?"

Now, Myrna looked away. "I'm sorry. I don't mean to hurt you. It surprises me that I can hurt you. You're so strong and rich and powerful. I guess I think nothing can hurt you."

Mark continued to stare into his wine glass, twirling it with his fingertips. He shook his head. When he spoke, his voice was thick. "That's what I meant in the car when I said you treated me like an ordinary mortal. Most people don't. Oh, yes. I can be hurt. Let me tell you something that happened just a couple of months ago.

"It was the Fourth of July. You remember the Fourth of July?" Myrna nodded. "Well, when I got home, Noreen was there, which didn't happen too often. She told me her father had died from a heart attack at the dinner table, that she had been trying to find me. Then, she said she wanted to make love. We hadn't slept together in years, and I can't remember when we last had sex. But I had just spent the evening with you and Scarlett, and I was so frustrated at being so close to you and not being able to do anything about it, that I said yes. We had sex right there on the floor. I won't dignify it as lovemaking. When we were finished, she made a crack about my—manhood—and laughed at me.

"Myrna. I didn't love her and she didn't love me. I shouldn't have given a damn about what she said, but it hurt worse than a kick in the groin. I moved out in the morning."

Myrna couldn't think of anything to say, except. "I'm sorry." After a long moment, she asked, "Did you ever love each other?"

"I guess in the beginning, we were attracted to each other. I confess I was more interested in her father's money to finance the manufacture of my invention. I got that back in spades. She spent our entire married life telling me how I wasn't really anybody, my invention would never have seen the light of day if it weren't for her father. He was really the one who made it a success." He set the glass down, hard. "I invented that switch when I was still a kid in college. I designed the manufacturing process, I sold the Army on it. I made sure the quality control never faltered. That pompous ass never did anything but preside over board meetings and brag about 'his' business. Then, he had the gall to go behind my back and try to sell it. I refused to give up the patent, which is in my name only, and that put a crimp in the deal. Thank god his pigheadedness killed him or we'd be in court for years."

Myrna held her breath through his angry comments. "What will happen now that he's dead and his daughter runs the company?"

"She owns it by three majority shares. I run it." He poured another glassful of wine and drank about half. "But I won't be around much longer. I have a nice deal in the works."

"What do you mean, you won't be around much longer? What about all your fancy words of a few minutes ago, about loving me and wanting to be a father to Scarlett?"

He stared at her, then took her hand. "I'm sorry. I wasn't thinking about what that might mean to you. I have a business deal in the works that will take me to the West Coast. I want you to come with me, as my wife. I guess that's why I'm getting kind of pushy about it."

Myrna's head spun. "And if I don't marry you? What will happen to my job? What will happen to the jobs of all the other people in the plant?"

"That's Noreen's problem."

"No, it isn't. Those people don't work there for fun. They need their jobs to put food on the table and a roof over their heads. Don't you ever think about that?"

Mark looked away and took another gulp of wine. "Darling, I'm covered with warts. Not physical ones. Moral ones. Not the least of which is not thinking about the people who work at the plant, the ones I don't know. I guess that's most of them. A business is all about money, profits. People who work there are just there to see that the business makes a profit."

Myrna slid away from Mark. "So, I and everyone else who works in the factory really are just part of the machinery, like everybody says."

"Sweetheart, I'm trying to be honest with you. That's reality."

"Not to me, it isn't. Not to Mary Jones, who's divorced from a drunk and who has three kids to support. Not to Katy Murphy, who's fifty-two years old and never married and has to support herself. Not to Tim Forrester, who has a wife and four kids and a 95-year-old mother to support. What are these people supposed to do when your ex-wife decides to fire them because she isn't getting enough money?"

"Sh-h," Mark said. "I know it's unfair, but that's the way it is."

"Sorry, I didn't know I'd started yelling. But it makes me so mad that good people are treated like "things" just because they aren't educated or rich. You say you want me to marry you. How can I marry you and move to lord-knows-where, knowing that people I've worked with for years will be out of work while I'm living like a queen?"

"Would they care if it was the other way around? Believe me, darling, any one of those women would jump at the chance to live like a queen and give the finger to those left behind."

"I don't know. Some would. Lydia wouldn't."

Mark's smile was not pretty. "No. Lydia wouldn't. Lydia would wade in up to her neck to knock down the company." He suddenly sighed and leaned back against the cushion. "I didn't come here to fight with you. Maybe you have a point, but think about my point, too. I don't have much of a choice. I could wrestle the company away from Noreen through a long, drawn-out lawsuit, but I don't really want to stay here. I've had another idea and I've proposed it to a company that likes it. I'm setting up a new plant to manufacture my new invention for them. It would be something that will change the future. I haven't been so excited about anything since I realized what the automatic switch could do. As far as jobs, my new plant will provide jobs for a lot of people in the Seattle area. They aren't the people you work with, but they are people who need good jobs. Are the people in Illinois more valuable than people in Washington?"

He brushed his hand across his hair. "Myrna, I'm a powerful man and a hard one. I tell someone with a doctorate from Harvard to jump, and he says 'How high.' I've argued down men with four gold stars on their uniforms. I've bulled my way through interrogations in the state house and Congress. I've had to make hard decisions to benefit the company, decisions that aren't popular, that put people out of work. I haven't always liked it, but if I have to fire a good friend—as much as I can have a good friend—to save five hundred jobs, I'll do it and not look back.

"But I promise you, if you decide to marry me, you will never see that side of me—unless there's a threat of some sort to you or Scarlett.

Then, I'll use it all to protect you. It's a male sort of thing." He grinned, and pounded his chest with his fists. "Me, Tarzan. You, Jane. Some nasty gorilla threatens you and I start swinging through trees."

Myrna folded her hands together under her chin and looked at him with a worshipful expression on her face. "Oh, Tarzan. What a wonderful man you are, and you swing through trees just like an ape. Jane feel so-o-o safe."

They fell against each other, laughing. "I think I've had too much to drink," Myrna said.

"The two glasses of champagne could make you a little tipsy, especially for not being used to it, but don't worry."

She sobered. "When you say you want a new life, you sound different. You sound kind of desperate, as if something terrible will happen if you don't get it. I don't want anything terrible to happen to you. I don't think I could deal with it if anything bad happened to you. It just hit me that I would feel almost as bad if something happened to you as I would if something happened to Scarlett. I feel like crying just thinking about it."

Mark stared. "Are you saying you love me?"

"I don't know. If that's what it means to love somebody, I guess so."

He took her hand and pulled her close, and then raised her hand to his lips. "You've just made me the happiest man on earth. New lives for both of us begin right this minute. We need more champagne to toast that."

Myrna grimaced. "I don't think so. I think they're waiting for us to leave."

Mark glanced at his watch. "No wonder. It's a quarter past ten. Come." He stood, removed his wallet and laid a stack of bills on the table, then helped Myrna out of the banquette. They nodded to the waiter and Angelo, and left.

Mark's hand was gentle on her arm as they walked toward the car. When they reached it, he took her hands and turned her to face him, then slid his arms to her waist, pulled her close and brushed his lips lightly across hers. Lightning burned through her body from mouth to groin and left her gasping. Her arms wrapped around him, the silk of his jacket against her palms, the rich, male smell of him sent the fire through her again. She lifted her head, her mouth searching. He found it and ate it like candy. Tongues twined and tasted. She felt his hardness and pressed against it. He pulled her even closer, kissed her hard, and then stepped back.

"I've got to stop or I'll take you right here on the pavement." He cupped her face with his soft, smooth hands, brushed his lips across hers. He reached for the car door and helped her inside, keeping one hand on her as if he couldn't release it. When she was seated, her kissed her again, and then closed the door and ran around the back of the car and got into the driver's seat, where he took her hand and brought it to his lips.

"My dearest, darling girl. I can't let you go. I wish I could fasten you to me, so I could touch every part of you and see you and smell you." She saw his smile flash in the dark. "Your hooks are so deep in me they'd have to be surgically removed."

Myrna squeezed his hand. "I-I've never felt like this before. I want you close, too. It's going to be hard not seeing you all the time. I don't know if I can hide it if I see you at work."

"Don't you dare hide your feelings when you see me at work. I know I'll light up like a Christmas tree when I see you."

He turned the key, started the car, backed it out of the parking place and turned toward the street. He put his free arm around her and pulled her close. She laid her head on his shoulder, soaking up his strength, almost daring to believe in his love.

The Rolls glided to the curb in front of Myrna's apartment and stopped. Mark kept his arm around Myrna, watching her asleep on his arm, impossibly long dark, curling lashes brushing her face. He bent and kissed forehead lightly. The lashes fluttered and her blue-violet eyes opened.

"You're home," he said.

She looked out the window at Mrs. Neumann's darkened apartment. Scarlett was safe. She turned to Mark and raised her face. She felt so good in his arms. His mouth was so soft, but so insistent and hungry. Oh, dear god, why had she ever wondered if she loved him.

Mark pulled away. "Time to go." He got out of the car, went around to her door and opened it. He put his arm around her and they tried to go up the stairs together, but it didn't work. They giggled at their struggle, trying to keep it quiet so they didn't wake Mrs. Neumann or Scarlett.

On the landing at the top of the stairs, they clung together. Mark brushed back her hair. "I would like nothing more than to take you to your bed and make love with you until noon, but I want our first time together to be special. I've been fantasizing about it for months."

"Oh? What are you fantasizing?"

"Mostly about your beautiful body naked in my arms, but also where that will happen." He kissed her hard. "But it will have to wait a couple of weeks. That deal I told you about? I have to go to Seattle to work on it. I'm leaving Monday night. But before I go, I'm having a telephone installed here." He touched her mouth with his finger when she started to protest. "I can't be away from you for two weeks without talking to you. I'd make a mess of the deal because all I'd be thinking about would be you. The telephone installer will be here Monday morning, and I will call you before I leave." He traced his finger around her face, and sobered. "One more time. Will you marry me?"

Myrna didn't hesitate. "Yes."

She thought her mouth would be permanently bruised, but so would his. It was hard to breathe in his embrace, but she wanted his arms around her forever.

He released her and stepped back. "I have to go." He unlocked the door and handed her the key. "I'll bring the ring from Seattle. And one other thing. As soon as I get back, I'm starting the legal process to adopt Scarlett. It will be my wedding present to her. A real, honest-to-god daddy."

Myrna stared at him, not trusting what she'd heard. "You-you're what?" She buried her face in her hands and sobbed. "I-I- . . ."

He tipped her chin up. "Hey. That was supposed to make you happy." He took her in his arms again and rocked her gently.

She untangled her arm from his chest and wiped her face. "Silly. Haven't you ever heard of crying for joy? I-I've never been so h-happy in my life," she hiccupped.

His kiss was soft and comforting, and his cheek was wet against hers. "Neither have I," he murmured. He kissed her once more and released her. "I do have to go. Sleep well. And remember. Me, Tarzan. You, Jane."

He turned and ran quickly and softly down the steps. At the bottom, he looked up and blew a kiss at her, and then strode to the car.

Head spinning, Myrna went inside and closed the door. She stood in the kitchen, as if she'd never seen it before. Was it only a few hours ago that she stood in this same place, jittery with nerves about the evening ahead, looking forward to it, and at the same time, terrified?

Had she really told him she'd marry him? How could the whole universe turn inside out in such a short time? Was she being honest when she said she loved him? She touched her mouth where she still felt his kiss. A pleasant shiver went through her. No doubts whatsoever.

Chapter 20

David Holman sat behind the big old desk in his office, a yellow legal pad in front of him, a pen in his right hand, trying to will his brain to think of something the pen could write on the pad. Small town politics. What was little Rockville most upset about and how could he promise to fix it? They didn't have any cops of their own, but depended on the Rosecrans County Sheriff's Department for law enforcement. But they liked it that way. Didn't have to pay . . . The phone rang, startling him. He sighed and picked up the phone.

"David, come in here. Right now," his father's voice said, and before he could respond he heard a click and silence.

That tone of his father's voice always set off his panic button. He took his suit jacket from the back of his chair and shoved one arm through a sleeve. He opened the door, struggling with the other sleeve, and rushed past his secretary, Shirley, without looking. He strode down the hall to his father's office, his stomach churning. He nodded at Gwen, his father's secretary, opened the door and entered the sumptuous office. Even from behind a desk, especially from behind that mammoth rosewood desk, David Holman II had the ability to shrink David Holman III into a six-year-old size. He wanted to run away and hide. With a start, he noticed the heavy, silver-haired man seated in the left chair in front of the desk; Paul Krueger, publisher of the Newport City Times.

He smiled and extended his hand. The older man took it with a grip of steel. "Morning, Paul. What brings you here so early? Father didn't say anything about an editorial board meeting today."

"Sit down, David," his father ordered. David sat in the right-hand chair. "Paul isn't here for a board meeting. He has something you need to see."

A number ten envelope lay on his father's desk. He picked it up and handed it to David.

The address was cut from newsprint and pasted to the envelope, like the one he got at the campaign office. He opened the envelope and removed a piece of paper, folded in half. Two photographs fell from the center, just like the photographs in his file drawer at the campaign office. He read the note and his heart began to pound. He couldn't seem to get enough air. He swallowed hard, licked his lips and made his mouth form a smile. "Cute kid. Crazy note."

"Paul called a little while ago and told me this came in his mail. Do you have any idea what this is about?"

David cleared his throat. "I got a similar note a month or so ago, and I guess it's the same woman who called my house awhile back and made the same accusation. You advised me to get an unlisted number. She called the office once and I told Shirley not to put her calls through if she called again. She has called and Shirley put her off. I guess this note to you is her way around that."

"Well, what do you have to say about those pictures?"

"What about them? It's a cute kid, but it has nothing to do with me. She's trying to extort money from me. If I knew who she was, I'd call the police."

David felt his father's dragon eyes bore into his. "Why would anybody accuse you of a thing like this?"

"You said yourself that crazy people come out of the woodwork during a campaign. Obviously, she wants money and thinks I'll give it to her. What can pictures of a little kid do to me?"

"If they get into the right hands, they can ruin you," Kroeger said.

"How?"

"Somebody can demand a paternity test."

"Why would I take one? I don't have any kids, this one or any other." David replied.

"Suppose Kretzmer got one of these. He'd make hay of any denial. You'd probably have to take a paternity test to prove you're telling the truth," Kroeger said. "If you refused, he could claim that proved you were lying.

As far as I'm concerned, it's a non-issue."

"It's not a non-issue if this woman is sending this stuff to the newspaper," said David II.

He turned to Kroeger. "You won't print it, will you?"

"There's nothing to print. There's no way to check it out. I just thought I ought to alert you," Kroeger replied. "By the way, if you were to pay her, how would you do it?"

David hesitated. "She gave me a phone number to call."

"What is the number?" Kroeger asked.

I don't remember," David replied, and straightened. "And if I did, I'm not about to give it to you."

"You don't trust me?"

"You do run a newspaper. It would make a juicy headline and sell a few papers," David III replied.

"David, if you have that number written down anywhere, destroy it. No reporters are going to get near that nut and destroy three generations of our family's public service," said his father

"Mind if I take the note?" Kroeger asked.

David handed the envelope back to Kroeger, who stood and turned to leave, and then turned back and laid it on David II's desk.

"Good morning, gentlemen," he said, and left.

David II waited until he heard the outer door close, then turned to his son. "Is there a possibility that this child could be yours?"

David shrugged. "If you're asking if I was a virgin when I married Carol, the answer is no. Like any normal young single guy, I sowed my wild oats in prep school and college, but that was way before this child was born. I was engaged to Carol six years ago, and I haven't looked at another woman since."

David II twirled his glasses. "I wish I could believe you. Now, get out of here and get back to work."

A week later, ten minutes before the law office closed for the day, David's phone rang. He picked it up, but before he could speak, his father's voice ordered, "Stay here until everyone's left the building, then I want to see you in my office." A click and the line hummed. David resisted the urge to slam the phone into the cradle, and instead replaced it carefully. Now what.

Less than fifteen minutes later, his father's voice roared from the next office. "David."

Rain splattered against the window behind him, the cloudy sky making an early twilight, darkening the room. He clicked on his desk lamp, creating a gold circle on his desk. The office was silent, no voices, no clatter of typewriters or doors opening and closing.

"Hold on, old man," he muttered.

When he felt in control of himself, he stood, straightened his jacket and tie, and strolled into his father's office. "Evening, Dad," he said, and slid into the leather client chair. The huge portraits of his father, his grandfather and his great-grandfather in their judicial robes stared at him from the wall behind his father's head, their green eyes narrowed, mouths stern, ready to pass judgment. There was a space for another portrait, his, beside his father's. It would be painted as soon as he was sworn into office as a representative. The artist had already been engaged.

His father's living face mimicked the portrait as he stared at David across the huge rosewood desk. The older man pulled his frameless glasses from his face and swung them back and forth in his fingertips, a pendulum marking time before the attack, green eyes drilling into his. When David was still too young to know that his eyes were the same green, he thought his father's eyes shot streaks of green fire. When he had misbehaved badly enough for his father's punishment, he had been made to sit in front of his father's desk in the study, exactly as now. When his father focused those green beams, David's head felt like it would explode with the fiery pain, and his body shook all over. When he told his mother, she had laughed and said it was "cute."

Now, pain thundered through his head, sweat filmed his face, his undershirt stuck to his back and the underarms of his gleaming white Egyptian cotton shirt were dark. Fine tremors rippled through his body.

His father finally spoke: "Al Torrence has been looking into things for me." The glasses didn't lose a beat. He could have been reciting the rules to a jury. "Rumor has it that Kretzmer got one of those letters and is digging into it, and those pictures. Rumor has it that the words 'sex scandal' have been spoken. You are under no illusions, I trust, what that rumor can do to your campaign." The glasses made a few arcs. "And what it can do to the reputation of the Holman family."

Much as his father wanted David in Congress, high office took second place to the Holman reputation.

David swallowed hard, took a deep breath to stop the shaking and tried to sound nonchalant. "As far as I know, the only problem is a crazy old woman with some fuzzy pictures making wild accusations to extort money from me."

"You got us into this mess, because your name is Holman. One Holman gets into trouble and the whole family is tainted. The older man's eyes narrowed as they drew bead on his son. The glasses still swung like a hypnotist's lure. "She's too persistent. There has to be something behind what she says or she wouldn't keep at it." He paused for several swings of the glasses. "Out with it. Something happened six years ago, and you know what it is. Now, I want to know. And. You. Will. Tell. Me. Now."

David clenched his jaw and took a deep breath. "Nothing happened six years ago, except that I married Carol. How many times do I have to tell you?"

"Ten thousand times, and I still wouldn't believe you. I can see it in your eyes. You know what it is. Now, out with it."

"I don't know what you're seeing in my eyes, but it surely has nothing to do with this situation."

The glasses dropped with a soft plop to the leather blotter, and David II leaned against the back of the big chair and closed his eyes. After a moment, he said, "You can't lie to me. I know every move you've made and every expression on your face and in your eyes since birth.

"If you won't admit to me what happened, I'll assume you don't care about this campaign, that you don't care about the Holman name, that you don't care about your wife. You know as well as I do that a sex scandal, in this district especially, will blow up in your face like an atom bomb.

The words spilled from David's mouth. "It was just once."

"So, you admit it. You had an affair. Did you know about the child?"

The word forced itself past David's voice box. "No."

David II leaned forward, "Why in the hell didn't you use protection?"

"There wasn't time."

"Time? What does time have to do with it? Were you on a schedule?"

David studied the edge of the desk, swallowed hard, sucked air into his lungs, and then looked into his father's eyes. "You're a man. You know there are times when you get so hard you can't wait. I had to have her. She was trying to get out of the car, and I couldn't let her. So, I grabbed her arm and pulled her back. And." He shrugged. "One thing led to another. Afterward, I took her home and I've never seen nor heard from her since. Actually, I forgot all about it."

The older man straightened in his chair as if yanked on a string. His fair skin flushed bright red, the lime green eyes narrowed to slits, the nostrils in his long patrician nose thinned as if to shut out a noxious smell, his lips twisted in disgust. He leaned forward, almost lying on the desktop, his eyes locked onto David's. His voice was a quiet deadly hiss.

"You raped her?"

David's stomach knotted, he couldn't breathe, his bowels stirred, a few drops of urine dampened his shorts. "You have to understand. You're a man. You have to have urges. I mean, she was absolutely gorgeous. I had to have her. I couldn't stop."

The father leaned back in his chair and studied his son, as if he were about to pronounce the death sentence on a child murderer.

"Don't you dare bring up this 'but you're a man' business with me." David II's voice was a hoarse croak. "A *man* controls his 'urges'. A *man* does not rape a woman, no matter what his urges."

"It wasn't rape," David protested.

The older man leaned on the desk again. "She was trying to get away. You pulled her back. Did she ever say 'Yes?'" David hung his head. "I thought so. It was sex without consent. The criminal law classes I took at Yale defined that as rape. I assume the same class was taught there when you attended." He sighed and shook his head. "What kind of man are you? What kind of son did I raise?" He made a face as if he had swallowed acid, and waved feebly at David. "Get out of my sight."

David stumbled to his feet and through the door, and ran to the men's room. He flung open the door to the stall and spewed into the toilet. When he finished, he leaned against the wall, weak and covered in cold sweat. His bowels and bladder suddenly seized in a violent cramp. He was barely able to yank his belt open, unzip and drop his pants, and fall to the slimy toilet seat. He sat there, breathing hard, too weak to move, surrounded by stink and filth.

The men's room door opened. "You in here?" came his father's voice.

"I'm sick," David replied.

A beat of silence. Then, "So am I. You make me sick." He paused. "I came in here to tell you I wash my hands of you. You are no son of mine. If even a hint of any scandal comes out, I will wipe you from my life. And that means my checkbook, your trust fund, and my will." The door closed. Hard.

David finally felt strong enough to stand. He flushed the toilet, and then went to the sink, stripped off his clothes and unrolled about three feet of toweling from the paper towel dispenser. He wadded it into a ball, and soaked it with water from the faucet, and washed himself. He threw his soiled underwear, shirt and tie into the trash bin and pulled on his trousers. The pants had somehow escaped the mess, except for some wrinkles. Thank god for the spare shirt and tie he always kept in his office. He went to the door, opened it a crack. Not a sound. The only light shone through his office door. His father was gone. Everyone was gone. Bare chested, he returned to his office, put on the clean shirt and tie and his suit jacket. He looked at himself in the foyer mirror, took a comb from the inside jacket pocket and ran it through his hair. Other than being a little pale, he decided he was presentable enough to go home.

How could he go home? Carol would see that he was upset and ask questions. He'd call and tell her he was working late to make time to recover. He made the call, then buried his face in his hands. Why had he ever made that stupid bet? Why had he followed through on it? Was there really a child?

He sat up. The time for 'wait and see' was past. Something had to be done—now. He wasn't concerned about the Holman reputation. He'd had that shoved down his throat since infancy and he could care less. Losing the House seat wouldn't be a too great a disappointment, although he had already made overtures to chairmen of key committees.

His father's words: "*I wash my hands of you —and that includes my checkbook, your trust fund, and my will. If even a hint of any scandal comes out, I will wipe you from my life*," rang loud in his mind. His father was trustee of the trust fund left him by his maternal grandmother, the source of most of his income, and his father's will made him the sole heir to the Holman fortune.

And Carol. My God, if Carol ever found out about the kid. . . He shook his head. That didn't bear thinking about.

His head still pounded and he felt weak and jittery, but he set his jaw and said out loud, "Pull yourself together and do something."

David slid open the desk drawer where he kept his basic information files and found the one that listed useful people and businesses and the notation: "Private Detectives." Tom Graziano in Chicago did a lot of work for the firm. He'd find that kid if anyone could. David glanced at his watch. After seven. He'd call Graziano first thing in the morning.

Chapter 21

"Here's the birth certificates you wanted, Mr. Kretzmer." George blinked and wiped a hand over his face to hide the fact that he had dozed off over a stack of affidavits. Margie, a tall, skinny, unfortunate-looking young woman stood in front of his desk, a long bony outthrust arm ending in a long-fingered hand holding a file folder.

George took the folder. "Thank you, Angie. How many did you find?"

"Six."

"That all?"

"All the girls."

"Thanks again." Angie nodded, made a military about-face and walked back into the outer office.

George opened the folder and leafed through the birth certificates for female babies born to unmarried women in 1947. Not too many girls who found themselves "in the family way" without a husband stayed in Newport City to give birth. Most of them went out of town to relatives or to homes for unwed mothers and gave their babies for adoption. Probably most of these girls had given their babies up, too. He heaved a big sigh. That meant hunting down each one in person, trying to talk to them about something they didn't want to talk about. Not something he really wanted to do, and he probably couldn't get it done before the debate. But then, the idea of getting a sex scandal on David Holman made it all more than worthwhile. He smiled and picked up the first birth certificate, suddenly full of energy.

Two days later, George had one more call to make. The others were all dead ends, most of them long gone. He read over the birth certificate: "Mother: Myrna Schroeder, 20. Father: Unknown. Address: 869 W. Spring St." He thumbed the worn telephone book on the desk, picked up the receiver and gave the operator a number. After a few rings, a voice like a rusty nail being pulled from an old board, answered. "Hullo."

"Is this Myrna Schroeder?" Kretzmer asked, although he doubted it was. This was an old woman. She couldn't possibly have a five-year-old child. It sounded like the voice on the pay phone.

"Who's askin'?"

"This is George Kretzmer, the County Clerk, and the Democratic candidate for the House of Representatives in Washington."

"I don't want to listen to no politicians," the voice said.

Quickly, before she could slam the receiver, he said, "I'm not calling as a politician. I'm looking for a Myrna Schroeder, who had a baby girl named Scarlett in 1947."

A long beat of silence before she replied. "What do you want with her?"

"I got a letter with a couple of pictures in it of a little girl that said the child was the illegitimate daughter of David Holman, my opponent."

"I don't know nothin' about no letter. My husband and me don't have nothin' to do with the little slut and her brat, don't even know where they live."

"So, you do know her?"

"You figured that when you called. The name's the same. My old man's her uncle. She's the bastard git of his kid sister, one of the kids killed racin' that train back in '27."

George suddenly remembered the wreck. Six teenagers, full of bootleg liquor, joyriding, had tried to race a train to the crossing and lost. Body parts had been scattered across the countryside. Even now, he shuddered at the memory. So, one of those kids had been Myrna Schroeder's mother. And now, Myrna was somehow connected to a scandal with David Holman III. "Thank you very much, Mrs. Schroeder." He hung up.

On the other end, Ada's hands shook as she put the receiver back on the wall phone's hook. That was close. Kretzmer took the bait, but she sure didn't want him connecting her with any note or any demand for money. Holman might keep it secret, but Kretzmer sure as shootin' wouldn't, and Kretzmer wouldn't pay the money. Not now. Stupid to send him that note.

Chapter 22

Myrna folded the top of the small brown sack that held her bologna sandwich, carefully cut in half diagonally and wrapped in waxed paper, and a nice fresh pear. Scarlett was already at Mrs. Neumann's, and she had fifteen minutes to catch her bus. She glanced around the small kitchen. Everything was put away and wiped clean. What could she do with herself for ten minutes?

A bell shrilled and she jumped, her heart pounding. The telephones. Every time they rang she just about jumped out of her skin. Mark had insisted on two: one in the bedroom and one in the living room, but they made enough noise to wake the dead. Nobody ever called her except Mark, and he didn't call until evening. She took the two strides to the living room where the cradle phone sat on a small end table, and picked it up.

"Hello."

"Miss Myrna Schroeder?" The woman's voice sounded efficient.

"Yes."

"I'm calling for Mr. Charles Furst, manager of First State Bank. Mr. Mark Weston has established a trust for you and you need to come to the bank to arrange accounts and sign some documents. When would be convenient for you?"

"I'm sorry," Myrna said. "I don't think I understood you. I don't know what you're talking about. Are you sure you have the right person?"

"You are Miss Myrna Schroeder? You are acquainted with Mr. Mark Weston?"

"Yes, to both, but I don't understand."

"Mr. Weston has established a trust fund for you. You need to open some bank accounts in order to use the money."

"What's a trust?"

"Mr. Furst will discuss all that with you when he speaks with you. How soon can you come in?"

"I don't know. I leave for work in. . ." she glanced at the clock over the sink. ". . .ten minutes."

"Can you come in on your way to work?"

"It'll make me late."

The voice took on a smug tone. "I believe you can afford to be late."

"I'm sorry?"

"The trust has a great deal of money in it. You need to make the arrangements immediately."

"I don't know anything about this, and Mr. Weston is out of town."

"We are aware of that. Mr. Furst will explain everything. Please stop at the bank before you go to work."

Myrna sighed. "All right. It'll be twenty minutes or so."

"Thank you. Mr. Furst looks forward to meeting you." The line went dead.

Myrna replaced the phone with shaking hands. "A great deal of money" the woman said. This was crazy. Eight minutes to catch the bus. She picked up the lunch sack and her purse, glanced around the apartment one more time, went out and locked the door behind her. She ran down the steps and around to Mrs. Neumann's front door. Scarlett opened it.

"Mama. We're going to the grocery store."

"That sounds like fun, sweetie. I'm leaving now. You be a good girl."

"You need anything from the store?" Mrs. Neumann loomed behind Scarlett.

"No. Thank you. I'll see you tonight." She hugged and kissed Scarlett, turned and walked quickly down the porch steps and toward the bus stop on the corner.

Fifteen minutes later, she opened the heavy door to First State Bank, a building that seemed to weigh down the corner of Holman Boulevard and Stephenson Street. A receptionist sat behind a desk just inside the door. "May I help you?"

"I'm here to see a Mr. Furst."

"Oh. Are you Miss Schroeder?"

REQUIEM IN RED
"Yes."

The young woman stood and said, "Come with me." She led Myrna behind the row of teller windows to a heavy wood door, and knocked. Another woman opened the door.

"Is this Miss Schroeder, Elsie?" Elsie nodded. "Thank you," she said and turned toward Myrna. Elsie left. "I'm Mrs. Bannerman, Mr. Furst's secretary. Please come in." Myrna followed her into a small room furnished with a desk, several leather chairs lined against a wall and a coffee table with business magazines arranged in a neat row.

Mrs. Bannerman rapped lightly on still another heavy door, opened it and stood beside it. "Mr. Furst. Miss Schroeder is here."

A small man, with a fringe of gray hair, almost hidden behind his huge desk, wore a black suit, white shirt and dark blue striped tie. He nodded at Myrna and stood. The edge of the desk reached his waist. "Come in, Miss Schroeder. I'm so pleased to meet you."

"How do you do," Myrna said and walked slowly toward the desk.

"Please sit down." He indicated one of two upholstered straight chairs facing the desk. When she was seated, he sat back behind the desk.

"Mr. Weston said this would come as a bit of a surprise to you. He was in a rush to leave and didn't have time to discuss it with you." Myrna couldn't think of anything to say. "Mr. Weston told me you and he are to be married. Is that right?" Myrna nodded. "My best wishes. Have you set a date?"

Myrna cleared her throat. "No. This just happened a couple of days ago and he had to leave right away."

"Well. He wanted you to be provided for until the wedding, especially since he will be out of town frequently, so his attorneys established a trust fund of fifty thousand dollars for you, with the bank as trustee."

"Fifty thousand dollars?" Myrna could hardly breathe. "What for?"

The little man smiled, a smirk really. "For your personal use until you are married."

"Fifty thousand dollars?" she repeated. "I wouldn't make that much money in ten years?"

"You are aware that Mr. Weston is a very wealthy man."

191

"Yes, but what has that to do with me?"

"You will be his wife. You will share that wealth. He wants you to have use of some until you are married—or after—if he wishes."

The room spun around Myrna. Long windows covered with heavy maroon draperies. They looked like velvet, an imposing round table surrounded by chairs, a pair of sofas with coffee tables in front of them on the long walls, like in Mark's office. Huge paintings of mountains hung on the walls. A double row of certificates and pictures of Mr. Furst with other people hung on the wall behind his desk. Fifty thousand dollars. It had to be a joke.

"I don't think I can take it, Mr. Furst," she said.

He stared. "I beg your pardon?"

"I don't need that much money, and I'm not married to Mark now."

Mr. Furst sat silent for a long time. Finally, he leaned forward, his arms on the desk. "You will need it, Miss Schroeder, in order to prepare yourself to live according to Mr. Weston's standards. Additionally, you don't have the option to refuse. The trust has been set up. The money is there in your name. Whether you choose to use it, is, of course, your decision. My responsibility is to help you open a couple of checking accounts and a line of credit so you can use it." He pressed a button on what Myrna recognized as the intercom on his desk. "Mrs. Bannerman, will you bring in the Weston papers?"

"Yes, sir," came the metallic reply. Moments later, Mrs. Bannerman entered the room with a file folder in one hand and placed it on Furst's desk. She turned and looked down her nose at Myrna before she left.

Mr. Furst explained each document before Myrna signed it, but it was still all a blur. When the last one was signed, he handed her a leather-covered checkbook. "I'll open a safety deposit box for you and put your copies of the documents in it."

Myrna picked up the checkbook, opened it and flipped through the pages. "I'm sorry to be so stupid, Mr. Furst, but I don't know how to write a check."

His eyes widened and he bit back a smile. "I'll show you." When he finished explaining the check-writing process, he stood. "Come. We'll open a safety deposit box."

Twenty minutes later, Myrna said goodbye to Mr. Furst, who bowed slightly and thanked her for coming in, and went back out on the street in a daze. The big clock on the sidewalk in front of Gerlanger's Jewelry Store showed that she was already a half-hour late for work. Her bus wouldn't come for another ten minutes, and it would be ten minutes after that until the bus got to the plant. Jack would have a fit. Well, he could just have his fit.

Her knees were weak and her head was fuzzy. The street she'd seen every day of her life, looked strange as she walked slowly toward the bus stop. She glanced at the storefront on her right, directly at the picture of David Holman. She felt the familiar spike of fear, but as suddenly, as if the spike split open the layer of fear in which she had wrapped around herself for so long, she felt Mark's presence like a shield around her and Scarlett. Now, even if David Holman learned about Scarlett, he could never take her away. Scarlett was safe.

And there on the sidewalk, with people walking past, with cars revving engines in the street beside her, honking horns, screeching to a stop at a red light, Myrna knew she loved Mark Weston, and that he loved her. Not the feeling of electricity when he was around or when she thought of him. That was "in love." As she knew, "in love," didn't last. The kind of love that kept people married for fifty years was different. Maybe the electricity was gone, but what replaced it was knowing and trusting that neither would deliberately hurt the other, that each would protect the other, that they could laugh and cry and fight and forgive. Tears brimmed her eyes, and she ached to have him near, to tell him.

The roar of a factory at work greeted Myrna as she pushed open the door to the second floor. She punched her time card and went to the empty break room, where she put her lunch in her locker. She ran a comb through her hair and washed her hands before going into Department 21. Jack looked up from his desk when she stepped through his office door.

"Welcome. Glad you could make it," he said.

"I called Joe and told him I'd be late. He said it was okay."

"Yeah. I know, but he doesn't have to make up an hour's lost rate. Get out there on number 25, and try to make it somewhere close to the night's rate." He looked down at the papers on the desk in dismissal.

"Yes, sir."

The sarcastic tone in Myrna's voice brought his head up. Myrna Schroeder never spoke that way. She smiled, and went to her machine.

At supper break, Betty poked Myrna in the back as she passed her in the hall. "Hey, you were almost an hour late. You ain't never been late before. Was this guy so good you couldn't tear yourself away?" She snickered and walked on.

Chapter 23

Myrna stood in her kitchen, looking for any speck of dirt that dared appear. She had walked through the living room and bedroom, inspecting them carefully. Scarlett was in the bathroom fastening her new black patent Mary Janes. She'd insisted, "I can do it myself."

Myrna wore the new silk dress the saleslady had called "lavender blue" and said the color matched her eyes. She had finally decided to spend some of what she thought of as "Mark's money" to buy clothes for Scarlett and herself for Mark's homecoming. First, she had taken Scarlett through the door of The Children's Store, where only the rich bought clothes for their children. Before Scarlett was born, she had stood and looked through the window at the exquisite knit sweaters and bonnets and booties for babies, at the frilly little dresses and trim little suits, longing to have something so beautiful for her baby.

The saleslady had smiled with her mouth, but her eyes slid up and down Myrna's thrift store skirt and blouse. "May I help you?" she'd asked in a tone that implied there was nothing in the store that Myrna could afford.

Myrna straightened and looked straight in the woman's eyes. "I'm looking for a party dress for my little girl, and the things to go with it." She pointed to a dress that hung on a nearby mannequin. It was made from baby blue cotton gingham as delicate as silk, with a sheer blue pinafore made from organdy fine enough to go through a needle, over it. "Do you have that in a size 6?"

"We do, Madame," She cleared her throat. "but it is a designer model and, well . . ."

"I'd like my daughter to try it on," Myrna said.

The clerk turned to go into the stockroom, when Scarlett said. "I don't want a blue dress, Mama. I want a pink one." The clerk stared, and then turned to Myrna and shook her head.

"You don't have it in pink?"

"Oh, yes. But, Madame, you must know as well as I that redheads, especially such flamboyant redheads, don't wear pink."

"Please get the pink."

"Very well." The clerk raised her eyebrows, but turned on her heel and disappeared into the stockroom. She reappeared a few moments later with the same dress in pink. Scarlett's face brightened like Christmas morning.

"Can she try it on?"

"Of course. Come with me to the dressing room." When Scarlett was dressed in the pink dress and the pinafore tied in a big bow in back, and her fiery curls fluffed out, she pirouetted in front of the three-way mirror. "I'm pretty," she said.

"Yes, you are," Myrna replied, deliberately ignoring the clerk. "Pink is a perfect color on you and the dress fits perfectly."

A stiff petticoat pouffed the skirt into a mushroom shape. "You look like Miss Muffat," said Myrna. Scarlett giggled and twirled to make the skirt flare.

"I'll take it, and the petticoat and a pair of pink socks."

At the cash register, the clerk said, "That will be fifty dollars and thirty-eight cents." Her hands paused about the register's keys as if she didn't want to waste her time entering the figures since Myrna obviously didn't have that kind of money.

Myrna removed the leather-bound checkbook from her thrift shop purse and wrote the check as Mr. Furst had instructed. She signed it and handed the check and the card Mr. Furst had given her to the clerk. The clerk's eyebrows arched when she read the card, and she immediately tapped the amount on the keys and punched "Enter." The cash register rang and the amount appeared in little popup squares in a window on the top. The clerk placed the check in the cash drawer and handed Myna the receipt before closing the drawer with a snap. "Thank you, Madame. Call again."

A little less intimidated, Myrna guided Scarlett, who carried the package with her dress as if it would vanish from sight, into Merlin's, another store she had never been brave enough to enter. It was quiet, with thick cream carpet on the floor, comfortable cream sofas placed in the center of the room in front of enormous vases of exotic flowers. Glass-topped coffee tables were set in front of the sofas and covered with tastefully arranged copies of *Vogue* and *Vanity Fair* and other fashion magazines. A small, ebony framed glass counter stood at the left of the door. A tall woman, her dark hair arranged in a shoulder length pageboy, smiled at Myrna from behind the counter. The same smile as the clerk in The Children's Store.

"I would like a dress to wear out to lunch in the country club." Myrna said.

When they walked out the door a half-hour later, leaving the clerk staring after them, Myrna carried a box with a lavender blue silk shirtwaist dress, a lace-trimmed silk slip to match and several pairs of nylon stockings, sheer as spider webs. Their next stop was the town's best shoe store, where Scarlett found the Mary Janes and Myrna bought a pair of gray pumps with two-inch heels, made from leather as soft as a baby's skin.

Now, they wore their new finery as they waited for Mark to come from the airport.

Christer, Mark's chef, general factotum and best friend, waited behind the wheel of the Mercedes Benz at Chicago's Midway Airport. Mark ran down the steps from the chartered plane and across the tarmac to the car. He opened the door and slid in beside Christer in the front seat.

"How was your flight?" Christer asked, as he started the car and steered it to the street.

"Smooth as silk. Not a bump on the whole trip."

"And the trip?"

"Things are moving right along. We found a location and ordered some of the machinery. We should be out of here by the first of the year. Is that okay with you and Inge?"

"Of course. Why wouldn't it be?" Christer's slight accent attested to his Norwegian birth. "Are you going home?"

"I want to pick up Miss Schroeder and her daughter, first, then we're going to lunch at the club." Mark gave Christer directions to Myrna's house and sat back. A long thin box covered in blue velvet pressed against his chest in the breast pocket of his jacket. He couldn't wait to see her face when she opened it. A smaller box rested in his jacket pocket. It was probably the first necklace Scarlett ever had. Myrna, too. At least, the first diamond necklace. He smiled as he thought of what the small box contained. The jeweler had done a great job to give him just what he asked for.

How would they react to his plans for the evening? Christer and Inge had been working since he left to turn one of the guest rooms into a perfect little girl's room, and he'd left strict instructions about what to do with his bedroom. Maybe it was too soon. Maybe Myrna wouldn't want Scarlett to go to his home. Maybe Scarlett wouldn't want to be parted from her mother. Why did he think they would be pleased at his surprise?

Christer stopped the car outside Myrna's apartment. "Not exactly the most elegant of neighborhoods," he said.

"The neighborhood doesn't reflect two people who live in it," Mark replied as he opened the door and got out. "We'll be down in a few."

He ran up the steps, breathing hard as he reached the top. He wasn't in the best of shape to be running up thirty steps. He rapped on the door. When Myrna opened it, he gasped.

"You are magnificent," he said. He folded her into his arms, breathing the faint scent of a new perfume. The lavender blue dress accented her eyes to perfection. He slid his hands from her back to where the shimmery fabric hugged her breasts and cupped the weight in his hands. Their mouths met and for a long moment, nothing else existed.

When they finally parted, Myrna breathed, "Welcome, home."

"That kind of welcome will guarantee me coming home faster than light." He held her away. "You are so beautiful in that dress. I could just look at you forever if I didn't have other things in mind."

Myrna stepped aside. "Someone else is beautiful, too."

Scarlett stood, wide-eyed, at the door to the bedroom. Mark, his arm still around Myrna's waist, caught his breath. "She certainly is. Scarlett, you look just like a red-haired Alice in Wonderland. I love that pink dress. You look like a beautiful doll all dressed to put under the Christmas tree."

Scarlett stood still, staring at Mark and Myrna, with a slight frown.

"Is something wrong?" Mark asked.

Scarlett looked at her Mary Janes. "Are you really going to be my daddy?" she asked, not looking up.

Mark gave Myrna's waist a squeeze, removed his arm and knelt to Scarlett's level, wincing as his knees cracked. "I'd like to be, if it's okay with you."

"Why?"

Mark paused. This was a question to answer carefully. Finally, he said, "I want to be your daddy because I love you and I love your Mama, and I want us to be a family."

"My daddy died in the war. I don't need a new one."

Mark looked up at Myrna, pleading. He grunted and stood to ease the ache in his knees. "This is something that needs more time to talk about," he said. "My friend, Christer, came to the airport to get me. He has other things to do, so I'd better arrange for his wife to come and get him while we talk. May I use your phone?"

Myrna shrugged. "You're paying for it."

Mark's felt as if he'd been slapped and he clamped down on an angry reply. "Let's not get into that," he said and strode into the living room. He called Inge and gave her directions to Myrna's apartment. "Now, let's sit down at the table," he said, after returning to the kitchen. "Things seem to go better when people sit around a table." He lifted Scarlett to the chair, her little body stiff with tension.

When they were settled, he looked at Myrna. "This is your territory."

Myrna took Scarlett's hand. "Honey, we talked about this before. Remember?" Scarlett nodded. "When somebody dies, they're gone. They're never coming back. Your daddy never knew you. He didn't even know you were going to be born. If he had lived to know that, he would have been very happy. If he had lived, he would love you very much and taken care of both of us. But he didn't." The lie had been repeated so many times, it almost seemed like the truth.

Scarlett's small face clouded. "Won't he be mad if I get a new daddy?"

"I'm sure he would be very happy that you are getting a new daddy, since he can't be your daddy."

199

Scarlett looked at her hands resting on the tabletop, her fingers playing an imaginary piano. Seconds crawled by as her fingers continued their arpeggios. Mark raised an eyebrow at Myrna. She shook her head, but finally said, "Honey, are you all right?"

Scarlett raised her head, two tracks of tears traced over the freckles on her cheeks. "I'm scared," she said, sniffing.

Myrna was at her side in a flash, picked her up and sat down in the chair with Scarlett in her lap. "Oh, sweetheart. I'm sorry. Of course, you're scared. It's scary when things change all of a sudden."

It was hard for Mark to speak around the lump in his throat. "It isn't going to happen right this minute. You'll have time to get to know me better. I want that more than anything. Right now, all that's important is that I love you and I love your Mama and I want us all to be together."

"Mama says you want to 'dopt me."

"Yes, I do. I can't be the Daddy who made you, but I can be a better Daddy if I adopt you. It won't hurt or anything. Your Mama and I will sign some papers and talk to some people and then we'll all go to a big place called a court. A man, called a judge, will say I can be your daddy. It won't be scary."

Scarlett looked at him, those unusual green eyes searching his face, fastening on his eyes as if trying to see inside him. She nodded. He reached across the table and took both her hands in his, marveling at how small and smooth they felt. "I love you Scarlett with all my heart, and I promise to make you safe and happy."

"That's okay," Scarlett said in a small, soft voice, pulling her hand away, looking down and snuggling close to Myrna.

They sat without speaking for a while, until Scarlett slid off Myrna's lap and walked around to Mark. "Can I sit on your lap?"

Mark felt a stone dissolve in his heart and reached to pick her up. "Any time." Her small body was light across his legs and his arms went around her as if he'd been doing it all his life. When he hugged her, she melted into his chest. He bent and kissed the top of her curls.

He reached into his jacket pocket, took out a small slim box and gave it to Scarlett. "This is for you. I brought it on the airplane, all the way from Seattle."

"What's Seattle?"

"It's a city a long way from here."

Scarlett pulled the lid off the box. Inside was a necklace of small pink pearls. "O-o-oh!" She looked at Myrna.

"It's all right, honey," said Myrna. "The necklace is yours. You can pick it up, and I'll put it on you,".

Scarlett carefully lifted the necklace from its satin lining and held it, lightly running one hand over the pearls. "They're so smooth." She slid off Mark's lap, went to her mother, and gave her the necklace. Myrna, fastened it around her neck.

"Go look in the mirror so you can see how it looks," Myrna said.

Scarlett slid off Myrna's lap, ran to the bedroom and climbed on the bed so she could see herself in the big mirror on the dresser. "Oh, Mama, it's so pretty with my new dress," she called. In a moment, she was back in the kitchen and stood at Mark's side, her head hung shyly. "Thank you, Mark."

Mark put his arm around her and held her close for a moment. "You are very welcome, Scarlett."

She ran to Myrna. "Aren't they pretty, Mama?"

Myrna bit her lip. "Almost as beautiful as you," she said and lifted Scarlett into her lap.

Mark took the square box from his breast pocket and slid it across the table. "I brought your Mama a present from Seattle, too." It wasn't the first gift of jewelry he had given a woman, but he found himself holding his breath, anxious for her to open the box, to see the expression on her face.

She gave him a quizzical smile, and lifted the lid. "Oh, Mark," she breathed, when she saw the deep fire in the large emerald cut diamond that hung from a fine silver chain. Later, she learned the chain was platinum, a metal she'd never heard of. "It's so beautiful."

Mark got up and went around the table, took the necklace from her and fastened it around her neck. "You make it more beautiful."

"Oh, Mama," Scarlett said, turning to look at the necklace. "It's so sparkly. It's almost as pretty as mine."

They all laughed. Scarlett slid off Myrna's lap and ran back into the bedroom to the mirror.

Mark put one hand in his other jacket pocket, opened a small box and worked an object out of it. He stood in front of Myrna, got down on one knee, praying it wouldn't crack, took Myrna's left hand in his and said, "Myrna Schroeder, I love you and I want you to be my wife. Will you marry me?"

"I thought that was all settled," Myrna said.

"It is," Mark replied, "but I want to do it perfectly. Will you marry me?"

Myrna held her breath for a long moment. "Yes," she said.

Mark slipped the ring from his hand to her ring finger, where the large emerald cut sapphire gleamed, a rich twilight blue, surrounded by a frame of diamond stars. Myrna gasped. "It's so beautiful. Just the color I love." She leaned over and kissed him gently. "Just as beautiful as the man I love."

He forced himself to stand without flinching, took her hands and raised her from the chair, wrapped his arms around her and drew her as close as he could get her. "I love you so much. I want to cover you with beautiful things. But most of all, I want to hold you like this." He bent his head until his lips met hers, soft and smooth and waiting.

David Holman eased onto a bar stool at the Sunset Country Club and within seconds Jeff, the barman, set a glass with two fingers of Johnnie Walker Black in front of him, accompanied by a tumbler of water. David lifted the glass in a salute to Jeff, and then tossed back the whiskey and chased it with half the water.

"Another one, Mr. Holman?"

"Sure," David replied. Jeff really didn't need to ask. David had the same drinks every day at lunchtime, five days a week. Today, he was meeting Jack Thurman, his campaign manager, for a strategy session that couldn't be handled in the campaign office or in the law office. When the second whiskey arrived, he sipped it, thinking how frosty the atmosphere had become at the law office since he had confessed his "sins" to his father. David II hadn't spoken to him since then, completely ignoring him at the office, walking past him without looking or speaking. Well, there wasn't much he could do about it. He couldn't go back and undo the whole episode.

David swiveled the bar stool to face the dining room, separated from the bar by a carpet in the colors of the sunset. At that moment, Karl, the maître 'd, escorted Mark Weston and a girl, whose face should have been on magazine covers, to a table. Mark really knew how to find beautiful women. As he admired the gorgeous girl, a flare of color caught his eye. A little girl held the woman's hand. A little girl with flaming red hair in a halo of tiny curls. He sucked in his breath and forgot to let it out. He knew without seeing that the color of her eyes would be the same as those that looked back at him from the mirror every morning, the same as those that stared in judgment from the wall behind his father's desk. The child in those pictures.

The woman was her, Myrna something, wearing a blue dress that fit her like water over a rock. What in hell was she doing with Mark Weston? But the kid. His eyes couldn't stay away from her in her pink dress. The old woman was right. The kid had the Holman red hair. How else did she look like him? He had to get out of here before someone saw the resemblance. "Tell Mr. Thurman I'll be back in an hour," he told Jeff, and dashed for the door.

Chapter 24

Myrna felt like she was about to step into a nest of snakes when Mark's hand at her back guided her lightly into the country club dining room with its window wall overlooking the golf course. She held tightly to Scarlett's hand. The maître' d led them to a table beside the window wall, and seated Myrna where she could see the golf course, bordered by trees that had begun to flame in fall colors. The maître d' brought a red leather booster seat for Scarlett.

'I feel like everyone is staring at us," she whispered to Mark, who was seated at her right.

He laughed. "They probably are. You and Scarlett light up the room. They haven't seen two such beautiful women in here in fifty years, I'll bet. Just ignore them for now." He turned to Scarlett. "Young lady. What would you like to eat?"

"Can I have macaroni and cheese?" It was her favorite food, which Myrna served only on special occasions.

"Of course,"

A tall, slim woman, her blonde hair in a perfect bouffant style, stopped beside the table and spoke to Mark, deliberately turning her back to Myrna.

"How nice to see you here. How are you doing as a single man?"

"Hello, Diana," Mark said. "I'd like you to meet my fiancée, Myrna Schroeder, and her daughter, Scarlett. Myrna, Diana Quinn. Her husband, Ted, is my Chief Financial Officer."

"Of course," Diana said, turning to face Myrna, and holding out her hand. "How nice to meet you," she said, barely touching Myrna's fingers. "And best wishes on your engagement." Before Myrna could reply, she turned back to Mark. "I hadn't heard of your engagement. It must have been very recent."

"It was. It took me a long time to screw up my courage to ask her. I was afraid she'd say 'no.' He took Myrna's hand and gave it a gentle squeeze. "I can hardly believe she said 'yes.'"

Diana made a mouth-only smile. "Isn't that nice." She turned back to Myrna. "Are you from Newport City? I don't believe I've seen you at the club or at any parties."

Mark squeezed Myrna's hand again. "Myrna works at Weston Switch. She hasn't been a part of the country club crowd, and she's not accustomed to sitting around doing nothing but drinking and tearing people apart."

Diana's face turned rigid and she bobbed her head at Myrna. 'Nice meeting you, Miss –uh. Sorry, your name slipped my mind. I must be getting old." She turned and walked quickly to another table where she joined another woman.

"What was that all about?" Myrna asked. "She didn't give me a chance to say a word."

"I'm her husband's boss, so she has to be a little careful how she behaves, and she sucked up to Noreen, so I'm sure she's had an earful of what a bastard I am. Don't worry about her. You are a thousand times the woman she is."

"Is that how all your friends are going to be?"

"Diana is NOT my friend. I don't like her and the whole useless crowd that believes they are so superior because their husbands have good jobs. Sadly, they are just one divorce away from the life you've been forced to live, and they'd be completely lost if that happened."

"Won't it be the same with me?"

"What do you mean?"

"If you decide to divorce me, I'll be right back where I started from.?

Mark stared. "Why would I divorce you? That would be like cutting myself in half."

"You might get tired of me. Diana made it really clear that she didn't think I was good enough."

A flicker of annoyance crossed Mark's face. "Myrna, stop thinking like that. I have no respect for parasites like Diana and the crowd she runs with. I fell in love with you because you aren't like her. You have taken the rotten life thrown to you and made something good for yourself and for Scarlett. You have courage and strength and a capacity to love someone for who they are. Or I should say love me for who I am inside, not the face I wear for everyone else. You have no idea how much that means to me." He turned to Scarlett who sat wide-eyed through the entire episode. "And you've brought me a beautiful daughter. What more can I ask?"

"That lady didn't like us very much," Scarlett said.

"I don't think she knows what she likes." Mark replied. "Besides, it doesn't make any difference. There are a lot of really nice people who do like us. Wait until we get to Seattle. That is a really cool city."

"Is it going to be like that in Seattle?" Myrna asked

"Well, in Seattle, I'm sure there are people like that, but it's a big enough city that we don't have to have anything to do with them. It isn't as big as Chicago, but it is a beautiful city and Washington is a spectacularly beautiful state, there's so much more to do than Newport City."

After lunch, Mark said, "I have another surprise for you. I'm going to take you to where I live, on my farm."

"A real farm with cows and other animals?" Scarlett asked, her eyes wide.

"That it is, and Scarlett, there are some new baby kitties you can see and pet, if you want."

Scarlett's green eyes sparkled with pleasure. "Kitties? Oh, I like kitties."

They returned to Myrna's apartment and changed clothes, then Mark drove them to the farm. He showed Scarlett where the kittens were and she immediately reached out to pet one. Mama cat hissed at her and she snatched her hand away.

"It's all right. She's just protecting her babies," Mark said. "Maybe if you just sat down beside them for a bit she'll get used to you and let you pet her and the kittens. Her name is Felicia."

Scarlett looked a little skeptical, but sat on the straw covered floor. "Mama kitty. I won't hurt you. I like you and your babies," she said. Myrna crouched beside her and spoke to Felicia. "Your babies are beautiful. You must be very proud of them."

"I'll be back in a minute," Mark said, and went to the farm manager's office in a corner of the barn. Thad, the manager, was bent over a ledger book on a small wooden desk. He ran one hand through his salt and pepper hair and shook his head.

"Problem?" Mark asked.

Thad swiveled his chair around. "Mark. I didn't know you were there." He glanced back at the ledger. "No. Nothing. Just my bad math."

"Your bad math. Yeah, sure. If there's a problem, we can discuss it later. If you can break away for a minute, I'd like you to meet someone."

"Here?"

Mark nodded and Thad got up and followed him to where Myrna and Scarlett were playing with the kittens.

Myrna stood up. "Thad. I'd like you to meet Myrna Schroeder. Myrna and I are going to be married. And this is her daughter, Scarlett, who will be my daughter soon after we're married."

Thad stared for a moment, then covered his surprise and made a little bow. "Nice to meet you Mrs. Schroeder, and best wishes."

"My name is Myrna," she said, and offered her hand, which he took in a gentle squeeze. "And thank you."

"Thad, is Harry around? I want to take Myrna up to the house and I'd like to have Harry show Scarlett around the farm. You know, the animals and things kids would like."

Thad raised his eyebrows. Harry, the farm hand, was not going to be happy babysitting. But Mark was the boss. "He's out in the shop working on the John Deere. I'll get him. Nice to meet you, Myrna and I hope you and Mark will be very happy." He turned and went out the side door and was back in a few minutes with a young blond man. Introductions were made, and Harry crouched down on the floor beside Scarlett and the kittens.

"I want to take you up to the house," Mark said. Myrna told Scarlett to be good for Harry and joined Mark. He took her hand and they walked up a slight incline to the back door of the butter yellow Victorian with its wrap-around porch, ornate dark green trim and peaked roof. There, she met Inge and Christer in a kitchen that smelled of good things cooking. Mark then led her upstairs and into a bedroom, freshly painted white, with a white canopy bed, covered with a pink bedspread and matching pillows where a menagerie of stuffed animals rested. A small table and chairs and an adult rocker were arranged along one wall and a white dresser was placed opposite the bed. Mark opened a door to a large walk-in closet filled with clothing in Scarlett's size.

"I can't believe this, Mark. It's so beautiful, and how did you know what kind of clothes to get her. There's so many she'll outgrow them before she can wear all of them. But she isn't going to be living here for a while. I can't take them all back to my apartment. There's no place to put them."

"I was hoping you would be living here," Mark said.

"Oh, no. That wouldn't be right. I don't want Scarlett to think I would live with you when I'm not married to you." A frown line appeared between Mark's brows, and Myrna cringed inwardly.

"Scarlett isn't going to know that. She'll just know she now lives in a beautiful house with a beautiful room and animals to play with and pretty clothes. She has no idea what being married is."

"I'm sorry. Everything is so nice and I appreciate all the work and everything, but I just can't."

Mark sighed. "We'll talk about that later," he said. He took her hand and added, "Come with me into our bedroom."

Myrna found it hard to breathe and she fought down an urge to run. She knew that sex would have to come sometime, and she flashed back to that awful night with David Holman. Still, she followed Mark into the next room. The walls were covered with blue wallpaper that looked like cloth. She touched it. It was cloth, and it felt like silk. The bed was huge, with a carved wood headboard and a silk bedspread that matched the wall covering. There was a fireplace in the wall facing the bed, with a loveseat in front of it and two upholstered chairs on either side. A dark wood coffee table stood in front of the sofa, and a small table and two chairs were placed against the wall to the right, with a vase of white chrysanthemums in the center. As in Scarlett's room, a door opened into an enormous walk-in closet, filled with women's clothing and Mark's. Windows draped in blue silk, looked over the back of the property. A huge bathroom with two sinks and two vanities, a large walk-in shower and an adjacent soaking tub was next to the bedroom.

"This is our room," Mark said.

"It's. . .It's. . .I just don't know what to say."

"Say you like it," Mark said, then guided her to the sofa, where she sat down and he sat beside her. He took both of her hands in his. "I want you and Scarlett to stay here tonight. Inge and Christer have prepared dinner, and Scarlett can sleep in her new bed. Then, I want to sleep with you and to make love with you."

"I-I don't know. I know sex is something that I'll have to do, but . . ."

Mark straightened and backed away. "You don't *have* to do anything," he snapped, "I thought you loved me. I thought you wanted to make love as much as I do; If not, I'll take you and Scarlett home right now and that will be that."

A lump settled in Myrna's chest. She would not cry. It was all too good to be true. She knew it all along. She wanted to get up and run out of this beautiful room, find Scarlett and find someone to take them home. Maybe one of the farm workers would do that. But she couldn't move and she couldn't speak. To speak would be to cry. Never to see Mark again. Never to have him hold her and kiss her until she felt like she was on fire, never to just sit and talk with him like a good friend. The thought made her feel hollow inside. But she was so scared. All she could think about was how David tore off her dress and hurt her, and how angry he was when she pulled away from him. What if she couldn't do it?

"Well, what is it?" Mark said. Myrna shook her head. "Say something."

Myrna swallowed. "I can't," she whispered.

"What do you mean, you can't. You spoke well enough to tell me you'd make love with me if you *had* to."

Myrna took a deep breath. "I'll cry if I talk," she said softly.

"Why? Because all the goodies will be gone?"

She gasped, struggled to pull the ring off her finger and threw it at him, then jumped up and ran to the door. "That was a rotten thing to say. Tell one of your men to take us home. I'll have all your stuff sent to your office. And I quit. I never want to see you or Weston Switch ever again."

Mark stood and ran after her. He caught her by the arm and pulled her to him. He wrapped his arms around her to hold her as she struggled to get away from him. He kissed her hard and demanding until she stopped fighting him. "Sorry. That was uncalled for. Come on, sit down again. We need to talk."

Back on the sofa, he said, "Now what is this all about?"

Myrna swallowed hard. "I'm scared," she said in a whisper. "When you kiss me and love me, I feel like I'm on fire, and I want you to touch me all over. But then, I think about that awful night when I got pregnant with Scarlett and I just freeze up. I can't go through that again."

"Oh, my God," he breathed. "Why didn't I think of that, and why didn't you tell me? That was rape, a vicious crime. I would never hurt you. It doesn't have to hurt. It can be wonderful and sweet and loving. Will you sleep with me tonight and let me show you?"

Myrna wiped her eyes with the back of her hand and nodded. "I know you won't hurt me." She paused. "I'll stay."

Mark pulled her close and his mouth found hers in a hungry kiss, and Myrna's body responded as if a magic button had been pushed. She couldn't get close enough and her body opened. It felt like they had melted into each other. Suddenly, Mark straightened and gently pushed Myrna away.

He traced her face with a gentle finger. "Lady, you don't have a thing to worry about. Your body is telling you, and me, you want me as much as I want you. But if we don't stop right now, we'll miss dinner and Scarlett will wonder what we're up to." He kissed her lightly and stood up. "Now, where the hell did that ring go?"

Myrna laughed and they both dropped to their knees and crawled around on the floor until the diamonds shot their fire from under the coffee table. Mark picked it up, and as they sat on the floor, he slipped it on her finger again. "Now, it doesn't come off until our wedding day." He helped her to her feet, then held her once again and kissed her. "Okay?"

With his arms around her, her cheek against the soft fabric of his jacket, the wonderful smell of him, Myrna felt completely safe and almost forgot her fear. Mark stepped back. "I have to stop this. Come on, let's get Scarlett and go down to dinner." He took her hand and they went to Scarlett's room.

Before they went into the bedroom, Myrna stopped, and turned to Mark. "I think it would be best if we took her to Mrs. Neumann's for the night. I'm afraid she'll wake up and be scared in a strange place. Do you mind?"

"Of course not," he said. "As soon as dinner is over, we'll take her. Do you have to call Mrs. Neuman?"

Myrna returned to their bedroom and called Mrs. Neumann, who said she would be delighted to have Scarlett spend the night.

"That's all settled," she said, and opened the door to Scarlett's new bedroom.

The little girl was lying on her new bed, on top of the bedspread, sound asleep, with a stuffed cat in her arms. Her patent leather Mary Janes were neatly placed on the floor beside the bed. "I hate to wake her," Myrna said.

"She'll be hungry when she wakes up, and confused in a strange house," Mark replied. "Better wake her now."

Myrna brushed the tumble of wild red curls. "Scarlett, honey, wake up. It's time for sup. . .er…dinner."

Scarlett moaned softly and hugged the stuffed cat closer.'

"Wake up, baby," Myrna said. Scarlett made a face, stretched and rubbed her eyes before opening them.

She looked around. "Where are we?"

We're at Mark's house. You're in a new bed that belongs just to you, but you have to get up now. It's dinner time."

Scarlett sat up and laid the stuffed toy on the pillow. "Go to sleep, kitty cat," she said, then slid off the bed. Myrna picked up her shoes and put them on her. Scarlett looked up and saw Mark, and for an instant her eyes went wide in surprise and a little fear. "Oh, I know who you are. You're going to be my new daddy," she said.

"That's right," Mark replied. "Are you hungry? Christer made something special for you."

Scarlett nodded and slid off the bed.

After dinner, Myrna told Scarlett, "I think you would sleep better if you went to Mrs. Neumann's tonight. I called her and she said she would really like it if you slept over.'

"Where are you going to sleep?" Scarlett's small face crinkled in a puzzled frown.

"I'm going to stay here tonight," Myrna replied. "Mark and I have some things to do." Mark coughed to stifle a laugh. "I'll be home to get you ready and walk you to school."

"Will Mrs. Neumann let me make cookies?"

"It's a little late for that right now. Maybe in the morning"

Scarlett thought for a moment, then said, "Okay."

Myrna found a large paper bag folded in a closet drawer and put the pajamas, the yellow dress, new socks and shoes and a pretty blue coat from the closet into it. "All right. You're all packed and ready to go. I'll bring some more of the new clothes in the morning."

After dinner, Scarlett said goodbye to Inge and Christer, then went out on the porch while Mark brought the Mercedes to the steps. By the time they reached Myrna's apartment, Scarlett was asleep. Mark carried her to Mrs. Neumann's porch and rang the doorbell.

"Ah, she is asleep already," Mrs. Neumann said. "I have the couch all made up for her."

"She had a nap, so she may wake up," Myrna said.

"That's all right. I will read her a story if she does."

Mark laid Scarlett on the sheet covered sofa, and Myrna pulled the blanket over her and kissed her forehead. "Night, night, darling."

Mark turned the car into the drive at the farm and touched the garage door opener. The door rolled open and he parked it. Myna got out and waited until Mark joined her, took her hand and went to the house.

"Why don't you go into the den. I left the television on, and you can watch while I pour us some wine?" She sat on the couch, kicked off her shoes and curled her legs under her. Canned laughter came from the television set, but Myrna paid no attention to it. Part of her body shivered in anticipation of what was to come, but part of her mind held on to the fear.

Mark set two glasses of deep red Pinot Noir on the end table and sat beside Myrna. He put his arm around her shoulders and pulled her close. His body close to hers wiped everything else out of her mind. He gently began to caress her breast. She gasped at the pleasure that coursed through her entire body, and lifted her face for his kiss. "I've waited so long for this," he whispered and his hungry mouth found hers.

He broke away. "That's enough," he said. "We don't need the wine." He stood, crossing the room to turn off the television and bank the fire. "We're not waiting any longer," he said, took her hands and raised her from the sofa. "Our bed awaits," he laughed. He put his arm around her waist and guided her up the stairs to the blue bedroom.

"Finally. We're alone, and there's no more waiting," Mark said. He took her in his arms, bent his head and kissed her gently. Myrna shivered. All the strange feelings deep in her body whenever Mark kissed her seemed to gather in one place and took control. "Yes," she said.

He unzipped her dress and slipped it over her shoulders. It dropped to the floor. He slid the straps of her slip off her arms and it fell on top of the dress. He unfastened her bra, but left it on. "O-oh. A garter belt." He smiled, picked up her clothing and laid them carefully over the back of the sofa. "Sit down," he said, and she sat on the edge of the bed. He unfastened the garters, carefully removed her stockings, kissed each of her feet, then reached under the garter belt and pulled off her panties, then tucked the garters under the fabric of the belt.

He sat beside her and took off his shoes and socks. His feet were long and slim. He stood, unbuttoned his shirt and tossed it across the sofa back, followed by his pants. Black curly hair covered his chest, arms and legs, tapered to a thin line that disappeared inside his jockey shorts. Myrna tensed for a second when she saw the bulge inside the shorts, remembering. Mark misunderstood the look on her face. "Yeah. I know I'm a furry bear, but it won't hurt."

"It's okay," she said. "I like it." Her fear vanished when he kissed her and pulled her down on the bed beside him. He cradled her in his arms, and his kisses became more insistent as he slipped the bra off her left arm, then the other. He caressed her breasts, then slid his hand down, over the garter belt and let his hand rest against her bush. Feeling the weight of his hand, warm and comfortable calmed her shivering. He bent over her and circled her left nipple with his tongue, sending bolts of electricity through her body. She arched her back, aching to get closer to him. His hand remained on her bush, but a finger went inside her vagina, rubbing slowly, gently. She felt herself getting wet, afraid for a moment she had wet herself, but the rubbing continued. He took her breast into his mouth and sucked it lightly. Myrna cried out and began to pant. Mark's finger continued to rub, slowly increasing the intensity until she was ready to scream.

He stopped, caressed her vulva and sat up. He reached across her to the bedside table and removed something from the drawer. "Will you take off my shorts?"

She sat up and he stood while she hooked her fingers around the elastic of his shorts and pulled them carefully over the bulge. He kicked them off and sat back down and slid a condom over the hard penis. "I want you pregnant, but not for a long time," he said, and pulled her back down on the bed. He kissed her on the mouth, his tongue finding hers and sucking it, then kissed each nipple and all the way down to her garter belt, which he unfastened and tossed on the floor. Again, he rested his hand on her bush and gently inserted his finger until she was writhing and panting. She was beyond thinking. Delicious sensation was all she knew. She reached for him, rubbing her hands across his chest, the soft hair, and beneath it, his hard nipples. Her legs spread of their own accord. Her body opened wide. Mark lowered himself between her legs, bracing himself on his forearms.

Myrna cried out, "Oh, please. I want you."

"My god, darling. I've waited such a long time. You are so beautiful." He entered her carefully, a little at a time. She raised her hips to take him. "Put your legs around me, sweetheart."

She did, and he slid into her and began to rock slowly. Myrna pulled her legs tightly around him, rocking with him until he began to thrust deeply. Her whole being was centered on the feel of his hardness deep inside her, building and building until it seemed she could never get enough. She lost any sense of control and cried in joy, her entire body shuddering again and again with pleasure that she had never imagined, Mark wrapped his arms under her and thrust hard and fast until he exploded, shouting "Darling Myrna." She felt the hardness begin to diminish, but she held him, not wanting him to move. He felt so good inside her – and on top of her. She never wanted to be separated from him. She ran her hands through his sweaty hair and kissed him hard. "I love you," she said.

Mark rolled to the side to take his weight off her, still inside her, and held her close, again caressing her breasts. He felt so good inside Myrna she didn't want to move and when he touched her swollen nipples, her body climaxed again.

"After that, I am your slave." Mark said. "I love you, Myrna, with my soul and with my body," Then he said, concerned, "Are you all right? I didn't frighten you?"

In response, Myrna moved closer so his penis was deeper insider her. "And I love you, soul and body. Nothing has ever felt so good. You couldn't possibly frighten me. I just want more and more."

"Me, too," he laughed, and kissed her mouth, her breasts, her belly, and pulled out of her to kiss where his ejaculation and her wetness mingled.

Myrna woke, confused for a moment by the strange bed and Mark's arm around her, one hand covering her left breast. Then she remembered the long night of lovemaking, and smiled. She eased Mark's hand away, and slipped carefully out of the bed. Asleep, he looked like an entirely different person. She bent and kissed his cheek. He muttered, and turned on his stomach, still sound asleep.

She picked up the silk robe and tiptoed into the bathroom, closing the door quietly. He must be tired, she thought, as he didn't move when she again tiptoed past the bed and opened the door.

Inge was setting the table when Myrna entered the kitchen. "Would you like a cup of coffee?" she asked.

"Yes, thank you." Myrna hesitated. "Mark said you bought all those beautiful clothes for Scarlett and me, and planned her bedroom."

Inge placed a steaming cup of coffee on the counter in front of Myrna. "I hope you don't mind. Mark asked me to do that, but I told him you would probably prefer to do it yourself. He said he wanted to surprise you."

"I can't imagine me buying clothes like that. I'd make all the wrong choices.'

Inge smiled. "I doubt that." She paused. "Christer and I are so glad for you and Mark. We have known him and worked for him for a long time and it is so good to see him happy. He is a good man, but he works too hard. Never takes time for himself. I think you will change that."

"Thank you," Myrna said. "I hope I can make him happy all our lives. That's all I really want. You are going to Seattle with us, too, he said. That's wonderful. I want to get to know you both better." She set the empty coffee cup down. "Great coffee. Now, I think I'd better get dressed."

Myrna offered to help Inge clear the coffee cups. "No, that is my duty," Inge said. "Christer will begin breakfast for you and Mark."

Myrna ran up the stairs and went into the bedroom. Mark was awake, and sitting on the edge of the bed.

"I didn't dream it. You were in my bed and we did make love all night." He reached out and pulled Myrna to him. "Come here, you amazing lover." He sat her on his lap and kissed her, opened the robe and brushed his hands over her breasts and on her mound. "I'm ready to start over."

"Well, I'm not just yet. Christer is preparing our breakfast, and I need a shower." She slid off his lap and pulled him to his feet.

"All right, but I'm not really hungry for food right now."

Myrna went into the bathroom, removed her robe, went into the large glass-enclosed shower and turned on the water. It was pleasantly warm and she took a handful of shampoo from the bottle on the shelf and soaped her hair. While the water poured over her head in a rinse and her eyes were closed, she felt Mark's hands rubbing her back. She shook the water from her eyes and turned. "What are you doing?"

"I'm bathing my beautiful princess," he said, gathering another handful of liquid soap and rubbing it over her breasts and her entire body, including between her legs and down to her feet. His naked body had a significant erection. Myrna took a handful of soap and began to wash him, including the erection. He pulled her to him and kissed her hard. She opened her legs to take him in, and they let the water slick their bodies as they moved to their own rhythm, until he shouted her name and she moaned in pleasure.

"That was the best shower I've ever had," Mark said, laughing. "God, what we've been missing."

Myrna caressed him. "Well, we won't miss it anymore," she said. "Come, we'd better get dressed. I have to get home in time for Scarlett to go to school, and I have to go to work this afternoon."

They stepped out of the shower and Mark picked up the thick towel and rubbed her hair and her body. "You won't be going to work," he said. "I want you and Scarlett to move in here right now."

"I can't do that. It would take Scarlett away from her school."

Mark began to dry himself with the towel. "You mean we can't get married until school is out next June? I plan to be in Seattle by first of the year. I want you and Scarlett with me."

"No. I want to get married right away, but I can't just uproot Scarlett right now and then again when we go to Seattle."

"I understand. We can work something out. But you aren't going back to Department 21. As far as I'm concerned, you're my wife in every way but the paperwork, and my wife is not working in Department 21."

"Give me a week or so to get things settled, please."

Mark snapped the towel. "I'll give you, and Jack, two weeks' notice. Then you will start preparing for our wedding and your role as my wife." He turned to her with a smile and cupped her face in his hands and kissed her hard, possessively. "There, that settles it. Now, I have to scrape off this beard, then we'll go see what magic Christer has prepared in his kitchen."

"I didn't know we were going to be staying all night, so I didn't bring any clothes," she said.

Mark turned, his face half covered with shaving soap, "Who do you think that closet full of clothes is for?"

"I thought that was for when after we're married."

He shook his head. "Silly girl. Go find something to wear."

Myrna found underwear in what Mark called her dresser and wrapped the silk robe around her. In the big walk-in closet, she looked through the two racks of dresses, blouses, jackets and slacks, even shoes, trying to find something to wear to work. "There's nothing here that I can wear in the plant. Nobody there wears stuff as expensive as this."

Mark, wearing nothing but jockey shorts, was in his closet. He pulled a light blue shirt from the hanger and put it on. "Well, find something to wear until you get back to your apartment. You can put on one of your old dresses there."

Myrna finally chose a gray wool skirt, a navy blue and white striped blouse and black pumps with a medium heel. She had found sheer nylon stockings in the dresser and a garter belt to hold them up. A full-length mirror on the wall had a padded bench near it. *I guess that means I get dressed in here, or do I take these things into the bedroom,*" she said softly to herself.

When she finished dressing and returned to the bedroom, Mark was knotting a navy and white striped tie. "Did you see a long, narrow jewelry box in the top drawer of your dresser?" he asked.

"No. Was I supposed to?"

"If you did, you did. If you didn't, you didn't," he replied with a smile. "Nothing 'supposed to' about it. Anyway, go get it out."

Myrna found the black velvet box, and opened it. A thin silver chain lay inside.

"That's a platinum chain," Mark said. "When you go to work in Department 21, put your ring on it and hide it inside whatever you're wearing. That's not the kind of jewelry that should be worn in a factory." He looked in the mirror and patted his tie. "Come here, I'll put it on you."

"Do I have to put the ring on it now?"

"No, silly. I just want to show you how to open and close the clasp." The chain was so fine she hardly felt it against her neck. "It's so thin. Won't it break?"

"No unless you pull on it really hard." He removed it and showed her how the clasp worked.

"I know the ring is expensive, but I did kind of want to show it off, especially so Betty would see it. It would make her turn green."

"Well, she can get green after the wedding when you won't be there anymore."

"Then, I won't see her do it."

"Do you really want to see her any more no matter what."

"Well, no. Not really."

"Okay. You look lovely in that outfit, but then you look nice in anything." He gave her a hug and kissed to top of her hair. "Have I told you I love you, and I'm so proud of you?"

"Not in the last ten minutes, and . . ." she took a big breath and said quietly, "I know now that I really, really love you. I can't even think about not being with you."

He put his arms around her and held her close. "Why didn't I find you a long time ago?" He kissed her hard, then stepped away and grinned. "No more of this. I have to go growl at the help. Except this morning I have a hard time growling."

Myrna laughed. It was kind of strange to hear him make a joke. "I'd better make the bed before I go down," she said

"Do you want to put Inge out of a job? Come on, I do have to go. I have a meeting in an hour."

A half hour later, the Mercedes stopped in front of Myrna's apartment

"See you later, darling. Love you." Mark said as Myrna opened the door and turned to get out.

"I love you, too," she replied as she stepped out of the car. She leaned back in just before she closed the door. "Just don't growl too loud at the help."

Mark laughed, engaged the gears, and drove off.

"You are home," Mrs. Neumann appeared at the railing of her porch. "I was worried a little."

"We were at Mr. Weston's house." Myrna held up her left hand. "See my beautiful ring."

Mrs. Neumann rushed down the porch to the steps to where Myrna stood. "You are engaged?"

Myna felt like her smile would split her face as she spread the fingers of her hand to display the ring.

Oh, my. So beautiful. So expensive." Mrs. Neumann gushed. "How soon will you be married."

"We haven't decided that yet. Soon, though," Myrna replied. "Well, I have to go get Scarlett settled."

Chapter 25

David Holman sat at his desk, staring at the legal pad in front of him, law books open but ignored. He was supposed to be writing a brief for a drunk driving trial, but his mind kept segueing into a picture of a small girl with red hair. He was sure the girl with Weston at the club was the one from the greasy spoon, and all he could see of the kid was that bright red hair tossed with curls that would look like his if he grew it long. Maybe he panicked for nothing. Mark Weston wouldn't be dating a girl like that, much less be marrying her as the scuttlebutt said. It had to have been a mistaken identity. With a sigh of relief, he turned back to the brief.

The words still blurred in front of him. He hadn't been able to concentrate on much of anything since his father's ultimatum. People in the office gave each other funny looks whenever his father passed him in the hall without looking at him. He had to lie to Carol when she wondered why his parents no longer invited them to their home or called.

But his mind wouldn't let go of the red-haired child. In the whole club restaurant, she and he were the only redheads. Did anyone else notice? Of course, lots of kids had red hair. Well, not really. Especially, the bright red with tight curls like his. Was she really his, the way the old bag said? Suddenly, the urge to see for himself was too strong to deny.

David glanced at the clock. Eleven o'clock. Almost lunch time. He couldn't wait for the detective to find her. Where could he find out where she lived, or where she went to school? If she went to school. Was she old enough? Maybe he could find out at the school board office. He reached for the phone book, looked up the administration building of Newport City's public schools and picked up the phone. When the operator answered, he said, "This is David Holman, of the Holman law firm. I need some information about a student for a case I'm working on, but I don't know which school she attends."

"I'll transfer you to Miss Perkins," the operator said, and the line went silent.

A few seconds later, a different voice identified herself as Miss Perkins, director of enrollment. David repeated his request, and added, "I think her last name is Schroeder."

Miss Perkins said she would have to look up the information, and he heard a drawer open and papers shuffled in the background. Then Miss Perkins' voice returned.

"We have a Michael Schroeder in the fifth grade at Adams Street School. The only girl is a Scarlett Schroeder in kindergarten at Henniman School."

"The girl is the one I'm looking for. Thank you for your help," David said, and hung up.

The school confirmed that Scarlett Schroeder was, indeed. a kindergartner at the school and that afternoon kindergarten students were dismissed at 3:00 p.m. David replaced the phone and leaned back in the chair, surprised at the excitement he felt.

The thought of lunch nauseated him, and he made himself work on the drunk driving brief until 2:30, when he told Shirley he had an appointment and left his office. Henniman School was only ten minutes away, and he parked across the street. A few cars were also parked in front of the school, and several women stood on the sidewalk. A bell rang, loud for something inside a building, then he noticed the big round bell high on the outside of the school. Seconds later, the door opened and a stream of small children poured through. They separated into different directions at the end of the walk to the entrance, some going to cars and others meeting mothers, he assumed.

David's breath caught in his throat. It had to be her. The red hair blazed like the sun. She stood talking to another little girl for a moment, then turned east alone, walked to the corner and stopped, looking around as if expecting someone. Moments later, a heavy-set woman, her gray hair pulled back in a bun, walked as fast as her stocky legs could move and crossed to the corner where the girl waited. She spoke to the child and took her hand and recrossed the street, David watched as the pair walked down the sidewalk, the child skipping beside the woman. Why wasn't her mother meeting her? Was that the woman who was sending the letters and pictures? She fit the way he imagined her, old and frumpy.

But the little girl, Scarlett was her name. He watched until he could see nothing but the red hair bouncing as she skipped. As he watched, his chest felt tight and it was suddenly hard to breathe. There could be no doubt. That was his child. That hair was the Holman identity in Newport City. It was always remarked in news stories on the radio and in the newspapers. If she had green eyes, that would cinch it. He had to get her up close so he could see her eyes and her face. Did she look like him? How could he get that close to her?

What was she like? From what he could see of her, she was cute and she had a lot of energy. Was she smart? She seemed to be happy. For a second, he had a crazy idea. Maybe he could approach Carol, carefully, and adopt her. Her mother was hooked up with Mark Weston. She might welcome a way to get rid of the child. Of course, Carol would see the resemblance right away. She, who wanted a baby more than anything else in the world, who had gone through all the medical stuff to make it happen, only to be told now that it never would. She who was adamant about not adopting, much less a child he had fathered on another woman. She'd kill him. Adoption was out. There was no way he could claim her without a scandal.

Scandal. That brought him back to earth. That's the only way this was going to end. He couldn't remember a time when he didn't know he was to be the best of all the Holmans. Grade school in his neighborhood school, a neighborhood where all the homes were almost as big and palatial as his, but when it came time for junior high school where he'd be thrown in with kids from all over town, he was shipped off to Randolph-Macon Academy in Virginia. High school was Groton School in Massachusetts. Then Yale and Yale Law, and finally back to Newport City to hone his legal skills. A proper marriage to Carol, the daughter of a prominent local doctor. Nothing ahead but Congress and ultimately, Chief Justice of the United States Supreme Court.

None of those plans included a red-haired little girl, the result of a stupid bet. He absolutely had to make sure the mother was the girl from the greasy spoon and that the kid really looked like him. Now, especially since, as rumor had it, her mother was going to marry Mark Weston. They'd be in the same social circle, going to the club. Sooner than later, someone would see the resemblance and the truth would be out. His father was angry now. If she showed up in the flesh, the old man would kill him.

Well, no point in sitting in the car, stewing about it. The bell rang again and bigger kids came through the door. Nobody waited for them. They were old enough to walk home by themselves. David started the car and drove away.

That night, he tried to make love with Carol, but for the first time in his life, he failed. She cried, blaming herself. "I'm only half a woman now. I can't even get you to make love with me." She turned on her side, and began to cry softly.

"It's not your fault,' he put his arm around her. "I've heard it happens sometimes as a guy gets older. I don't care about not having babies. Please, don't cry.""

Carol pulled farther away from him and buried her face in the pillow, still sobbing. "I don't believe you."

David rolled to his back and put his arm across his forehead, Carol's sobs fueling his guilt. The weeping finally stopped and her deep breathing told him she was asleep. He finally fell asleep, only to dream about a red haired little girl, and his father's blazing eyes when he saw her for the first time, and he would see her. There was no doubt about it. He woke in a sweat. Careful not to wake Carol, he got out of bed and tiptoed downstairs to the den. He went to the liquor cabinet and opened the first decanter he came to. The fiery whiskey burned his throat but he poured a second and a third until he didn't feel anything anymore. What was he going to do? Why had he gotten himself into this mess? How could he get out?

He picked up the newspaper. Maybe he could read himself to sleep. A small headline on an inside page caught his eye. *"Child dies after fall from a swing."* The story told of a boy who fell out of a swing in Holman Park where the family had gone to picnic. The child had suffered a skull fracture and died a day later.

Suddenly, David sat up straight in his chair. Of course. A perfect solution. He swallowed the last of the whiskey in the glass, got up, went back to bed and fell asleep at once,

Chapter 26

Myrna and Scarlett, dressed in their ordinary clothes, swung hands as they walked to the little park nearby. Fall was announcing its approach with bright reds and yellows among the dark green leaves, like the first gray hairs reminding the recently-young of mortality. The air even smelled like fall, crisper, cleaner. A smattering of leaves had fallen to the sidewalk, and Myrna and Scarlett scuffed through them. "I like the scrunchy sound the leaves make when I step on them," Scarlett said.

When they reached the little park, Scarlett dropped her hand and ran to the swings, rocking in the light wind. Myrna set the brown paper bag with their lunch on the picnic table in front of the swing set.

"Mama push me," Scarlett called, climbing into a swing and pumping her legs to get a start. Myrna stood behind her and pushed, sending Scarlett's skirt fluttering behind, her short legs pumping hard. "Higher, Mama."

The swing was at least four feet off the ground at the top of the arc. "That's high enough," Myrna said, and stepped away. She let Scarlett pump until she got tired and the swing slowed to a stop.

Scarlett slid out of the swing. "I want to go down the slide now,"

"All right, but that's the last. It's time to eat. Aren't you hungry?"

Scarlett answered by running to the slide. Her legs stretched from one step to the next until she reached the top, sat down and pushed. "Whee!" she shouted as she slid down.

Myrna shook her head in wonder. When she was Scarlett's age and Uncle Ernie took her to the park, she was too scared to go down the slide. Once, she even got to the top, but the sight of that silver path that ended a long way down made her cry and back down the steps, much to the disgust of the kids behind her. "Crybaby." "Scaredy cat," they had taunted. Nothing frightened Scarlett.

After their picnic of baloney sandwiches, an apple and one of Mrs. Neumann's oatmeal cookies each, they scuffed home through the leaves, laughing. Scarlett put on her new yellow dress. She pirouetted, making the skirt ripple around her legs. "Now, I have two new dresses. Can I wear my pink dress tomorrow?"

"No. You might tear it or get it dirty or something," Myrna replied.

"I wouldn't spoil it. I would be very careful."

"I'm sorry. It isn't a school dress. I don't wear my pretty blue dress to work, do I? It's a special dress and I don't want anything to happen to it."

"But you're gonna visit my class and I want to look real pretty."

"That's nice sweetie," Myrna said, "but you look nice in the new yellow dress."

Scarlett put on her yellow dress and her brown school shoes, and proudly tied the laces all by herself, and they again walked through the leaves to Henniman Elementary School. The smell of old shoes and chalk dust took Myrna back to her own grade school days; school was the only place where she was happy. Scarlett tugged Myrna's hand to her classroom.

"Miss Ellison. My Mama's come to visit," she called to the petite young woman behind the desk.

"Isn't that nice, Scarlett." Miss Ellison had blonde hair and a round sweet face. "So nice of you to visit, Mrs. Schroeder. I love to have parents visit. Then they have a better feel for where their child spends the day. Scarlett, come take your mother to the Visitor's Chair." She smiled at Myrna. "The Visitor's Chair is a special honor. It's the only adult-sized chair in the room besides mine, and I won't torture parents by having them sit in one of the children's chairs." She giggled. "Your knees would be on your chin. Besides, it's a real thrill for a child to escort a parent to the Visitor's Chair."

Scarlett seemed an inch taller as she led Myrna to the Visitor's Chair in the back of the room and later when she introduced her to the class. Miss Ellison told the children to sit on the story rug, and that Scarlett's mother would read the story. Myrna gasped. She couldn't sit in front of all those little children and read a story; she might make a mistake. Myrna opened her mouth to tell Miss Ellison she couldn't possibly read, but Scarlett looked at her, beaming, her eyes sparkling with pride. Myrna went to the story circle and folded herself into the tiny chair. Miss Ellison handed her *The Little Engine That Could.* As she read, the children chuffed and huffed along with the little train, and cheered when he got up the mountain.

"Very good, Mrs. Schroeder," said Miss Ellison.

After supper, Scarlett cuddled in Myrna's lap on the sofa for her favorite story, *A Dog Named Joe*. When Myrna closed the book, Scarlett looked into her eyes. "When we go to live at Daddy Mark's house, can I have a puppy, Mama?"

Myrna tickled her tummy. "I thought you liked the kittens."

"I do, but I like puppies, too."

"Well, right now, it's time for bed." She gave Scarlett a light pat on her bottom. "So, go brush your teeth and get your jammies on." Scarlett made a face, but slid off Myrna's lap and ran to the bathroom.

Scarlett climbed into bed. "'Night Mama. Today was the bestest day ever."

"I thought so too, sweetie." Myrna kissed the soft, cool cheek and gave the cover a pat. "'Night, 'night, sweetheart."

Myrna closed the bedroom door and went to the kitchen sink to wash the plate and drinking glass from Scarlett's bedtime snack. It felt like she'd walked a mile. Why was she so tired? Then, she smiled. She hadn't had a whole lot of sleep last night. It had been a wonderful day with Scarlett, especially when she'd read the story to the children. She'd see the pride on Scarlett's face if she lived to be a thousand. Scarlett was such a good little girl, and smart.

Dreams really do come true, she thought. She could almost forgive David Holman. Without that awful night, she would never have had Scarlett. And never in a million years would she believe that a man like Mark would want her. She looked at the ring on her finger, a mysterious looking star in the middle of the gorgeous blue, and all those diamonds flashing fire around it. She went into the living room and turned the radio on low, to a nice music station. She sat on the sofa, tucked her legs under her, picked up a magazine and waited for Mark's call.

Myrna was up early Tuesday morning, tiptoeing so as not to wake Scarlett. She filled the bushel basket with dirty clothes from the bathroom hamper and carried them downstairs to Mrs. Neumann's outside basement door. Mrs. Neumann was the cleanest person Myrna knew, even more than Ada who scrubbed the floor so hard they had to replace the linoleum every couple of years. The cellar's damp musty odor made her cough when she opened the door. The old round, pea green washing machine was set against the built-in laundry tubs, and Myrna connected the hose to the faucet and began to fill the washer. Thank heaven, Mrs. Neumann let her use the washing machine, and, that she had hot water. When the washer was full, she poured a cupful of Rinso into it and turned it on. The agitator quickly turned the soap powder to froth and Myrna carefully put each item of white laundry into the water. While the washer churned the clothing, Myrna filled the two sinks with cold water for rinsing.

"Mama. Where's my play dress?" Scarlett stood in the doorway, blinking.

"What are you doing outside in your pajamas? You'll catch your death."

"I couldn't find my play dress. I'm hungry. Can I get some Corn Flakes and listen to Mister Whisker?"

"Just a minute, honey. I'll be right there and go up and make you some breakfast. I thought you'd sleep longer."

After breakfast, the play dress was found, and Scarlett followed Myrna to the basement, where she watched when Myrna turned on the wringer, pulled a dripping dishtowel from the water and fed it between the rollers.

Scarlett giggled. "It's raining into the washing machine. Can I put the clothes through the wringer, Mama?"

"The wringer's dangerous, sweetie, but why don't you stand by the sink and put the clothes into the rinse water."

When the wash was finished Myrna emptied the sinks and drained the water from the washer into a bucket, then poured it into the sink.

"Come on, Scarlett, get that bag with the clothespins and you can hand me the clothes while I hang them on the line."

Because it was raining Myrna hung the laundry on ropes strung across the basement. They'd take forever to dry. It would be nice to have one of those new automatic clothes dryers. Maybe, when she was married to Mark. . .

Myrna fixed a light lunch and made a sandwich to take to work. Scarlett put on her yellow dress again, a brown coat and wooly red cap. Myrna sighed as she shrugged into her tired old navy blue coat on and tied a scarf around her head. She dreaded putting on her coat for the first time every fall. It meant that winter was just around the corner.

"Go get the umbrella, Scarlett, and your rubbers."

"I don't like rubbers. They make my shoes hurt."

"Wet shoes and wet feet feel even worse. Now get them, and I'll help you put them on."

Today, there was no scuffing of leaves. The pretty, crispy leaves of yesterday were a soggy mess of muck on the sidewalk, and they had to walk carefully lest they slip and fall.

"'Bye, sweetie," Myrna said as they reach the entrance walk to the school. "Remember to wait for Mrs. Neumann. Don't walk home by yourself." She stooped to kiss Scarlett's cheek, cool and damp from the rain. "I wish I could go visit your class again, but you be a good girl and do what Miss Ellison says."

"Okay." Scarlett turned. "Oh, there's Margaret Ann. Margaret Ann, wait up."

Myrna watched as Scarlett ran toward the door where Margaret Ann waited. For a moment two heads, one gleaming black and one that brought fire to the dreary day, bent together, then separated. A big boy flung the door open and ran outside. Scarlett caught it and held it for Margaret Ann to go inside, then suddenly turned toward Myrna and waved before she disappeared into the building. Myrna glimpsed a flare of fiery hair as the door swung shut.

She turned, and, head bent against the rain, walked to the corner and stood huddled in her coat to wait for the bus. The weather fit her mood, gloomy and wet. God, but she hated going back to that place with its stink and its noise, and Betty and her crowd. A wheeze of brakes roused her, and she swung aboard the bus as soon as the doors opened. She could stay home, like yesterday. Mark's money made it possible, but she just couldn't bring herself to spend it. A nagging little voice in the back of her mind still didn't quite trust him. Even the beautiful ring, which nestled between her breasts on its platinum chain, wasn't enough to quiet the voice.

229

"Hi, Myrna. Nice weather for ducks." Bill, the driver, grinned at her as her dime rattled through the fare box. "Got the little redhead off to school?"

Bill had been driving the bus since Myrna was old enough to ride it alone. "I don't even think the ducks would like this weather," she said. She sat in the first seat opposite the driver. "I visited Scarlett's class yesterday. Her teacher's real nice."

"Hey, I bet that was fun, and I bet she was proud as a peacock."

Myrna allowed a smile at the memory. "She seemed like it. She had to get up in front of the class and introduce me, and she took me to a special guest chair and I got to read a story to the class."

"You should have been a teacher."

"Hardly likely. I only got past the second year of high school."

"And now you're stuck at Weston Automatic Switch Company like half the people in town."

Myrna smiled, and thought, Not for long.

Chapter 27

David Holman sat at his desk, apparently busy with his drunk driving brief, but he couldn't think of anything but that newspaper story he'd read last night. The boy getting killed by a fall from a swing. When he got up this morning, he noticed that Carol went through the motions of fixing coffee and setting out cereal, but hadn't said much beyond, "Good morning.' He didn't pay her much attention. She'd get over his failure the night before. His mind was spinning. How could he get that kid to a swing set? That little park had one, he was sure. They all did. He had made plans this morning, but would they work. They had to work. His life, literally, depended on it.

It was finally two-thirty in in the afternoon. He cleared his desk It was time to act. His breathing became shallow and fast. Sweat formed a light film on his face. His bladder sent an urgent message. He picked up his briefcase, where he'd stowed a hat to hide his hair, folded his coat over his arm and left his office. "I'm off," he told Shirley. "See you in the morning." She smiled and nodded and returned to her typing. David stopped in the men's room, then ran down the steps to the first floor, avoiding the elevator. He walked quickly to the parking lot behind the building to his reserved space and got in the Cadillac.

As soon as he closed the door, he opened the briefcase and removed the black fedora. It appeared crushed, but he ran his hand around the inside and the brim and the folds disappeared. An ordinary black hat, a half-size larger than normal. It would cover his hair, but not be too obvious that it was too large. He put it on and looked in the rearview mirror to see whether any stray red hairs were visible. He tilted it slightly to one side and looked again. No hair. Finally, he slid his hand around the brim to make a fashionable snap-brim. One last check in the mirror. The hat looked good. He smiled. He'd have to wear a hat more often. But now, it was time to go.

David parked a block down the street from the school, got out of the car, crossed the street and walked to where several women waited for their children. "Hello," he said to a young woman, her hand on a stroller where a toddler slept. "My wife sent me to pick up our daughter, but I forgot to ask whether I should go into the building or wait outside."

"We wait out here," he woman said. "The school doesn't want us inside."

"Thank you," David replied. "Do you come every day?"

"Oh, yes, Bobby would get scared and cry, if I wasn't waiting for him."

"Do many kids do that? Cry, I mean."

The woman grimaced. "Not many. I don't know why Bobby gets so scared."

The big bell rang, and moment later a flood of young children poured out of the door. The woman, quickly pushed the stroller toward the walkway from the school, catching the hand of a small black-haired boy. Suddenly, he realized it may not have been such a good idea to talk to her. She would remember him.

What would he do if that old woman showed up right now? She apparently was late the other day. He looked down the street and didn't see anyone. Where was the kid? Maybe she didn't come to school today. Then he saw her, red curls bouncing as she spoke to another little girl, obviously very intent on what they were saying. They broke apart and the little redhead came down the sidewalk toward him.

Seeing her triggered a feeling that for a second grabbed his stomach. He had made this child. She existed because of him. *His* child. The only one he would ever have. For a moment, he dismissed his father's ultimatum and the complete disaster she would bring. He longed for that little red-haired girl. As suddenly, the emotion passed like an ocean wave reaching shore.

David walked up to her and took her hand, as if he were a parent. She looked up at him, startled, pulled her hand away and started to run. His long strides quickly caught up with her and he took her hand again, this time holding it tight so she couldn't get away.

"Let me go," she said, tugging at his hand.

One of the other mothers looked at them strangely as she walked past with her little girl, but continued toward a car parked nearby.

"Now, just settle down, Scarlett," David said. "I just want to talk to you."

"I don't know you, and my Mama said I wasn't supposed to talk to people I don't know."

"Your Mama is right, but I'm special. I know your Mama very well. Is your grandma coming to meet you today?"

"I don't have a grandma."

"Oh. Somebody told me your grandma met you after school every day."

"That's Mrs. Neumann. She lives downstairs and she takes care of me at night while Mama goes to work."

"Do you see Mrs. Neumann?"

Scarlett looked down the street. No one was in sight. "Sometimes, she's a little late. She like to listen to Stella Dallas on the radio and sometimes she forgets. She said I mustn't tell Mama."

"Do you keep many secrets from your Mama?"

"No, but Mrs. Neumann gives me a cookie or buys me an ice cream cone if I do."

Still holding the child's hand tightly, he looked at her carefully while they talked. His blood ran cold. There was no denying the small version of the face that looked back at him in the mirror. And the green eyes. They had the same flashing quality as his father's. Dragon eyes. No question. This child could ruin his life.

How could he get her to go to the park, a block away? "

"Scarlett, let's walk down the street together. Maybe we'll meet Mrs. Neumann coming after you." He started to walk. Scarlett resisted but his grip was too strong and she soon walked beside him. He looked down at her. "You know, Scarlett. I have a surprise for you. I know something about you that you don't."

"What's the surprise?"

David slowed his pace and looked down at her. "Did your Mama ever tell you about your Daddy?"

"My Daddy died in the war. My Mama told me."

"Your Mama said that because she wanted to protect you," he said. Was that too big a word for a little kid? "You see, your daddy didn't know about you. Your Mama told him, but she thought she was telling a joke. Know how I know that?" The red curls shook. "I know that, because I'm your daddy. That's the truth."

Scarlett stopped, and he gripped her hand harder. "'Tis not." Fire flashed from the green eyes, just like his father. "I'm going to have a new daddy now. Daddy Mark." She turned away, ready to go back to the corner.

David gripped her hand hard and pulled her back. "That's nice, but I really am your real daddy."

"I don't even know you." She pulled harder, struggling to get away. "Let me go. Go away."

David looked around. All the children and parents were gone. He pulled her back. She didn't reply, and the green eyes flashed fire.

This was harder than he had imagined. "See that white car over there? That's my car. Why don't we go there and wait?"

"My Mama said not to get in cars."

David sighed. Now what? He still had a tight grip on her hand. "I'll bet there are swings at the park down the street. Would you like to go there until Mrs. Neumann comes? Your Mama wouldn't want you standing on the corner by yourself all this time."

Scarlett stopped struggling and looked up at him. "OK."

David heaved a sigh of relief and she obediently walked beside him to the park a block away. A swing set was located at the far end of the park from the street. A picnic table sat a few feet in front of it. "Do you like to swing?"

Scarlett ran to the swing set, hopped on one and pumped her legs to make it start. "I'll push you," David said and trotted to stand behind her.

He pulled the swing back, surprised at her weight. She looked like she was light as a feather. He gave the swing a tentative push and she rocked away from him, pumping the air with her legs.

"Higher," she shouted, as the swing came back into David's hands. He made a strong push and she soared away from him, giggling. That was a positive sign. He pushed again, harder each time until the swing was nearly at the same height as the bar that held it. By now, Scarlett was shrieking with excitement, her short legs stretching as far as they could to make herself go higher. This would be easier than he thought.

It started to rain, and David slipped in the mud under the swing. Scarlett laughed as the swing went so high the chain buckled a little. David stepped back and jumped as the swing reversed. He grabbed the chain and held it. Scarlett screamed as she slid off the seat and lost her hold on the chain. She flew through the air, still screaming. There was a soft thud, like a melon dropping, and the screaming stopped.

David let go of the swing and ran to where Scarlett lay beside the picnic table. Her head was at a peculiar angle and there was a bloody gash at her right temple. Her eyes were rolled up into their sockets. He knelt and felt her carotid artery for a pulse. There was a slight flutter under his fingers. Then nothing.

Chapter 28

Myrna sat at her machine, hands automatically feeding parts to the die and hitting the actuator buttons. The beautiful sapphire ring felt warm on its platinum chain between her breasts, and she felt an excitement in her lower parts as she relived the night with Mark. How gentle he was, careful to make sure she was all right, that she had nothing to fear. And it was going to be that way for the rest of her life. It was hard to believe.

She looked up, something catching the corner of her eye: the company nurse in her crisp white dress, starched cap, white stockings and shoes, strode through the wide department door. The nurse walked directly to Jack, who was standing beside Betty's riveter, talking to her. The nurse spoke to him and they went inside the office and Jack closed the door. Myrna watched through the window as they talked, Jack picked up the phone and spoke briefly, then hung up. He and the nurse stood in the office, not speaking. What on earth was going on, Myrna thought.

Lydia stood beside her machine, alert, her eyes riveted on the office, as was every eye in the office. Suddenly, Mark Weston strode through the doorway. He glanced at Myrna and made a twisted smile as he turned the doorknob and went into Jack's office. The three talked together briefly, then Mark opened the door and walked to Myrna's machine. He stood beside her and rubbed his hand lightly across her back. "Come with me. We're all going to my office. We need a place where we can talk privately," he said.

"What about?"

"Something that doesn't need the whole department listening in," Mark said.

Myrna said nothing, but her heart was pounding faster than she thought anyone's heart could go. Why would they want to talk to her privately? She hesitated.

"Myrna, it's important," Mark said."

Lydia suddenly appeared beside the group. "If you have anything to say, say it to me."

"This doesn't concern you," he said.

"If it concerns Myrna, I'm going to be there," Lydia said.

Jack clenched his fists and Myrna heard him take several deep breaths. "All right," he said. "Anne, come back into the office. Lydia, you too. Myrna, we'll be back in a minute."

Lydia joined Mark, the nurse and Jack in Jack's office, and after talking a few seconds behind the closed door, Mark returned to Myrna's machine. She couldn't move. What had she done? Why didn't they talk to her?

"It's okay, Myrna," Lydia said. "We'll all go to Weston's office." Her face looked sad, not angry.

A gentle hand touched her arm. "Come, darling, I'm right here and I'll help you," Mark said.

"What do I need help for," she said.

"Please, honey, just come with us," Mark said.

Myrna sighed, shut off the machine and stood. "All right."

Mark took her hand and squeezed it. He kept a tight hold on her hand as the five of them made a strange, silent parade to Mark's elevator and rode it to the fifth floor.

They walked into the office, and Mark pointed to the black leather sofas. Jack, Lydia and Anne arranged themselves on the one with its back to the office, their expressions grim, and Myrna and Mark sat on the one against the wall, across the big glass coffee table. Myrna's heart began to pound again.

Nobody spoke. On the opposite sofa, Lydia sat with folded hands in her lap, her eyes on Myrna, the sad expression still on her face. Jack stared at the floor, legs spread, his hands folded between his knees. Anne, the nurse, stared over Myrna's head.

Finally, Mark squeezed her hand and said. "About an hour ago, Anne got a phone call from the police, Mrs. Neumann called them." He swallowed, took a breath and continued. "Scarlett didn't come home from school."

Myrna shook her head. "What did you say? Scarlett doesn't 'come home' from school. Mrs. Neumann goes to meet her there."

Mark repeated what he had said, speaking softly. "Scarlett wasn't where Mrs. Neumann usually meets her."

"Where is she?"

"They don't know." Mark continued, "Mrs. Neumann went to the school, but it was closed, and she called Scarlett's name until a neighbor came and asked what was wrong. They've been searching around the school and around the neighborhood ever since, but nobody's seen her. That's when Mrs. Neumann called the police. They've been searching, too, and haven't found her."

"But it's dark."

"That's what worries them. The police want you to go home so they can talk to you."

Myrna shook her head. "Scarlett can't be missing. I've told her and told her to always wait for Mrs. Neumann. She's such a good girl. She always minds me."

"Mrs. Neumann was late to pick up Scarlett," Mark said. "She had gotten engrossed in a soap opera on the radio and forgot the time."

"How late?"

"A half hour."

"A half hour? And Scarlett was standing there in the rain for a half hour? "Maybe she went somewhere to stay dry."

Mark touched her arm. "Come on. I'll take you home and you can talk to the police. They can answer your questions."

Jack turned to Lydia. 'You can go back to the floor, and get her coat."

Lydia stood up and went around the coffee table to Myrna, sat beside her and put her arms around her. "I am so sorry, honey."

Myrna buried her face on Lydia's shoulder and held her. She smelled like Lux soap with a touch of metal. "I'm so scared."

"I know you are, baby. Just have faith that everything's all right." Lydia stood and walked to the elevator door where Anne waited. Anne pushed the button and the door opened. They got in, the door whispered shut and the machine purred as it went down.

Myrna stared ahead. The big room blurred, the grandfather clock bonged as if it was a hundred miles away, but all she saw was a little red-haired girl standing on a street corner in the rain, waiting and waiting for someone who didn't come, maybe crying for her Mama. Did someone take her? There were all sorts of perverts running around. Myrna stuffed her fist into her mouth at the thought.

"Darling, we have to go. You'll feel better at home where you can talk to the police." Mark's hand on her arm was gentle, but insistent. She made herself stand up and let him guide her to where Jack stood beside the elevator door, which slid open just as they reached it.

Lydia stood beside the elevator when it reached the first floor, holding Myrna's coat and purse. Mark murmured "Thanks" and took the coat. He raised Myrna's right arm and slid it into the coat sleeve, and she reflexively put the left arm into the other sleeve. Where had her coat come from? "I'll get the car," he said, kissed her on the cheek and left.

Lydia guided her to the front door and to the Mercedes-Benz, opened the door and helped her get seated. Mark nodded his thanks, as Lydia closed the door, and turned the car away from the curb. A blast of cold air on Myrna's legs meant that he'd turned on the heater.

"It'll warm up in a minute," he said.

Myrna heard herself saying, "How could she be missing?"

"You know kids," Mark replied. "She probably met a new friend and went home with her, never thinking about waiting for Mrs. Neumann."

"But that isn't like her. I warned her and warned her to always wait for Mrs. Neumann."

Mark grunted. "And the one day Mrs. Neumann can't pull herself away from that damned soap opera, Scarlett goes missing."

Myrna leaned back against the seat and closed her eyes. She saw Scarlett's hair, bright even in the rain, as she and her friend . . . what was her name? . . . went into the school. Just a few hours ago? Her face all pink and happy as she went higher and higher on the swing. Yesterday?

"Here we are."

Myrna opened her eyes. Every light was on in Mrs. Neumann's part of the house. A police car, with its big light bulb on the roof was parked in front of Mark's car. She didn't want to get out of it, didn't want to go into that house, didn't want to see the police. Her own apartment, upstairs, was dark. Oh, God. Where was Scarlett?

Mark opened the door and Myrna got out on legs made of Jell-O. He held her around the waist as they walked across the tiny lawn and up on the porch. Mark punched the doorbell. She shivered. Maybe they found Scarlett. Maybe she would come running to the door.

The door opened, the light blinding Myrna for a moment. When she could see, it was a hulk in a rumpled suit. He stepped aside to let Myrna and Mark into the house. Myrna looked around the room, but no red hair shone from a corner. Only Mrs. Neumann rocking back and forth in her old rocker, sobbing into a handkerchief. When she saw Myrna, she dropped the handkerchief, ran to her and flung her arms round her.

"Oh, Myrna. I'm so sorry. It's all my fault. I'd rather die than have something like this happen."

Myrna disengaged from the woman's arms. "What happened? Why didn't you call me right away?"

The questions restarted the tears. "Oh, Myna. Please forgive me. I didn't mean harm. Amy just found out she was pregnant and she was afraid to tell George, and I couldn't leave the radio until I found out what he would say. When it was over, I realized that I was late meeting Scarlett, so I went just as fast as I could walk, but when I got to the corner she wasn't there. I went to the school and it was locked. I knocked on some neighbors' doors, but none of them had seen her. I came back home, calling her all the time, but she didn't come. When I got home, I called the police right away. I didn't call you because I didn't want you to worry. I supposed the police would find her right away. Then Sergeant Brown came back and said they couldn't find a trace of her, and I called the plant." The rush of tears started again. "I'm so sorry, Myrna. I love that child like my own. I don't know why I was so careless.'

The police officer cleared his throat. "Miss. The Mrs. here says you live upstairs. Why don't we go to your place?" Myrna nodded, numb.

Mark's arm was around her again, and Sergeant Brown followed them upstairs. Myrna unlocked the door and turned on the kitchen light. Scarlett's cereal bowl from breakfast, neatly rinsed, sat on the sink drainboard. "The living room's in here." She led the way, turned on the lights and sat heavily on the couch. Mark sat beside her, Sergeant Brown in the overstuffed chair opposite them.

"The Mrs. didn't seem to know any of Scarlett's friends. Maybe you could help us with that. By the way, I'm Sergeant Brown."

Myrna answered questions for what seemed like hours. Sergeant Brown telephoned the parents of Scarlett's friends that Myrna could remember. He called the teacher. The answer was the same from all. No one had seen Scarlett after she left school.

Oh my God, she thought. All the time I was thinking about our wonderful weekend, Scarlett was calling for me, hurt, needing me. I should have been thinking about Scarlett.

A heavy tread sounded on the stairs, followed by a loud hammering on the door. Sergeant Brown went to the door and another plain clothes policeman followed Sergeant Brown into the living room and sat down in the chair Sergeant Brown had left. Myrna couldn't get the words out fast enough. "Have they found her? Was she at a friend's house?"

Brown sat in the straight chair opposite the other officer. He looked at Myna, sighed heavily and looked at the floor through his folded hands. He cleared his throat. "This is Lieutenant Carpenter, Miss Schroeder. I'm afraid we have some bad news." Myrna bit her lip. Sergeant Brown squinted and he leaned forward, pulling a handkerchief from his inside coat pocket and held it out to her. "Here, Miss Schroeder."

Mark took it and gently dabbed blood from Myrna's mouth. Why was he doing that? She touched her lip and was startled to see blood on her finger and realized she had bitten her lip, which beat with pain. She looked back at the sergeant. The pain beat hard, like her heart; her stomach shook and she couldn't take a deep enough breath. Why didn't he say more? No. Let him be quiet. It was better not to know. That's what Ada always said.

The lieutenant cleared his throat and leaned forward, closer to Myrna. He, too, seemed to have a hard time deciding what to say, like he didn't want to say it. He was a big man, like Sergeant Brown, but younger and thinner, and his blue eyes looked sad. To Myrna, the only sound in the room was her pounding heart.

He made a big sigh, then looked directly at Myrna. His hands clung to each other. He cleared his throat, but when he opened his mouth, nothing came out. He harrumphed again and took a deep breath, and used it to say, "Miss Schroeder, I'm real sorry to have to tell you this. One of our patrolmen found your little girl's body. At least, it fits the description."

A heavy weight settled on Myrna's chest so hard she couldn't breathe. She went numb all over.

"At least, he found the body of a small red-haired girl in the little park near the school. She was lying in front of the swing set. It looks like she fell from the swing and hit her head on the picnic table."

A shaky faint voice came from somewhere. "Body?" The faint, shaky voice was hers.

Lieutenant looked away and Sergeant Brown studied his shoes. The lieutenant addressed the floor. "Yes, ma'am. The little girl he found is dead"

Myrna saw his mouth move, heard words, but all of a sudden, she was looking down on the room, like it was a dollhouse; one that has an open roof and you can look into the rooms. Everything was dollhouse size, too. There was the lieutenant, bent over in his chair, his hands still clasped, Sergeant Brown looking at her, a worried expression on his face. She saw herself sitting on the couch, and Mark sitting next to her with his arm around her. That was funny. How could she be sitting on the couch when she was up here, looking down on it all? As suddenly as she found herself on the ceiling, she was sitting on the couch. She could feel the scratchy cloth against her legs, and the weight of Mark's arm around her. He always smelled so nice, like a summer day.

"Myrna." Mark's voice was right in her ear, soft and sad. "Are you all right?"

Why shouldn't she be all right? She wanted to turn and tell him that, but she seemed to be made of glass; if she so much as twitched she would shatter into a million pieces. There was a soft roar, like what you heard when you put a seashell to your ear. Mark's arm squeezed tight. She tensed. He could break her.

"Myrna. Say something."

An enormous lump lodged in her chest, growing like a balloon. If she opened her mouth, it would burst and everything would come pouring out.

"Myrna?" Mark's voice sounded scared. Maybe she had better try to talk.

The balloon did burst and the words gushed out. "It couldn't be Scarlett. The little girl's. . ," She paused, took a breath, letting it out as "body." She swallowed, and continued. "I walked her to school this afternoon. I saw her talk to Margaret Ann. I saw her go into the school. Ask her teacher. She's in school."

The old man, Sergeant Brown, wasn't it, raised his head, his face looked like something was pulling it down. "We did talk to her teacher. School was out a long time ago. It's nine o'clock at night. We don't have a positive identification, but I'm sure it was your little girl. Is there someone in your family who could go to the hospital tomorrow and identify her? Your parents?"

"I don't have any parents. I just called them that. Ada and Ernie are my aunt and uncle.

" Why don't I call them," Sergeant Brown said.

"I don't want them anywhere near Scarlett."

"It's just to go look at her and tell us if that's who it is. It isn't something you should see."

"I'll go," Mark said. "I was going to adopt her, so she's almost my daughter."

"I want to go, just to tell you it isn't Scarlett. I know it isn't." Myrna couldn't sit any longer. She stood and started toward the kitchen. "See. There are her dishes from breakfast. Her jammies are on the bed. I can show them to you. She's a good girl. She always folds them up neatly and puts them on the bed."

Lieutenant Carpenter stood, and Sergeant Brown lumbered to his feet. "Maybe you should lie down, Miss Schroeder, get some rest," said the lieutenant. "I know this has been a shock to you. Is there anybody you want to stay with you?"

"No. I don't want to lie down." The glass that encased Myrna cracked a little, admitting a flame that burned right through her whole body. "O-o-oh God, why did Mrs. Neumann have to listen to that show? What happened to my little girl? Scarlett! Come to Mama. I can't lose you!"

Mark's arm was around her again, guiding her toward the bedroom. "No! I can't go there. Not without Scarlett." The two policemen were talking, but the sounds were beyond her. She was back on the couch and somebody lifted her feet up so she had to lie down. She closed her eyes. Maybe the pain would go away.

"Myrna." It was a woman's voice, soft and gentle. Myrna opened her eyes.

"Lydia? How did you get here?"

Lydia knelt beside the couch. "I told Jack I needed to come, and he brought me. He had to go back," she said. "And Mark's taking us both to my house."

"No." Mark's executive voice. "I'll take you home, but I'm taking her to the farm, where I live, and where she will soon be living."

"No, yourself," Lydia snapped in the same tone of voice. "She needs a woman, a mother, right now. My Mama knows her and she knows Scarlett, and she loves them both. She knows exactly what to do." She turned back to Myrna. "I called Mama and she has a bed all ready for you, and some hot tea and soup, and Mama does not take 'no' for an answer."

Chapter 29

David Holman drove aimlessly along the narrow two-lane highway, windshield wipers slapping away the sheets of rain sluicing down the Cadillac's windshield. The twin beams of the headlights illuminated only rain. David wasn't quite sure where he was, and he didn't much care. Just as long as it was away from . . .

From what? He had to think hard before he remembered. The red haired little girl. Scarlett. His little girl. Lying limp, her head twisted and bloody, on the wet ground. That telltale red hair floating around her head like a halo. She had green eyes. Dragon eyes, just like his father, like his. But he couldn't see the green. All he could see were the whites. Why was that? The crooked way her head tilted. The blood on her head. The flutter in her artery when he touched it. And then the flutter stopped. He'd killed his own child. The truth grabbed him in the gut, and the car slewed sideways. Wrestling it under control took his mind off the memory for a moment, but as soon as it was traveling straight, the panic returned. There must be a side road around here somewhere, he thought. I've got to get off the highway and think this through.

He hunched over the steering wheel, to stare through the rain and dark. A swath of gravel interrupted the roadside grass. He turned the wheel hard, narrowly missing the ditch, and drove a quarter-mile along the gravel tracks that passed for a road, stopped and turned off the lights. The rain and the dark closed around him. He lay back against the seat, limp, exhausted. Nausea swept through him and he opened the door and retched, but nothing came up; he'd rid himself of it all in the park.

He closed the door and rubbed his hand over his wet hair. That damned red hair. That's what caused all this. Why couldn't she have had her mother's genes? Black hair. He remembered that much. What in the name of Christ am I going to do? It had seemed like such a good idea. Just like killing a rattler that threatened him. That's what it was. Self-defense. That crazy old woman could destroy his whole life, even Carol's. Especially Carol's.

Nobody would ever know. Kids fell out of swings every day. It'd even be a relief to her mother. No more stigma. Life would be easier for her. She'd have all Weston's money. He relaxed a little. His stomach stopped shaking. Yes, that was it. Put it out of your mind. It didn't happen.

David looked at the dashboard clock. Six-thirty. God, Carol would be wondering what happened to him. He always called when he was going to be late for dinner. The panic came back. Can't stay here all night. What if someone comes down the road? I'd have to back out. That would give them plenty of time to get the license number.

He turned the key and the car purred to life, the lights bored through beams of raindrops, he shifted into reverse and slowly backed down the road until the taillights picked up the sheen of the wet highway. He turned right, backed onto the highway into the right lane, straightened the car, directed it back to Newport City, and stepped on the accelerator until the speedometer hit 70 miles per hour.

Twenty minutes later David let himself into his office. Everyone was gone. No one stuck around after five, not even his father. He strode across the dark waiting room to his private office, unlocked the door and switched on the desk lamp before he settled into the big leather chair. Maybe he'd better close the blinds, so no light showed into the street. The chair's springs squawked, and he felt a sweat break out. The pictures, the notes. Paul Kroeger. Who else did she send them to? Stop it. Get hold of yourself. You're a Holman. She's the bastard kid of a nobody. Who else in this town would ever connect you with her? Except her mother. Why couldn't he ever remember her name? Myrna. The kid's last name was Schroeder. Had to be her mother's name. That's it. No. Better make an effort to forget so you don't blurt it out at the wrong time.

He picked up the phone and gave his home number to the operator. "Hi, honey," he said. "Sorry I'm late. I was busy with a client and forgot the time. I'll be home in about a half-hour. Will that ruin dinner?"

Carol assured him dinner wasn't ruined, but she'd say that even if a roast had baked to cardboard. The sound of her voice brought him back to here and now. Nothing happened this afternoon. He spent the time with a client, in the client's home, on a confidential matter.

Chapter 30

Sarah's kitchen was warm and filled with the smell of a well-loved home, the kind of home Myrna wanted for Scarlett. Mark's arm around her waist guided her to a chair at the table.

"Sit down before you fall down," Lydia said.

Sarah placed a plate holding a bowl of golden soup on it in front of Myrna, fragrant steam curling from the soup. A row of soda crackers curved around the bowl. Mark sat opposite her, watching carefully.

"I know you don't feel like eating, but you must remain strong and this chicken soup will help," Sarah said. "When you're finished, I have some tea that will help you sleep. The bed's already made up."

Myrna knew she should say something, but couldn't get the words together. The soup smelled good, but her throat felt like a noose had snugged around it.

"Open your mouth." Mark held a spoonful of soup. Myrna opened her mouth and he slipped the spoon in. She swallowed the hot soup, rich with chicken flavor, hot and salty. It melted away the noose and smoothed out the spasms in her stomach.

"I'll take the spoon," she said. She ate slowly, savoring each spoonful, until the bowl was empty. The plate and bowl disappeared, replaced by a thin china cup, white, painted with pretty blue flowers, on a matching saucer. The tea was golden, too, and it tasted like spearmint gum. It tasted almost like the soup going down, only sharper.

When the cup was empty, Sarah said, "That's enough for now," and removed it. "Now, come with me." Myrna felt Sarah's arm around her and she stood, letting Sarah lead her. Lydia and Mark followed them upstairs.

"You can wait in the hall," Lydia told Mark. "There's a chair over by the window. He nodded and went to the chair, but stood and stared out at the darkness.

The big bed, made from some dark wood, stood in the middle of the small room, a white sheet was folded at a sharp angle across a blanket the blue of a summer sky. Thick pillows in their starched white cases, waited. Sarah lifted a nightgown, white, sprigged with pink flowers, from the bed and Lydia helped Myrna take her clothes off. The nightgown was soft on her body. Sarah turned down the sheet and Myrna eased under it.

The sheets were cool and smooth. The pillow comforted Myrna's hot, aching head. Sarah pulled the sheet and the soft blanket over her, and brushed a stray hair from her face with a cool, smooth hand.

"This feels good," she said. "I don't think I'll sleep, though."

Sarah smiled. "We'll go out now." She switched on the small lamp on the dresser, snapped off the overhead light, and then she and Lydia went out, closing the door behind them.

Mark stood beside the door. "Can I go in?"

"For just a few minutes,' Sarah said. "The tea will put her to sleep soon."

"Did you put something in it?" he asked.

"No. It's just an old-fashioned tea that helps you sleep."

Mark opened the door quietly and tiptoed into the bedroom.

Myrna turned on her stomach, wrapped her arms around the pillow and let the tears flow. Scarlett couldn't be dead. Not her baby. She'd worked so hard to make a good life for her. She was such a happy little girl, so good. Even when she had tantrums, she was really a good girl. How could she be dead?

A warm hand brushed across her cheek, and a gentle kiss followed. "That's a girl. Cry it out." Mark said.

Suddenly, his cheek was close to hers, scratchy, and wet. Wet? He was crying, too.

The next morning, Myrna sat in a hard, wooden chair between Mark and Sarah in the basement of the hospital, in the coroner's no-nonsense office. Lydia sat in another beside the big window with a heavy curtain drawn across it. The place smelled like bleach and something sickeningly sweet that clung to the back of Myrna's throat. The tan walls had no pictures, no certificates on it. Except for a half-dozen chairs like the one she sat on, placed against two walls, the only furniture in the room was a naked desk. Not even a grain of dust marred its dark shiny surface.

A white blur appeared outside the frosted glass of the door a moment before the door opened to reveal a man, who stood there for a moment as if waiting for applause. His ball of a head was trimmed with a fringe of dark hair. Heavy black-framed glasses were anchored around large flat ears.

Thin, frowning lips announced, "I'm Louis Ousley. Miss Schroeder." The "miss" was stressed ever so slightly.

His chin rested on a pillow of fat hiding his neck. The long white coat, buttoned from hem to the roll of fat seemed to wear him. Cuffed black trousers beneath the coat attached themselves to small feet in mirror bright black shoes. He looked like a toy that had a ball for a head, a bell-shaped body, and stiff legs that swung, like the clapper.

The shoes and legs made quick movements in Myrna's direction and a stiff white arm stuck out. When Myrna didn't shake the extended hand, it fell back in place. "Miss Schroeder," he said. ""Are you here to identify the child found in Holman Park last night?"

Ousley paused. Myrna nodded.

"We all are," said Mark, standing.

"She's my little girl. I'll identify her" said Myrna.

"In a moment," Ousley said. "First, I want you to know that although she died under unusual circumstances, we won't do an autopsy. Cause of death is obvious. She fell out of a swing and her head struck the picnic table. Her neck was broken and her skull was fractured. An unfortunate accident." He turned toward another door. "Please follow me."

"Wait a minute," Mark said. "It sounds like you don't really know the cause of death. I think you need to do an autopsy."

"It's pretty obvious," said Ousley, "and it would save Miss Schroeder considerable money."

"Money is no barrier." said Mark. "Do it."

Ousley paused, looking at Myrna and the two Negro women, and Mark. "You look familiar," he said to Mark," then said, "I know. You're Mark Weston."

"I'm Miss Schroeder's fiancé." Mark replied, in his executive voice.

Ousley swallowed. "Oh."

**Myrna stood and Mark stepped to her side and held her.

The coroner's small black feet under the bell of his lab coat led them to a large, cold clammy room that smelled like the waiting room. Myrna looked at the floor.

Ousley led them to a hospital cart covered with a sheet. A few ridges and lumps indicated a small body under it. He gently drew the sheet away from the head, and then stood at the foot of the cart like a sentry.

The halo of bright red hair fanned across the cart. Scarlett's eyes were closed and she could have been sleeping, except for the bloody smear on her forehead and her open mouth. Her small face had a smudge of dirt on it, and Myrna reached to brush it away. Her fingers, expecting to feel the warm satin skin, recoiled at the cold unyielding touch.

"Oh, no. Oh, god, no. Scarlett, wake up. It's Mama. Oh, please." The room spun and her legs gave way."

"Myrna," said a soft deep voice. She opened her eyes. She was lying on a narrow bed. The white paint on the ceiling, the cold damp smell of disinfectant was no place she knew. "Myrna," the voice repeated. She turned her head. A handsome man, his dark curly hair frosted with silver around his ears spoke to her.

"I'm Mark," he said. "Remember?"

Myrna remembered. Everything. Pain struck her like a wall of water, sweeping her away, spinning her every which way, nothing to hold on to. No way to stop it. A warm hand in hers stopped the spinning.

"You're in the hospital," Mark said, gently squeezing her hand, "You fainted. Are you feeling better now?"

Myrna rolled her head from side to side on the pillow. Pain pushed her under water, and a heavy weight pressed against her chest. She closed her eyes again. "Scarlett was on that cart. Her face was cold. So cold."

"Cry, dear. It helps," a soft woman's voice said.

How do you cry when everything inside you is dead, except the pain? Why couldn't she faint again? It was the only way to escape the pain,

Mark's warm hand massaged her arm. "It's all right. As soon as you feel strong enough to stand, we'll take you to Sarah's house. She can take care of you."

Myrna tried to make herself blank again, to bring back the merciful darkness. She almost succeeded, when angry voices from another room startled her awake. She couldn't make out what they were saying.

Mark went to the door and opened it a crack. "What is going on out here? Don't you know we have a sick girl in here? Have some care for her." He closed the door carefully and returned to Myrna's side.

Myrna made herself sit up. "I want to go home. I don't like this place."

"It isn't a good place for you, or anybody else, for that matter. Here, let me help you," Mark said. He put her shoes on her feet, and held her coat while she slid her arms into the sleeves. He held her around the waist while she waited for the room to settle down. Sarah opened the door to the hall. The three people there stopped speaking, as if someone had turned off a radio, and stared at Myrna.

Lydia, a young man with a notebook, and a policeman. Lydia glared at the reporter and the cop, as if she would like to punch them. "There's nothing here to interest the newspaper," she said.

"When a young kid dies in a weird way, it's news," the reporter said. "What was her name? Are those her parents?" he asked, indicating Myrna and Mark. He looked again. "Mark Weston. What're you doing here?"

"None of your business," Lydia snapped. "Get out of here." She turned to the officer. "Can't you get him out of here so these people can leave in peace?"

The policeman shrugged and said, "There's nothin' here for your rag, Tony. Get out of here."

"There's plenty here. Mark Weston for one," he said. "I'm not going anywhere."

Mark gripped Myrna's arm tightly. "Come on, ladies. Just ignore this nosey guy." He told Myrna to put her head down and led her at a fast walk out of the hospital and to his car, parked a few feet away. Lydia and Sarah flanked Myrna, so the reporter couldn't reach her.

Myrna would remember the next few days in blurred images, like a speeded-up movie. Sarah's warm blanket of comfort and care, Lydia on the phone, giving prickly answers to nosey people. People with sad faces. People bringing food. People saying words that Myrna never remembered. She supposed she answered them. Mark crying.

There was the funeral parlor with Mr. Ousley, wearing a black suit, who poured oily words over her and tried to lead her to a big room where a small white casket sat in front of a bank of more flowers than Myrna had ever seen. She flinched at his touch; Mark immediately took her arm. Mr. Ousley shrunk under his glare.

"Now, it's going to be hard, Myrna, but we're right here," Mark said, as they walked toward the white box. The closer she got to the white box, the worse the flowers smelled, like the time she sprayed her arm with all the perfumes in Morris's Department Store. The colors washed together until nothing was in focus but the white box.

"My, doesn't she look pretty," Sarah said.

Myrna studied the sheaf of pink roses that lay on the closed half of the box, tied with a pink bow that said "Mama," in gold paper letters. A lid, lined with quilted pink satin, was propped open next to the flowers. Myrna squeezed her eyes shut until a few rainbow sparkles floated across the black.

"Myrna, please look at her," Sarah urged gently. "You need to say goodbye to her."

Myrna shook her head. "I don't want to say goodbye to her. I don't want her to go away."

"I know, my dear, but one day you'll want to remember that you did."

Myrna took a deep breath past the lump in her chest. She opened her eyes and looked at the lid, then let her gaze find the pink satin pillow where flame red hair flared. She'd never see that red flame again. Don't think that. The blood had been wiped off the face, and her mouth was made into a little smile. Rouge colored her cheeks and pink lipstick her mouth. Lydia had gone to the apartment and gotten Scarlett's favorite pink dress, the one with the pinafore, and pink socks. She wore it now, with Mark's necklace on her breast. Her arms cuddled the stuffed cat from her bed at the farm.

Myrna turned away. What lay there on the pink cushion was not Scarlett; it was a doll made to look something like her.

The next night, there was something called a visitation, where she had to stand for hours while people came by and shook her hand or hugged her, or just stood there with a strange smile, saying, "I'm so sorry." The next day was the service, all sad music on a tinny organ, and a preacher saying something she never remembered. She sat in a small room with a curtain in front of it, with Mark, Sarah and Lydia beside her. When the preacher stopped talking, the room outside the curtained-off place got quiet. She heard heavy footsteps on the carpet, then a click. The lid on the box that held Scarlett had been closed. Something snapped in her head, as if the part of her brain that was Scarlett had broken off. She stayed in her soft chair, waiting for a reason to stand up.

"Come, Myrna. We have to go to the cemetery now. The cars are waiting," Mark said. His hand was gentle, but strong on Myrna's arm. Mark's hands were always strong, and with Lydia on the other side, she stood and put one foot ahead of the other until they went through a door. Mr. Ousley held the door open to a black car. Ahead of it was the big black hearse where the small white casket was buried under flowers.

The car followed the hearse to the cemetery behind a motorcycle policeman. The cemetery was a short way out of town, a flat place with a few trees and statues and wilted bouquets of flowers here and there. The hearse and the car stopped beside a tent on high poles that covered a hole in the ground. Myrna's shoe heels sank into the wet ground. It had rained ever since Scarlett. . ., but today the sun made the grass glow and warmed the September air.

David Holman drove slowly along Lincoln Street, past the Ousley Funeral Home. The parking lot looked full and cars lined both sides of the street. People were still going into the funeral home. Good God! Even Mark Weston. Weston looked up at the same moment and their eyes held for a second. David quickly looked ahead. Why would somebody like Weston go to this kid's funeral? Weston had taken the girl and the kid to the club.

Word had it that he was serious about somebody after his divorce. Strange a hot shot like Weston would pick a nobody like that girl, especially a girl that had a kid. More to the point, did Weston recognize him? He continued down the street. No law against driving on a public street. He could have any reason for coming this way. Cut it out! No reason for Mark Weston or anyone else to be suspicious of him.

He drove around the block from the funeral home and found a parking space a couple of doors away. What was going on in there? Were they talking about her red hair? That's the sort of stuff they said in funerals. Would anybody be there that would get the connection with him? After an eternity, people came out and got in their cars and left. Should he leave, too?

A frisson of fear ran down his spine when the motorcycle cop came down the drive, followed by the hearse, which turned right out of the driveway and would pass by where he was parked. David ducked down into the well of the passenger's seat as the police escort passed, followed by the hood of the big hearse that eased toward his windshield and slid past. He sat up and looked through the rear-view mirror. The cop was still escorting the hearse.

A glimpse of white caught his eye through the big window in the rear of the hearse, a small white casket almost completely covered with flowers. Tears filled his eyes and a lump gripped his chest. He couldn't turn away until the hearse was gone. A limousine followed the hearse. The family. Again, he bent low over the passenger seat, as if he were looking for something, so if Myrna were looking his way, she wouldn't see him. When he straightened, the hearse and limousine were out of sight, but he was locked into his parking space by a long line of slow moving cars.

Suddenly he was beyond caring whether anyone saw him. The pressure in his chest was too great. He lay his arms on the steering wheel, buried his head in them and sobbed. After a few minutes, he sat up, wiped his eyes and face with a handkerchief, started the car and drove back to his office. It was done. Nothing could change it. At least, now he could move on without worry. The threat was gone.

At the cemetery, the preacher talked some more and threw a handful of dirt on top of the small, pristine casket. Myrna wanted to scream, "Don't get it dirty." Wide straps held the white box over a deep, dark hole like a swing, That's where her baby was going to be, covered up with all that dirt Myrna thought. Mr. Ousley handed Myrna a rose from the casket and whispered to her to put it over the dirt.

254

Myrna dropped the flower onto the casket. She would never see her baby smile, hear her laugh or cry, never kiss her sleeping face. Never. Never. Never. She couldn't move. Why couldn't they put her in the hole with Scarlett?

"I know, darling," said Mark, his arm strong around her arm.

The strong arm led Myrna away from the hole, away from the people, away from the white box. They walked to a car, a large black one with a winged figure on the front. Mark slid into the back seat beside her, and Sarah on the other side. Lydia sat next to her mother.

"Mr. Weston thought it would be better if you went straight home instead of having to ride in that funeral car," said Sarah.

They walked into the house, greeted with an overpowering smell of food that made Myrna want to throw up. The big dining room table, which had been stretched as far as it would go, was covered with dishes of food. From the kitchen, Myrna heard laughter and the rattle and chime of china and glassware; the rich smell of coffee filled the air.

Sarah helped Myrna up the stairs and into the bedroom; she took off Myrna's shoes and Myrna let the soft mattress receive her exhausted body. Sarah pulled the blanket over her and drew the window shade. "You rest now. Try to sleep if you can," she said, then the door closed with a soft click.

Chapter 31

Mark Weston sat in a stiff overstuffed chair, his empty coffee cup dangling from his index finger, watching the stairs. Most of the horde that packed the McIntire's first floor was gone.

"Would you like another cup of coffee or a piece of cake, Mr. Weston?" Sarah McIntire stood beside him, holding a sleek silver coffee pot.

Mark stood. "No, thank you and please call me Mark. Actually, I'd better be going. I just hoped I'd get to see Myrna again."

"She was exhausted. The last time I looked in on her she was sound asleep." She turned; "Lydia, will you get Mr. Weston's coat?"

Sarah accompanied him to the hallway, and Lydia brought the coat and held it at arm's length, as if she couldn't tolerate being any closer. He put it on and had just finished slipping the top button through the hole, when the front door swung open, as if blown by a strong wind.

A woman planted her feet inside the sill. She was built like a concrete block, and was about the same color. Her coat was concrete gray, and a shapeless gray felt hat had been slapped down over gray hair twisted into a tight bun at the nape of her neck.

Ada Schroeder, Mark realized, watching fascinated as her face turned from red to purple. God, was she going to have a stroke right here? Those icy little eyes searched the hallway and the living room beyond.

"Where is she?"

The house went silent. People in the other room looked up and stared, then froze like the old game of Statues. After a moment, a woman looked at the cup she held halfway to her mouth, and set it down with an embarrassed laugh. The hum and buzz of subdued conversation restarted; something china crashed in the kitchen.

Lydia stood in front of the woman, arms akimbo, her face inches from the other. "Who the hell are you?"

"I want to talk to her. And you damn well know who I mean." The woman raised her right arm and jerked her thumb at someone behind her "Ernie, shut the door."

Mark saw the man behind her for the first time. Ernie Schroeder. He wore a green plaid jacket and a black stocking cap pulled down to his ears. His face was blank, closed tight. The door closed quietly, although in the shouting match between the two women it could have slammed hard and no one would have heard.

Mark glanced up at the stairs while the women yelled at each other. Myrna stood there in her stocking feet, gripping the banister with both hands as if she were strangling it. As he watched, her face transformed from Snow White to the Evil Queen.

The two women saw her at the same time. "There you are," Ada yelled. "Come on down here. You're coming home with me. I been looking for you ever since I first heard. How come I had to read about it in the paper? I had to tell everybody I didn't know nothin' about the brat. That was bad enough, but then I find out you're livin' with these niggers . . ."

"Shut up," Myrna screamed. She let herself down to the next step, still gripping the banister. "Scarlett's out there in the cold, under the ground hardly two hours." Another step down. "And you barge in here callin' my dead baby names." She stood on the bottom step, eye-to-eye with the woman. "Why ain't it you out there?" Tears poured down Myrna's face. "You ugly, evil old witch. If it wouldn't mess up Sarah's floor, I'd stick a blade in your fat gut right here and now and wash my hands in your blood.

"You push your way into this house and call the people who live here names. I've had more love and kindness from Sarah and Lydia in the last few days than I ever had from you in my whole life. Get out of my sight. I never want to see you again or hear you again or smell you again."

Myrna suddenly collapsed onto the step and buried her face in her hands, sobbing as if her heart would come out of her body. Sarah took a step toward her, but Mark was there first. He sat on the step and cradled Myrna in his arms, crooning.

The woman opened her mouth. Lydia stepped behind Ernie and opened the door. "Out," she said.

Ada raked her gaze over Myrna and everyone else, then turned on her heel. "Go on, Ernie. We know when we ain't wanted," she said, and shoved him outside. The house shook when she slammed the door.

Mark started to breathe again. He helped Myrna to her feet and up the stairs. "It's all right, baby. You just cry it out. Scarlett would be so proud of you telling that old bag off."

Sarah followed. "Now, we'll get those clothes off of you and get you into bed, and I'll bring you a cup of tea so you can sleep."

"Will she be all right?" Mark asked Lydia.

"It was good for her," Lydia said. She allowed herself a little smile. "And the way she told that old bitch off did my heart good. Who were those people?" she asked.

"The people who raised her; her aunt and uncle." Mark said."

"Good God, what a childhood she must have had."

"Yeah, she did. She learned how to keep her mouth shut and how to try to please everyone." Mark's mouth set in a grim line. "Even the bastard that gave her Scarlett."

Sarah came down the stairs. "I think she'll sleep now."

Mark pulled up his collar up. "Well, I must be going," he said. "Thank you for all you've done for Myrna. I'll call in a little while to see how she is. I'll come by in the morning."

Sarah nodded and put her hand on his arm as she opened the door. "Myrna's a fine woman. We'll take good care of her, and you're welcome here whenever you want to come."

The crisp September air slapped him awake. He breathed deep, clearing the stuffiness of the overheated house from his lungs. Snow tonight, he thought, as he searched through his pockets for the car keys.

"It didn't do no good, and you made Myrna mad."

Mark stopped. He could just make out the silhouettes of a man and woman standing beside a car parked in front of the next house on his left. The man's tone was hesitant, as if he weren't accustomed to speaking his mind.

"Who cares? I don't want her in that house with those niggers. People are gonna talk."

Mark winced. Who could forget that voice? He listened more carefully. "Besides, there's insurance money from the kid, and I'm gonna see that I get some of it. She owes me. Takin' care of her all those years, and then her brat."

The man, Ernie, didn't answer; he just walked around the car to the driver's side and got in. The old bitch got in the other side, and the car drove away from the curb, past Mark and disappeared down the street.

Mark discovered that his hands were clenched inside his pockets and he was breathing hard. How had Myrna turned out to be the sweet person she was after enduring abuse like that all her life? He doubted there was insurance money for Scarlett, but he'd check it out. If there was, he'd make sure that old hag didn't get her hands on it. He got into the car, turned the key in the ignition and roared away from the curb like an Indy driver.

By the time he reached the stop sign two blocks away, Mark's temper had cooled enough to realize he didn't know where he was going. He didn't want to go back to Pleasant Meadow. It was too far from Myrna. There was always the office, and God knew he'd neglected his work since Scarlett's death. There were always clothes kept there in case of a quick trip.

Lights blazed from the factory windows and the muffled thump and roar of working machinery greeted Mark as he let himself in the door, the door he'd opened into Myrna. His private elevator hummed its way to the fifth floor and the doors opened into his office. He flipped a switch and two table lamps glowed. He tossed his coat over the back of a chair, loosened his tie and sat down at the desk. He took the glass and bottle of Glen Livet from the liquor drawer, and half-filled the glass. No booze at the McIntire's. "Thou shalt not drink strong spirits," appeared to be Sarah McIntire's eleventh commandment.

He leaned back in the chair, closed his eyes and stretched his legs under the desk, crossing them at the ankle, and savored the whiskey's smooth fire. Home, at last. Only here, in this room, at night, alone, with the muffled sounds of the machines as background music, could he feel. Here, he could laugh and cry, rage and get drunk. Mark emptied the glass and poured another.

This was the first time he'd really been alone since all the craziness that began with Ed's death. It had been one crisis after another. Not the kind of crisis he was used to, that he could solve with a decision or throw money at. His emotions stirred around like a pot of Everything Soup that Mary made when he was growing up. If he didn't get the ingredients all sorted out, each vegetable in its proper place, he'd go crazy.

In the "Noreen" slot:" Her Majesty, chairwoman of the board, majority stockholder, ex-wife. In the "Business" slot: Sell the patent to Noreen. He didn't need it any more. The Seattle proposition was getting better and better. Really exciting to be in on the ground floor of a history making project. Another swallow of Glen Livet. In the "Personal" slot: Scarlett. Just thinking her name struck him with a hammer blow. You don't go to funerals for little kids. Tears came to his eyes. Weird. She was so bright and funny. It would have been fun to raise her. The tears ran down his face. He wiped his hand across his face.

That called for another drink. How did the glass get empty so quickly? He filled it to the top and squinted at the bottle. Not much left. Where was he? "Personal." "Myrna?" No. Myrna wasn't in any slot. She was the whole shebang, the whole enchilada. That amazing night, and then . . . Oops, boy, don't go there. He tossed off what was left in the glass.

Back to work. This kind of problem he could deal with. After an hour or so the print on the pages began to run together. He absentmindedly patted his shirt pocket, still squinting at the paper. Glasses. Coat pocket. Not wearing the coat. Where was it? He looked up, frowning. Oh, there, where he'd tossed it. That meant getting out of this chair and walking to the sofa. He pushed himself out of the desk chair and found his way to where the jacket hung over the sofa. He patted down the jacket until he found the glasses case, took them out and managed to hook them over his ears, then returned to the desk.

Glasses just made the bad news worse. He wanted to stay right here and get even drunker than he already was. Jeez. It was quiet. Must be past midnight. Everything was shut down. He pulled the glasses off one ear, letting them hang from the other, and rubbed his face. Every muscle in his body ached and his head was muddled. All that Glen Livet, he guessed. He stood, swayed a little, yanked the glasses off his ear and dropped them on the desk, pulled off his tie and draped it over the glasses, fumbled his way the couch and collapsed on it

Self-pity inserted itself between waking and passing out. Why did it always happen that when he thought his dreams had come true, they were smashed? Sure, the business was fantastically successful, but always was Noreen's and Ed's constant put-down. Never, did they appreciate the lifestyle his creation brought them. Always complaining about something. Always throwing Ed's initial financial support in his face. Then, he found Myrna and Scarlett and thought they were the answer to the gnawing loneliness. And now. . .

He closed his eyes and Myrna's haunted, ashen face appeared. Will she ever get over it? I wouldn't, if it was my child, he thought. Hell, she was my child, in my mind anyway. Why? Why? Why?

Why? Of course. Mark sat up, his mind cleared. Scarlett would not have gone alone to the playground in the rain. If Mrs. Neumann hadn't shown up in ten or fifteen minutes, a long time for a five-year-old, she would have started to go home. Her mother walked her to school, and Mrs. Neumann walked her home. She knew the way. No way, would she have veered off a block to the playground and the swings. Furthermore, she couldn't have swung herself high enough to fall out of the swing against the picnic table. Scarlett didn't die accidentally. She was murdered.

Chapter 32

The lighted face of David Holman's alarm clock told him he had finally dropped off to sleep for a half hour. Two days had passed after Scarlett's funeral, each night longer than the one before, Sleep had become a memory. Each night seemed forty hours long. Carol worried because he wasn't sleeping. How could he tell her that the minute he closed his eyes, a small pretty face, framed by red hair as curly as his, looked up at him. Her little girl voice, exhorting him to push her higher, rang in his ears. The pretty little face in an awkward twist, the red curly hair flung above it, her head at a funny angle. No breath from her nostrils; no heartbeat in her chest. But most of all, he felt her weight on the swing as he held it, then the sudden release of the weight and the chains holding the swing going slack. The wet melon smack as her head hit the picnic table. He couldn't keep his eyes closed, he couldn't breathe, sweat soaked the sheets. He got out of bed and tiptoed to the door, trying not to wake Carol.

He turned on the light to the den, closed the door and went to the liquor cabinet. The first bottle he touched, whatever it was, he took, sprawled into his big leather armchair, unscrewed the cap and swigged the fiery whiskey like he'd just found water after a week in the desert.

David, old boy, he said softly, you know what you are? You're a killer, a murderer. You've committed infanticide. Your own child. Aren't you proud of yourself?

He swigged more from the bottle.

What kind of man kills his own flesh and blood? Something lower than the lowest. Someone the devil reserved the best seat in hell for. So, you want to be a United States Representative, maybe then United States Supreme Court Justice and with the right roll of the dice, Chief Justice, just like grandpa wanted. Couldn't miss, with Pop's reputation and Grandpa's memory greasing the way.

I can hear myself now, handing down my opinion on whether to grant a stay of execution for a man who killed his child. "This man has committed the most heinous of crimes. The child he killed, his own flesh and blood, got no stay of execution. Justice demands that he receive the same tender mercy he gave his child. The prisoner shall be executed at the date and time set by the trial judge."

A light tap on the door, which then opened a crack, and Carol said, "David, may I come in? Are you all right?"

David quickly sat up and set the bottle on the floor. "I'm fine. Come on in."

"What are you doing down here at this hour? It's two o'clock."

"I have a knotty case going to trial in a couple of days. It keeps spinning around in my head as soon as I hit the pillow."

She came close, bent over and kissed him gently on the cheek. "I'm so sorry, dearest. How can I help?" David took her hand and caressed it, then kissed it. "You can help by going back to bed. I won't be much longer."

"Are you sure you're, all right? You smell like a distillery."

He coughed a laugh. "Well, I have had a drink. It relaxes me."

She kissed him on the mouth, and he pulled her close and returned the kiss. "I could keep this up until morning, but it won't get the work done." He gave her a light slap on the fanny, and said, "Now, back to bed with you."

"All right," she said, smiling. "If you're going to get nasty about it." She closed the door quietly and David heard her footsteps disappear up the stairs.

David buried his face in his hands. "My God, what have I done?" How could he make up for it? He was thirty-six; how many years would he have to live with this thing gnawing at him? He took another long pull from the whiskey bottle and lay back in the chair, and closed his eyes. He fell asleep with the lights on.

"Honey. Wake up. Breakfast's ready."

David plowed his way to muzzy wakefulness. Carol stood over him, her hand on his arm. He rubbed his hand over his scratchy face and blinked at the bright light. Sunshine. His head felt like a bass drum was beating inside it and his mouth tasted like something in a cesspool. "I'm sorry," he said. "I guess I drank a little too much and passed out down here."

"The coffee's hot and strong. Come on."

"That sounds reasonable. I'll have to get myself shaped up before I go into the office."

Three cups of scalding black coffee later his eyes focused for the first time, but the drum was still pounding in his head. Carol sat across the table, behind the morning paper.

"The funeral for that little girl they found in the park was yesterday. The paper said the child's mother worked at Weston Switch, and that the company was closed for it. That's odd. They just closed a few weeks ago for Mr. Best's funeral. I wonder if that's a new company policy. Closing for funerals."

Dunno." David put down the coffee cup. "I've got to shower and get to the office. Thanks for putting up with me these last couple of days. Once the trial's over, I'll be okay."

"Of course," Carol said, putting down the paper and giving him a smile. "You seem to be getting a lot of difficult cases lately. Is your dad slowing down and giving you the heavy ones?"

"Dad slowing down? Hardly. I just seem to draw the heavy ones. Well, off to the salt mines." He picked up his briefcase, kissed her and walked to the garage.

Tonight, he'd take Carol to dinner in Riverton, tell her he won his case. She'd ask him about it. Somehow, he'd have to come up with a good story.

Chapter 33

Lieutenant Carpenter leaned back in the visitor's chair in front of Mark's desk. When Mark Weston called, people answered, but he wasn't sure what the president of Weston Automatic Switch wanted with the police, him, specifically.

"Thanks for coming," Mark said. "As you can imagine, I've had little on my mind but Scarlett's death, and last night I had a sort of epiphany. I'd like to run it by you." He repeated his thoughts about Scarlett not going to play on the swings alone when Mrs. Neumann wasn't waiting for her after school.

"I've been thinking that way ever since we found her," Carpenter said. "Besides, a little kid couldn't get the swing high enough on her own to cause a fall that far from it, nor would she have been going fast enough to break her neck if she did fall."

"My thoughts, exactly," Mark said.

"I had my guys check the ground around the swings. It was all pretty muddy, but under the swing closest to the picnic table, there's a big skid mark, like somebody stopped, but kept sliding in the mud."

"But why would anybody want to kill a five-year-old girl?"

"There's a lot of perverts out there," Carpenter said. "Maybe he lured her to the swing set, somehow expecting to abuse her, but she tried to get away and he shoved her into the table. Right now, we have no idea."

"Do you have any other clues as to what happened?" Mark asked.

"Not a lot, but we're not giving up. This hit all the guys hard. They want nothing more than to catch the guy who did it."

They talked a few minutes longer, then Mark stood and so did Carpenter, and extended his hand. The detective shook it, surprised at the strength behind it.

"Thanks again for coming, and keep me posted," Mark said.

"I will," Carpenter said, then grinned. "By the way, where do you buy your shoes?"

"My shoes?"

"That skid mark had a shoe print on it, a really unusual one. Just curious."

Mark shrugged. "I get my shoes from a shoemaker in New York. His name is Giovanni Fertitta. Came here from Italy to escape Mussolini." He paused, his face turning dark. "You're accusing me?"

"Shoe print we found was from a handmade shoe. A rich man's shoe." Carpenter grinned. "Your alibi checks out. We know you were here that afternoon."

Mark smiled through clenched teeth. "Glad to know that. Thanks again for coming." He stood behind his desk until the detective was gone. "Damn cop, trying to make me look like a fool," he muttered,

Myrna lay in bed and watched the immense golden harvest moon work its way up the black cold sky. A bright moon to shine down on Scarlett where she slept in the cemetery. Three nights there already. Five days since she'd kissed her goodbye. Five days since she watched that bright head light up the dark school hallway. Five days since she'd heard her say, "Mama." Six nights since she'd felt the small warm body next to her in the bed. Pain wrapped itself around Myrna and squeezed until she had no breath left. Tears were all dried up for now, only the pain was left.

Questions whirled around her brain. Why am I still alive, still breathing? What's the point of being alive when you're all alone? Scarlett was the only reason I had to work, to find a place to live, to go home from work, to live. What difference does it make whether I wake up in the morning? Who's to care? Oh, dear God. Why did you have to take Scarlett? She was a good little girl, a loving little girl? Why take her and let me live? Why take her and let a mean, ugly, fat slob like Ada live? It makes no sense. No sense. No sense. Life makes no sense.

The moon was now high in the heavens, gleaming, a night-light for people who couldn't sleep. A cold light cutting through clear, cold air, making sharp edges on the shadows. And Scarlett lay in that white box, deep under the cold ground. Myrna's arms ached to hold her child, warm her, sing her to sleep. And now she never would, her mind said. Her heart and soul, whatever a soul was, couldn't agree with her mind. It was too much, as if she'd slipped off the edge of an abyss and floated down into nothing.

The moon was gone and the sun shot a beam across Myrna's face. She had gone to sleep. She slid her feet out from under the covers, and pulled them quickly back inside. It was cold. She made herself sit up and put her legs out. The thick white terry cloth robe that Sarah had loaned her hung over the rocking chair in the corner. There were slippers somewhere. Right at her feet. She put them on and dashed to the rocker, pulled on the robe and went into the bathroom. The aroma of coffee floated upstairs and she followed it down to the kitchen.

Sarah stood at the stove, hair perfectly arranged, wearing a neat blue housedress with white flowers and a matching blue apron. "Good morning, Myrna. It's so good to see you up. Are you feeling better?" She smiled and filled a thick white mug with the steaming black brew, placed it on a thick white saucer and set it in front of Myrna. "There now. That should get rid of the cobwebs."

"Thank you." The coffee was strong, bitter and warmed Myrna through. "Is Lydia up yet?"

Sarah laughed. "Land, no. She won't stir for another two hours. Her excuse is that she works nights, but I know that she just likes to sleep late. She prowls at night, like a cat."

"Which reminds me," Myrna said. "I think I'll go to the apartment today. I have to get my things out of there and start looking for a place to live."

Sarah spun around to face her, a frown erasing her smile. "You have a place to live. Right here. Lydia and I will get your things."

"I appreciate that. I've never known anyone so kind, but I can't butt into your family. I could go live with Mark, but right now, I just can't. It would be like I'm being happy while Scarlett's—dead."

"I can understand about living with Mark right now, but you are family to Lydia and me." Sarah paused. "Or don't you want to be part of a colored family?"

Myrna flinched as if Sarah had slapped her. She opened her mouth but nothing came out.

Sarah's stern face melted, and she ran to Myrna and put her arm around her. "Oh, honey. I'm so sorry. What was I thinking? And you hardly aware of the time of day. Oh, please, forgive me."

Myrna wrapped herself in the embrace and then put her head on Sarah's shoulder. "It's all right. It's been a hard time. You didn't even know me, but you took me in and comforted me like nobody ever has. Brown is a warm color, a loving color. If I could, I'd turn my skin brown. Being a part of your family would make me proud."

Sarah kissed her cheek and stood. "That's settled then."

"One thing, though," Myrna said, hesitating. "I appreciate your wanting to get the things from my apartment, but I need to go there myself and pack them away. I want to see it one more time just the way it was when I left with her that last time. You can keep Mrs. Neumann away from me, though. I'll give you the rent money and you can pay her. I just don't want to see her or have anything to do with her."

"That we can do. Now, let's get some food into you. Did you ever have grits?"

"Sarah, just before I went to sleep last night I thought about how it's going to be without Scarlett." Myrna swallowed down the lump in her throat. "I don't know how I can go on. I've spent my whole life trying to do the right thing to please other people, but I never could. Scarlett was the most wonderful thing to happen to me in my whole life, and now she's been taken away from me for no good reason. For no reason at all." She hesitated. "I really don't see much point in living."

Sarah stopped stirring the grits and turned to face Myrna, still holding the spoon. She turned off the burner and put the spoon in the pan, then sat down.

"Child," she said softly, covering Myrna's hand with her own, "I can understand you feeling like that. Your heart's gone out of you. I can tell you all the clichés and platitudes that people say when somebody tells them what you just said, because they don't know how to answer. I don't know how to answer, either, except that you are a good person, a valuable person.

"There was no reason for Scarlett to die. It was an accident, just like if I stepped in front of a bus because I wasn't looking. I'd probably die. That's life. But you are still alive. You are young. You have Mark. Dying because Scarlett died won't help her or bring her back, but if you stay alive there are so many things you can do to keep her memory alive."

"What things?"

"I can't tell you right now, but when all of us have time to recover from this tragedy, when we can think right again, something will show itself. I believe that with my whole soul." She took Myrna's chin in her hand and kissed her cheek. Her lips were soft as velvet and cool.

Myrna stared at her fingernails and picked at a loose cuticle. "Thank you for saying such nice things about me. I like the idea of doing something to make Scarlett's memory alive; it's almost like she didn't die. I'll think about it."

She looked up, and for the first time noticed the concern in Sarah's dark brown eyes, the worry lines in her forehead and cheeks, felt the warm, soft hand on her own. The sun shone through the bright window glass, framed by starched white curtains trimmed with red and white checked ruffles. The red and white checked tablecloth where she sat was crisp and smooth, and the sweet corn smell from the pot on the stove, how the stove and refrigerator and sink all gleamed white. Deep inside, tense muscles eased, her heart slowed its beat, she sighed, deep and long.

Myrna smiled. "You know? Those grits smell good. And I'm hungry."

Sarah patted Myrna's hand and smiled. "I'd better get them on the table." She stood slowly and arched her back a little. "My back sure doesn't take to sitting this time of the morning."

Shortly after noon, Lydia pulled her rusted '35 Chevy to the curb in front of Myrna's apartment, and stopped. She turned to Myrna. "You ready?" Myrna nodded, and Lydia looked over her arm into the back seat. "You coming, Mama?"

"Of course. And you let me do the talkin'. You're bound to mouth off and make her mad."

Myrna's heart thumped against her ribs and her palms felt clammy. She fumbled through her purse for the key to the apartment and walked toward the steps like a soldier on parade. By the time she reached the top of the stairs, she was winded and her knees felt like they were made of rubber. She slid the key into the lock and turned it, but couldn't make herself turn the knob. After a moment, she took a deep breath and opened the door. A gust of Lysol made her cough. She stepped inside, hesitating beside the open door, and looked left at the sink, steeling herself for the sight of the cereal bowl and spoon Scarlett had left there.

The bowl and spoon were gone. What happened to them? Who had come into her apartment? Lydia and Sarah followed her, and she slammed the door closed, and strode into the bedroom. The pink chenille bedspread was smooth and tucked over the pillows, just the way she'd left it that morning, but Scarlett's flower-sprigged white pajamas weren't folded on top of her pillow as they had been.

Who dared to touch Scarlett's p. js?

She flung open the closet door. Two of Scarlett's school dresses hung there. The other one and the coat, the police had taken, and she was wearing her dress-up dress in that pink satin bed under the ground. At least, nothing was missing from the closet. She yanked open the dresser drawer where Scarlett's things were kept. Small underpants were folded and stacked in a neat pile; her socks were folded together like balls. She closed the drawer and looked around the room. Scarlett's toys were placed tidily in the big cardboard box she used for a toy box. Scarlett was a neat little girl, except for her toys. Somebody else had rearranged them in the box.

In the living room, the big chair where Sgt. Brown had sat that night was turned in a different direction from the way Myrna kept it. The cushions on the davenport had been fluffed up, and there wasn't a grain of dust anywhere.

Mrs. Neumann had been up here, cleaning, getting the apartment ready for a new tenant, even before Myrna told her she wasn't coming back. Myrna clenched her fists until her nails dug into her palms.

The door opened. "Myrna, where are you?" It was Lydia.

"In the living room. And mad enough to kill. I'd like to go down there and beat on that woman until there was nothing left of her."

"What are you talking about?"

"She came in here and cleaned. She put Scarlett's things away. She took her cereal bowl and spoon off the kitchen sink. She had no right."

"Mrs. Neumann did that?"

"Look around. It's like we never lived here."

The door closed. "What's the matter?" Sarah asked, as she came into the living room.

"That old biddy came in here and cleaned it all up, even moved Scarlett's things," Lydia said.

The sobs came, as suddenly as a fit of vomiting. The rage and tears heaved out until Myrna's throat was raw and she couldn't breathe. When she quieted at last, Sarah wiped her wet face with a spotless white man-sized handkerchief, then gave it to Myrna, who blew her nose.

Sarah put her arms around Myrna and held her close. "There, there baby."

"I'm sorry," she said. "I don't what came over me."

"Sorrow came over you," said Sarah. "And it's about time. You don't cry and all that grief's gonna poison you."

"I'd like to go back down there and give that old biddy a piece of my mind," Lydia said.

"She didn't have anything bad in mind," Sarah replied. "She's an old woman in a lot of pain. She probably thought she was doing a good thing."

"Did you give her the rent money?" Myrna asked, her voice hoarse.

"She wouldn't take it," Sarah said. "Said it was the least she could do. Lydia, did you bring up those sacks?"

"They're right here. Come on, Myrna. We'll help you gather up your things and Scarlett's."

"I wonder if Mrs. Neumann would get mad if I took that bowl and spoon?"

"You take it. I'll tell her," Lydia said.

Myrna identified the cereal bowl in the cupboard from the crack along the bottom; the other bowl had a chip out of the side. Myrna had worried that it might break some more and Scarlett might swallow a piece of china. She opened the utensil drawer. Four spoons were laid inside each other. Which was the one Scarlett used? They were all alike.

"What's the matter, honey?" Sarah asked.

"I don't know which spoon it is."

Sarah looked in the drawer. "If Mrs. Neumann washed and dried it, it's probably the one on top."

Myrna took the top spoon and closed the drawer. Lydia came out of the bedroom. "I got everything of yours out of here, even the toys. What about the bathroom?"

"I forgot about the bathroom. Her toothbrush and comb are in there, if *she* didn't put them somewhere."

The small toothbrush was still in the drinking glass on the sink. Lydia put it in the grocery bag and looked all around the bathroom for anything that might belong to Myrna, then went into the kitchen. "I think we've got everything. Let's get out of here."

Back at Sarah's house, Myrna smoothed the tablecloth and set the three plates around the table. She picked up the silverware and placed one fork at the left edge of a plate, and nearly dropped the knife when a heavy pounding came from the door.

"I'll get it," she called to Sarah, and opened the door. A tall, beefy man stood there. Myrna stared. She had to swallow hard before she managed to whisper, "Sergeant Brown. What's wrong?"

The Sergeant took off his hat. "Hello, Miss Schroeder. Can I come in? We've learned something about little Scarlett's death that you should know from me before seeing it in the paper.

"Of course," said Sarah, at Myrna's elbow. Myrna moved aside and the sergeant stepped carefully over the threshold and wiped his feet on the small throw rug.

Sarah led them to the living room and offered him a chair. He eased himself into the sturdy upholstered chair beside the sofa. Myrna sat on the sofa, with Sarah beside her.

"What is it?" Sarah asked.

The sergeant clasped his hands and heaved a sigh. "The lieutenant wasn't satisfied that Scarlett fell accidentally and he went back to the park the next morning. Our people and the medics stirred up the ground a lot, but right under the swing, it looked like somebody slid in the mud, coming to a stop and sinking into the mud, making a deep footprint of a man's shoe, and just a couple of steps behind the swing, was another print. We made casts of them. They matched. They're expensive shoes, maybe handmade. Shouldn't be too hard to trace."

"What does that mean?" asked Myrna.

"It means some rich man murdered Scarlett," said Sarah, who had followed Myrna to the door. Her voice was flat, controlled.

"Murdered?" It sounded like a foreign word to Myrna's ears. "Why would anybody murder Scarlett?"

Sergeant Brown harrumphed. "There's filthy trash out there, rich and not so rich, who do just about anything to a little girl."

Myrna shook her head slowly. "No. Nobody touched my little girl, *like that*. I don't believe that. She was a good little girl. She wouldn't do that."

Sarah knelt in front of Myrna's chair and took her hand. "Hush, love. Scarlett was a baby. She couldn't do anything wrong if she tried. The sergeant didn't say anything had happened to her. Whoever it was, maybe was just working up to it."

Sudden agony squeezed Myrna's stomach and she clamped her hand over her mouth and ran to the downstairs bathroom. Everything she'd eaten in days, it seemed, came up and she finally sagged to the floor, covered with cold sweat. Sarah sat beside her and held her.

Myrna buried her face in her hands and screamed, raking her fingernails down her face until blood oozed out of long scratches.

Sergeant Brown's gruff voice asked, "Can I do something?"

From a distance, she heard Lydia. "You better go now, and thank you for coming." Sarah kissed Myrna's hair and rocked her, there on the floor next to the toilet.

Chapter 34

Myrna lay in bed, staring out at the gray sky, at the skeleton of the oak tree that swayed in the strong wind but her mind saw a low hill almost bare of trees, stiff dead flowers stuck out of metal tubes in the ground. Garden of Memories, the new cemetery in Newport City that was supposed to make you happy to be there, strolling around among the graves. Myrna's inner eye saw only a narrow rectangle of dirt, covered with a mound of frozen flowers tied with frozen ribbons. Under that pile of wasted flowers and dirt, hidden in a concrete box, stretched out on a pink satin cushion inside a white box, was Myrna's reason for living.

Why should she get out of bed? Scarlett couldn't get out of her pink satin bed. Why should she eat? Scarlett couldn't eat. Why should she go to work? It was a smelly, ugly place; so noisy it made you deaf. Scarlett wasn't here to feed and clothe.

Myrna had lost track of time. A doctor had come, after Sergeant Brown was there about the murder, but she had no idea how long ago that had been. Sarah made her take the pills he'd left, but Myrna didn't know what the pills were for; she was just as empty and numb as before. Only now, she couldn't seem to make herself do anything. She did get up and go downstairs to eat. Otherwise, Sarah would have brought food to her on a tray and she didn't want that. She just lay there in bed, cold, as Scarlett was cold. Mark came every day after work and stayed late, but she couldn't even respond to him.

Downstairs, Sarah, Lydia and Mark sat at the kitchen table, coffee getting cold in their cups.

"I swear I don't know what to do any more," Sarah said. "It's been a week and a half since that policeman told her that Scarlett was murdered. It's worse than when she died. She just lies there in that bed and stares out the window. When I try to talk to her, it's like she has to come back from a long way away. The doctor says the shock's worn off and she finally has to face what happened."

Sarah insisted Mark have dinner with them every night, since he came to see Myrna anyway. The couple who worked for him had gone to Seattle to set up the condominium he'd bought, and to set up the one they had purchased for themselves. No sense in him going to a restaurant and then coming back.

"I think she needs to get back to work," Lydia declared. "It'll keep her mind off what's happened."

"Nothing's going to take her mind off what happened," Sarah retorted. "Not if she lives to be a thousand years old."

"I didn't mean that. Of course, she won't get her mind off of it, but if she's at work, she at least has to think about something else."

She really doesn't have to work," Mark said. "She has the trust fund I set up for her and after we're married, she won't work." Lydia glared at him. "All right. I know. It will be good for her. The money doesn't matter."

"Just make it sound like it does," Lydia said. Mark sighed, rubbed his chin and nodded.

"First, we have to get her out of that bed," said Sarah.

Lydia stood. "There's no time like the present. Let's see. This is Friday. If we can get her out of bed and moving around, she might be strong enough by Monday night to go to work for at least a couple of hours."

Sarah started to get out of her chair. "No, Mama. You stay right here. I might have to get a little mean, and you'd try to stop me. I won't hurt her, but I may have to talk turkey to her. Mark, you too. Tell her, she'll lose her job if she doesn't get back to work on Monday. Lay it on thick."

"I've already told Jack she would be leaving by now," Mark said.

"Well, untell him," Lydia snapped.

"I'll see," Mark replied.

"I don't know," Sarah began.

"I do," Lydia replied. "Come on, Mark."

Lydia went up the stairs, Mark following with a heavy tread. Lydia knocked sharply on Myrna's door. A weak "Come in," responded, and she opened the door and went inside.

Myrna turned her head away from the window, and her eyes opened wide in surprise when she saw Mark with Lydia. She pushed herself to a sitting position. "I thought it was Sarah with my medicine." Lydia stood beside the bed, and Mark sat at the foot. He reached to touch Myrna's hand and she snatched it away.

"That's no way to treat Mark. He loves you and wants to help you. He still wants to marry you, although I can't see why after you've pushed him away for weeks," Lydia said.

Mark looked up at Lydia, who stood beside the bed, hands on her hips, a sneer on her face. "Now, just a damn . . ."

Lydia turned her head away from Myrna and winked. Mark leaned back. "Do you need some medicine?" he asked.

"What do you need medicine for?" Lydia snapped. "You sure aren't sick, a little peakéd maybe, but who wouldn't be after lying in bed for a week and a half."

"I don't feel sick, like the flu or something. I don't know what the medicine's for," Myrna replied. "It's just too much work to move."

"Now, you sound like Betty's brother-in-law. You know the one I'm talkin' about."

A smile brushed across Myrna's lips. "You mean, Henry? The one who's always too sick to work?"

"You got it."

"But I'm not like that."

Lydia's coffee and cream face twisted like she'd tasted a bit of something sour. "Well, not exactly like that. I'm sure it's real pleasant to have Mama fussin' over you like a baby."

Myrna sat a little straighter. "I don't mean for her to fuss."

"Of course not. Mama just naturally loves to fuss. She should've had fourteen kids, so there would always be a baby around to fuss over."

A blush of color came to Myrna's face and she sat a little straighter. "I'm not being a baby." She wilted. "I just can't think."

"You've been doing too much thinking," said Lydia. "Time you got around to some 'doing.' You're going to work on Monday." She looked at Mark.

Mark made his face stern. "We all feel sorry for you, Myrna. Nobody can imagine what you've been through, but the plant doesn't have feelings and neither do the parts nor the people who buy the switches. We need you. If you can't come back now, even for just a couple of hours like Lydia said, we'll have to find somebody else."

Myrna's eyes widened. "I'm fired?"

"No, no. If you can come back just a couple of hours a day and work up, that's fine." He looked at the floor and shrugged. "Of course, if you really aren't up to it, I s'pose we could ask for a sick leave, but hourly workers don't usually get sick leave. You wouldn't be fired, exactly. We just might not have a job for you when you're ready to come back."

Myrna looked from one to the other. The blank expression in her eyes turned to panic. "Not have a job? What can I do? I don't have any money and I can't sponge off you and Sarah forever."

Lydia erased any expression from her face. "Well, if you don't remember, Mark gave you a bundle of money, but if you don't want to take that you'll just have to go on relief, or go back to your aunt and uncle."

Myrna sat up straight, her jaw set, her eyes flashing. "Never. I don't need Mark's money. I'll scrub floors before I go on relief, and, I don't have an aunt and uncle."

Lydia shrugged. "Suit yourself."

"Mark, can I come back Monday?"

"Sure, if you feel up to it," he said, and cringed at the glare Lydia shot at him.

"Not, 'if you feel up to it,'" Lydia snapped. "You'll be there on Monday. On time, ready to work at whatever Jack tells you to do, even if it's the kick press."

"I won't let him put you on the kick press," Mark said quickly. "Maybe the bench where you won't have to work so hard, and for just a couple of hours."

"It'll be the kick press if that's what they need her on," Lydia said. "Myrna how do you think Betty and Sophie and Bessie would take it if you started getting soft jobs?" Myrna made a face and shuddered. "That's what I thought."

"All right. I'll try," Myrna said, adding, "I don't want people to stare at me or to treat me different."

"I'll see to it," Mark said.

"Hallelujah!" Lydia shouted. She leaned over the bed and hugged Myrna. "Now, get out of that bed, lazybones. Mark, beat it. Come on, honey, I'll get you some clothes. You probably forgot what they feel like."

Monday afternoon, Myrna and Lydia swung off the bus at the factory's entrance. A weary sun in the ice-blue sky of October cast the factory's heavy shadow over the street. Myrna glanced up. The building loomed over her, top-heavy, waiting to crush her. She cringed, pulled her coat tight and followed Lydia through the door.

Inside, the fluorescent glare canceled time. It laid bare every dirty crack in the pea green plaster. They went up the four worn concrete steps to the guard's station. He looked up in surprise. "Hey, Myrna. Good to see you back." She smiled and nodded.

"Hurry up," Lydia called, already halfway to the second floor.

"It's only three-thirty," Myrna replied.

"Yeah. And we've got to be on those machines at four-oh-five on the dot. You know what a stickler Jack is for starting on time."

Even after two days of long daily walks, Myrna still felt wobbly and her knees objected to climbing the stairs. She was panting when she reached the time clock on the second floor.

She automatically pulled her time card from the 'OUT" slot, punched it into the clock at three thirty-five and slipped the card into the "IN" slot. She glanced around at the pea green walls, the pea green machines standing like rows of soldiers at attention. The tang of oil in the air irritated her nostrils. Everything was the same, but yet, it wasn't. It was almost like her first day here when she felt like she'd stepped into a strange world.

Come on," Lydia said. Myrna followed, hung her coat on the rack outside the break room, drew a deep breath and went into the room. It hadn't changed either. The same people sat in the same chairs; the sound level of the conversation was that of people accustomed to talking over the noise of heavy machinery. It stopped the instant

Myrna stepped through the door. She felt like two dozen pairs of eyes were boring holes through her.

Lydia was just behind her. "What's the matter? You guys see a ghost or something?"

Betty, directly across the room, put on a smile. "Hi, Myrna. Good to see you back." Myrna paid attention to the "MYRNA."

"It's good to be back."

Sophie stood. "Here., You can have this chair." There were a dozen empty chairs.

"Thanks, Sophie, but Lydia and I can sit here."

They went to the chairs against the wall and sat down. The conversation picked up again, but not so loud, about husbands and the job.

"Do you know what that kid of mine did Saturday night?" Elsie began. Betty shook her head and nodded toward Myrna. Elsie looked at her lap and twisted her hands.

"What did your kid do this time, Else?" Lydia asked, in a voice that could have been heard over all the machines in the building.

"Uh-well-uh. I forgot. I mean, I don't want Myrna to feel bad."

"Why should Myrna feel bad? It's your kid."

Elsie swallowed hard. "Well, Suzanne told me she was going to the library to study with Amy. The library closes at nine, and Suzanne wasn't home yet at nine-thirty, so I called Amy's folks. Amy was home. Had been all night. Her mother made her get on the phone and tell what she knew about Suzanne. Suzanne had told her Bob Switzer had asked her out, and that she was going even though Pete and I said she couldn't date until she was sixteen.

"I tell you, Pete and I was waiting when she breezed in at ten-thirty. I never seen Pete so mad. And that kid stood there and talked right back to him. Said she'd go out whenever and with whoever she pleased, and nothing we could do would stop her. I thought Pete was going to belt her right there."

Everyone was all ears as Elsie told her story. "What did you do about it?" Elaine asked, and everyone nodded.

"Well, Pete told her that until she could keep a civil tongue in her head and until she did as she was told, she couldn't leave the house without one of us with her. I have to walk her to school in the morning and Pete walks her home after work. It's a good thing he gets off at two. If she has to go to the library, one of us will go with her. We'll do this for a month, then she can go to school and come home alone, but if she's late to school or late coming home, we go right back to square one."

"Good idea." "Smart." "I'm gonna try that with my kid."

The klaxon sounded, and one by one, the women got up, scraping the metal chairs against the concrete floor, shuffling their feet, stretching in dread of sitting in one place for four hours, and lined up outside the door. Lydia stood right behind Myrna. Sophie, in front of Myrna, turned around and said softly, "I'm real sorry about your little girl."

"Thank you." Myrna blinked back tears. Lydia squeezed her arm.

Tom gave Myrna a tight smile, glanced at the clipboard and said, "Number 28." Myrna nodded and walked into the department, her breath coming in tight little gasps, her heart racing, back at the same chair at the same machine she'd left the night Scarlett went missing. She couldn't bring herself to sit down. The last time she sat in that chair, her world ended. She blinked back sudden tears, set her jaw, and sat down. Her hand, of its own accord, hit the button and the press roared the life. Before she knew it, the small thin wires were in her left hand and her right began feeding them under the hammer, her foot tripped the hammer and it slammed down, crimping the wire. Her fingers flicked it into the bin. The next wire was already in the die. Soon, the rhythm established itself: seat, crash, toss; seat, crash, toss, and the counter above the machine advanced numbers as rapidly as the second hand on a clock.

A fragment of Myrna's attention monitored the action, but she made herself blank out all conscious thought. Whenever a memory of Jack coming out of his office toward her or a nurse's white uniform threatened to intrude, she forced it out. There was no need to think, no need to feel as long as the machine pounded out its stentorian beat.

"How's it going?"

Jack's voice made her miss a wire. "O. K.," she replied, watching the machine as she reestablished the rhythm. She felt his hand rest on her arm and squeeze it gently as he walked away. Seat, crash, toss; seat, crash, toss. The beat returned and Myrna zoned out once more.

The klaxon's braying got her attention, and sudden quiet descended. Suppertime. Myrna shut off the press and stood. Her back ached from sitting on the hard chair, in one position so long.

Lydia appeared beside her. "How do you feel?"

Myrna twisted a bit. "My back's sore, but I'm all right, I guess." She glanced at the counter. "Looks like I'm making rate."

Lydia grinned. "I knew you could do it. You ready to go home or do you want to go to supper?"

"It feels kind of good to be doing something. I'll go to supper."

"Let's go eat. My treat tonight," Lydia said.

"You've been treating me for weeks. Let me buy tonight."

"O.K., girl, you're on. I'm gonna get the most expensive thing on the menu." Myrna laughed as Lydia took her arm. "Hey, that's a nice sound you make. Come on. I'm starved. Can't wait for some of the salty Salisbury steak and watery mashed potatoes and lumpy gravy." Myrna laughed again, putting down a flash of guilt. It was all right to laugh. Scarlett would laugh.

Chapter 35

"Hey, Myrna. This ain't a kick press. All ya gotta do is barely touch the pedal." Tom stood beside her, ready to transfer the box of completed parts with an empty one.

"I know that," she snapped and stomped hard on the pedal again. "I like to hit it hard."

"Jeez. What bit you?"

She tuned him out. In the hazy background of her mind she took note that the box was empty again and she let her fingers return to their job. Who would kill Scarlett? Why? Always why. The word buzzed around in her head all the time she was awake and often in her dreams, now in time with the rhythm of the press. Someday, she'd find who did it. And when she did . . .

She pictured the monster who had laid his filthy hands on Scarlett's soft, smooth skin. He was big, had to be to push the swing that high and that hard, fat, his gut hanging over his belt, and he had greasy black hair. She stood in front of him, butcher knife raised, and when he laughed at a little bitty thing like her threatening a big, strong man like him, she'd shove the knife right through all that lard straight into his heart. No, that was too easy. He'd die right away. She'd stick him in the belly, right where it hung over his pants, and watch it pop like a balloon, spilling all his guts. He'd look surprised and then fall down and try to hold his guts in with his hands, like she'd heard wounded soldiers did in the war. He'd beg her to get help. Beg for her forgiveness. Tell her he was sorry. She would smile, wipe the knife handle clean and toss it on the ground, turn around and walk away.

Myrna felt a hand on her arm and flinched.

Cleanup time," said Tom. He glanced at the counter. "Man, you must be after a raise."

"I could use one," Myrna snapped. She filled out her count slip for the night and gave it to him. "Where's Lydia?"

He jerked his head toward the door. "She quit on time. Not one second of unpaid overtime for that darkie."

Myrna spun around, her hand raised to slap him. Suddenly realizing what would happen if she did, she curled her fists and said through clenched teeth, "Don't you ever call her that."

He raised his free hand in mock surrender. "Okay, okay. I didn't mean nothin' by it." He looked hard at her. "What's with you, Myrna? Where's my quiet, sweet little Myrna?"

"I'm not your Myrna, nor your quiet, sweet little anything." She picked up her purse and stalked through the door.

Lydia stood beside the door to the break room with her coat on. "You planning to spend the night?"

"Lay off," Myrna snapped. "Tom is bad enough. I don't have to hear it from you."

"Whoa. What bit you?"

"That two-bit, double-toed jerk and his filthy mouth."

"Tom? I agree that he's a jerk, but what did he do to get you this mad?"

"Never mind. I get so sick of hearing him bad-mouthing everybody and everything." Myrna yanked her coat off the hanger and shrugged it on.

"Just ignore him. Come on. The cab won't wait." Lydia walked toward the time clock, and Myrna fell into step beside her

Myrna pushed her time card into the clock. It rang, and she put the card into the "out" slot.

Lydia pushed open the stair door. "Come on, I want to get out of here. she said as they ran down the stairs.

They squeezed into the crowd of women huddled together in the small entry waiting for the cabs. The weak light over the door illuminated snow, slanting parallel to the ground. "Hey, October fifteenth and it's snowing already," someone said. The door opened with a shotgun blast of icy air and hard snow pellets, and a red-nosed man with his collar up around his ears. "My, God, Ed, did you have to let in the whole outdoors?" Betty shouted.

Ed shrugged and grinned as he armed his way through the crowd of women and up the stairs.

"East side one is here," the guard called.

Myrna stumbled against Lydia as Judy shoved her from behind.

"Judy, quit shoving," Lydia snapped. "Nobody's gonna take your precious front seat."

Maggie climbed into the back seat, her two hundred plus pounds taking up half the seat. Myrna and Lydia wedged themselves into the other half. Myrna felt like the inside of a sandwich.

"Hey, Bob, don't you ever clean this thing?" Maggie said. "It stinks like a year's worth of old cigarette smoke and beer and puke."

"It gets you where you're goin' don't it, and you don't have to pay for it," Bob replied, and made a careful U-turn on the snowy street instead of his usual crack-the-whip spin.

The cab straightened and roared toward the bridge. "Not only is this thing filthy, but when are you gonna get a muffler? You're lucky the cops haven't picked you up," Maggie said.

Bob ignored her.

Lydia turned toward the window. The only sound was the roaring muffler. Myrna stared through the windshield between Bob's and Judy's heads. Snow swirled in the streetlights throwing everything behind them into a ghost landscape. The cab slowed and stopped where a bare bulb lit a sagging porch and a door with a torn screen. Judy got out without saying goodnight, slammed the door, as usual, and walked carefully up the snow-covered sidewalk and the porch steps.

The next stop was Lydia's and Myrna's, where pale light shone from a rear downstairs window. Sarah had the coffee on. Lydia put some muscle behind the door as she slammed it shut and followed Myrna's footprints in the snow to the house, as the cab's unmuffled roar echoed in the quiet street.

In the kitchen, Sarah poured three cups of steaming coffee, set one each in front of Myrna and Lydia, then placed one on the table for herself and sat down. "You two look like you've stepped into a bear trap."

"Could be," Lydia said.

"I guess I'm in a bad mood," Myrna said.

Sarah folded her arms on the table and leaned toward Myrna and Lydia. "You're just tired. Everything will look better after you've had some sleep. Drink your coffee and forget about it."

Chapter 36

The door to Mark Weston's private elevator slid shut behind him, and he tossed his overcoat and scarf on the sofa, wiped his hand over his face and punched the intercom button on his desk.

Joanne's voice promptly said, "Good morning, Mr. Weston. How was your drive?

"Lousy. They can't get that new road built too soon for me." Mark glanced at his watch. "It's almost noon. Anything I should know before the execs meeting at 1:30?"

"No, sir. Things have been going smoothly while you were away. Shall I have lunch sent in?"

"Thanks. Whatever's on the menu downstairs."

"Right away, sir."

An amplified click signaled that she had disconnected. Mark's black leather chair squawked as he sat down and picked up his private phone and gave the operator a number.

"Good morning, Sarah. This is Mark. May I speak to Myrna?"

"She and Lydia are out shopping, Mark. I'll have her call you when she gets home." Sarah said. "How's Chicago?"

Mark sighed. "Chicago's Chicago. Dirty and loud," he said. "I'm going to be tied up in a meeting all afternoon. I'm in the middle of a complicated business situation. How is she, Sarah?"

"She seems to be better. As you know, she worked last night."

"Well, tell her I'll call her when my meeting ends."

"Of course."

Mark leaned back in the chair. Damn. He'd spent half the time on the drive from Chicago planning what he would say to her see if she'd go to dinner on Saturday. Maybe get back to the farm."

A light tap on the door preceded Joanne with a tray. The smell of coffee brought him to attention, and the spicy scent of chili, with a hint of corn bread, made his mouth water. His stomach responded with a growl. "Thanks, Joanne. I'm hungrier than I realized."

Myrna and Lydia finished their shopping and turned into Charlie's Burger Emporium for lunch. After they finished their meal and put on their coats, they went to the door and handed their money to the sullen teen at the cash register. Myrna had her hand on the door knob, when the sound of a dish crashing to the floor behind the curtain that concealed the kitchen stopped her. Heads at the counter jerked up and swiveled toward the sound, then back to glare at Lydia. A second crash followed, then another, as if someone were breaking one dish at a time.

"Somebody's going to get fired," Myrna said.

Lydia's face was rigid; her eyes had narrowed to slits. "Let's get out of here," she said as the crockery continued to break.

Outside, Lydia strode away from the restaurant, head down, plowing against the wind, shoulders hunched, her hands stuffed into her coat pockets. Myrna had to run to keep up with her.

"What was that all about?" Myrna said, between gasps for breath.

"You said somebody's going to get fired," Lydia said, not changing stride or expression. "He'll probably get a raise."

"A raise? For breaking dishes?"

"For breaking dishes that a nigger ate off of, and dishes of a white person who'd eat with a nigger."

"I never heard of such a thing."

"That's 'cause you're white. And now white folks think you're just as much of a nigger as I am for being friends with one, not to mention living in the same house with two of 'em.

"That's dumb."

"Tell them."

They continued in silence until they reached the downtown bus stop, next to a photography studio, its window filled with portraits of pretty women, handsome men and adorable children, even a stately Irish setter.

"I can't believe somebody would spend money to have a picture taken of a dog," Myrna said.

Lydia shrugged. "When you've got money, you spend it on anything you want. Here's our bus."

When they got home, Sarah greeted them, and smiled at their packages "Did you leave anything in the stores? By the way, Myrna. Mark called. He sounded disappointed when you weren't here."

Myrna hung her coat in the closet and turned around. "What did he want?"

"To talk to you. He asked how you were, and said he was going to be busy the rest of the day but that he'd call you soon."

"Okay," she said. "We ate at Charlie's burger place, and people broke dishes when we started to leave."

Sarah's gaze bored into Lydia, who stood in front of the hall mirror smoothing back her hair. "What's that?"

"Guess they don't like colored folks' germs. They didn't mind takin' our money, though."

Sarah pursed her lips and set her jaw. "Some day . . ."

"I didn't know people treated Negro people like that," Myrna said.

"Didn't you learn anything from your dear Aunt Ada? She didn't make any secret of how she felt about us," Lydia said.

"She talked that way all the time. I never paid any attention to it. Actually, I never paid any attention to much of what she said."

"Well, we can't solve the problem standing here. We've only got an hour to catch the bus to work," Lydia said, starting up the stairs.

"Myrna," Sarah said, putting a hand on her arm. "I'm sorry you had to go through that, but I'm afraid it won't get any better as long as you're with us."

"Then I'll have to be as tough as you are," Myrna replied

Chapter 37

David Holman leaned over the bathroom sink to peer at his reflection in the mirror. The black circles under his eyes made him look like he'd gone nine rounds with Joe Louis. His cheekbones stuck out like hatchet blades. He knew he'd lost weight; he'd taken his belt in two notches and the waistbands on his pants looked ruffled, but he felt sick all the time, now.

Not to mention his performance in the bedroom. Like last night.

He'd gone to bed long after Carol, but when he stretched out on the smooth, cool sheets, she had pressed against him, rubbing his rump with her soft, furry mound. Her nipples brushed his back. He groaned and rolled to meet her, palming those soft heavy breasts. She wrapped her legs around him, pressing her wet opening against him. The tip of her tongue circled his nipples.

"Oh, honey, I feel so ripe," she whispered. "I know it could be now."

The fire in him went out, as if he'd been doused with a bucket of ice water. He tried, suckling her breasts, kissing that wet place, rich with her ripening, but what usually aroused him beyond endurance was faintly disgusting. He kissed her mouth tenderly, and gently disengaged.

"I'm sorry, sweetheart. I just can't."

Carol turned away so she faced the wall. He could tell she was crying, silently, so as not to let him know. He touched her arm. She flinched and moved even farther toward the wall.

He turned his back to hers and stared at the sheen in the dark that was the window. The face was there again, his face, softer, rounder, sweet, infinitely sweet and innocent, crowned with that telltale blaze of red-gold hair. The Holman green eyes. She always smiled at him, that ghost-face in the window, in his nightmares, in his law books; wherever he went, whatever he did. The thought of another small face like his, crowned with red-gold hair, in Carol's arms, at her breast, those warm full breasts that begged to nurture a child . . .

Even this morning, the face that looked back at him from the mirror had a greenish cast. He took the Gillette electric razor from its holder on the wall, and concentrated on the razor's buzz and the slight tug on his whiskers.

Dressed in a proper lawyer/politician's navy suit of featherweight wool, a shirt so white it hurt the eyes, the collar of perfect stiffness, a navy silk tie with discreet red figures in it, black shoes that shone like mirrors. He followed the fragrance of coffee downstairs. Coffee was the only thing that didn't nauseate him. The shining chrome electric coffee pot sat on a tile trivet on the counter, a white oversized mug, in a matching saucer waited beside it.

"Carol," he called. There was no answer. "Carol? Where are you?" He walked through the downstairs, but didn't find her. Then, he noticed the note beside the morning paper on the breakfast table. *"Darling, I have tried everything I know to bring you back to me, but nothing seems to work. I have to go away for a while so I can think. I don't know what I've done, and you're so far away. I can't seem to reach you. I love you so much. Carol."*

David's knees turned to water. He sat down at the table and stared at the note, as if reading it over and over would erase it and Carol would be there in her pink robe, smiling at him from across the table. He wanted to lay his head on the table and cry, howl and scream, like a child whose puppy has been killed by a car. But he couldn't. He had a case at trial this morning and he had to show up at headquarters later. He could make an excuse. They could delay the case. Lawyers do occasionally get sick. He'd only half-promised Barbara he'd stop in at headquarters. He got up, finally, disconnected the coffee pot. He couldn't even think about drinking what she had made, from the cup she had put out. He picked up his briefcase and strode to the garage. Her car, the turquoise Thunderbird she loved so much, was gone. The empty space struck him like a blow to the chest.

David stared at the vacant stall, slight tremors shaking his entire body. He couldn't blame her. Last night must have been the last straw for her. He made himself walk around his Cadillac, open the door and slide under the steering wheel. It would be so easy. Just keep the garage door shut, open the windows, turn the key and step on the accelerator. The invisible, silent killer would put him to sleep, to sleep for a change and never wake up. Never see that smiling face. Never hear that ugly voice, threatening. Never see Carol's accusing eyes. So easy.

He turned the key and stepped on the pedal. The big motor roared to life, then settled into a soft purr. David sat behind the wheel for a moment, then opened the door, got out and opened the garage door.

He returned to the car and stared through the windshield. But he had to see Carol again. Had to make her believe his behavior had nothing to do with her, that he was the evil one, that she had married a monster. How could he do that? What could he do? He glanced at the briefcase. Work. Work always obliterated everything else from his mind, even the face. When he worked on a case, nothing else existed. And Jack Herndon needed him with all his wits intact to save his business from a crippling lawsuit. David straightened his arms, gave a tug to his tie, and put the car in reverse.

The trial had gone well, and Jack Herndon was a happy man, the kind of happy that might translate into money for David's campaign, and David repressed the urge to run down the grooved concrete steps of the ancient courthouse. His long strides took him back to his office in five minutes. "We won it," he said, grinning, to Shirley, his secretary. "Lunch is on me."

Shirley was an attractive fifty-two and had been a fixture at the firm since she graduated from Newport City High School. "Congratulations, and thank you." She riffled through her notebook. "I think that woman you said not to let through, called."

"Did she say anything?"

"She just said, 'Tell the cheat I ain't forgot him. It's about that little girl.' Does that make any sense to you?"

David's euphoria evaporated; he wanted to turn and run, but he managed to keep his expression straight, smiled, in fact. "That wouldn't make sense to anyone. Just another crank." He took a step toward his office, and said, "By the way, I'm going to lunch with Jack Herndon, then I'm off to party headquarters." Shirley nodded, and David went into his office and closed the door. He tossed his briefcase on a chair and sat at his desk. He'd thought he was rid of her, of the phone calls that always seemed to come at unexpected times and places. When will it stop? Who is she? And today of all days. Carol's note came roaring back into his brain and he leaned on the desk, burying his head in his hands.

He made himself go into his private bathroom and wash his face and hands. It wouldn't do to show up bleary-eyed at campaign headquarters nor to lunch with Herndon. He scrutinized his face in the mirror, decided he was presentable and snapped the light off.

291

One advantage of a small town was that you could walk to anyplace downtown in a few minutes, and David liked to walk; it stretched his legs after hours in the courtroom or behind his desk, and the crisp air washed the fuzz from his brain. Today, he walked to his campaign headquarters without feeling the stretch of his muscles and his brain wasn't fuzzy, it was a maelstrom. He almost walked right past the place. He opened the door and a dozen female heads looked up.

"David," Barbara caroled and strode toward him, her hand outstretched. "I'm so glad you dropped by." He shook her hand, and she swept her left arm to include the women at the tables sorting envelopes. "These wonderful ladies come every day to get out the mailing. They will be so happy to meet you." She tugged on his arm and he followed her down the rows of tables.

"This is Joan van Naaman, Audrey Schmidt, Barbara Bender, Nancy Eberhart, Phyllis Aumont, Antonia Scarpelli, Agnes Schwartzenhagen, one of our most dedicated volunteers," Barbara said. The required pep talk only took five minutes; he flashed the Smile one more time and fled out the door.

A loud ringing penetrated David's brain and he opened his eyes. What was he doing on the floor? What was that noise? Oh, yes, the alarm clock. It would keep getting louder until someone shut it off. He pushed himself slowly to his feet, balanced with a hand on the footboard of the bed, and held on to it as he rounded the bed, reached for the loudly ringing clock, and pushed the button that shut it off. He collapsed back on the bed and closed his eyes. His head was pounding. The picture again. It wouldn't go away. Every time he closed his eyes, there it was. Scarlett lying on the ground like a broken doll, that red hair flaming around her head. Whoever found her had to notice the red hair.

His little girl. He had started her life. He had ended her life.

A heavy ball filled his chest. He couldn't breathe. Was he having a heart attack? Tears filled his eyes and flowed onto the bedding. He gasped and moaned, rolling over to his stomach, great sobs seemed to come from the ball in his chest. The sobs became heavy, gasping screams. Why? Why? All this time, and nobody ever said anything. Why did it have to come now? Why did it have to come at all? One nasty old lady. He imagined her as ugly. Why did she have to ruin his life? Finally, the screams diminished back into sobs and stopped. The lump in his chest was gone. As suddenly as the spasm of grief had come, it disappeared, leaving him wilted. No way was he going to court today. Spent, he fell asleep.

David woke an hour later, feeling a little better. He had to go to court. He couldn't change his work habits or his campaign mode. It would look strange and questions would be asked. He sat up, rubbed his eyes, got his feet on the floor, stood and turned to the bathroom. A shower would clear his head.

Chapter 38

A bell chimed softly at the front of the bus, and it slowed for the stop outside Weston Automatic Switch Company. "Well, here we are, ready to do or die to put a bunch of money into Mark Weston's many bank accounts," Lydia said loud enough for the entire bus to hear as she pulled herself to her feet.

Every woman in the break room leaned toward Betty, hanging on every word, as Myrna and Lydia walked in after hanging their coats on the coat rack in the hall. ". . . said he told her about this doctor in Dubuque who'd do it cheap," Betty said in a hushed voice. "He took her up there on Wednesday . . ."

"So that's why neither one of them was at work Wednesday," Georgia interrupted. A dozen heads turned toward her and a dozen pairs of eyes glared her into silence. "Sorry," she murmured and shrunk back into her chair.

The klaxon blared. The women glanced through the window into the hallway, then turned back to Betty. "Well, what happened?"

Betty hauled herself to her feet. "I'll tell you later. Right now, we better get out there. Tim'll have a cat fit."

Myrna got in line behind Lydia, who maneuvered herself behind Betty. "What's this all about?" Lydia asked.

"I just got in on the tail end," Betty said. "Jim knocked up Edie, then got her an abortion in Dubuque and bailed after the abortion didn't seem to work"

"Asshole," Lydia muttered.

Shortly before supper break, Myrna was thinking about Edie and the abortion, her hand blurring as she fed wires into her machine, when Jack tapped her on the shoulder. She stopped and looked up at him. "Come into the office," he said. Her heart stuttered. What happened now? She shut off the machine and followed him into his office. He waved his hand for her to sit in the visitor's chair. He sat behind his desk and folded his hands on it. "Mark Weston just called. He wants you to come to his office." Jack looked at his hands. "He said you won't be coming back. Did you know that?"

Myrna shook her head, but said, "He did tell me he gave you my notice a while back."

"He did, but he didn't put a date on it." Jack looked hard at her. "Is this what you really want? To marry him?"

"Yes, I do."

"I know he can be charming and he can turn a girl's head. I've seen it more than once. He'll wine and dine her a few times and she gets all excited, and then he drops her like a hot potato."

Myrna reached for the platinum chain around her neck and pulled the ring from under her blouse. "Does this look like he's going to dump me?"

Jack's eyes went wide when he saw the ring. "That looks pretty serious."

"I know all about the women and his nasty treatment of many people," Myrna continued. "I also see a side of him very few ever have. He's a good, kind and gentle man. He planned to adopt Scarlett, and he's been there for me all through this nightmare." She paused. "He needs loving. And so do I."

Jack sighed. "O. K. I just wanted to make sure you knew what he can be like. I don't want you hurt."

"Thank you, but I trust him and his love for me."

"Well, it's been good having you in the department. We'll miss you," Jack stood and so did Myrna.

"Thank you," she replied. "You've been a good boss." She walked out of the office and turned her back on Department 21 for the last time. In the hall, she took her coat from the hanger and went to Mark's elevator.

Mark waited beside the elevator as the door opened and Myrna stepped out. He opened his arms and she walked into them for his embrace. "Everything all right?" he asked.

"Fine. Jack just had a little talk with me, warning me about you."

"Oh, he did. Well, that's his privilege. Were you warned off?"

"What do you think?"

Mark kept his arm around her as they walked to the sofa. "Do me a favor, please. Take the ring off the chain." She slipped the chain over her head. He took it and opened the fastener, slid the ring off, picked up Myrna's left hand and slipped the ring on her third finger. "Now. You'll never have to take it off again." He wrapped his arm around her and held her close, his right hand cupping her breast as he kissed her. "Oh, dear God, how I love you," he said when they both came up for air.

"The feeling is mutual," Myrna replied.

Mark sat back. "I'll have to stop that right now or I won't be able to," he said, kissing her cheek. "I have some business to discuss with you, so I can't do that."

"Business?"

"First, we'll go to dinner in Riverton. Then we'll come back and stay at the farm for the night. Is that all right with you?" Myrna smiled and nodded. "I have to go to Seattle next week, and I want you to go with me. We have to pick out a place to live and stop in at the University of Washington so you can meet the professor who is going to tutor you." He paused. "I would really like it if you would come live at the farm with me until we're married. How do you feel about that?"

Myrna sat straight, her eyes wide. "A professor? To tutor me?" When Mark nodded, she covered her mouth and closed her eyes to hide the tears, but they leaked down her face. "You mean I can get my high school diploma?"

"And after that your college degree."

She took his face in both hands and kissed him, tears still running down her face. "I don't know what to say, except 'thank you.'"

"You say thank you with every breath you take, but you don't have to thank me. Your smile lights up my life; Even though you're crying now, I assume they're tears of joy." He brushed the tears from her face. "Now, you didn't answer my question about moving to the farm."

"I've been thinking about what to do next. Lydia and Sarah have been so good to me, and I don't want to hurt their feelings, but I really do need to be on my own. The idea of being your wife hasn't really sunk in, until just a few minutes ago."

"You have doubts?'"

"It isn't that. Losing Scarlett shut out everything else. I'm just now understanding that I have to learn to live without her." She blinked back tears. "The idea of being married to you and living with you wasn't quite real. Now, since Jack called me into the office and I walked away from Department 21 for the last time, and coming up here, I'm beginning to understand that it's really going to happen." She held out her hands and he took them. "I'd love to come live with you at the farm."

He held her tight again and kissed her gently, tenderly. "You really do love me."

She laughed, "Of course. Why would I put up with you if I didn't"?

"Call Sarah and let her know you won't be there tonight." s

"I need to tell Lydia, too."

"Of course." He tapped the tip of her nose and got up.

The day after returning from Seattle, they sat in Sarah's kitchen over cups of coffee and streusel coffee cake. "The flight was so exciting," Myrna said. "Everything on the ground was tiny, like toys, and it was so exciting being above the clouds. The sky was so blue. And Seattle is such a nice city, so much water and you can see Mount Rainier. I never imagined anything like it. And Professor Cassidy at the University was so nice. He said he looked forward to being my tutor. And Mark bought this big building right on Lake Washington. We'll live on the whole top floor and Christer and Inge will have their own apartment two floors down. And . . ."

Lydia grinned and said, "I can see how excited you are,"

"Remember what we came here for?" Mark prompted.

Myrna hung her head. "Sorry. I guess I got carried away," she said. "What we were thinking about was Thanksgiving. It's only a couple of weeks away, and we'd like to have you come to the farm for Thanksgiving dinner."

Lydia and Sarah exchanged a look. "We were going to ask you to come here"

"We are so thankful for all you've done so much for us, we can't think of anything we want more than to have you come to our home, and to meet Inge and Christer," Myrna said.

Chapter 39

Carol Holman turned the key in the locked door to her home. She'd looked through the garage windows to make sure David's car was gone. She knew he had a rally scheduled in Buena Vista at two o'clock, but from what she'd heard, he was paying little attention to his campaign these days. A pang of sorrow caught her throat when she walked into the living room she had decorated so carefully. She loved this house. It always seemed to protect her, to welcome her. No more.

She started up the stairs to her sewing room, the room that in her dreams she'd decorated as a nursery. Those dreams were bitter nightmares now. No one wanted children more, but her arms remained empty until even David rejected her, and the questions never changed. Why? What was she being punished for?

She disconnected the power cord from the sewing machine and wrapped it around the machine. The carrier was in the closet and she turned to get it when the phone on a small table beside the door rang. She hesitated. Should she answer it? There was no reason not to. This was still her house. She picked it up. "Hello."

"This David Holman's house?" The voice sounded female, but it was deep and coarse. It could be a man.

"Who's calling, please?"

"Never mind. I want to talk to David Holman."

"He isn't here. If you give me your name, I can leave a message for him."

"He don't need my name. Are you a maid?"

Carol hesitated. "I'm not a maid. I'm Mrs. Holman. Now, if you'd be so kind as to give me your name."

"Mrs. Holman. Now that's even better." When Carol didn't answer, the voice continued. "Just tell your hubby it's his friend whose been callin'. Tell him time is running out. 'Course, I suppose he's told you all about it, him bein' such a good husband like all the ads say."

Carol knew she should hang up, but her hand was locked on the phone. "He tells me many things. What, specifically are you speaking of?"

"My ain't we hoity-toity! Sound like a school teacher. Sounds like he ain't told you nothin'. Maybe it's time you knew."

"What are you talking about?"

"Did you know your wonderful hubby had him a little fling 'long about six, seven years ago, and that little fling just happened to make a baby?" Carol felt the blood drain from her head; the voice scratched across her mind like a fingernail across a blackboard. "Little girl. She's dead now. Killed a month ago in some kind of accident. Her pitcher was in the paper. She looked just like her daddy, red hair and all."

"No. You're lying. Why would you say such a thing to me?"

"I figured you ought to know."

Carol threw the phone to the floor and dropped to her knees, screaming and sobbing at the same time. The story in the newspaper about the little girl in the park. It said something about her red hair. The Holman red hair. Of course. David made a baby. With somebody else. Why didn't he tell me? Maybe we could have taken the child. No. It was all her fault. She'd failed him, failed herself. All his lies about not caring whether she had a baby. All lies. He'd gone out and made a baby with someone else. It proved she was a freak, her whole life a waste.

Finally, there were no more tears left, only a raw throat and broken fingernails where she'd clawed the rough carpet. She was exhausted, but she made herself stand, then picked her way down the stairs and out of the door. Her head felt like it was filled with foam. Her ears rang. It was hard to see, but she started the car and backed it down the driveway without thought. She turned into the street and drove away.

The little turquoise Thunderbird sped along the narrow two-lane highway toward Buena Vista. Carol didn't consciously know that was where she was going; the car seemed to be guiding itself. She didn't see passing cars, didn't see the huge old oak trees lining the river bank, didn't see the river. The car kept going, around sharp curves, even passing slower moving vehicles. She didn't notice the sign by the road that read, "Buena Vista," nor the increasing number of houses. The car went up the grade to the high bridge in the center of the small town. The steering wheel suddenly jerked sharply to the right. The Thunderbird flew through the pedestrian rail. Carol's head hit the steering wheel and the world went dark. She never knew the car plummeted down, down, down until it hit the water as hard as a concrete wall, then slowly slid beneath the surface.

David stood beside the lectern on the stage in the Buena Vista Grange Hall, holding a glass of green punch in his left hand, shaking hands with well-wishers with his right, practiced smiles and bland words. It had been a good speech. His campaign manager was pleased, relieved that David was back in form. The glooms seemed to be over.

The door opened with a dramatic bang and a uniformed sheriff's deputy strode into the room and toward the village magistrate. "Car's in the river. Went off the bridge." Conversation stopped mid-sentence. Everyone knew what the announcement meant. Nobody survived a fall off the old fifty-foot high bridge.

The shocked silence lasted only a moment, then the building buzzed with questions. "Anybody see it?" "Who was it?" "Are they draggin'?"

"Betty and Cliff Amworth were walkin' along the river path and saw the whole thing. They said the car sort of jerked off the road and through the rail, like somebody wanted to crash it. It was a turquoise blue Thunderbird," the deputy said.

David felt the breath go out of him, and the green brew in his glass made miniature waves. A turquoise Thunderbird. It couldn't have been Carol. What would she be doing in Buena Vista? She didn't know anybody here. She didn't even know he was here, did she? Besides, there were thousands of turquoise Thunderbirds on the road.

The room emptied, leaving David and his campaign manager standing alone. "Well, should we go see what happened? Although I doubt if there's anything to see at this point," Steve said.

David forced himself to pay attention. "I suppose so. It would seem strange if we just went away. It'd look like we didn't care."

"Now you're thinking like a candidate." Steve paused and looked hard at David. "You all right? You look like you've seen a ghost."

David made himself smile and glanced at the glass. "I'm fine. I just took a swig of this poison. Maybe we ought to hire a taster." Steve laughed.

Steve drove them to where parked cars lined both sides of the road leading to the bridge. He turned into a vacant driveway and shut off the ignition. They got out of the car and walked to the bridge, where a wide gap, bristling with jagged metal pipes and broken, bent wires, bore witness to where the car went through. There were no skid marks on the roadway, indicating that the driver had tried to stop. They peered over the intact part of the rail and saw a small motorboat in the water and a tow truck backed up close to the edge. Deputies in the boat seized the grapple from the tow truck and moved downstream near the riverbank. The river was relatively shallow at that point, and David thought he could see automobile wheels just under the surface. Please, he thought. Please don't let it be Carol.

It was hard to breathe. His teeth chattered. His stomach began to shake.

Chapter 40

David slammed the door between the garage and the kitchen and stood in the dark kitchen, shaking, his hands clenched, breathing deep and ragged. How could they? His own family. On the worst day of his life.

His father seated at the head of the long mahogany dining table, like a king, after the blur of Carol's funeral, after the endless reception. He was, in fact, the king of the Holman family, his pronouncements never challenged, his orders obeyed instantly. He had pushed his chair back slightly, signaling the end of the meal, and said, "David, you have been extremely foolish."

David had come out of his mental fog. "Foolish?"

"Yes, foolish, to summarily shut down your campaign. Now, get on the radio and put an announcement in the newspaper immediately to rescind your remarks. Tell the people you really didn't mean it, that Carol would want you to go on."

"You're not serious."

The rest of the family had gone still. No one so much as swallowed.

"Of course, I'm serious. There's no question about your election now. You'll have everyone's sympathy after Carol's unfortunate death and admiration for continuing the fight to bring good representation to the people of the thirty-third district. It's a shoo-in."

"You mean I'm supposed to use Carol's death to get myself elected to Congress? No, I'm not going to go on with the campaign. I won't do that to Carol's memory." David had stood, pushing back his chair so hard it fell, strode from the room and had run out of the door without his coat.

Now, he stood in Carol's kitchen, so often warm and fragrant with the meals she had prepared, just like the evening he'd received that first phone call. If he just hadn't answered the phone. If he hadn't been home. If he hadn't taken that stupid bet. None of this would have happened.

His muscles tensed with the urge to run through the house, pounding walls, smashing things, screaming, but he couldn't move. It was a living nightmare, trying to escape some unidentifiable monster chasing him down fog-filled streets not knowing where he was or where he was going.

The last time he had been in the house was right after Carol's body had been taken from the car. Was it only five days ago? He'd gone upstairs to the bedroom and noticed the door to Carol's sewing room ajar. The room that was supposed to have been the nursery. He hadn't been in that room since she had left. The lights were on. He hadn't turned them on.

There was the sewing machine, the cord wrapped around it, the carrying case on the floor. So, she had come when he was gone to get her sewing machine. The first pang of grief took his breath. He stood there, motionless, not knowing what to do, expecting the pain to last forever, but it subsided momentarily, and he noticed that the phone was on the floor, as if she'd dropped it and run. Who could have had that effect on her?

He needed a drink, a good stiff one and went into the living room to the bar. The phone rang. He paused; it was probably his father, continuing his tirade. He continued toward the bar, the phone's ringing following him. He filled a highball glass with whatever came to hand and took a slug. It burned all the way down and the phone continued to ring. He grabbed it, just to stop the sound. "I'm not getting back in the campaign," he shouted into it.

"Nobody asked you to."

David sobered instantly. That raspy, ugly voice. He started to hang up, then replied, "What do you want?"

"Same as always, only this time, I'll add another ten thousand. You might as well pay it. It'll just get more expensive the more you stall."

"How dare you threaten me tonight of all nights."

"Why? Because of your wife's funeral? That bothers you? I heard she left you. Is that when you told her about the brat?"

"I never told . . . You. You were the one who called and she answered the phone. You told her about the child. You killed her."

"I didn't think it was anything she didn't already know. Good husband that you were, I figured you'd have told her all about it a long time ago. I figured she might be able to persuade you to pay up. She wouldn't want you to ruin your run for Congress."

"You killed her."

"From what I hear, she killed herself. That was too bad. Shoulda been you. But then, I wouldn'ta got my money, so I guess it's a good thing it was her."

David tossed down another swallow of scotch while the bitch spoke, and suddenly, the mental fog disappeared. "You're right. I've had enough. How much do you want?"

He could hear the smile in her voice. "Now, that's more like it. I'll take a hundred and fifty thousand in cash."

"All right. It will take a little time, but I can have it by tomorrow night. How about meeting me at that little park at Compton and Chicago. You know, where the child was killed."

"Why do you want to meet there?"

"It's fitting. Besides, this time I'm calling the shots. You be there at seven o'clock sharp, or no money."

She didn't answer immediately, but finally he heard a heavy sigh and she said, "All right," and broke the connection.

David replaced the handset and smiled. The next drink, he savored slowly.

Chapter 41

A street light made a weak cone of light at the corner where Scarlett had waited for her babysitter to walk her home from school. The small park was shadows of strange shapes. David checked his watch. The bitch had one minute to the deadline. Part of him hoped she wouldn't come, but he wanted to see her face, if it was as ugly as her voice. Headlights came toward him on the street and an old Chevy stopped at the corner. A thick human shape got out and waddled to the sidewalk. The Chevy pulled away. David waited until the headlights were gone, got out of his Cadillac and strode across to the corner.

The shape had its back to him.

"I'm David Holman."

She turned, a face puffed with fat that squeezed her eyes to slits. Her mouth turned down in a perpetual scowl. Her hair was covered with a black wool headscarf tied under her third chin. A black coat was buttoned to the top. "I know who you are," said the familiar grating voice.

"You have the advantage of me. Under the circumstances, don't you think you should give me your name?"

She was silent, apparently thinking about it, then she shrugged. "You've got no reason to turn me in," she said, finally. "My name is Ada."

"Ada, what?"

"You don't need to know that."

"You don't need that hundred and fifty thousand."

She thought a moment longer. "Ada Schroeder."

"Schroeder? Myrna Schroeder? Are you her mother?"

The scowl straightened to a thin line, supposed to be a smile. "No, sir. I'm proud that I never birthed that slut. She's just like her mother, though, a slut from the get-go, and that little brat would have been just like the both of them."

A flash of anger tinged David's reply. "Now I remember. Myrna's aunt. Well, I can't say I'm pleased to meet you." He steeled himself to touch her arm and take a step toward the playground area of the park.

Ada pulled her arm free. "What are you doin'? Give me the money. My husband'll be back in fifteen minutes and I don't want you to be anywhere around when he gets here."

David took her arm again, clenched it tightly and made her take a few steps. "You aren't in charge any more. You'd better walk. I'll drag you if I have to."

She glared at him and walked slowly, his hand still firmly around her arm. When they reached the playground, he walked her to the swings. "Here's where 'that brat' died," he said, pointing to the ground. "She loved to swing high, kept telling me to swing her higher, so I did. Then, when she was at a high peak, I grabbed the chains and held them. She went flying out of the swing and her head hit a picnic table that was there. When I went to check on her, a trickle of blood was running out of her mouth. Her eyes were open, but she didn't see anything. She had a slight pulse, and then it stopped. I left."

"You killed her?" Ada's eyes were wide, like a trapped rabbit.

"You know the answer."

"You didn't want nobody to know you had a kid?"

"Why else are we here?"

Ada looked toward the street and took a step. "That's worth a lot more than a hundred fifty thousand, she said." David tightened his grip on her arm. She tried to pull away. "Gimme the money. I got to go. My husband will be here any minute."

"You won't be here when he comes. You're coming with me." He steered her away from the playground and back to his car, opened the door and pushed her. She struggled to get into the seat. David slammed the door and ran around to the driver's side and slid behind the wheel. "Don't try anything funny," he said, as the engine roared to life. "Remember, I've killed my own child. It wouldn't be hard at all to kill you. Actually, it would be a pleasure."

Ada huddled into the corner of the passenger seat and they drove in silence until David pulled the car to the curb in front of the police station and shut off the motor. Ada put her hand on the door opener, but David's hand clamped around her arm.

"Don't try anything. Slide under the steering wheel and get out." He got out, still holding her tightly as she struggled over the gearshift lever and under the steering wheel. When she was out, he slammed the door and guided her toward the police station door.

The desk sergeant looked up, surprised to see David Holman holding a woman like a prisoner. "Hi, counselor. What've you got here?"

"This is Ada Schroeder. She's a blackmailer. Me, you know. I'm a murderer."

The sergeant's eyes popped and he swallowed hard. "Blackmailer? Murderer? You?"

"She's a killer, too, but more by accident than intent. She's been blackmailing me for months. She met me tonight to collect a hundred and fifty thousand dollars. I'm a killer by intent. I killed my daughter, Scarlett Schroeder." The words sounded ridiculous to David as he spoke them. Why didn't he keep his mouth shut?

The sergeant's thick black eyebrows met in the middle as he tried to make sense of what he heard. "I don't understand. I have to call the lieutenant." He picked up the phone, spoke quietly, then hung up. "Lieutenant Carpenter will be here in a sec. Meanwhile, come inside here." A buzzer sounded, and David opened the gate that separated the reception area from the rest of the police station and pushed Ada through.

An impossibly tall plainclothes officer, a large pistol holstered on a belt around his ample waist, filled the narrow hallway. "Hi, there, Mr. Holman. What's this the sergeant said? You've got a blackmailer and murderer here?"

"Correct," David said.

"Well, bring her back to my office."

"I'll come with her. Mrs. Schroeder is the blackmailer."

Lieutenant Carpenter frowned. "Are you her lawyer?"

"No," David said.

"He killed his kid. He told me." Ada shrieked. "Lock him up, not me. I didn't do nothin'"

Carpenter looked hard at David. "What *is* she saying? Why did you bring her in? Why are you here?"

David looked at the floor. "She's telling the truth. Or at least part of it. She's been harassing me for months, trying to extort money from me. I told her I'd meet her tonight to give her the money." He wiped his hand across his face. "I didn't know about the child. I panicked." He paused and looked at the floor again. "I-I had to see for myself. I found out where she went to school and I went there. I saw this little girl with red hair, and I waited until the next day and went back. Something drove me. I had to see her up close, maybe talk to her. I couldn't think of anything else. When she waited for her babysitter after school, I talked to her. There was no question. She looked just like me. She was my child.

"I knew if Ada made the connection from a picture, so could others, especially if they saw her in person. If it got out, my campaign would have been over. My father would disown me. My wife would kill me. The only solution I could think of was to remove her. I read something in the paper about a child dying after a fall from a swing. That park was close to the school, so I talked her into going there to swing. When it got really high I held it and the momentum threw her out. She hit the picnic table. When I got to her, she had a pulse but it stopped." He looked Carpenter in the eye. "I killed my daughter, Scarlett Schroeder." He looked away from Carpenter and stared at the floor and said softly, "My life has been pure hell ever since. Prison would be a relief."

Carpenter clenched his jaw and glared first at Ada, then David. "Murder is a capital crime," he said. He picked up his phone and called the sergeant at the desk. "Get detective Brown up here, and tell him to bring two sets of cuffs."

Chapter 42

Mark Weston pushed his glasses to his forehead, scrubbed his face with his hands, propped his elbows on the big desk and held his head. God, divesting his interest in the company was harder than building it in the first place. He glanced at the tall, walnut grandfather clock in the far corner of the office. Eight o'clock. He'd been at it all day and now, three hours after everyone else had gone home, he was still a long way from finished. Would he have it ready for the board in two weeks?

The phone rang, startling the glasses back down on his face, and he picked up the handset. "Weston."

"Mark, this is Jim Cahill. Hold your seat. I just got a call from David Holman Two."

"Dave's father?"

"Yes. He wants me to defend Dave. Seems like Dave confessed to the murder of Scarlett Schroeder, the little girl who was found dead in the playground last fall."

"My adopted daughter." A brief silence answered him, then Cahill said, "Sorry. I didn't know." Mark changed his tone, and continued. "*Dave* confessed to her murder? I thought she had been murdered and so did the cops, but Dave Holman . . .?"

"Said he was the kid's father. An old biddy, said she was the kid's great-aunt, and was trying to extort money from him. Said she would go public with pictures that could prove it. Dave was scared for his election bid. Admitted he had a one-nighter with a girl some six, seven years ago. The kid looked just like him," Cahill said.

"Seems weird. But, in this business, weird is normal," Cahill continued. "Well, I called you because I heard you're engaged to the child's mother. Could you break the news to her? I'd hate for her to hear it on the news."

"Sure. I can do that." He paused. "Well, thanks for letting me know. And thanks for your thoughtfulness. I appreciate it. By the way, are you going to defend him?"

"I don't know. I told David Two I'd have to think about it. He wasn't happy. He wants his golden boy out of jail NOW."

"Well, lots of luck if you do. You'll need it," Mark said. He pressed the button to disconnect the call, then reconnected and started to give the personal number of the farm, but quickly hung it up. Myrna would be asleep. This was not something to tell her over the phone in the middle of the night. He placed the papers in file folders and left them on the desk, put on his coat, took his car keys from the pocket, went to the elevator and pressed the "down" button.

A half-hour later, Mark drove the car into the barn garage and turned off the engine. He walked quickly to the house and ran up the stairs to their bedroom. Myrna was asleep, the covers pulled to her chin. Mark looked at her for a moment. She was so beautiful and in sleep she looked so peaceful. It was hard to wake her. He bent to her and kissed her cheek. Her eyes flew open and she looked confused for a moment.

"Mark." She rubbed her eyes and sat up, and looked at the bedside clock. "Are you just getting home? I waited as long as I could, but I just couldn't stay awake."

Mark took off his coat and laid it on the back of the love seat, and sat on the edge of the bed "It was time I quit. Everything was beginning to blur, but something came up that you need to know.

Myrna's eyes went wide.

"I got a phone call a short time ago that concerns you, and I didn't want to tell you on the phone," Mark said. "I really don't know an easy way to say it." He pushed a lock of her hair away from her face. "The call was from a lawyer friend of mine. He said Dave Holman's father called him and asked him to defend Dave on a murder charge.

"Murder? David Holman? That's strange."

Mark took a deep breath. "He confessed to killing Scarlett."

Myrna gasped and the room blurred. There was a small whimpering sound and Myrna realized she made it. "Sh-sh-sh. I'm right here," Mark said, lying down beside her and wrapping his arms around her.

"Why would he do that? Scarlett was . . ."

"His child?" Mark finished for her.

Myrna turned to face him. "Why do you say that?"

"Not hard. She looked just like him. I wondered about it for a long time."

"But you never said anything."

"I knew you'd tell me when you were ready."

"I-I was going to tell you after we had moved to Seattle. You said you'd kill the person who raped me, a-and I was afraid to say anything while we were still in Newport City."

Mark held her close and kissed her. "I'd like to, but I think he's hurt himself enough. His wife killed herself, they think, and instead of bringing glory and honor to his family, they'll have to hang their heads in shame. He'll maybe get the electric chair, unless his old man can find somebody to make a deal. Frankly, I won't shed any tears." He paused. "There's more."

"More? How could there be more? David killed my baby so he wouldn't lose an election? Because she looked so much like him." She covered her face and sobbed. "When will it end? Why is this going on and on and on?"

"One more thing, and it's the end for you. We are going a long way from here. I refuse to allow you to be dragged back for a trial, if there is one. We're going to start a new life. We'll always have Scarlett in our hearts, but the best thing we can do is put David Holman and Ada Schroeder out of our minds as if they don't exist."

"Ada? What does she have to do with this"

"That's the 'more'. Ada saw Dave's campaign picture in a window and realized Scarlett looked just like him, so she's been trying to extort money from him for months. Tonight, Dave tricked her into thinking he was going to pay her and ended up taking her to the police, where he confessed and implicated Ada."

Myrna gasped. "Ada killed my baby? For money?" She clenched her fists. "She's hated Scarlett and me all our lives, and now she's destroyed my only reason for living. Her and her greed. I hope they put her in the electric chair and are slow to turn the juice up high so she suffers and suffers and suffers. I'd kill her myself, with my bare hands, if I got near her."

"I know, sweetheart. As I said, Scarlett will always be in our hearts, but we won't dirty her memory by thinking about David Holman and Ada Schroeder. We will erase them from our minds."

Mark folded her in his arms and patted her back as she sobbed in his arms. "You have me, sweetheart. I'm here now, and I'll always be here. I'll take care of you and keep the bad things away." He rocked her gently, as a child.

After no more tears remained, Myrna sat up and wiped her eyes with the back of her hands. Mark handed her a large white handkerchief that smelled of him. She made a lopsided smile. "You're right. We won't spoil Scarlett's memory by thinking about them."

"Are you all right now?" Mark asked. Myrna smiled and nodded. "Then, I'll get out of these clothes and show you how quickly we can erase the bad stuff."

In the morning, Myrna called Lydia and told her what had happened.

"Both of you come on over right now. Mama and I want to hear all about it," Lydia said.

Myrna and Mark repeated the story over big cups of Sarah's black coffee.

"How are you feeling?" Lydia asked.

"Shaky. It's so hard to believe."

The phone rang, and Sarah said, "Some man has been calling, asking for you. He won't give his name, but he said it's important. That's probably him."

"Do you want me to answer it?" Mark asked.

Myrna shook her head and went to the phone. "The McIntire residence."

"Myrna, that you?" said the raspy voice.

"Yes, Ernie. Sarah said you've been calling. What do you want?"

"It's Ada. She's in jail."

"Yes, I know."

"How'd you know?"

"Mark told me."

"Figures," Ernie said. "Well, that cop said she blackmailed that red-headed lawyer about Scarlett. He claims he killed Scarlett because of what Ada told him. They won't let her go. I thought maybe your boyfriend, might help get her out."

Myrna couldn't make herself speak. Ada, who'd help raise Scarlett from the time she was born, had killed her, as if she'd been the one who'd pushed her out of the swing. She held out the phone to Mark, who was beside her in an instant and took the phone. "Who is this and what do you want? What did you tell Myrna?"

"Who the hell are you?"

"This is Mark Weston. I'm sure you remember me"

"Yeah. I was just askin' Myrna, maybe you could help us out.".

Mark's hand tightened around the phone. "With what?"

"Bail my wife out of jail or find her a good lawyer or somethin'"

"Why would I do that?"

"Well, you likin' Myrna and all, and we are her only kin."

"Too bad you didn't think of that a long time ago. As far as we're concerned, your wife can spend the rest of her life in some dirty, low-class prison with all the rest of the killers, and if either of you ever come near Myrna or try to speak to her in person or on the phone, I'll have you in jail. Do you understand?"

"Never would've happened if Myrna'd behaved herself instead of actin' the slut. It's all her fault. You'll find out what a sorry mess you've got yourself into with that one, Mr. Rich Man."

"Do you understand what I told you?"

"I sure did. After all we done for Myrna and her kid, she's turned on us like a snake."

Mark slammed the phone into the cradle. "That sonofabitch."

"What happened?" Sarah asked.

"Ada's in jail for trying to extort money from Dave Holman. Ernie wanted me to bail her out or find a lawyer for her."

Sarah covered her mouth with her hand. "Oh, dear God. When will it end for you?"

Mark smiled. "It ends right now, and on a happier note, I have an announcement that you will be the first to hear. I've decided to give a ten per cent raise to everyone in the plant, except the execs, before I leave."

Lydia looked up suspiciously. "Yeah. Sure. You're going to give a ten per cent raise to everyone at Weston Switch?"

Mark cleared his throat for attention. "That's the idea. As a farewell gift from me and a wedding gift from Myrna and me. First of all, I'm resigning from the company at the end of the year. The Weston Automatic Switch Company will soon be the 'Best Automatic Switch Company,' and Myrna and I will be leaving Newport as soon as we're married."

"Have you thought about any wedding plans yet/" Sarah asked.

"Not really. Too much has happened, too fast," Myrna replied.

Lydia interrupted. "That sounds fantastic. But Seattle's so far away. We'll never see Myrna. And you, of course."

Myrna covered Sarah's hand with her own. "You two are the only reason I have for staying in Newport, and you have done enough for me. Sarah, you'll always be my Mama, and Lydia, you'll always be my sister. I'm not going anywhere that you can't come, and maybe I can come to see you."

Chapter 43

Lydia pushed back her chair and cleared her throat. "Well, I have an announcement to make, too, although not as spectacular as yours." They all turned to her. "You're not the only ones leaving Weston Switch. Mama, I know you want me to stay here, but Newport City is not for me. I've decided to go back to school and get my master's, maybe even a doctorate in some sort of social services program. I've loved living with you and I hesitate to leave you, but I'm going crazy here. I hope you will forgive me."

Sarah took a long swallow of coffee and carefully set the cup back in its saucer. "Honey, there's nothing to forgive," she said, finally. "I've loved having you here, but I didn't work all those years to put you through college to have you come here and work in a factory. I want you to do the best you can." She smiled. "I can just hear it now. My daughter, *Doctor* Lydia McIntire."

"That's great Lydia," Mark said. "Where will you go to school?"

"I haven't decided yet," she said.

"Why not check out the University of Washington in Seattle?"

"I never thought of that. It's so far away."

"Not really." Mark smiled and squeezed Myrna's hand. "Maybe we could persuade Sarah to come with us. Seattle's a great city, not too big, but big enough, and a good place to live."

Myrna's eyes brightened. "That would be wonderful. Neither Mark nor I have any family, and you would be family there. Oh, please think about it."

"Well, first I have to apply to the university and then be accepted," Lydia said. "But that would be the answer to a prayer—if I said prayers."

"What were your grades at the U of I?" Mark asked.

Lydia turned to her mother. Sarah sat up a little straighter and smiled, her expression full of pride. "Straight A all the way through. She graduated second in her class."

"With that on your resume, you'll be a shoo-in, and I know a guy or two who can put in a good word, Mark said.

Lydia turned to Sarah. "Would you be willing to pull up stakes and move West?"

"It's awfully sudden. I never gave much thought to moving again, but I do kind of miss living in a city. I'll give it some serious thought."

"What about the union?" Myrna asked.

"I've already talked to Betty about taking it on. She'll make a great union organizer, and once it's voted in, a great president."

"Betty?" Myrna was incredulous. "I thought she was in the company's pocket?"

Lydia glanced at Mark. "Not since that letter from Mark's ex. Betty doesn't trust her now that she's head of the company."

"Now that you all have the company sorted out," Sarah interjected. "We have a wedding to plan."

Myrna, Sarah and Lydia went to the tiny shop in Chicago, where an old friend of Sarah's was dressmaker to the rich and famous. She designed a slim, strapless wedding gown with a short train and cropped jacket with a Snow White collar in a silk charmeuse heavy as cream. Matching shoes were ordered as well as a wardrobe fit for a wealthy man's wife.

The Rev. Clarence Fontaine, pastor of Sarah's church, worked two hours into his hectic Christmas Eve schedule to perform the ceremony in Sarah's home.

The Christmas tree in the corner beside the front window filled the living room with soft colors and a spicy pine fragrance, and candles flickered in the center of evergreen rings on the small portable altar Rev. Fontaine used for traveling tent meetings. Esther Jones, the church pianist, began the crashing chords of the "Wedding March" from Lohengrin. Lydia, wearing a Christmas red gown, designed like the wedding dress, carrying white roses, came slowly down the stairs and crossed the living room to the altar.

Myrna stood at the head of the stairs, shaking so the white orchid on her small white Bible trembled. Behind the filmy veil, she blinked back the tears, as in her mind's eye, she could see a tiny girl in a long pale pink dress, her hair a flaming halo, preceding her, scattering rose petals on the steps. The music commanded, and she glided down the stairs, her eyes drawn to Mark, handsome in his black tuxedo, who watched with wonder and a wide smile as she came toward him. Inge and Christer, returned from Seattle after organizing the new condominiums, were the only guests.

Sarah lifted Myrna's veil and presented her to Mark.

Hours later, the wedding dress lay carefully across Myrna's bed in Sarah's house, the Rev. Fontaine and his gear packed up and gone, the wedding supper finished, the Silver Ghost in its heated garage, Inge and Christer in their cottage, Myrna and Mark were finally alone in their bedroom at the farm.

"Lydia and Sarah gave me this beautiful nightgown," Myrna said, placing a gift box on a chair.

Mark turned, placed his hands around her waist and pulled her close. "No nightgowns. Nothing is going to get between me and that beautiful body." He lifted her until her face was close to his, then his mouth was on hers, gentle at first, then demanding and hard. Flame seared through her, she wrapped her arms around his neck and their tongues found each other. Mark set her back on her feet without taking his mouth from her, and fumbled for the zipper on the back of her dress. It fell to the floor, followed by her half-slip and her bra. Her panties went last in a small pink puddle. He stood back and looked at her, his eyes ablaze with desire. "Oh, my god," he breathed. "you are absolutely perfect." He dropped his suit coat and struggled to release his necktie. Myrna laughed, reached for it and loosened the knot and began to unbutton his shirt, "Don't bother," he said.

Myrna pulled his tie free. "I don't want a big old shirt to get between you and me, either, Take it off, or I will." He ripped the front open, popping a few buttons, then pulled her down on the bed.

He caressed her face and kissed her tenderly. "Mrs. Weston. Do you have any idea how much I love you?"

"No, Mr. Weston," she replied, laughing. "Can you show me?"

Shortly before noon the next day, Mark and Myrna stood beside the steps that led to the open door of the chartered DC-6 at Chicago's

Midway Airport. Lydia and Sarah stood beside them, wind howling down the skyscraper canyons, whipping their coats.

"Sorry ladies, but it's time to get aboard," Mark said.

Myrna hugged Sarah and Lydia. "Love you both. Just think, in a couple of months you'll living in the same building as we do, getting Lydia ready for her graduate classes at the University of Washington. Wasn't that acceptance letter the best Christmas present?"

"Yes, thanks to Mark's intervention," Lydia replied.

Mark hugged each woman, put his hand on Myrna's back. They climbed the steps, turned and waved, then stepped into the plane. The door closed behind them.

The smiling stewardess in her navy blue suit with wings on the chest, took Myrna's sable coat and Mark's overcoat, then led them into the cabin, which was fitted out like a living room. Myrna slid into the chair facing the cockpit on the port side, while Mark sat across the glass coffee table from her. The engines started with a roar, Myrna watched the two propellers on her side blur into opaque spinning circles as the plane followed the ground crewman's orange wand onto the runway. It crouched there for a few moments, then slowly crept forward, picking up speed bouncing along the rough tarmac until the roar reached a screaming pitch.

The bouncing suddenly stopped and the cabin pitched up. In seconds, they were above the clouds over Chicago into the clear blue and bright sun of the heavens. The left wing dipped and the nose turned west to Seattle.

Made in the USA
San Bernardino, CA
05 March 2018